There's No Place Like Oz by Leann Belle

First Printing, 2023

Book Design and Cover Art by Leann Belle

There's No Place Like OZ

Vicious Wonders Book Two

By Leann Belle

Content Warnings

While there are many moments of fun and spice in this story, this is a DARK work of fiction. Proceed with caution if you're not comfortable with the following concepts:

Content warnings include (**May include spoilers**): Dubious Consent, Gore, Violence, Kidnapping, References to Cannibalism (not depicted), Murder of minor characters, Fear and Blood used in sexual context, Voyeurism, Exhibitionism, Threats of dismemberment (not depicted), Knife Play, Blood Play, Choking

CHAPTER 1

DOROTHY

I clenched my little black Scotty dog tightly against my chest, bracing him as the wheels of the plane connected with tarmac. He whimpered, and I forced myself to loosen my hold, trying not to hurt him in the process of finding my own comfort.

"Welcome to Wichita, Kansas. The current time is 3:43 PM, and the temperature is seventy-nine degrees with a chance of thunderstorms." The pilot announced in a gentle voice over the PA. I let Toto relax on my lap while the rest of the passengers began the usual hustle and bustle. Half the crowd stood up way too early, then they waited around for five minutes in awkward positions until they could pull their luggage from the overhead and get off the plane. I waited for the whole cabin to clear out before I placed Toto on the floor and retrieved my carry-on.

I'd barely needed to bring it, really. I think I had less coming back than I had when I'd took off for the big city ten years ago. All I had left was some basic, comfortable clothing and treats for Toto.

It was all I really needed these days. I'd dreamed of owning the entire world when I first set foot in Hollywood. If only I had known all I'd be walking away with was a bushel of emotional scars. It was a blessing in disguise when my dear Aunt Em had asked me to come home to help her on the farm for a while. It meant I didn't have to admit that I *wanted* to come home, and it meant I didn't have to admit I was doing so a failure with my head hung low. Instead, I got to tell myself and everyone else that I was just here because I was a good daughter. Considering Aunt Em had raised me from the time I was barely old enough to walk, it only felt fair that I would come home to help her when she needed me. She was my Aunt only by title and blood, but she was my mother in every real sense.

I disembarked from the plane, nodding politely to the stewardess on the way out, while Toto lead the way into the terminal. Compared to LAX, this airport was a breeze to navigate. Aunt Em and my Uncle Henry were waiting for me as I stepped out of the arrivals gate, and I climbed into the back seat of their pickup.

"It feels like it's been ages, Dorothy." Aunt Em said as I buckled my seat belt. "You look good! You've really grown into a woman since I last saw you."

I smiled meekly, though there was nothing happy about that compliment to me anymore. I was eighteen when I left, and now I was ten years older, and a lifetime less optimistic or confident. I could see my unmade face and the first sign of my dark roots reflecting in the window. Every flaw and every blemish on my skin reflected prominently, and even with their tummy control, my comfortable black leggings didn't make me feel any better about myself. The oversized cashmere sweater that hung off one shoulder wasn't very flattering either. There was nothing about me that looked *good enough* right now. Not for a red carpet and not for life.

"I see you have a friend now." My aunt continued, nodding at my little dog. "Not sure he'll make a very good cattle dog, but I'm sure he looks cute in a purse."

"This is Toto." I ruffled Toto's fur, and he curled up on the car seat against my thigh. "Honestly, he's the best guy I met in that whole city." I added with a forced laugh. I said nothing about the underhanded jab at his perceived usefulness. I certainly wasn't going to tell her that he was certified as my emotional support dog.

Aunt Em was very traditional, and I knew she'd find me silly. Mental health was just something you were supposed to soldier through out here, and I'd already been judged enough. It was easier to just withhold truth as needed these days.

I loved my Aunt dearly, but sometimes love meant being careful not to rock the boat too much. Though it served to remind me just how little I fit in back here. Calling it home just because I grew up here was painfully ironic on the best of days.

"I can only imagine. Though you must have met a few nice people on set when you were recording for that commercial for... uh... what was it again?" She looked up as she searched her mental database. I opted to put both of us out of our misery.

"Toilet paper." I couldn't help blushing as I said it. I had moved to Hollywood to become an actress. I was convinced I could make it big if I was just around the right people with the right connections going to the right parties, but the closest I ever got to being famous was getting picked for the lead role in a TV pilot that never sold, a few straight to cable low budget movies, and acting in a commercial for soft quilted two ply. Maybe I messed up when I refused to listen to that fuck-stick of a B-Movie director when he suggested my career would definitely take off if I just got enough plastic surgery.

"Did you meet anyone really famous?" She asked in that star struck way everyone always did when I told them I lived in Hollywood.

The image of coats and cocktail dresses flashed through my mind. I could still taste the bitter flavor of his lips, mixed with whiskey, tobacco, and weed. And I could still feel the bruises on my wrists from when he'd tied me up for the shoot he'd sold to a seedy porn site without telling me. I shook my head to banish the thought. If only they knew what a shit hole that place really was.

"No one too interesting." I replied dismissively, hoping she wouldn't ask me to elaborate. I stroked Toto to subtly calm my increasing heart rate, then I did my best to change the subject. "How much of the harvest is left?"

"Not much." My uncle chimed in, and I was grateful to talk about anything but my last few years. "But we would love some help with stockpiling wood for the coming winter. It's supposed to be a real bad one this year, and your aunty here can't chop as fast as she used to."

"I only have to chop as fast as you can carry them, and you can't carry as many logs as you used to either, old man." Aunt Em glared playfully at her husband, and he grinned back at his lovely wife. That brought a legitimate smile to my face. They were always so sweet together. I wished *I* had someone like that. A forever best friend who supported me even when I was at my worst or most broken. Despite the number of times I'd joked that 'all men are dogs.' I would have given my right breast to meet a guy who was half as loving and loyal.

It was hard to even imagine going on a date with someone without constantly having to worry about ulterior motives. It was hard to find genuine friendship or expect any sort of commitment when half my encounters ended with discussions of what I'd get if I let them do this or that to me. I'd rather be single if my options were a bunch of men who only wanted to use me as a pretty cum receptacle.

I shook my head in an attempt to throw off the constant nagging of depression that was always eating at me nowadays. "It's a good thing I'm a professional wood chopper." I said, receiving both of their nods of agreement.

I was *damn* good at chopping firewood, actually. That was something positive I could still be proud of. There was a technique to it, and I perfected it over the years of keeping warmth in our run down old homestead while growing up. I had to get good at it, after all, since it seemed like I was always the only one who was cold, and they never wanted to put enough wood on the fire to fix that. As much as I resented the life I'd just left, I was definitely going to miss my perfect thermostat that I could always have set to just below boiling.

We arrived at the old cabin in the country, and Toto was quick to jump on my lap and stare out the window. His little tail wagged wildly at all the new sights and sounds. The livestock, the open fields, the blue skies—It really was beautiful in its own way.

Maybe Kansas wasn't so bad.

After a long afternoon of catching up with my family on the perceived glitz and glam of city life, I was more than ready to retire to my room. It was a small homestead, comprised of little more than a kitchen/living room combo for the main compartment, then one full sized bedroom for my aunt and uncle, and a smaller bedroom for a child, where I laid on my old twin bed. It was a far cry from the luxury of a California King, but it was familiar. It smelled of the lilac detergent that Aunt Em always used, and the good memories of my childhood were enough to make this more comforting than the beds that all the money in the world could buy.

I sighed, then I rolled over onto my stomach and buried my face in my pillow. Almost immediately, my sweet little Scotty dog hopped up onto the bed and squirmed into his position between my arms. I burrowed my face into his scraggly black fur. "What do you think, Toto?" I spoke into his small, snuggly body. "I'm sorry I failed you so badly, but it might be nice to take a little while to reset, don't you think?"

Toto whined empathetically, and I buried my face further into his warmth.

Really, even though these weren't the circumstances that I'd hoped to return home under, this wasn't going to be so bad. I liked the exercise of hucking hay bales and I felt kind of big and tough when I was running the tractors. It was simple and pleasant compared to the social obligations of hustling for gigs and constant wining and dining, and that's exactly what I liked about it. Though I knew at some point it would start to get boring, and I'd be desperate for some sort of mental stimulation and big dreams and ambitions again, but for now, I'd bear with it.

I'd started to drift off when a sudden crack of thunder jolted me back into consciousness. I squeezed Toto harder as the wind started to howl. Tornados weren't a thing back in California, and it was one of many things that I didn't miss about living in the plains. I'd nearly forgotten about it, to be honest. If I never had to hide in a basement from the weather again, it would be too soon.

Another loud crack and the rain let loose, pounding on the roof of this old farmhouse. Water dripped in from every imperfect seal in the homestead, of which there were so very, very many. Toto ran from my arms and took shelter under the bed, and I shot up and darted into the den.

"Aunt Em!" I called into an oddly empty house. "Uncle?" I searched the whole homestead—which didn't take very long considering its size. "Aunt Em? Where are you?"

With no one in sight, I opened the door, despite knowing better, and rain came rushing into the house sideways. I was drenched in a matter of seconds, while the winds ripped the doorknob from my grip. The wooden door broke on its hinges, and it slammed into the side of the house. My gaze shot frantically around the field, trying to find where my Aunt and Uncle must have gone on this most treacherous night. It was too dark to see very far, and the entrance to the cellar was on the other side of the house, so it wasn't visible either. *They must have darted for the storm cellar.*

Though I couldn't imagine they would do such a thing without me, but perhaps there was too little time, and they figured I was old and mature enough to know what to do. I frowned as I shielded myself from the violent deluge with my arms in front of my eyes.

It was then that a massive cyclone came into view. It sucked in the dark clouds, and rain, and lightning like a black hole, twisting and destroying everything that neared its path. My jaw dropped, and I forced myself to close it again. Though that only made it more apparent how much my lips were quivering. It was far too slow that I processed the fear I was feeling so deep in my gut.

Right, the storm cellar. I had to get to the storm cellar.

"Toto! Come here, Toto!" I yelled back into the house, hoping he would come to me by choice and save me the precious seconds I would need. But he remained in the room, cowering under the bed. "Dammit!" I shouted, but still I rushed back to the room. Toto was the only good thing about my life lately, and I wouldn't risk losing him. I reached under the bed, and he backed up out of range. I tried again, and he whimpered.

"I don't have time for this. Please just come here, Toto." I pleaded in near tears. Water was dripping on my legs as I squirmed further under the bed. A loud and violent gust pounded at the thick log walls of the house, as if to warn me that I was running out of time. With a last desperate stretch, I managed to get a grip under Toto's tiny body, and I hauled him out from beneath the bed. Just as I was getting back on my feet, I swear the whole goddamn house moved, and I was thrown right back onto the ground.

I scrambled for footing once more, but as though I was staring at a surrealist painting, the room started to spin and warp before my eyes. I blinked rapidly, trying to bring the scene into a coherent view, not believing at all what I was seeing, but the world kept spinning. The walls began to melt into each other in a twisting blur. It was like I'd set out on the worst possible acid trip, and someone mixed in mushrooms and molly along the way. I gave up trying to stand, and just braced myself on the floor.

I clutched Toto tightly against my chest, and I squeezed my eyes shut, hoping when I opened them again, this vision would have all been a dream. I shivered as wind penetrated the walls, rapidly drying the water from my wet clothing.

Then the room started to warm. A gentle, comfortable heat blew into the cracks until the whole place was blazing hot, and the water penetrating every opening in the old wood was now instantly turning into steam.

Toto barked at the distorted world around us, and I clutched him more tightly. Sweat coated my body, and the heat was so intense, I could barely breathe. It felt like pure fire in my lungs, while the roar of wind completely commandeered the sound waves. My senses were being assaulted from every angle, and I was already too overwhelmed to act. The spinning intensified. The wind howled.

If one were to manifest the word chaos into a visceral reality, this would be it. I must have been captured by the cyclone. Ridiculous as it sounded, that was the only thing that made sense to me right now.

Wood started to splinter around me, as though the old house was folding in on itself, and the speed of the cyclone picked up yet another several miles per hour, The G-forces threw me against the wall, and I lost my hold on Toto. He yelped as he hit the opposing log barrier.

Then we spun and spun and spun as though we were in a Gravitron at a demented carnival.

I was on the verge of puking when those intensifying forces of gravity in this rapid twister snapped the logs behind me. The deafening gusts of wild winds, pounding rain, and the roar of unending thunder were the last things I heard before I blacked out completely.

CHAPTER 2

DOROTHY

The warmth of a summer sun engulfed my face, the whizzing of powerful winds hit my back, and the bright red image of light penetrating my eyelids filled my vision as I came back to consciousness rather abruptly. I opened my eyes slowly, blinking gently to regulate the amount of brightness hitting my eyes after what felt like a long rest. The clouds in the sky were obscured by a combination of the dryness of my eyes and the fluttering of my eyelashes.

I forced myself to keep them open as I rotated in suspended motion, and wind whipped into my dried corneas at an alarming rate. It was then that I realized I was freefalling through a bright blue sky, and much unlike the whipping winds of the plains, it was pure gravity that was creating this powerful gust.

I patted my chest, feeling around for a ripcord, as if I'd had any chance of having put on a parachute at some point.

Because Aunty Em's homestead would have such a thing, and who doesn't put on a parachute when a Tornado comes through...

I sighed at my own ridiculousness, then I flailed about in hopes of getting a hold of something to slow my descent.

I was surrounded by random bits of wood and logs, splintered and broken by the cyclone, careening to the ground at the same rate I was. I reached for a large log, and I pulled myself through the air to get a better hold on it. I wrapped my arms and legs around the broken wood like I was a koala bear, and I rode the thing down on the vague, absurd notion that it might help break my fall somehow.

The green grass was still distant, and I was still picking up momentum. I had no clue how I got here or how I was going to survive this. I was almost so overwhelmed, I didn't have time to register what that impact would mean once it came.

I couldn't believe I was supposed to die here. I just couldn't.

I chewed on my lip, hoping a blanket or sheet would suddenly appear as a makeshift parachute, but by physics, the chances of a sheet catching up to me while I held onto a heavy log were not very strong.

So instead, I just tried not to look down at my impending doom. I told myself this was a dream once again, but the sensations were all far too acute and vivid for that to be true.

I made the fatal mistake of glancing downward, and the ground had gotten even closer. Toto was nowhere to be seen. I could only hope he had somehow been spared this same bizarre fate.

Just as I began saying my prayers to whatever gods did or didn't exist, something that looked startlingly similar to a woman on a broomstick crossed my field of vision. She was just be-bopping along like there wasn't a violent rain of jagged wood careening through the sky above her. She was like a witch from a storybook—black hat with a yellow band, blond hair flowing behind her, stripy black and yellow socks, a tight little black dress, and six inch red stilettos to give the whole outfit some pop.

I blinked several times to assure I was seeing what I thought I was seeing.

If that's a magic broomstick, that might be my chance. There was no time to think about whether that made sense or not. This was a time to act.

I released the log, then I pressed my arms to my side and straightened my legs, and I honed my aerodynamics like a javelin, hoping to catch her before she flew away. I never would have imagined learning to skydive for a role in that thriller that I didn't get would have saved my life one day, but here we were. I outpaced the falling log, then I went darting downward toward her broom. I held my hands forward and prepared to catch it before I fell.

Closer. Closer.

Her speed was a touch too fast. My timing was going to be just wrong.

Fuck!

"Hey!" I yelled to get her attention.

The witch upturned her face, revealing a near undead paleness to her skin, so light she was almost blue, while her irises were an eerie neon yellow. Her shifted attention was just enough distraction to get her to slow down. In a fraction of a second, I was catching the tail end of her broomstick and wrenching myself on top of it.

"Who are you?! How did you get here?" The woman's surprise could only be described as a shriek. She bucked her broom trying to knock me off, but I held on for dear life. "Get off!" She shouted. But like fucking *hell* was I going to be doing any such thing. When choosing between falling to my death or being mildly annoying to a stranger, I was going with the mild annoyance.

The witch twisted the broom around viciously, and I fought the urge to smirk at her fruitless attempts to throw me. I wasn't good at a lot of things, but I'd just say I earned the attention I got whenever I sat down on a mechanical bull in a bar. I think I made more money off of every Chad and Cletus who doubted me those days than I did my whole time in LA.

She jerked the broom again, and before I could tell her to just give up and drop me off, the log I'd been holding spoke for me. I watched in what felt like slow motion as the giant girth of wood smacked straight into her, and took her off the broom with a violent squishing noise.

I cringed at the sound, but had little time to process it as the broom shattered in half along with her. The magical transport now broken, we began drifting downward towards the ground again. I held on, while the log careened with increasing velocity, and my half of the broom floated down softly on what must have been the last of its enchantment.

The log struck the earth with a boom that sent shockwaves through the grass, and I was set gently beside it by my magical cleaning instrument.

I hopped off, then I rushed over to the log, where this witch laid skewered beneath shards of wood.

Blood coated every splinter, and heat and color dropped from my cheeks. A deep cold and deathly pale terror took my whole body. This was all my fault. I needed to save her.

"I'm sorry, I'm sorry, I'm so, so sorry!" I pleaded as I knelt down and gripped one of the smaller splinters that had javelined through her chest. I used every ounce of strength I had to rip it from her flesh, immediately making everything… completely worse.

Cold blood erupted from her chest like a geyser, splashing into my face and coating my fluffy oversized sweater.

"Shit shit shit—I'm sorry about that too." I said with desperate apology before plunging the stake back into her wound.

Brilliant Dorothy. Plug the hole by stabbing her again. WHAT COULD GO WRONG?

I admonished myself for my own dumb logic, but before I could do anything else to help her, I caught the angry glare of the witch as she sneered at me with the last of her life. Then, as though she was a pool toy with a pin prick, she began deflating and shriveling. Her whole body curled into itself until her body disappeared entirely. Those hot red stilettos on her feet clomped onto the ground as the only proof she had existed at all. The red dye, on what I assumed was a fine leather, began oozing into the grass, and the heels began shrinking and retracting like they were drawing in a telescope.

After a moment, they stopped shifting and they stilled in the grass in the form of silver flats. Very cute and comfortable looking silver flats, if I was being honest.

But I would never think such a thing, because that would be like robbing a corpse, and I was not a mid-century pirate or a Viking who pillaged my kills.

Also I wasn't a killer despite any possible implication of what just happened. *Which... did that really happen?* I looked down at the grass where the witch once lay, and there was no trace of her body left. No trace other than the crimson that stained my clothing. It all felt so surreal, I still couldn't register what was happening as anything more than a lucid dream.

Maybe I died in that tornado and this was heaven.

Fuck, if this is what heaven is like then Aunty is going to be pissed at all the times she avoided eating shellfish just to get into a place like this.

Maybe it was presumptuous to assume I would go to heaven in the first place in hindsight. I think after a few years in Hollywood, most people were going to hell. That uncomfortable limbo in between would be a lucky mercy for me after I skipped out on my boob job appointment to fly home to Kansas *after* letting that asshole front the deposit just out of pure spite. I might have gone through with it if it had been something I actually wanted for myself, but considering I was getting surgery just because some director said he'd give me my big break if I let him mold me into his version of a perfect fuck toy, I think I'd made the right choice.

The amount of times I was used as an *imperfect* fuck toy was still not going to look strong on my angelic resume though.

I huffed and stood up, now feeling so annoyed I'd nearly forgotten where I was or how chaotic the whole thing had been. I glanced down at my ruined sweater with irritation. It should have been horror that filled me, but none of this made enough sense to feel real.

With a harrumph, I turned to survey my surroundings.

When you set aside the violence of my entrance, it was really quite beautiful around me. Birdsong filled my ears, and soft grass brushed against my ankles and my bare feet as I curled my toes into the ground. I licked my chapped lips, tasting the trace residue of a lingering summer storm: a familiar flavor that I didn't much mind especially when topped with sunshine.

A perfect blue sky on a perfect day. I shifted my weight from one leg to the other in grass that was soft and springy. The sun felt good as it dried the remnants of the storm and the witch from my now ruined clothing. It might have felt incredibly peaceful if not for the still raining logs and splintered branches of the farm house hitting the ground around me.

I breathed in a three count, then I exhaled twice as slow until the last clunk and thwack of falling wood came to silence.

I glanced upwards to assure the last of the homestead was done with its descent, then I turned cautiously on my heel to look around some more. Where I was or what had happened to Aunt Em, Uncle Henry, or Toto, I couldn't begin to say. I knew for *sure* I wasn't in Kansas though.

I could see massive, rocky, snow peaked mountains in the distance, first of all. And there sure as fuck weren't anything that resembled real mountains in Kansas. The vast jungles across the horizon line, where I could see the fanned leaves of towering ferns and palm trees left me to think that this wasn't somewhere in Colorado, either.

I touched my face to verify I could physically feel it, just to officially negate any remaining hope that this was a dream, while I slowly took in my more immediate surroundings. I seemed to be in a small town of some sort. There were little bitty houses that looked like they were built from bricks, mud, and grass. Very simple and very primitive. Almost Hobbit-like, really. Was I back on set for that straight to cable Cave Man RomCom? I'd already dismissed the possibility of a lucid dream, but that didn't mean it couldn't still be a lucid nightmare…

I dusted myself off, scattering wood shavings back to whence they came, and I began combing the wild mess of my highlighted and no longer straightened hair. The streaks of lighter and darker blond from my last bleach and style session shimmered in the sun like locks of pure gold, while the frizz of my never-quite-even curls was a lost cause under this heavy humidity. But still, I liked my natural curls. I'd straightened them for years to better match the aesthetic of the other models and actresses I saw in the waiting rooms, and it was almost refreshing to see them so loose and free for once.

Pretty.

I smiled silently at the thought that had become far too rare when I regarded myself. I kept combing, then I started braiding this rats nest best I could.

I'd nearly made myself presentable by the time people began emerging from the houses.

They were rather small figures, probably something like three feet tall at most. And they all gawked at me, wide-eyed, as if I'd just landed from the heavens. I suppose I kind of had. They all approached with slack-jawed wonder sparkling in their eyes.

I pursed my lips, not quite certain what was going on. Perhaps they'd never seen someone who towered as high as my wild and massive five foot four—a height that was far too diminutive for the runway modeling I'd once dreamed of, yet made me a giant today.

I glanced down at my clothing again, reminding myself of the sheer amount of blood staining my sweater. *Well, this probably doesn't appear very kosher*. Not sure how I was going to explain this.

I wrapped my arms around my sweater in an attempt to cover my crimes from the forty or fifty pairs of little prying eyes, suddenly feeling incredibly nervous and self-conscious.

They stared me down with their shock and horror, and I experienced stage fright far beyond anything I'd felt back when I first signed up for improv. I took one awkward step back, only to have them swarm in ever closer.

Small as they were, these folks weren't proportioned like dwarves. They were more like kindergartners with adult facial features, complete with wrinkles and facial hair.

"You killed her…" A man with a twisty mustache muttered.

Fuck. "I-it was an acci—"

"You saved us all, great sorceress." A woman with thinning white hair and the tiniest, cutest eye glasses I'd ever seen interrupted me. She shook her head without giving me a chance to process any part of that ridiculous statement. "What a battle. The way you fought for her broom and stabbed the Wicked Witch of the East again and again even once she was down. Why it was so savage. What a sight to behold!"

"I uh… That's not…" I blinked rapidly. *Not my proudest moment here.* "No I—"

"Our hero." One of the little people said.

"A great hero." Another echoed the sentiment.

"Not even the Good Witch of the North dared to stand against Grunhilda of the East." A younger looking woman professed with adoration.

And then they all got on their knees and they all bowed deeply with the utmost respect, while I continued to process what in the unholy fuck was happening. It probably wasn't a good time to mention that I'd been trying to save the witch when I pulled that stick out of her. But better to be seen as a successful vigilante than a bumbling accomplice.

"Will you set us free, great sorceress?" The elderly woman raised her head. She took to her feet and stepped forward.

24

"Uh…" *Well, this is awkward.* "I mean… I'm not going to tell you how to live your lives or anything." I attempted another step back, feeling awfully crowded all of a sudden. I wasn't exactly privy to whatever this Grunhilda chick had put them through, but enslaving a bunch of itty bitty people shockingly didn't rank on my list of morally acceptable activities. Not the least of which because I wasn't a sorceress at all, so I'd be pretty easily overthrown if they ever got uppity.

This is *definitely* not Kansas. Country folk were many things, but they were definitely not the types to bow to much of anyone for much of anything. I knew— assumed, rather—that they weren't dangerous, but I was still at a total loss as to how I was supposed to react here. Their wide eyes were all jabbing into me like the staring equivalent of acupuncture, and I didn't even know what Grunhilda did to deserve their hate.

"Sure. You're free. You're welcome." I tried, hoping I'd read their social cues right.

Cheering and oohing and aahing erupted from the group. "How can we ever repay you great sorceress?"

"I just want to go home. I have no idea where I am or how I got here…" I stopped myself from saying much more on the basis that, right now, they respected me, and I felt it would be wise not to ruin that. My mouth wasn't good for much beyond digging my own grave, as I'd discovered over the last decade. It got me a handful of auditions, I suppose, but that was usually less from reading the part and more from… Right, well, we don't need to think about that right now.

Not feeling terribly comfortable with the way they were all still staring and crowding and making a commotion over me, I low key glanced around for an out— any out at all—but there were so damn many of these guys.

Where was Toto when I needed him? He may not be big, but neither were they, and I could've used his inflated sense of size and protectiveness right about now.

"Where is your home?" The little old lady asked. She seemed to be the leader of sorts. She asked the most questions, and no one ever dared interrupt her. I hoped that when I was her age, I'd be able to command that kind of respect. Especially since I didn't seem to get too much now. I would not look back on my twenties with any love lost.

"It's in Kansas." I tried first. They all glanced among each other with befuddlement. I couldn't really blame them. If I didn't have a need to know Kansas, I probably wouldn't have ever heard of it either. "I would settle for Hollywood. Los Angeles? Do you know where that is?" I tried second. The one and only good thing I could count on about California was that most people in the world had at least heard of it. That, and the fact that, if I did make it back to LA, there were plenty of flights *out of it*.

But no. That just left them even more confused. I supposed that these little hubble houses may not have televisions. Or electricity for that matter. I sighed deeply then tried a new angle. "How about we start with: Where are we right now?"

"Oh, that's easy. This is Oz!" The woman announced proudly.

"Like, Australia?" I pursed my lips. *How the hell did I get to Australia?*

That same confused look returned to her brow. "No, Oz is just Oz. I don't know this Australia." *Alrighty, well that wasn't very helpful.* She pondered for a moment, then came up with a single raised finger as she found her aha

26

moment. "But if you put on Grunhilda's shoes, you can go anywhere you want!"

I frowned. *Wow, what a solution. I can just walk home. No shit.*

I fought the urge to roll my eyes, then I glanced back at the location of the long vanished corpse. Her shoes were still sparkling under that fine sunlight. They were quite pretty with their silver. They didn't look terribly comfortable, but I couldn't remember the last time I wore shoes that were. So, for no logical reason, I sat down and I tried on the shoes, hoping she'd meant they'd magically take me where I wanted to go, and not that they were literally just damn shoes that I had to walk in. I was still barefoot anyway, so if I wanted to go anywhere, it only made sense to use what was available. None of these little people's shoes would fit my size seven-and-a-half feet, after all.

The silver shoe wrapped nicely around my foot. *Shockingly comfortable, actually.* They seemed to magically resize themselves until they fit perfectly. They were cute, and they went well with my black leggings.

My leggings that were soaked in death and starting to smell like it.

"The shoes have chosen you." She nodded, then she approached me while I was still on the floor and our gazes were more level.

In the background, the little people cheered to see the shoes on new feet. Their mouths all twisted in smiles, and they jumped up and down and high fived among them. "What a wondrous day!" The woman cried out. "You truly are the sorceress of whom the prophecies foretold!"

"The sorceress! The sorceress!" The others cheered. I cringed at the weird way they now seemed to be eyeing me.

"The sorceress who will now save us from famine!" The woman added.

"Uhh…." *Not really sure how I'm going to do that…*

"The sorceress who will use her enchanted blood to feed the fields!" The cheers continued.

"Wait, what—"

A violent impact connected with my head so hard and fast, I didn't even have time to register where it had come from.

CHAPTER 3

DOROTHY

I came to, sprawled out on something that was unexpectedly plush and comfortable. I rolled my head to the side opposite the painful throbbing from the impact sight. Small furry fibers brushed my cheek with a welcoming warmth.

I squeezed my eyes tightly together, then I gathered the courage to open them, peeking carefully through only one side to start. I had a blanket on me, I now realized. A comfortable blanket that was soft and fuzzy and slightly weighted. What an unexpected bit of hospitality from the people who just knocked me out cold with a blunt impact. Maybe I deserved that after brutally murdering their queen. For people who sounded so happy to see her gone, they sure had a strange way of expressing appreciation.

I sat up and I rubbed my head while I surveyed my surroundings. I was in a room. A very tiny one. Four even walls, spaced maybe six or seven feet apart and built from stone. Moss gathered in the corners, where moisture dripped in through the unsealed cracks. A small bed, big enough only for a munchkin or a dog like Toto, was against one wall, while a dim fireplace brought in warmth and light.

It felt like a combination between a cabin and that old fashioned dungeon I'd seen on set in the low budget fantasy movie I played in as a delusional prisoner. Well, other than the fluffy rug of unknown animal fur beneath me. I supposed since I was their alleged savior, they wanted me comfortable while I was awaiting execution.

I sighed, then I cautiously got to me feet, testing my steadiness while holding onto the end of the bed frame for balance.

I wasn't injured other than the pounding headache, so that was good. I also still had the silver shoes on my feet, which was pleasantly unexpected. My leggings and my sweater were gone, however, and in their place was a clean blue sun dress with white polka dots. The hem only reached down to about mid-thigh. This was probably a full length dress on a munchkin woman. If I were to wager a bet, they were the only clean clothes they had that would fit my frame. I'd complain, but it was better than being soaked in someone else's blood.

Another deep breath and I patted myself down. The shoes went well with the dress, and my hair was now washed and neatly braided. Rather than think about the violation of having been bathed and redressed, I focused on the pops of my gold highlights in each link of my braids reflecting the flames of the fireplace. I was looking rather Little House on the Prairie up in this bitch.

Could be worse, I thought. And the universe was quick to confirm that sentiment, when the door flew open, and a horde of tiny men shoved a man into my box with me to make it worse.

A beautiful, striking, prince charming of a man. He was tall and a normal human height, with mid-length black hair that fell gently over his ears and accentuated his strong jaw that was smooth and clean, and a sharp, angular nose that rested between two high and defined cheekbones. Meeting my gaze was a pair of dark brown eyes, as enticing as the most decadent chocolate, that reflected my same surprise and worry.

"A sorcerer, a sorcerer!" The munchkins proclaimed. Before I could get a single word in, the door slammed shut and he was stumbling into the room. I took a step back in a too-late attempt to brace myself, when he hit right into me and sent us both toppling over. My back hit that fuzzy carpet, and I let out an embarrassing squeak when the coarseness of this man's simple, all black tunic hit my chest. His slim and muscular physique was heavy and hard as it pressed down on top of me.

He wrenched himself up, so he was now hovering over my body with a hand placed beside each side of my head. He looked down into my eyes with those deep brown spheres, then without saying a word, he leaned in close… and he sniffed me.

"What the hell!?" I came to my senses, and I pushed this pretty, pretty man away from me.

I admonished myself for even having such a thought. I'd just been hit upside the head with a club, and now I was stuck under the hard body of a stranger, and I was thinking about how hot he was instead of how fucking dangerous this was? *Get it together, Dorothy. You're not that hard up for a good lay.*

"Are you okay?" That sexy voice hit my ears, and I shook sense back into myself and crawled out from under him. The corners of his lips dipped into a frown.

"Y-yeah. I'm fine." I muttered as I sat up straight. "It looks like we're in the same fucked up boat, so I'm not going to blame you for tripping."

The man nodded. "I'm just glad to see you're safe. I was so worried." His tone reflected that sentiment genuinely, much to my confusion. He reached out and brushed the hair from my eyes gently. He tucked the loose strands behind my ear.

Before I could react, he closed the distance between us again, and he wrapped me in a warm, tight, powerful hug. I sat there stiffly in confusion. An unexplained heat and sense of relaxation bubbled through my whole body while I waited for him to release me and explain who he was and what the hell was going on.

He held me for several moments before he let those hands move to my shoulders. He braced me there, never breaking that intense eye contact. "I hope you weren't too frightened without me, Dorothy."

What the fuck? "I wasn't... I mean, I don't know... Wait what?" I was completely taken aback by that. "How did you know my name?" I stared at him in disbelief.

32

This dark haired Adonis furrowed his brow. "I suppose you wouldn't recognize me." His tone was a verbal frown. "It's Tobias—" He caught himself, then started again. "Sorry, *Toto*. But in this form, please use my full name."

"To… to…" I blinked rapidly. "Toto like… my dog?"

"Yes." He said, hooking his finger through a red choker that I was just now noticing. A choker that was actually a dog collar, and a dog collar that had a little charm on it with my contact info, and contact info that was there because I had put it on my dog, and…

WHAT IN THE ACTUAL FUCK.

I was internally screaming as I stared at this dark prince in front of me who literally just proclaimed to be MY LITERAL FUCKING DOG. *What is even happening right now?*

"You're Toto?!" My voice was shrill to the point it even annoyed me.

"Yes. Toto." His cheeks flushed at the cute little Scotty dog name. "But if you don't mind using Tobias…" He insisted again. When he swallowed, his Adam's apple visibly bobbed. Because Toto had an Adam's apple now. Because he was a dark haired male model. Because he wasn't a Scotty dog.

"Toto." I repeated. Stunned. *Fucking stunned.*

CHAPTER 4

"TOTO"

TOBIAS

Dorothy stared at me in abject horror, as if I'd just told her it was time to go to the vet. In the dim lighting, I could sense it more than I could even see it. She was always one to wear her emotions on her sleeve, and the subtle increase of her heart rate and shallowness of her breathing were loud and clear in my ears. I shook my head, then I stood up, still getting used to this awkwardly balanced human body. I stretched my long arms and flexed my rather useful fingers.

"Why are you afraid of me?" I asked with a frown. "I'm here to protect you, Dorothy."

"Y-you're... You can't be..."

I sighed. I didn't like seeing my lady so terrified. It wasn't an expression I'd never seen, unfortunately, but it was something I always tried to protect her from. I wanted to be the one to guard her from that kind of pain, and it hurt so much more to know my existence now caused her more anxiety than it healed. "When the cyclone took us to this... wherever this is."

"Oz." She managed to correct me despite her shock. Correcting people who were wrong was something she was always good at. I liked that about Dorothy.

"Right, after the cyclone hit and we ended up in this *Oz*, I woke up in this form, while being carried by a bunch of strange tiny people. While normally I could have squirmed out of their grasp—perhaps even bit or scratched at them if need be—I couldn't seem to figure out how to work my new body." I frowned. I'd felt pretty helpless and pathetic at that moment. "They kept chatting between each other that I was *'the sorcerer that would save them'* and it left me thinking they don't have dogs here in Oz at all."

"A sorcerer, huh? At least they're consistent, I suppose." Dorothy placed a hand on her chest. She closed her eyes, and she breathed in and out for several counts. "Okay, so you're Toto. My dog. In human form."

"Yes," I ran a hand through my soft black hair, which was now only on top of my head. "I know this is all very confusing, but I just want you to know that I pledged my life to protect you from the day you chose me as yours, and I will not go back on that promise no matter what my physical body looks like."

She blinked several times, still trying to register everything that was happening here. I had a lot to process too, but I could worry about my own struggles later. There was a reason I was her emotional support, and I knew how much she genuinely needed me for that purpose. I watched her carefully when I noticed the slight quiver to her lip and the very slight increase to her breathing rate. I could hear the pounding in her chest as it reached an elevated level.

Shit.

I closed the distance between us, not giving her any more time to protest, and I swept her up into my arms. I squeezed her tightly against my chest, not wanting to watch her crash over to the other side of a full blown panic attack. I shared my warmth, and I pressed her cheek against my slow, steady heartbeat, while I stroked her hair gently.

"It's okay. You're okay." I whispered into her golden locks. That seemed to help. Her breathing started to normalize, and her otherwise rigid body began to relax into my arms.

This was nice, if I was being honest. Initially, I'd been rather distraught over this new form, but I'd never realized how badly I wanted to be able to hold her when she was sad until right now when I had the size and articulation to do so. She felt good, warm, and secure there. She fit just right in the crux of my shoulder, and her delicate body seemed so small and soft against me

Maybe this was how it felt for her when she used to hug me in dog form. It was soothing. Comfortable. Pleasant.

I buried my face in her hair and took in her scent of rain, guava fruit shampoo, and her natural smell, and I felt my own mind come to a calming ease.

"You really are Toto." She said into my shoulder, nuzzling me there. I could feel the slight dampness of her tears as she wiped them on my tunic.

"Yes." I confirmed while I held her.

"You're warm like him, and you're soft like him, and you have the same energy as him. I can sense his heart and soul in you." She started the list in a way that made me think it was more for herself than for me. "I'm so glad you're okay." She wrapped her arms around me too now, and she squeezed the muscles of my back. "If you had gotten hurt, I don't know what I would have done."

"I feel the same about you, Dorothy." I relaxed completely, feeling fortunate she'd accepted me in earnest. "Now let's figure out how to get out of here and get back to Kansas."

I let her go, and she stumbled backwards a few steps. I could see the way her eyes were combing my entire being, trying to understand and memorize my new form. She took a deep breath and started over. "Yes. Let's figure out how to go home."

CHAPTER 5

DOROTHY

Once the initial shock of it all had worn off, I was grateful to be here with Toto. No matter what happened in this wild place, at least I knew for sure that he was someone on my side. If I could count on nothing else, I could certainly count on that.

But now that his identity had been established, we really did need to figure out how to get out of here. If they thought I was some sort of sorceress and they planned to… uh… use my blood to feed their crops, I didn't know how good my chances of survival were.

As I came down from my panic, I took a moment to search for possible escapes. I'd tried the door already, and it was locked tight, while there were no windows to break, dirt to tunnel through, or broken stones to pull away. Chances were likely we would be imprisoned in this small room until they'd decided what to do with us. Fortunately, the fireplace provided plenty of light to what was otherwise a drab, simple, and rather small place that felt even more cramped now that there were two of us.

I should have started calculating some elaborate plan, but as the high and adrenaline of shock had started to wane, I realized exactly how emotionally and physically exhausted I was. I wouldn't be coming up with anything tonight, and sleep might do me more good than relentless fear and stress.

The bed was far too small for either of us to sleep in though, and I would feel guilty taking the rug, since Toto was much larger than I was. At best, maybe I could manage the bed if I stayed in fetal position all night. Not the most appealing, and the blanket itself wasn't even big enough to cover my legs, but I didn't have many alternatives.

Toto—ahem, *Tobias* frowned as he watched my internal debate, easily read by the way my face was darting back and forth between the bed and the rug. His attractive brow furrowed again. It was still such a strange concept to me that my little Scotty dog was now a six foot one, tall, dark, and handsome stranger.

"Take what you can of the bed. I'll sleep on the floor." He said with a gentle nod. "The fire should be plenty for me to keep warm."

"Oh, no, that wouldn't be fair. I can't—"

He didn't even wait for me to finish my protests before he positioned himself on the floor at the foot of the tiny bed. He used his arm as a pillow, and he settled in to the rug. It was a strange sight. I had to keep reminding myself he was used to being a dog, and this new body was probably just as confusing for him as it was for me.

So I listened, and I climbed onto the little bed, and I scrunched myself up as small as I could, pressing my knees tightly against my chest, and hugging them there so I wouldn't accidentally sprawl out over the edge and kick him in the head.

I closed my eyes and we both did our best to get some rest.

… Yet, even in all the turmoil and strife of the day, it was still difficult to fall asleep. I was beyond exhausted, but my mind was utterly restless.

I opened my eyes again and stared at the wall for several moments, accepting the futility of rest. I had no clue what was to become of me when the morning came, and I my anxiety wouldn't let me forget it.

But it wasn't just that. Even though I'd been single for so long, I just…

I wasn't used to sleeping alone.

"It's weird trying to sleep without the warmth of my little Toto teddy bear." I spoke cautiously through tentative desperation. Though he was human now, I still kind of wanted that warmth. He was still my best boy deep down, regardless of his new body, and… I needed Toto. I hadn't gotten him as a service dog because I'd simply wanted to take him everywhere. His support was the difference between my ability to function in my day to day versus being an emotional wreck. "I-I mean, it would probably be awkward now but—"

Before I could say another word, Tobias was at my side and hoisting me into a princess hold. Then he laid me down on the floor with him and held me tight against his body, wrapping me in the full length of his warmth like he was a cocoon around a tiny little caterpillar. My eyes widened at the sensation of firm pecs and well-built abs behind me, while I was cradled between some very powerful biceps.

"I'll always keep you safe, Dorothy. Taking care of your mental health will never be awkward." He whispered gently into my hair. His low, calm voice made me shiver. But having his soothing body heat was everything I needed in that moment. I should have been too embarrassed to sleep, but I really did feel safe with Tobias.

The gentle crackle of the fireplace was like a peaceful lullaby, and the rise and fall of his chest was like a mother rocking her baby to sleep. I was out in a near instant under the most restful comfort.

The next morning, we woke to see a platter in our room, slipped in while we'd both been resting, I presumed. It was a breakfast of meat and eggs and veggies that were tinged with a purple hue. Even if someone had been there to explain, I wasn't going to ask what kind of animal they came from. I likely wouldn't have heard of it anyway.

My stomach grumbled, but I didn't trust the food before me. Tobias, however, was quick to indulge. He picked up his portion and dug right in with his fingers, shoveling potato-like chunks into his mouth.

"It's actually really good." He said enthusiastically.

"Aren't you worried it could be poisoned or drugged?" I asked with a frown.

Tobias shook his head. "No. I would smell it if it was."

He had a point. Just because his body appeared human, that didn't mean that he had lost his heightened senses. That could be a useful tool from here on out, I thought.

Still, I hesitated, partially out of distrust and partially because I was too scared to have an appetite. On the contrary, the sight of the strange food almost made me sick just imagining ingesting it. Instead, I offered Tobias to indulge in both of our meals, figuring it would help to keep him at full strength. He had a dog's stomach after all, and I had a much more sensitive constitution even on a good day.

Tobias finished the food, while I sat on the bed in anticipation. I didn't know if they'd keep us here for several more days, or if they had more immediate plans to kick start their agriculture, but the uncertainty of it all was almost more terrifying than the threats themselves.

I was sitting in my nerves when the sound of a turning lock caught both of our attention. The door suddenly flew open, slamming into the inside wall with a loud bang. I jumped at the noise, and barely had time to collect myself before a swarm of munchkins filled the room, and immediately took hold of us.

Tobias and I both struggled in their grasp. He tried his best to fight them off, but by sheer numbers, there was nothing either of us could do. Eight men wrestled Tobias to the floor, and I watched in horror as they struck him over the head, hard enough to silence him. It was probably safe to say the food hadn't been drugged considering the need for such violence. In hindsight, if they were going to bleed us out to feed the fields, they couldn't risk tainting our bodies.

What a comfort... I internally hissed at such awful thoughts.

Six more men had their mitts on me, and after seeing what they'd done to Tobias, I resigned to my fate. It wouldn't do me much good to sustain injuries in a fruitless battle. If *he* couldn't stop them, my chances were below abysmal, and escaping would only be more difficult if I ended up hurt or unconscious.

No, this was strategic. I'd preserve my strength for whatever they had planned for us, and I'd use it to free myself after the fact.

The munchkins hauled us out of what I soon discovered was the basement of one of their hubble houses, then they marched us across a farmer's expansive, undulating field. The hills were comprised of thousands, if not millions, of small bean plants sown in orderly rows. It seemed so ordinary, all things considered. It almost felt a little bit like Kansas in some ways. Our captors surmounted one of the small hills, giving me a much better view of the valley. I'd stopped struggling, and Tobias was limp under the march of the eight men who carried his body through the crops.

In the distance, a rugged cross jutted out of the ground like a spear that had been thrown into the earth from the heavens. As we neared, I got a full view of the crossbeam that formed a rugged crucifix, which was nailed into the surface with bent, over long spikes. The unfinished wood was wrapped heavily in barbed wire that glistened in the light of the still rising sun.

Every blade and coiled string of metal sparkled with pure but subtle violence, and as we rounded that wooden monument of pain, still in the grasp of these awful little men, we saw a man that was already imprisoned upon one of the planks. He hung silently and limply in the field like a corpse who'd been repurposed as a scarecrow.

He was quite a sight. His skin was heavily scarred by the barbed wire, with cut marks across his neck and wrists and shoulders as though he'd been stitched back together after being torn limb from limb. He wore a dark sleeveless shirt, similar to that of the munchkins, but lengthened to match his much more substantial height, and a pair of jeans sat nicely on a trim waist. His head hung as though he was either sleeping or dead—I certainly hoped for the former and not the latter, though the pale greyish hue to his skin and the lack of obvious breathing didn't give me much confidence. Framing his face was a mess of wild black hair that shot out in every which way, all sprawling out from the bottom of a darkly dyed, wide brim straw hat.

My eyes widened as I took him in. He was a strange juxtaposition of calm and torture. His long eyelashes rested softly over his nicely sculpted cheekbones, and his pale blue lips were parted just a touch.

Is that… is that what they're about to do to us?

Tobias was thrown onto the ground, still unconscious, while the munchkins who carried him began building a new cross. They built two of them, side by side, using primitive hammers and poorly secured nails. My carriers held me down on the floor, assuring I didn't escape while the others began hoisting Tobias onto his mount.

Fuck—There was no chance that I would be able to get out of bindings like that. I jerked and thrashed in a fight for my life when I saw exactly how inescapable my prison was about to be. This wasn't simply a captive situation. This was a human sacrifice situation. They were about to turn us into pretty scarecrows to protect their crops, and I wanted no part of it.

I kicked and bit at my captors, who seemed about as fazed as a horse with a fly on its back, while a few of the small men climbed atop the cross they'd chosen for Tobias. The men on the floor hoisted his unconscious body upward, handing him off to those mounted up high, and the munchkins got to work on fastening his wrists to the wood with the barbed wire. I watched the way the metal barbs cut his flesh, and red dripped from the sharp points.

"Stop!" I cried out. "Stop, you can't do this!" I knew it was futile, but I couldn't help myself. "I'm your hero. I'm not a scarecrow. We can be so much more useful to you if you let us live." My voice broke in sobs as they began securing Toto's other wrist. His head held limply, while another munchkin wrapped the wire around his neck.

"You saved us from the Wicked Witch's control, and for that we are eternally grateful." A munchkin spoke harshly into my ear. "And as such a selfless person, we now thank you as you save our food supply from the witch's evil crows that still remain to torment us."

No matter how hard I fought, I was completely overpowered. My throat burned under my heavy crying. I was never strong enough when I needed to be. That was par for the course. "You—You're the ones who are evil!" I shot back. "There has to be a better way."

"This is the only way. The prophecies have foretold this, and the prophecies are never wrong." The munchkins, who had just finished securing Tobias to the cross, jumped down, then they started climbing atop the crucifix that would be mine. "We need a sorceress's blood to scare away a witch's demons, and you are a sorceress strong enough to defeat their master. Your life force will feed the earth, and her minions won't dare come here so long as your body hangs."

I glanced between the unconscious Tobias and the man who died in these bindings, and my heart rate accelerated out of control. I made one last ditch effort to get free, while firm hands began hoisting me upwards.

No use.

They secured me on a pair of hooks, supporting me beneath my underarms, then they held me there while others started to tie the wire around me,

"Let me go!" I screamed through my tears knowing it would fall on deaf ears. "I'm not a sorceress. My blood isn't magic."

"Of course it is." The man who tightened bindings on my right wrist spoke casually. He yanked the wire tight until he was satisfied by the depth of the punctures. "The prophecy clearly foretold that a sorceress would save us from the wicked witch and famine. And here you are."

"I'm not…" The barbs on my ankles cut in as deeply and easily as needles through cotton cushion, pinning me to the cross like I was a butterfly about to be dissected. "I'm just a girl from the country. I shouldn't be here at all." I stopped struggling in an effort to minimize damage. They were determined to keep me trapped, and there was little I could do to stop them now. "Don't you think if I had magic I would be throwing you all off of me right now!?"

They ignored me. Reason didn't work on these people. My other wrist was shoved against the wooden cross beam, and the wire was tightened down. My neck and torso were next, and I screamed when those tiny blades cut into me. My blood dripped down through my bust. I held my breath and focused on keeping as still on my hooks as possible, lest gravity deal me the final blow.

The men jumped down from the cross, and they all stopped to admire their handiwork. My eyes were watering out of control, mixing salty tears with my dribbles of blood, and I bit into my quivering lip in an attempt to deny them the satisfaction of being outwardly broken.

I couldn't believe that this was how I was going to die. Breathing was enough to cut myself on the barbs, and every slight shift of my body made it worse. The metal scraped over my skin viciously and without forgiveness.

A circle of blackbirds circled overhead like buzzards waiting for an animal to give up their last breath.

I glanced to my right, moving only my eyes, where Toto hung limp and silent in my periphery. A painful and horrible sight, where my only respite was that he wasn't conscious to be living this horror like I was. I couldn't bear to see him like that.

So I shifted my gaze to my left, where the dead man hung instead, letting the reality of my fate sink in with the visual.

Which was when I noticed that this dead man… had started to stir.

CHAPTER 6

"THE SCARECROW"

CROWE

I lifted my eyelids only a sliver, allowing me to easily observe without giving away my current state of consciousness. I'd been hanging in this field for the better part of a month—if my count of the sunrises has been accurate—but this was the first time I'd ever been treated with company. The man was likely alive yet unconscious. The woman, conversely, was *obviously* alive and very feisty. She was flailing about, kicking and screaming bloody murder. The munchkins *were* bloody murderers, incidentally, so I supposed I could forgive the shrillness of her whines. Her words dripped with panic, and her yelps and cries of pain spoke to someone suffering the disadvantages of mortal flesh.

I was like that once. I'm fairly certain, anyway. Though I barely remembered a time when I was just a man.

A sorceress is what they called her, but that couldn't be true. If she *was* a sorceress, she would have surely been able to defend herself. Weak as she was, Grunhilda never would have been held by these little trolls for long, and the other witches all had their own parlor tricks that could put an uppity munchkin in their place.

Surprise, surprise that they would confuse a human for a god, considering the level of munchkin intellect. They wouldn't be able to tell a magician from a dormouse with their logic and observational skills. There was a reason that ten thousand of these strong, able-bodied people had cowered under the rule of one tired woman with little more than the ability to raise a few corpses, make tiny flames

48

from her fingertips, and fly around on a broomstick. If they were strong enough to capture me, after all, of course they were capable of a coup d'état. They just would have needed half a brain to organize, and I doubted whether there was even a fraction of that collectively among the whole lot.

Yet here *I* was, pinned to a crucifix in the middle of a field, because my dearest Hildy thought to tell everyone that my blood would save them, all because we'd broken up over a silly little disagreement over the merits of indiscriminate torture.

Oz hath no fury like a wicked witch scorned.

But I digress. More significant than my cursed love life was this new company who joined me as fellow scarecrows. The dark haired man was a sight to behold. He was about as tall as I was, beautifully symmetrical, and it was obvious how nicely sculpted his body was, even under the raggedy tunic he'd been dressed in. A fine specimen to be sure, but by no stretch was he a scary one. The crows wouldn't be afraid of such a man. He looked far too kind and too delicate.

And then there was this young woman. Her hair was a waterfall of color, from soft browns to sparkling streaks of gold, and her eyes were a mesmerizing blue, shining behind the heavy gloss of tears. I won't say I liked seeing a woman cry, *per say*, but I did find that vulnerability and fear in her voice and expressions rather... enticing. Perhaps I'd simply been nailed to this post for far too long, because just the image of her so helpless and desperate and scared was doing something to me.

I fought a chuckle that would draw attention to the fact that I was still alive. *You're a sick man, Crowe.*

Though perhaps if Hildy hadn't performed a magical lobotomy with her bare hands, stealing away my guilt, compassion, and humanity in the process, I wouldn't be thinking something so horribly depraved. *But what can you do. We all have our crosses to bear.*

Hildy liked me better this way after all. An orgasm was so much more satisfying when you nearly died in its pursuit, and I certainly had no qualms with the possibility of nearly (or completely) killing her. My only regret was that I never pushed her near death all the way to actual death. I'd have to fix that at some point.

I returned my attention to this girl on the pike, where I combed my gaze down her body until I reached the shoes that adorned her little feet.

Silver shoes. Shoes that hadn't been flat or neutral in color in ages.

The witch's shoes.

Curious. How did she come upon those?

The detestable little trolls turned their back on us as they began gathering up their tools, and I opened my eyes and moved my head just enough to catch the attention of the sobbing girl at my side. I motioned towards the distracted munchkins with my chin, allowing the barbs to scrape along the raw skin of my neck. I'd long since bled out up here, so there was no mess from my usual cuts and bruises.

"Don't squirm too much, or you'll bleed out faster." I whispered, low enough that the little bastards wouldn't hear. I twisted the corners of my lips upward with deceptive gentleness. "Oz would be bereft to lose a beauty like you. And *I* would be bereft to lose your company before I've even gotten to enjoy it."

She blinked those pretty little doe eyes, dispelling the tears, and regaining some sort of composure. How funny that I would give someone calm. Perhaps I could be that savior she was crying for. "I don't want to bleed out up here." Her words were less quiet, though the munchkins were blatantly ignoring her. "My blood isn't magic." The break in her voice was begging me to give her hope.

Mmmm, sweet girl, there is no hope in Oz. But lucky for her, I *had* grown most tired of this post.

"Don't be so certain." I winked. "Magic takes many, many forms."

I would be more than happy to show her an example. I tugged forward on my right wrist until the barbed wire was taut against my bloodless flesh. The metal cut in deeper and deeper, slicing through my muscle like it was a knife in soft, warm brie, up until my restraints hit bone. She watched, wide eyed, as I began to saw at my wrist, using the barbs to sever tendon and cartilage. I wrenched the connecting tissue back and forth until my hand was completely severed. It fell to the floor, separate my body, with the fingers still twitching and pulsing.

The look of absolute *horror* in her agape lips and dilated pupils was most adorable and innocent. I was guessing she'd never met a cursed corpse who had fucked the immortality out of a witch before. How lucky that I could be her first.

The thunk of my hand on the ground got the attention of the miniature monsters, and I extended my palm-free arm as they turned to face me.

"Can you get that for me?" I asked ever so casually. "I seem to have dropped it."

The munchkins looked at me. They looked at the hand. They looked at the expectant and impatient glint in my eyes. Then, like the idiots they always were, the toughest among them bent down, picked it up, and presented it to me.

Magic instantly reconnected it to my wrist, and I flexed my fingers to assure the full and perfect joining of my nerves. Then, using my now free arm, I pressed back on the cross that held me, and I shoved myself forward, allowing the wires to cut through me on every point of contact. My ankles, my stomach, my neck. I nonchalantly chopped myself into pieces, then I tumbled into the weeds as a fully disassembled man.

I laid still for a moment, just to revel in the sweet melody of disgust and surprise from my audience. I never wanted to miss a good opportunity to shock and awe.

A munchkin tip toed up to my scattered parts with caution. I waited until he was too close to escape, then I willed myself to snap back together swiftly and suddenly. The magic reassembled me in perfect form in an instant, and I used my newly freed body to knock the nearby munchkin to the ground with a well-placed chop on the back of his neck. His jaw hit a rock at the most perfect angle, and I slammed my heel down on the stupid thing's head in an expertly executed curb stomp. I waited for the siren song of sharp, horrified gasps that followed.

Music.

This immortal body was the one good thing that came of my failed relationship. She thought eternity would be torture, but oh how I enjoyed the power it gave me.

I rolled my shoulders, then I glanced at the little army. They had all taken a step back, defensive in stance as they regarded me. I could have likely freed myself like this much sooner, but I hadn't had much reason to. Very little motivated me these days. Something about losing your soul and sentimentality will do that to a person.

But what I lacked in drive, I made up for in sadism. I grinned widely, showing my sharply pointed teeth that

52

had been ground into shape by my barbaric hosts. They thought fangs might scare the crows, but they seemed much more useful for terrorizing these little bastards.

"Boo."

That single word had them scrambling for their tools—wrenches, hammers, pitchforks, anything they could use as a weapon. I wasn't going to give them the time to gather their wits, however.

With a nod of my head and a wave of my hand, the crows that circled overhead darted downward, bearing talons and beaks, while flapping their powerful wings at the munchkins. The crows had come to respect me in our many long talks on a dull day. The munchkins had lamented my inability to protect their crops from the birds, and now they were about to lament *their* inability to protect themselves from me.

I yanked the barbed wire from the cross, and I whipped it in a violent circle. The slaughter was effortless. One, two, ten—I took them out one by one, not sustaining so much as a single hit.

I cackled at the sight, feeling rather satisfied up until a pitchfork came careening through my back. The cursed little troll gored me through and sent me stumbling forward. I hit the dry dirt chest first, and the pitchfork punctured the earth like I was a steak on a sponge cake. The successful munchkin hopped atop me in his attempt to feel like a big man.

What a victory.

He really thought he did something there.

I placed my hands on the ground beside myself, and I pressed through my biceps to lift myself from the ground. I rose up on hands and knees, making no effort to remove the fork from my torso. No, I let it penetrate my body further, dragging myself upward along the pointed length of its spikes, just to show how much I *didn't fucking care.*

The Munchkin's eyes grew wide. He fell from my back, hit the ground, and scooted back on his butt, trying to make distance. Though this display of dominance had him so entranced, he didn't think to get up and run for his stupid fucking life.

He remained mesmerized as I continued to stand, leaving the fork lodged in the ground, just so I could make a show of tearing myself through the entire length of the handle. It was a shameless flex of intimidation and power.

On my feet, I used both hands to feed the handle of the pitchfork the rest of the way through my chest, then I yanked the decorative end from my body with a pop. It was a lightweight and easy to use tool in my hand. I twirled it in my grip and pointed the sharp end at my host.

The stupid imp started to whimper, but he was paralyzed by the image. I laughed in a tone that only beget horror, then I lunged it through him swift and hard.

"Didn't quite work out how you imagined there, now did it?" I smirked while I hoisted my enemy to the sun.

I quite enjoyed a good slaughter. It had been far too long. When I worked and lived as Hildy's whore, I was tasked with keeping the little men in line often. But now that I was Hildy's exile, I'd instead been tasked with nothing but cultivating my boredom. "Such a shame that you couldn't have amused me longer."

With that, I walked my grip down the handle until I had the little dying thing good and close. Then, unceremoniously, I bit into his neck and drank him dry of his essence until a warmth started to return to my flesh. It wasn't much, and the blood wouldn't last long in my system, but it was enough to feel alive again. I slammed the pitchfork into the ground when I was done with him, savoring the final grunt and gurgle as the last of the air in his lungs was expunged.

My chest healed near instantaneously, closing the open hole as if I'd simply stuck my finger into a pile of loose sand. I dusted myself off, then I smiled gently at the carnage around me. Ten little trolls, slaughtered by their own scarecrow. What foolish little demons. The munchkins were heinous things after all. No one would miss them, other than their equally heinous families, and I certainly had no love lost for any of them.

Once I'd stretched and found myself satisfied by this freedom, I turned to face my new companions. I fixated on this woman who was so very fetching in painful bondage. Dangerously fetching. "Thank you for drawing the munchkins up here for me. I'd been meaning to do that for weeks now." I removed my straw hat and took a deep bow. My long and messy black hair hid my face. Advantageous, as I may have scared her if she saw the expression I let slip. I would prefer this lovely little toy not have any inkling of the things I wanted to do to her.

"Crowe is my name." I added. "To what do I owe the pleasure of your presence, my sweet girl?"

CHAPTER 7

⊙ DOROTHY ⊙

There were dead bodies everywhere, and the field was dyed a deep, dark red. I stared at the horrific battlefield before me, too numb to acknowledge the zombie-like man at my feet, smiling so pleasantly up at me.

"Your name, my lady?" He said in a way that was so polite that the contrast of it was jarring. He gazed into me with two eyes that were completely black, save the red irises that formed glowing rings in their center. He may have been the devil himself for all I knew. I stopped believing in god a long, long time ago, but since arriving in Oz, I'd become less and less certain that this was not, in fact, purgatory.

"D-Dorothy." I managed. "My name is Dorothy." I spoke carefully, trying not to exacerbate the wounds around my neck. The barbs had dug in deep enough already.

"Dorothy. I've never heard such a name." Crowe rubbed his chin while he looked me over. "From where did you get it?"

"Kansas. I'm from the United States."

The scarecrow pondered that for a moment. "I've never heard of such a *place* either. What are these states united against, exactly? Are you also ruled by witches?"

"I'd say we're ruled by demons, mostly." I muttered to myself. If I'd learned anything since I'd arrived, he'd likely take that statement literally. But then, I'm not sure I didn't mean it literally. I dismissed the thought, then addressed him again. "Would you mind helping me down?"

It was hard to say if he was on my side or not, but if he wasn't on the side of the munchkins, then that was good enough for me.

"Would I mind, indeed." He reached out a lukewarm hand and danced his fingertips lightly along the side of my calf. I shuddered at the sudden contact, only causing the wire to cut into me more. He used the lightest pressure as he danced those fingers up to the hem of my skirt. I fidgeted again. That only got a low chuckle out of him. "Are you scared of me, Dorothy?" He asked with amusement.

"I-I don't know." I bit my lip, uncomfortable with the tingles his touch was sending through me. "I don't know if you're saving me or going to hurt me more." I attempted to pry into his intentions, hoping for the former, but mentally preparing for the latter.

"Well, *I* would certainly be afraid of me if I were you." He lifted my skirt an inch, never removing those cool fingers from my skin, and my heart beat picked up just from the look in his eyes. But then he stopped short and let his exploration of my legs drift back downward. He feathered light taps down my skin, then he drew small circles around my ankle bones. "After all, whether I help you or hurt you, sweet girl, all depends on if you can tell me *where* you got these silver shoes." His smile revealed shark teeth, and I swallowed into the painful sting of my restraints.

If he wasn't on the munchkin's side, that could very well mean that he was on the wicked Grunhilda's side, and telling him I'd knocked the woman off her broom and murdered her with my house probably wouldn't go over that well.

"Th-they were a gift." I lied, but it was painfully obvious that I'd done so. My acting skills should have been much better than this, but fear had a way of shutting down any such talents. That was one of my many, many failings when I'd been on set.

He laughed again. Always so amused, yet it felt innately sinister in nature. "Sweetheart, I am *incapable* of reading or comprehending emotions, and even I can tell that's a damn lie." He stroked the top of my foot with the back of his fingernails, drawing lines down to the edge of my shoe, then he traced the rim of silver until he was back up to my ankles. With a suddenness that made me jump in my bondage, he took a firm grip of my legs. His fingers pressed into my skin so roughly I was certain he'd leave bruises. "I know who these belong to, and I know how important they are to her. They would never be given away as a gift. Certainly not to some pretty little thing from wherever the fuck Kansas is."

His grip tightened until it hurt nearly as much as the barbed wire.

"Okay okay okay—I *took* them from the Wicked Witch of the East." I confessed immediately. The only thing I handled worse than pain was keeping secrets. "I... I killed her. On accident, I mean, she's dead from a series of unfortunate events that were only partially my fault, and I was barefoot, and the shoes fit me so... so I kept them." This explanation was terrible, but at least it was honest. The last twenty-four hours had been such a sensory overload that I was still registering the reality of my role in her death. Saying it out loud was the first time I'd started to process it.

I closed my eyes tightly, bracing myself for the anger and vengeance that might come next, but instead, that confession elicited a laugh that was much more gentle than the last. His grip slackened. I opened my eyes again to meet a playful smile.

"Accidentally? How does one *accidentally* murder the most powerful woman in Oz?" He motioned to the slaughter around him with a tip of his chin. "I could see someone *accidentally* slaughtering the pathetic imps that she governs, but... my dearest Hildy?"

DEAREST Hildy? Fuck.

"W-was she your lover?" The nerves caught in my throat. I very much wished he would let me down, but the longer this conversation went on, the less he seemed likely to do anything of the sort.

"She was a lover of something." He eyed me with a curiosity that didn't feel menacing, but he still made no effort to untie me. "When your choices for companionship are a devil in a black dress or…" He jerked his head slightly to motion towards the munchkins. "A gaggle of goblins in flannel, let's just say you choose the devil."

"Are you going to punish me for killing her?" I tried next. And *that* laugh was deep and guttural.

Crowe shook his head, as though he was unable to contain his amusement at such a question. He locked in eye contact with those devilish red rings, while he began drawing circles against my muscles with his thumbs. His grip moved upwards again, massaging me along the way, kneading and squeezing up my calves. It was becoming difficult to focus on anything other than the way he was touching me. "Do you like being punished, Dorothy?" The scarecrow asked in a low whisper.

I swallowed, but I didn't respond.

"That's not a no." He smirked, but still I didn't respond. So he rolled his neck, drawing attention to the scar that circled his skin. It looked as though he'd been decapitated and sewn back together. "My *dearest* Grunhilda quite enjoyed the way I punished her. She gave me many gifts when I was her whore, and not the least of which was an immortal body that long outlived my heart and my conscience." His fingers slipped just under my skirt this time, climbing up just high enough to hide his hands completely. He now rubbed those circles on the sensitive skin of my inner thighs. "Don't be so tense, sweetheart. Her death is delightful news. I simply needed you to confirm it for me."

Comforting. I didn't know why that was the first word to settle in my mind, but it was. His little circles inched dangerously higher. I clenched my thighs together, stopping the ascent before he felt something I'd rather him not notice. "S-so how about you help me down as a thank you?"

Crowe released me suddenly, then he touched a finger to his lips in thought. "I suppose such a thing does owe you my gratitude." That sharp smile sent shivers through me. "Fine then. You can consider me in your debt, Sweet Dorothy. And I am a man who always pays his debts."

"Thank you." I managed to say as he began gingerly undoing my bindings. He freed my ankles, then he started on my waist, my neck, then my wrists. When the last wire was unraveled, he lifted me from the hooks that held me in place, and he set me softly on the ground. Just like that, I was saved.

I rubbed my neck absently where the barbs had injured me, then I turned to Tobias with a start. "I'm sorry, can you please help me get him down, too?"

Crowe nodded, then he joined my efforts of unraveling the barbs. I appreciated his superior strength as he lifted Tobias from his hooks and placed him safely on the ground.

I checked his pulse first, for fear he may have taken too hard a hit to the head. The gentle beating of his heart gave me calm, and I shook him lightly to wake him up. Tobias groaned as he blinked himself awake.

With a start, he sprung to his feet in a stance that was ready to fight. "Dorothy, are you alright? Who is this?" He growled.

I nodded. "I'm quite alright, thanks to our new friend." I motioned to Crowe, who took a bow in response. "Tobias, this is Crowe. Crowe, this is Tobias. My... uh..."

"Her friend and protector." Tobias immediately stepped between us. He placed a hand on my chest and pressed me slightly behind him. "Did you do this?" He asked with measured caution while surveying the miniature warzone. It reminded me of when Toto used to defend me from our house guests by barking wildly between us. Only now his bark was much deeper, and something told me his bite was much more severe.

"They did it to themselves, really." Crowe shrugged nonchalantly. "As you clearly experienced, the munchkins are a stupid and superstitious people. If you'd preferred, I could have let them bleed you out, but I decided I would rather have your continued company. A woman who is so callous as to wear the shoes of someone she murdered, after all, is someone worth protecting."

Tobias eased his defenses. It was barely perceptible, but I noticed.

"I see." He said. "So you mean Dorothy no harm."

Crowe glanced playfully upward. "I mean lots of harm, honestly. The more harm I can share, the more joy I find. But your sweet girl has put me in her debt, so if she so prefers, I'll save my violence for the rest of Oz."

"Yes, I *would* prefer that." I said with a quick wave of my hand.

"Then it's done." He added with an elegant tip of his hat. "I will protect you both so long as you should want it."

Tobias seemed to accept that response. Even if there were thinly veiled threats in all of Crowe's words, I think so long as Toto believed *I* was safe, he didn't care if harm could come to himself. Still, if Tobias was willing to accept Crowe, than that was all the confirmation I needed. I trusted his judge of character much better than I trusted my own, after all.

I took a step forward, now beside Tobias instead of behind him. "I appreciate the offer, but I'm not sure how you're going to help us." I frowned, and I continued. "I would love your protection as we make our way back to Kansas, but I don't even know what direction we should be travelling. It could be south or north or east or west…"

"Well, there's no witch in the east anymore, so that would be a safe direction." Crowe pondered. "But if it will get you to Kansas or not, I couldn't say. I know of someone who might be able to though."

"Who's that?" Tobias asked with unhidden suspicion.

"The Wizard of Oz, of course. He's the ruler of all of Oz, and he should, thusly, know of our neighboring nations. If anyone can help you find Kansas again, it should be him."

"The Wizard of Oz…" I repeated the title. "Is he evil like the witch? Or the munchkins?"

The scarecrow shrugged. "No clue, I've never met him. He hasn't granted audience to anyone… ever, actually. But they say that he's all seeing, all mighty, and all powerful. I can't see any reason he wouldn't want to meet with someone as lovely as you, sweet Dorothy."

Toto chewed his lip for a moment, then he muttered quietly. "If he's all powerful, I wonder if he can turn me back into my old form?"

"Sure, why not?" Crowe's demeanor was much more friendly now. "Or at least he better be able to, since I've been planning to ask him to return my conscience and compassion. Grunhilda took a lot from me when she reached into my brain, and I lost even more when she exiled me to this post. Now that she's dead, I'd like to build a life in this post-Hildy world too, if you don't mind me tagging along."

"How do we find this Wizard though?" I pursed my lips. It all sounded great in theory, but I knew where this Wizard lived about as well as I knew where Kansas was.

"The Wizard lives in the Emerald City, placed firmly in the center of the continent." Crowe's local knowledge was already becoming a great asset. "A brick road connects the north, west, east, and south kingdoms to the heart of Oz that governs it all. If we follow that path, we'll certainly find it." With that, he swept his hand to the west, where the distant gold of the path glistened under the now fully risen sun. The way the light reflected off the bright yellow bricks made it impossible to miss, even with vegetation blocking the view.

Toto glanced at me, and I glanced at him. Then I took a deep breath and placed my first foot forward. "Then I guess we're off to see the Wizard." I said with finality. *The Wizard of Oz. I hope he's kinder than these munchkins.*

Chapter 8

"TOTO"

TOBIAS

I didn't know what to think of this new companion. He barely looked like he was alive, and he had no natural warmth to make me reassess that impression. He had no heart, he didn't breathe, he didn't sweat—he did nothing that helped me to get a read on him. Dorothy was so quick to accept him, but over the last couple of years since I'd been watching over her, she'd been quick to accept a lot of men, so that didn't mean much in the grand scheme. I'd seen her fall in with some terrible, narcissistic people in the past, and I would hate for that to happen in such a strange new environment.

Crowe also wasn't giving off any sense of hostility, however, so in theory, he was passing some of my most basic evaluations. Whatever happened, at least now I was strong enough to protect her. This was my opportunity to do better than I could when I possessed a body so small and frail. Whether that meant talking her down from a panic attack or tearing her enemies apart, I was open to whatever it took to be that man for her.

We walked together through the field, hill after hill, always getting nearer and nearer to the shiny brick road. When we'd at last reached its edge, I had to say this so called *'yellow'* was quite impressive. The bricks that made up the pathway were bright and vibrant, glistening like Dorothy's lovely hair, while also heavily contrasting with the darker color that made up the grass, or the color of the sky that was the same as Dorothy's kind eyes.

It was overwhelming all these new sights and sounds. Spending my whole life in the body of a color blind dog, I'd never realized what I was missing out on. But now that I had this new form, my soul felt like it could truly stretch out. It felt right. Almost familiar and comfortable and freeing.

I was seeing everything in a new light now, really. My lady was so vivid in her mannerisms and her bright, captivating colors. Her soft lips, her tanned skin, her multi-colored hair, her gently swaying dress that caught the breeze in animated ruffles—she was a vision of goodness and beauty, yet she was also so small and vulnerable.

"I present to you the road of yellow brick." Crowe interrupted my thoughts with a tilt of his chin. I eyed him as his lips curled into a smile. He always seemed happy in an unexplainably cruel way. I needed to get more of a read on him.

We began to walk the path, and I took position between he and Dorothy. "So how did you lose your humanity, Scarecrow?" I prodded carefully, curious to how he might respond.

Crowe cocked his head to the side before he answered. "Do you want me to show you?" The way he asked almost seemed serious, and the way his sharp teeth shone in the sun had me immediately on my guard.

"I don't think anyone wants the gory details." Dorothy stepped in, and immediately he softened his gait. *Interesting.* While I had obvious reason to listen to my lady, I couldn't understand what had him obeying so quickly and without argument. Dorothy was certainly special, and she did have a way of making people respond to her, even if I'd had to sit helplessly by as she attracted the wrong attention one too many times. It was hard to say yet where Crowe fell on the spectrum. Something about him still felt a touch unhinged for my taste. I would have to stay vigilant around him.

CHaPTER 9

DOROTHY

The Yellow Brick Road was long and arduous, made so much worse by uneven paving and missing bricks. I barely got to enjoy the scenery; I was so busy keeping my eyes on the ground in front of me. The glare of the yellow in the bright Oz sun made it difficult to see the pitfalls until you were tripping in them, and I had to say, I was not at all impressed with the handiwork.

This was probably built by those munchkins. Such awful little things.

Though in the rare instance I did get to take a break long enough to look around, Oz was quite beautiful. It was similar to the world I was used to, yet completely different and fantastic at the same time. The fern trees that were speckled sporadically in the horizon were bright and billowing, wafting in the soft breeze like they were waving hello to passersby. To the West I could see mountains that were dark and foreboding, complete with black thunderclouds lighting up the sky. To the South, there was the distant illusion of sand dunes and cacti. To the east was the tropical ghetto of the munchkins, and to the North, it was flat enough that I couldn't make out any obvious landmarks. At this distance, I could only see the tallest and most prominent features, but it was enough to make Oz appear a rather diverse and interesting place.

I inhaled deeply, taking in the scent of flowers and fresh air around me. Far removed from the smell of the city, and far removed from the smell of the farm. In this moment of calm, I felt like I could finally find my bearings.

Oz had been overwhelming since the moment I'd arrived, and I'd been bombarded with so much stimuli, I hadn't gotten to truly appreciate my predicament.

This seemed to be some sort of fantasy world, and apparently it existed on the other side of a cyclone. I didn't *think* I was dead, but I could never say for sure. Though I would assume that pain and death wouldn't be a thing here if it was an actual form of the underworld, and Crowe had mentioned he was immortal. I'd like to argue that this wasn't really happening in some delusional yet logical way, but there's a point in life where you just have to stare at your reality, no matter how horrifying it may be, and accept that this is your mountain to climb or fall off of. To say it was any worse than a movie set was a stretch anyway. I could roll with these kinds of punches. I've pretended to be a warrior princess before, after all.

This is real, and I'm going to survive. I said to myself in silent affirmation. My therapist had told me I could manifest whatever I wanted for myself so long as I believed it. I was still working on the genuineness of those beliefs, but it couldn't hurt to try chanting them. I was a "sorceress" now, after all.

Maybe if the munchkins kept calling me that, that would become true one day, too.

Head up and eyes forward, I trained my gaze on the road ahead. What should I expect of the Emerald City? I couldn't begin to imagine. Would this Wizard of Oz be a normal sized person like Tobias and Crowe? Would the city be full of more of these munchkin types? Did country munchkins and city munchkins have very different cultures like we did in the States? I had so many questions, yet I knew neither of my companions could answer them. We were all at least a little in the dark in this place. Though Crowe was a local, I didn't know that he got to explore anything other than the Wicked Witch's vagina, and Tobias was about as lost as I was.

I glanced between them. Tobias walked beside me, his eyes always scanning the horizon for potential enemies, while Crowe took several steps ahead, unbothered by anything that might go on behind him. I couldn't help but notice the way Tobias would occasionally stare at our new party member but not saying anything. I knew he was withholding his opinion for my sake, but it was still a bit comical to see the way words would bubble up, he'd prepare himself to voice them, then he'd frown and shake his head and say nothing. Tobias was really expressive in his face and in his general mannerisms. He seemed to wear his heart on his sleeve, and I already liked that about this human version of him.

I felt like I'd picked up an entourage. My personal bodyguards. I smiled to myself, trying not to focus on the fact that one of them was magically animated zombie with evil black eyes and that the other was technically my toy puppy. If you ignored that though…

Right, great to have some companions who I liked and trusted anyway.

I continued walking and walking, listening to nothing but the sound of rustling leaves, gentle breezes, and my silver shoes tapping on the brick. It was peaceful and calm, really. Like going on a nice hike through a new place, enjoying the unusual view of ferns and mountains and blue skies. I'd been dealing with a lot of tension in my day to day life, and this was a welcome comfort despite the circumstances. A bizarre way for the universe to give me what I needed, but I could still appreciate the effort.

We continued on for hours, engaging in little more than small talk and observations as we went.

"How far is this Emerald City exactly?" I asked Crowe up ahead.

"Far." Crowe said with a shrug. "I'm not sure how far, since I've never been, but from what I understand, it takes days on a broom. Potentially weeks on foot."

"Weeks?" I frowned at the ground. My stomach rumbled as if to remind me of my missed breakfast. "Is there any way to get food for these weeks? Any plants that are edible or streams with some trout? I know how to fish. I don't like hunting, but if I had to, I could do that too. My uncle taught me to dress a deer as a kid, and I'm good at cooking. I'm just going to need *something* to eat here."

"Eat?" Crowe stared at me, and his eyes blinked rapidly. "I miss eating." He added with a sense of nostalgia. "If you want, we could probably roast some munchkins. I'm not sure how they compare to a deer, and I personally find them a bit stringy, but they'll get the job done. Might be the only job they can get done, really."

My whole stomach lurched at the mere suggestion. If my face had turned green, I wouldn't have been terribly surprised. "No, I think I'm good on that."

"Hmmm, suit yourself." Crowe shrugged, ever so nonchalantly. Maybe he really was missing his humanity. Though how you remove such a thing from a person, I couldn't begin to guess, but there were very few things in Oz that were matching with my general expectations. Considering I'd watched him saw off his own head a couple hours ago, that was hardly farfetched. "So is eating something you *have* to do? Or is that more like a preference?" He tilted his head to the side inquisitively.

"More like I'll die if I don't." I scrunched my nose. "Weren't you ever human? I'm not sure I'm understanding what you Oz people are at this point."

"I believe so, but I don't recall much about it." Crowe looked up at the sky in pondering. "When Hildy lobotomized me, I lost some memories along the way. I can tell you what her pussy tastes like, but I'd be hard pressed to tell you anything else I've done prior to being strung up on that post."

"I see." I frowned at that. This Witch truly did sound rather wicked. Maybe not the most heinous person I've *ever* encountered, but certainly in the top ten... maybe top twenty, actually. I could think of ten slime balls too awful to be outranked.

We continued to walk, and my stomach continued to rumble. I glanced at the plants beside the path, hoping one of them might have some sort of fruit or berry, but despite the lushness of the foliage, there wasn't anything that appeared to be edible.

Tobias kept his eyes forward. I assumed he would need food soon too, but I didn't know much about his new body yet. Since this was Oz and all, he could be more like the scarecrow than a regular man for all I knew. He'd eaten both of our breakfasts, though, so at the very least, he'd probably sustain himself longer than I would today.

We walked on and on and on, until my legs grew tired, and the sun was starting to dip down over the horizon. "How about sleep. Do you need sleep?" I caught up to Crowe again, who seemed terribly unbothered by the distance we'd walked.

Crowe's mouth flattened in a line. His demonic eyes looked somehow less threatening when paired with such an awkward expression. "You have to sleep, too?"

"I'm sorry to be such an inconvenience." I shook my head, not at *all* sorry to be such an inconvenience.

"I didn't mean it like that, sweet girl." Crowe frowned, as though he was capable of emotion. "I meant it more to say there are some terrifying creatures in these woods, and I can't see how you'll safely fall unconscious for hour after hour after hour while the land is veiled by darkness. Such vulnerability is a death wish."

"It's a good thing I travel with a scarecrow who doesn't need sleep who promised to protect me then, eh?" I smiled sweetly. I'd seen enough of his fighting ability to be pretty confident we'd be fine, though I had little concept of what might even lurk in woods like these.

"I suppose it is." Crowe pursed his lips, then we fell back into silence. We kept walking a few more yards, when Crowe at last turned to Toto, looking rather distraught. "Do you sleep too?"

"Yes." Tobias said with exasperation.

"And you eat?" Crowe's brows were furrowed in a way that was comically perplexed for his innately demonic face.

"Oh my god." I threw my head back and let out a heavy sigh. "You are literally the only immortal, organ-less zombie here. The rest of us have to actually maintain our bodies."

"That's unfortunate." Crowe seemed genuinely perplexed and let down. "It's not like you're the first person I've ever had to be careful with, but I'm a bit disappointed, I'll admit."

"Why?" Tobias scrunched up his nose.

"Because being gentle and careful isn't really my thing." He spoke matter-of-factly and did not elaborate. "But I suppose I'll manage." Brief as it was, I couldn't help but notice the way his gaze fell on my silver shoes. And in that moment, I wondered if he was only going to be loyal so long as I had them in my possession. Maybe they were enchanted, and he had to be loyal to whoever wore them. That would explain his extended service to someone who he seemed to despise.

But that wasn't a question I was going to ask. So long as he helped us get home, there was no reason to question him. I'd just accept this temporary alliance for what I knew it was.

"Why don't we stop here so we can build a shelter while we still have a little daylight." Tobias nodded toward a clearing in the trees. It was a large circle of uncharacteristically sparse vegetation, where random stumps still protruded from the ground as if the forest had been cleared by a woodsman. "It'll be easier to see attackers approaching if they have to run through open grass."

"Fair enough." Crowe nodded. "I wouldn't mind a break anyway."

CHAPTER 10

"TOTO"

TOBIAS

I broke some branches off a nearby tree, and I used the strong wood to build a tiny shelter of leaves and twigs and mud. It was rugged and simple, but I knew Dorothy didn't mind things like that. She wasn't one to need heavy pampering or big luxuries, even if she had fallen down a bit of a rabbit hole in Hollywood. No matter what happened, she'd always kept to her roots, and I loved that about her. She could wear a nice gown without losing her "roll your sleeves up and get it done" personality, for better or for worse.

Once the largest part of the structure was secure, I took off my tunic and laid it across the springy greenery. It wouldn't cover the ground completely, but it would be more comfortable for her than lying directly in the grass. I spread the material smoothly then looked up at Dorothy who'd been watching my handiwork the whole time.

"Will this work?" I asked. "Or wait, I can use my pants, too." I began unbuckling my belt, and immediately Dorothy threw up her hands and shook her head rapidly.

"No—no that's fine. The shirt's plenty. Keep your pants on." She said through a bright red flush that filled her entire face. I stared at her for several seconds when the reason she was blushing finally hit me. A heat filled my own cheeks, and I turned my face away hoping she hadn't noticed.

"Of course." I nodded while not wanting to share the strained smile on my face. *Did Dorothy see me like that?* This body was rather similar to the kind of men she used to tumble with. I swallowed, not even wanting to think such a thing about my lady. "Get comfortable, and I'll go get some water for the night." I tipped my chin in the direction of a distant stream that she may not have been able to hear as well as I could. It was a good excuse to walk away.

"Thanks, Tobias." Her voice was soft and gentle. And so was the hand she placed on my head. She pulled away without ruffling my hair, and I frowned at this strangeness between us. I didn't want it to be awkward, and I hoped this new form wouldn't ruin the relationship we had.

She climbed into the tent and curled up on my shirt, looking so cute and so content, and that was my cue to go for a walk.

Crowe stood against a tree not far from our little tent. He met my gaze as I neared his position.

"I'm going to go get some water… Which I assume you also don't need." I told him with a nod. Crowe was a strange anomaly, and tonight would be our first chance to see if he was sincere in protecting Dorothy. If he was, we could continue this journey together merrily. If he wasn't, I'd find a way to pin him to a post that he wouldn't be able to free himself from.

"You assume correctly." His eyes scanned my expression as though he was trying to read something in it. A ghost of a smile touched his lips. "Though I must ask, while I'm trying so very hard to understand you mortals and your human bodies: is cuddling with the girl also something you *need* in order to survive, Puppy Dog?" His tone was blatantly teasing and antagonistic, and I wasn't going to let him rattle me that easily.

"It is." I confirmed without missing a beat. "In fact, touch starvation can cause havoc on the human body, to the point an infant can die from not receiving affection." This was all true, and a large portion of why Dorothy had been allowed to keep me as her emotional support. "In addition, shared body heat throughout the night not only promotes better quality sleep, but it prevents hypothermia when sleeping outside without adequate insulation."

"Fascinating." Still that smirk of his remained. "You had better touch her good and hard then, because I would hate to be up all night, fighting demons and wild cats, only to have her die without your heat."

The implication wasn't lost on me, and I knew he was just trying to get a rise out of me. The fact that it was working wasn't something I could say I was proud of. I swallowed, and I broke eye contact, then I walked past Crowe, not wanting to speak another word to him lest he find some other way to twist my words. My relationship with Dorothy was still that of protector and friend, and nothing else. I'd never look at her like some kind of outlet for pleasure like so many men had done to her in the past. While she was beautiful and kind and loving and deserving of all the attention she got, I was not going to betray her in that way.

But this new body of mine seemed to react to her in a way I wasn't used to, and she seemed to look at me in a way she never used to, and I didn't know what to make of it at this point.

I strolled down to the stream, and I built a small vessel to transport the water using more sticks, mud, and leaves. It wasn't perfect, but the leaves were tightly woven enough that they would keep the water reasonably clean, and I could build her a small fire to boil out any bacteria.

I stared down into the little bowl, and for the first time since taking this form, I saw my reflection clear as day. My strong jaw, my dark hair, the lean muscles of my bare chest… I hooked a finger through the red collar around my neck, and I slipped along the inside of the leather until I hooked the dog tag connected to the central metal ring. "Tobias – Answers to Toto. Service Dog" was written cutely on the tag.

My lips downturned for a reason that was difficult to explain. I was born to take care of her, and I would always and forever do exactly that. I wouldn't ever let myself be one of the men she feared or resented. I was proud to be her partner and protector.

So why did I now feel so complicated?

Wanting to get out of my own head, I lifted the water over my shoulder, then I walked back to camp. Crowe still stood idly against a tree, and I chose not to speak to him. That smile on his face as I placed water beside the tent and crawled inside was enough communication.

Dorothy was already half asleep when I pulled down the cover of leaves on the doorway. She shivered, and I reached over to pull her into the warmth of my chest.

But then I stopped myself. She was defenseless and I had all the power here. It… it was inappropriate to hold her like that now. Last night, I'd simply wanted to calm her anxiety, but if I did that when she didn't absolutely need my touch, would I be taking advantage of her? Would I be just as bad as the last man who hurt her?

"Tobias." Her soft voice broke me out of my train of thought. I forced my nerves down, but I didn't speak. "Will you help keep me warm tonight?" There was a shake to her voice. She sounded embarrassed but desperate.

Without a blanket, perhaps she was. That would explain such a question.

"Of course, Dorothy." *Right. That settles it.* I nudged up next to her, and I pulled her into my chest, encompassing her like she was a small spoon. I couldn't let the scarecrow or anyone else get in my head about why I was sleeping with Dorothy. She needed me, and I was there for her, and it didn't have to be any more complicated than that.

CHAPTER 11

"THE SCARECROW"

CROWE

Dorothy and Tobias were off doing the devil knows what in that makeshift tent, while I was officially on guard duty for the duration of the trip. I leaned against a tall tree, and I stared at the half moon sky in boredom. It felt a bit like being a scarecrow again, to be quite honest. Equally as banal and equally as lacking in real threats. It was going to take forever to get to the Emerald City if we had to stop every single day. *Humans, I swear.*

Which I would have been perfectly content with if not for the fact that, first of all, standing around while a pretty girl slept felt like a wasted opportunity for the both of us to have a good time, and second of all, not killing anything for hours at a time was a waste of my talents. It would be nice if some sort of monster could show up. Maybe destroy the tent, attack my friends, give me something to get riled up about. I was craving a song of gushing blood and screams like a vague itch for something salty, and it was starting to make me question myself. While I didn't have much of a conscience these days, I did still have needs. Just because I couldn't feel guilt, doesn't mean I didn't want to feel *something*. Rage and pleasure were typically my go-to's—*I'm not sure if they're separate things, really*—and I wouldn't mind someone enraging me right now.

I wondered if, like eating food and needing to sleep, these were things Dorothy and Tobias craved sometimes, too. The taste of violence was so satisfying, if didn't at least *think* about it, they must not have ever tried it. I'd have to ask and get to know them better in the morning. I would hate to find us incompatible as companions.

I sighed. A crow fluttered down to me and I outstretched my hand to give him a perch. The silky black bird settled in on my forearm and began cleaning itself with its beak. I kept steady and stable while it fluttered its lovely dark feathers. "Anything fun to kill around here, little buddy?" I asked my winged company. The birds had long become my cohorts since my days in the pasture. I had a knack for befriending detestable creatures.

It lifted its head and shared with me a view into those little black marble-like eyes. Just enough so I could sense the answer of *"nothing that provides any real sport."*

I rolled my head to the side, pressing my cheek to the bark of the tree, and I stared at the little tent. The material rustled just a touch. *I hope Tobias is fucking her in there, but they're probably just cuddling. Maybe even legitimately sleeping.* He seemed a bit too meek to make a move on her anyway. A wolf in battle and a golden retriever in bed. Boring.

Boring boring *boring.*

I drifted my gaze to the empty horizon, when the crow launched itself from my arm and flew over to another perch just a few feet away. An odd perch. Not a tree. Not a rock. It almost looked like some sort of statue.

I shoved myself off the tree, and I paced over to this curious object. The closer I got, the more clear its shape came into view. It was a man, I thought. I couldn't sense a heartbeat or breathing, but it definitely wasn't just a simple sculpture. I got nearer still, and the little moonlight there was caught on a metallic glint.

Less boring.

I placed my hand on his face, and I felt along the contours. Smooth, cold, and hard. He was taller than me and intensely muscular. A metal mask was wrapped around the bottom half of his face like a muzzle on a vicious dog, and his hair was short and slicked back, revealing the irritation in his expression. Likely the last look he'd had before he was frozen in place by whatever magic put him here.

I dropped my palm to his neck, then I slid it along his shoulder. *Such* muscle. He was built like a god, truly. I bet he could murder someone with his bare fingers. *Twist and break bones, dig through flesh…*

My cock twitched at the thought, which only made me want to explore a touch more. With a wide palm, I took in the firm and thick muscles in his chest, then the defined abdominals that created hills and valleys in his smooth yet petrified skin. As my touch reached the waist of his pants, I smirked to myself. *I wonder…*

Over the clothing, I cupped him between his legs, then I lifted my eyes to his. "Plenty to play with here, tin soldier."

His eyes shot open, and my gaze was met by shining silver. The expression in his brow remained rather perturbed. I couldn't say if that was because his face was stuck like that, or if it was a genuine and current sentiment.

So of course I had to test it. I dipped my grip a little lower, sliding my fingertips beneath his balls. A flicker of irritation. I chuckled. "Let me guess," I purred as I removed my hand from his substantial cock and returned it to his metal muzzled cheek, "you used to play with a wicked witch, and now you're a cursed doll just like me. Blink once for yes. Twice if I'm somehow wrong."

He said nothing, I presumed because his jaw had been frozen, but he did give me one single, satisfying blink. I was always right about these things.

"That's what I thought. These witches are so predictable." I shook my head in feigned disgust. Though I had fared better than most of their fuck dolls. I'd only been bled out and robbed of my soul, but I could still function like a normal person in most other ways. More or less. "I know you weren't Hildy's toy. So which one cursed you? Eloise in the North? Gwen in the West?" No response. I should have known. "Sasha in the South."

There was the blink I was waiting for. "Sasha. You poor thing." I chuckled. She had a... reputation. Not the least of which when it came to her penchant for disemboweling and dismembering her playthings. But for him to be alive-ish and standing, rather than being granted the mercy of a swift death, he had likely done something as offensive as I had. "You must have really fucked up to end up in this region. The so called good witches of the North and South never step into the Wicked West or the Evil East. So what exactly did she do to you, tin man?" I felt along his muzzle. There was no apparent way to remove it. It seemed to be adhered to his face. "Did she take your voice?"

The tin soldier's gaze fell over my shoulder. I turned to see what he was so fixated on.

But a few feet away, there on the forest floor, buried in the leaves of a small fern, was a glowing bottle. It would have been impossible to see from any other angle but his. If I were to guess, it was his chance and salvation, and Sasha placed it there so he could forever see hope so close yet so far. Devious. Almost delightful. I might have even called her brilliantly evil if not for the fact that I would never side with one of Oz's witches.

So instead, I'd call her a cruel bitch and help out.

83

I fished what appeared to be a small satchel with a bottle of lotion from the brush, and I returned to my little statue. His silver eyes reflected relief as I pumped some lotion into my hands and started to rub his shoulders. His body softened under this moisturizing massage, and he physically relaxed into my touch. Such a tough, strong man, yet he was completely at my mercy.

Hmmm, I should be abusing this more.

I really should have been, but I was admittedly enjoying this softening of his body more than I should. I ran lotioned hands down his biceps, and I felt his firm muscles flex in my grip. I made it down to his elbows, and his heavy forearms dropped limply at his side as soon as I freed his flesh. I gave him a wry smile before shifting my efforts to his chest, his abs, his… neck. I was sweet enough to come up to his face and free his muscles so he could share his expressions with me, and when that brow softened, I only then made my way to his hands. Once the entirety of his upper body was free, I presented him with the bottle of remaining lotion.

"I would happily finish the job for you, but if I keep rubbing you like this, you might learn some things about yourself you're not quite comfortable with." I smirked. A flush in his cheeks implied he might already be comfortable with such a thing, but he took the suggestion and went to work freeing the lower half of his body.

He slipped his lathered hands into his pants, and he rubbed on his thigh muscles with noticeable pressure, working thick quads until they flexed and relaxed. He seemed to hesitate as he moved back up to his hips, and as he rounded his body to squeeze his glutes. Paralyzed or not, it would be inaccurate to describe any of the areas he rubbed as truly *softening*. The Southern Witch had some preferences, indeed.

He made it down to his calves and his feet, finishing the last of his legs, yet he was very pointedly avoiding one very specific area.

"Don't suffer on my account." I said, taking a step back to lean against the tree and watch. "Just pretend you don't have an audience."

The tin man flushed. He swallowed through his freed neck. I lifted an eyebrow as he still hesitated to touch himself in the only place that was still hard as steel. He must have now been *quite* uncomfortable.

"Do you want me to do it for you?" I certainly wouldn't have minded. Man or woman, I was never terribly picky. A nice cock was fun for everyone, and fucking moans through someone was always pleasurable. I was never one to turn down a hot, tight playground.

He shook his head, so I leaned back and held that very uncomfortable eye contact just to watch him fidget. With a flash of deviance, he nudged his pants just enough to let me see what we were playing with today. He wrapped his fingers around a thick, long, erect cock lined in metal barbells, one step of metal piercing through every inch. *Interesting.*

The flesh of his palm caught on every rung of the ladder as he relieved himself with a shaky stroke. I couldn't see much of his expression behind that metal muzzle, but I knew it was a satisfied one.

"Go on. Keep working it in. You want more than just your surface level nerves free." I added with a smirk. He narrowed his gaze, looking rather fierce as he complied. Spiteful yet willing. *I think I wouldn't mind this one's company on a longer term basis.*

I held eye contact, more interested in watching the micro-shifts in his expression than the physical act itself.

There was something satisfying about watching people *feel*. Whether themselves or deep pain, it was something I'd long lost, and I held nothing but envy for those who could experience large and overwhelming sensations.

His expression remained steady, as though he was trying to keep it together while he lost himself. I'm sure he'd worked the lotion in enough by now, but he'd walked himself right to the edge in the process and couldn't stop when he was so very, very close.

He turned his head and he closed his eyes, and I frowned as the window to his mind closed so suddenly. He expressed himself so vividly through those silver irises, and I wanted more. "Now, now." I said with a shake of my head, before I pushed off the tree again. I paced over to my new friend, and I lifted his chin back to face mine again. "It's cruel not to share." I whispered against his muzzle. His eyes opened slowly, though under the weight of those pretty dark lashes, he only let me in half way. Not enough.

I wrapped my fingers around his knuckles, and I squeezed his grip until it was tight around his cock, driving those barbells into his palm. That got him to open his eyes all the way. I drew small circles on his wrist with my thumb until he eased up his rigid tension, then I decided to help. Still gripping his hand, I began to guide the motion in slow and steady strokes. "Eyes on me." I picked up the pace. "Let me take you to the other side."

He grabbed onto my shoulder, gripping me with bruising strength, but he still met my intensity with that sparkling silver. That was confirmation enough for me. I pushed him further and further. Though I don't think he could speak, his muffled moans were telling enough on their own. The slickness of his dribbling pre-cum lubricated the ride, and his hand slid easily up and down his shaft. My iron grip assured he didn't get lazy, while I braced his hip with my other hand to assure he could pump hard and strong until he gave in completely.

A tensing of his brow and a squint of his eyes marked his release. His cock tensed in my grip, and a thick heat coated both of our palms. I held him there, not letting him collapse despite the shake in his legs. He'd probably not used those muscles in a while. I could relate to that feeling.

So I held him there for several moments as he gathered his wits about him. He nuzzled into my shoulder until he could right himself, then he reluctantly removed his hand from his softened, partially metal cock. I released my hold on him and dragged my hand upward, smearing his come across his stomach to clean my palm.

"They say it's good for your skin, and yours seems rather dry." I rubbed it in, then I licked the remaining residue from my skin. He didn't protest, but the blush that was nearly visible even with his metal mask was telling. "Crowe." I stated simply. "I'm on my way to see the Wizard in the Emerald City in hopes of undoing the curses bestowed upon me by the Wicked Witch of the East. Would you like to come?"

He nodded. <*"You can call me Talos."*> The words were spoken directly into my mind, and I was taken aback when I realized what he'd done. <*"Now that we've shared this connection, I can speak to you this way."*>

I pursed my lips. "And here I just thought you enjoyed a bit of voyeurism, but I see you were rather calculating with this seduction."

<*"No, you were just easy."*>

I'm not sure that I liked this communication string. Words like that should never be in my head, even if spoken by someone else. "I see." My eyes narrowed in irritation, but it wasn't worth a fight. "Well, my offer still stands. I assume you'd like your ability to speak back without having to come on someone first," *though there are worse things.* "Will you join me on my journey, Talos?"

He simply nodded. And I took a step back.

"Excellent, then come join me in standing guard. It'll be nice to pass the nights with someone else who doesn't need food and sleep."

Talos stared at me quizzically, but I had the whole night to fill him in on the situation with Dorothy and Tobias. While I disliked his invasion of my mind space, I supposed it was worth the inconvenience to have a companion to help me pass the boredom of traveling with humans.

I'm sure the sweet girl would be fine with it. She seemed rather open to help and friendship in a way that was admittedly rather dangerous. But I liked watching her get herself into danger anyway. She was hotter when she was scared, and first impressions left me thinking she was certainly trusting enough to walk into these sorts of traps.

Excellent. A most successful and not boring night this would be.

CHAPTER 12

DOROTHY

I awoke in the warm snuggle of Toto's arms, cocooned in the comfort of his body warmth. Despite the strangeness of my life at present, these last few nights were oddly the best sleep I'd ever gotten. I should have been nervous and scared and constantly jumping at every little sound, knowing I had no real protection in this thin palm tent, yet I felt safer than I had when I lived alone in that Hollywood apartment with the best security system I could afford.

Maybe I just needed to get away from that environment, or maybe it was because my sweet dog was now tough, handsome, and protective. I'd always considered myself a feminist, but I'd have to admit that there was something deep down in my soul that liked the feeling of having a big, strong man who wanted to keep me safe and cared for instead of bringing me harm. Trying to stand as an equal in a male run industry didn't give me a lot of warm fuzzy feelings in regards to men, and it certainly didn't make me see that half of the species as protectors. But Tobias wasn't like them. He had the body of a model with the heart of a dog, making him an unconditional friend and companion who I knew I could trust, even in this new form.

I snuggled into the intimacy of my big spoon, and he stirred just slightly. I rolled over on his arm to meet his slowly opening eyes. "Good morning." I said with a soft smile.

He returned the expression. "Did you sleep well, Dorothy?"

I nodded, and he took that as his cue to sit up and give me space. I missed the warmth as soon as it was gone, but it was probably about time we got back on the road anyway.

I straightened out my dress, then I crawled out of our makeshift shelter. Tobias followed, taking a small pot of water he'd gathered the night before, and starting a fire to get it boiling to disinfect it. I appreciated his ingrained survival ability. I didn't entirely understand how or when he learned it, but I just assumed it was the natural instinct of animals.

The warm sun met my face, and I stretched out towards its pleasant rays. This really wasn't so bad. It wasn't high luxury living, but it was slowly bringing me back to the roots that I needed. I smiled broadly, not thinking at all about the chaos of Oz, until I turned to see Crowe leaning against a tree, staring into the distance with a look of utter disinterest on his emotionless face. And beside him was…

"Who are you?" I blurted as I realized my weird, undead, unsleeping and uneating companions had multiplied overnight. The new one had dark, slicked back hair and silver eyes that were almost metallic in nature. More notable was the metal mask that covered the bottom half of his face like he was some sort of cyborg ninja, and most notable of all were his muscles sculpted by the gods themselves. He was shirtless and he was fucking ripped like a body builder on competition day.

But his ranking at the top of my hotness scale was not the point. The point was that I had no clue who he was or why he was here or where he came from or even if he was safe.

He stared at me for several moments, then he looked to Crowe, then back at me without saying a word.

"Crowe, who is this?" I tried again.

Crowe shrugged. "Talos." Was all he said.

"Is he... a friend of yours?" I waved a hand to demand he speed up the sharing of information. Crowe already seemed a bit off, so I wasn't sure how much I wanted to meet his friends. But then, the one and only good thing I could say right now was that we had slept safely last night, so maybe I shouldn't judge yet.

Crowe glanced at his companion. "I don't have friends, but he's more interesting than you and the dog in the middle of the night." My expression flattened, and I waited with puffed up cheeks for him to elaborate. An annoyed enough scrunching of my eyebrows finally got him to take the hint. "If you *must* know, I found him in the woods while I was standing watch. He's also been cursed by one of the four witches, and he would also like to see the Wizard to reverse his damage. I didn't think you'd mind if I invited him along."

I blinked several times.

"I... I guess I don't." I mean, I wanted to say he looked harmless enough, but I was pretty sure he could suffocate someone just by flexing. On the other hand, harmless was less helpful than being powerful in a place like this, so having another strong brute at my side would probably guarantee a safer journey to the Emerald City. If he needed help as much as the rest of us did, it didn't make sense to kick him off the team just because I wasn't expecting him.

I paused for several moments to contemplate this new development, when it finally dawned on me. "Wait, so does he... not talk?"

Crowe glanced at Talos again, then he returned his gaze to me. "The Witch of the South took his tongue, but we've formed a sort of unspoken trauma bond. I can be his translator." The singsong way he said it was nearly comical and somewhat uncharacteristic, but again, who was I to judge this weird friendship. If Crowe trusted him, I guess that was good enough for me, even if I didn't really trust Crowe himself.

I glanced over at Tobias, who had a squiggly and unreadable expression on his face as he held the now boiling pot of water over the flame. He shrugged his shoulders in a way that said *"your call, Dorothy,"* and I internally groaned at having to make all of these judge-of-character decisions myself.

"Well, then, the more the merrier…" I apparently said.

"Agreed." Crowe nodded, then he stood up and dusted the grass from his jeans. He offered Talos a hand, and that's how we ended up traveling with the weird, silent giant.

Chapter 13

"THE TIN MAN"

TALOS

Dorothy, Tobias, Crowe. These were my new travel partners. Crowe had saved my life, and I appreciated that fact, while the other two seemed to be plucky enough. I'd like to be able to speak to them myself, but it would require… some commitment I wasn't prepared to make. As it stood, Crowe had no idea what he'd walked into, but I didn't regret trapping him. There was no other reasonable way to break Sasha's spell, considering I'd been in that spot for months on end without so much as seeing a munchkin walk by on the yellow road. Where Crowe had been granted an immortal body and a loss of his conscience, I had metal bones and lost any need for my vital organs to stay functioning. Being able to survive a night in bed with women who needed their partner to have those traits to get off typically wasn't a recipe for healthy connection. There weren't many among us who had survived such abuse, and only those who had could truly empathize.

Beside, I'd need him for communication when we at last found the Wizard. He'd serve as my translator for a while. I'd have plenty of opportunity to get a better read on him as we went.

As for the other two, Tobias walked with a certain guardedness to his every step. I couldn't tell if he'd been abused or if he was simply overprotective and over cautious. It could go either way in a place like this, though I didn't think either of that pair was *from* this place. Dorothy, for example, was much too sweet and demure compared to the witches of Oz. She smiled, and not only when she was killing someone, and she had a range of expressions that danced along her brows when she spoke. I liked how simple and animated she was, and I had a feeling there was more to her than surface appearances.

I'd like to get to know her spirit better, but it would be difficult not being able to speak to her. Not having visible use of my mouth made that even more trying. I wished I could get this muzzle off.

We'd have to find ways to communicate with our bodies and our eyes. Sasha liked to communicate with her blades, but that was hardly a model I wanted to perpetuate and pass on to others. The only time I wanted to use a knife again was to sever her head from her pretty neck. For these two, I'd settle for hand signals.

We continued on toward the Emerald City, entering a wood speckled with fruit and flower trees. Dorothy's big blue eyes took in the image like she was staring at a masterpiece. Which made sense in hindsight. She probably needed to actually eat.

She glanced up at an apple that was a solid foot out of her reach. Noticing her interest, I caught up to her and plucked it from the tree.

"You need to keep your strength up." I wanted to say to her, but my words were, as always, trapped inside. She was an outlier from our kind, and something in my gut told me she was the only real hope we'd have to convince the Wizard to help the more cursed among us. It wasn't like I or the scarecrow had anything to offer the Wizard—even in the form of simply being good people. Whereas this girl may.

"He wants you to keep your strength up." Crowe stepped in, sharing a brief nod with me in understanding. I smiled behind my muzzle, though no one but him would know that. He stared into my eyes for a few moments, then he continued to serve as my voice. "This is a bit tough to explain to an outsider, but he and I are both what's considered a cursed puppet. If we were ever human like you or... uh..." Crowe glanced at Toto, "well, like *you*, Dorothy, we have no recollection of anything we'd done prior to being kidnapped and rewired by a witch, and as such, the rulers of Oz don't look fondly upon us. Munchkins may be the bottom of the food chain, but they are still given free will. He and I, on the other hand, lived in mighty castles as little more than toys for our masters. We have more physical strength, yet far less freedom to use it." He tried to explain. I nodded again to thank him.

"I see." Dorothy frowned: a look that didn't suit her face. I didn't like it on her at all. "So you're like actors being forced to play a role by a director who only cares about his own gratification." I could hear her heart beat pick up as she said the words. As if that was some sort of cue, Tobias reached over and took Dorothy's hand. He rubbed small circles on her wrist with his thumb, and that same heart rate slowed again. *Interesting.*

"I suppose that's a good way to put it. Only the director can make you do anything they want, and the consequences for speaking up are... severe." Crowe rubbed his neck. Those were his own words, but his face never showed any emotion. Wicked joy, perhaps, but that was a pre-programmed feeling for all of us.

"No, I think it still sounds about the same." Dorothy pursed her lips, and I couldn't help but notice the nervous way she wrapped an arm around her torso as a small form of protection. Like she was hugging herself. Perhaps Oz wasn't the only place that had some form of cursed puppets.

I plucked another apple from the tree, then I tossed it to her dark haired companion and looked to Crowe.

"Let's stop for a moment so you two can eat. The forest up ahead is full of wildlife and is notoriously treacherous." Crowe said aloud for me. "That was from Talos, by the way. I don't particularly care if you eat."

Dorothy rolled her eyes at Crowe, then she looked at me and gave me the softest smile I'd ever seen. If my heart was still beating, it might have skipped a tick or two for that. A strange thought.

I picked a few more apples from the tree, and I situated myself on the floor with my companions. Tobias dug into his fruit, and Dorothy ate slowly, perhaps trying to appear a touch more dignified. I watched them both, studying the very guarded way Tobias' eyes would shoot toward any subtle sound of rustling leaves or light breezes, and the differently guarded way that Dorothy would cover her mouth while she chewed, as if not wanting anyone to see her when she was less than proper and perfect.

I wasn't a fan of perfect, personally. I think she would be more beautiful a bit disheveled and ruffled.

"I feel the same." Crowe communicated directly into my mind while remaining outwardly silent. I was glad he'd figured out he didn't need to speak out loud to talk to me. *"She would be beautiful bathed in a wicked witch's blood."*

"You'd said she killed your witch though, no?" I stared at him inquisitively. *"Though your curse wasn't broken simply by killing her. Isn't that odd?"*

"I don't know. I've never heard of anyone murdering a witch before, so it's hard to say what's normal." Crowe licked his lips as his gaze fell back on Dorothy, who was sitting cross legged beside Tobias. I watched the movement of his eyes as they dipped down to the little silver shoes that rested on her feet. *"Though I suspect that she might BE my wicked witch now."*

My eyes widened at the implication. If Dorothy had Grunhilda's power... Was that why Crowe was travelling with her? Was he compelled to be by her side, or was he simply doing what was natural to him? Figuring he may be honest with me in this silent channel, I made clear eye contact with the Scarecrow. *"So then, are you travelling with her to protect her, or are you hoping she might..."*

He grinned widely, showing off his sharpened fangs that lined his entire jaw, and I nodded in clear understanding. Dorothy was not a wicked witch, but so long as she wore those silver shoes, she had the potential to be. I didn't know if her death could bring relief to Crowe, but I was curious enough to stick around and find that out. We could only hope the same corruption would never touch Dorothy's spirit like it did the most fabled Grunhilda.

Chapter 14

DOROTHY

What a strange turn of events this has been. I supposed Oz was at least more interesting than life on the homestead might have been, but it was difficult to even try and find any sort of normalcy with all these strange characters along for the ride. This was starting to feel like being a cat lady, but instead of accidentally rescuing an always growing number of stray kittens, I was rescuing hot psychopaths with trauma. They should call me the deranged man whisperer. Maybe the emotionally unavailable pied piper, who drew all the soulless killers of Oz away from their kingdoms.

Was that really so different than the men I'd attracted in the past? I glanced between my companions, then I returned my focus to this small gaggle of apples we'd gathered. They were unusually sweet, almost resembling honey more than fruit. Every bite was a pleasant combination of crisp and juicy, and it made me realize exactly how dehydrated I'd been. It was nice to get my strength back.

Talos handed me another apple since my stomach was still grumbling after the first, and his soft, silver eyes seemed to smile as he did so. I accepted the fruit, but I hesitated to take another bite. I should still be in an excessive calorie deficit, but they were so sweet, for all I knew I could have been eating pure sugar. I had no idea the nutritional or caloric density of these strange Oz fruits either.

I shook my head, trying my hardest to dismiss the notion. My body fat percentage was the last thing I should be thinking about right now, yet it was so hard to turn it off. Even now that I was out of that world of obsessive fitness, where my body was required to be a few levels thinner than perfect, and I counted every bite I took against my workouts, I still twitched at the thought that I might eat too much on accident just because I'd been in near starvation mode over the last day or two. I already had a tendency towards binge eating after growing up not always certain where our next meal might come from, and it had taken years to un-train my brain from clearing my plate just in case there wouldn't be more later.

So instead, I trained myself to leave the table still hungry, which at the moment, I was starting to realize wasn't any healthier.

Tobias rested a hand on my knee. His palm was warm, and the simple, gentle contact instantly put me at ease. He crunched into another fruit, and I frowned at how obsessive I was being. This was going to be a long journey, and I needed to focus on what was important. The Wizard likely wasn't going to send me packing if I gained a pound or two, and I couldn't imagine my companions would think less of me for eating enough to avoid fainting on the road. If anything, Crowe would just end up more confused as to how human bodies work if I'd eaten yet still couldn't function.

That thought amused me, and my heart felt a touch lighter. I barely knew these men, Toto included, really, yet I felt so comfortable with them already. Tobias was proving to be reliable and kind. Crowe was strange, a touch terrifying, literally a psychopath, yet not at all threatening towards myself. And Talos, while he'd not spoken a word, exuded a kindness and carefulness through his eyes and body language that put me at ease. I'd never felt this comfortable around men before, and I hoped it wasn't misguided trust.

I bit into the second apple, trying to convince myself that chasing away hunger pains wasn't a sign of poor discipline, and I made myself eat until I felt completely satiated this time. Slowly but surely, I needed to undo all of this unhealthy thinking that I'd decided I had to govern myself with. All of the things that were fine for others to enjoy but weren't acceptable for me had to *become* 'acceptable for me.' This would be a long journey, and all I could ask was that it also might be a healing one.

"That was delicious. Thank you, Talos." I said with a friendly smile.

He nodded, then he began packing spares for later in a satchel slung over his shoulder. He tucked aside a small bottle to make room for more.

Crowe stood in as his voice to respond, guessing my question before I could ask. "His witch had turned his bones to tin and placed a paralysis spell on him. The lotion is an antidote of sorts." His demonic eyes rolled from his companion back to myself. "Lots of other uses for a good lubricant though, if that's more what you were thinking."

"I-I see." My cheeks immediately flushed, and while it was difficult to tell, it looked like Talos' cheeks may have too.

"Creaky hinges and such, you know." Crowe added with an obnoxious amount of neutrality. "Anywho," his voice shifted immediately to something more singsong, "I hope that was enough, because the forest gets much more dense from here, and who knows what might live in those trees."

"Are there a lot of wild animals in Oz?" There was still so little I knew about this place, even if it felt like I'd been here an eternity already.

"I wonder" was all Crowe said. If Talos wanted to share more information, Crowe wasn't offering to translate anymore. I wished I could speak with him directly, since he seemed the more reasonable of the two. Though that was only a vague assumption.

A warm hand fell on my shoulder, and Tobias gave me a gentle but reassuring smile. "It won't matter what Oz has to throw at us, so long as you stay by my side, Dorothy."

Genuinely comforting. He helped me to my feet, and we all turned to face the long stretch of yellow bricks before us. The golden shine of the cobbled road disappeared beneath the heavy shadows of the coming woods, and I wondered if anything I encountered could possibly be any worse than what was already behind me.

Or what was already beside me.

The darkness swallowed me whole beneath the heavy shade of the trees. The uneven, ill-constructed roadway didn't inspire much confidence as I near tripped on the crooked lip of every brick, and it was difficult to see my companions even when I could hear their footsteps still so close. I'd come to identify each of my men by the sound of their walk. Tobias was light and quick, Talos' step was heavy and focused, while Crowe was completely silent, save the near inaudible shifting of fabric as he moved. This made it easy to identify every sound that wasn't one of them, which was why every rustle of leaves had me on edge.

Yet, there were still no signs of any alleged beasts. For all I knew, Crowe could have made that part up just to scare me. He seemed the type to find amusement in the terror of others. We'd not encountered another creature since our last stand against the munchkins, so I should have relaxed. If anything came at us, Toto would hear it first, after all, and he would keep me safe.

I felt my way through the blackness, where I started to notice I'd lost some pace behind the others. It was likely that they had much better eyesight in these sorts of low light settings. I was the only plain, boring, ordinary human among us, and that was starting to feel like a disadvantage when the road rounded a sharp bend, and I completely lost sense of Crowe and Talos.

The snap of a twig caught in my ear, and I fixated on the direction of the sound. Not that I could see what was coming, but I swore I heard something moving, and I wanted to be ready. I opened my mouth but hesitated to speak. What was it they said you were supposed to do when you encountered a wild animal on a trail again? Was I supposed to stay quiet to not alert it, or was I supposed to make noise to scare it away? I hadn't paid much attention to bear safety techniques when I was hiking Runyon Canyon on the regular, and in all the lessons I'd had in fishing and wood chopping in Kansas, I knew more about safety around cattle than I did around rattle snakes or wildcats.

Another barely discernable squish of mud, and I dead froze. The sounds of my companion's steps continued, likely having not yet noticed the way my feet had stopped and my heartbeat was in my ears.

I took an unsteady step back.

"Dorothy? What's wrong?" Tobias' voice seemed distant as a violent thud of a hard, muscular body slammed into me from the side with all the force of being tackled by a charging bison. All the air was forcefully knocked from my lungs, and I went tumbling into a bush. The loud snapping of branches was accompanied by a whirlwind of leaves flying in the wake of impact.

My wits were nowhere to be found when my assailant had me over his shoulder and began dashing through the foliage with a near feline nimbleness, jumping and dodging trees and ferns and splashing through rivers. If my friends were giving chase, I couldn't hear them amidst such chaos. Grass and leaves whizzed by below me.

"Help!" I kicked my feet and beat on his back with closed fists, hopelessly shouting for him to put me down but ultimately being unsuccessful. I had no idea how far he'd taken me when he at last came to a sudden stop. Darkness grew darker when I realized we had reached a cave in the trees.

He hauled me through a pitch black opening, where I was greeted by an eerie chorus of dead silence until we reached a small, crackling camp fire. Such a simple thing provided uncharacteristic warmth and comforting light in the otherwise imposing tunnel. It was then that he unceremoniously threw me face first into the mud.

I tried to scramble away, but he grabbed me by the ankle, dragged me beneath him, then wasted no time settling on top my back. My assailant pinned me with hard palm pressing my cheek more deeply into the wet and squishy ground. I thrashed best I could, but my position had me at a distinct disadvantage. The weight let up only long enough for him to flip me over and jerk my wrists over my head. He trapped them both under a single heavy hand.

His other hand covered my mouth before I had a chance to so much as scream. My friends would notice I was missing though. They would come for me. I didn't know about Crowe or Talos, but Tobias would. Toto would never let me down. I'm sure he could follow my scent. Or at least I hoped he could.

"Don't scream." My attacker growled the words, low and deep. I blinked up at him, trying to dispel the traces of dirt from my eyelashes. In the warm but low light, all I could make out was that he was blond with mid length dreadlocks tied back behind his head, and his eyes were slitted by a sharp pupil in an orb of gold. A scar across his cheek rested atop a short gold beard that was barely more than stubble. He was muscular yet lean, and he was bare-chested, other than the intricately patterned tattoo that snaked down thick biceps and a defined chest. He wore furs and leathers from the waist down, and if not for the cascade of small hoop earrings adorning each ear, he'd appear entirely primitive.

A Viking, I thought. *I've been kidnapped by a Viking.*

I squirmed in his grasp, and he tightened his grip on my mouth. His fingers dug into my cheeks, while the tips of his razor sharp nails extended until they just barely broke skin.

He blinked down at me for seconds that felt like minutes, and his lips pursed as if he wasn't entirely pleased with what he was seeing.

"Wait, you're not a munchkin." He said with genuine surprise. He leaned in close and started sniffing along my neck. "Not a Kalidah." I felt his tongue slide along my jugular. "And you don't taste like a witch either."

He removed his hand from my mouth, though he kept my wrists pinned, and he stared into me with discriminating irritation. "Well fuck, I was hoping you were a munchkin. I haven't had a decent meal in weeks, and now I don't even know if you're something venomous or not."

While I was fairly certain I was perfectly edible, that was not something I was going to argue with right now. Instead, I decided this was a good opportunity to scream loud enough for Tobias to hear me. I opened my mouth, but a simple rise of his finger, demonstrating the way his sharp black claws extended to a killing length, was enough to scare me back into silence.

"You'll be dead before they find you if you make a sound." He added plainly, as if it wouldn't bother him in the slightest to murder someone. It probably wouldn't if he ate munchkins. While I wasn't fond of the people from my first encounter, they still resembled humans far too closely for me to be comfortable seeing them as food.

I bit my lip as he shifted his hips on top of mine then began drawing a line down my neck. He pressed in just enough to break skin, and I watched the smallest droplets of blood bead in his black nails. I swallowed, and I whimpered, but the severe look in his eye told me not to make a sound louder than that.

"What a strange thing you are. You aren't a shifter, and you're much too pretty to be one of *them*." He continued down to my bust line. He drew a line over to my shoulder, then he retracted his claws and nudged the material down.

A shifter? I wanted to ask, but I didn't dare speak yet. Instead, I kept my eyes on his, trying not to acknowledge the heat he'd started to build inside me with this exploratory touch. I held my breath as I felt the soft material of my dress start to slide down my breasts. A slightly more forceful tug got the bust line over my firmed nipples, exposing me completely to his view.

There was no lust in that gaze though. Only… curiosity? *Why is that look so disarming?*

"Different." He muttered as he cupped my breast and squeezed. My nipples were pebbled in his hand, and that seemed to only amuse him more. He kneaded me gently, rolling that sensitive peak between his coarse fingers. "You're not cold or hard like the women I'm used to." He traced circles around my areolas with his thumb. "So pleasant to the touch. I wonder if you're this soft and warm on the inside too."

My breathing hitched again on those words. I couldn't tell if his idea of "inside" meant goring me or fucking me, but I wasn't going to ask him to clarify.

"What exactly are you?" His tone was a purr, and I fidgeted as my body responded to his voice and caress. His movements were so unexpectedly gentle, and he seemed to have a good sense of where and how to touch me to get me hot and bothered instead of simply scared. Thoughts like that may have been the most disturbing part of this whole situation. "You can answer now." He said, still sending small shockwaves through me as he kneaded and played with my breasts.

"I-I'm human." I said unsteadily, while I watched him drift his hand further downward. He applied steady pressure, feeling me through my clothes. "Just a regular human trying to get through the woods. I'm not trying to intrude." I attempted next, but my voice fell off into a practical squeak. He was exploring me, but the more he sniffed and prodded and felt his way around, the more animalistic it felt. It was like a predator determining if my flesh was worth eating. Vicious and hungry and terrifying, even if the dampness he'd started building between my legs was betraying that sentiment.

"Human, huh." His thin lips cocked in a half smile. "I think I might like humans." With a suddenness, his hand was back up to my neck, and he was squeezing firmly enough to keep me from calling out, yet with enough restraint that I could still breathe if I focused hard enough. "I've hunted in these woods for quite some time, and I've never encountered anything quite like you."

I jerked in his grasp again, bowing my back against the floor and pressing my head back into the mud to try and create some amount of distance between his squeezing force and my wind pipe. He just chuckled and shook his head. I was completely overpowered. He was heavy and he was strong.

"Shhh, don't struggle, little human. I just want to test a theory." The grin that slipped across his lips was one of pure deviance. He lifted his hips so he was now hovering over me, and he removed the hand from my neck to slip it, instead, under my skirt.

I bit my trembling lip and closed my eyes as those exploring fingers found their way in between my legs. "You see, I'm used to women who have bodies like stone and blood like ice." He traced my entrance, then he nudged my panties to the side. "Pleasuring them is about as enjoyable as fucking a frozen pipe." He effortlessly slipped his first finger into me, and I didn't want to explain why I was so incredibly wet already. I couldn't help the gasp that sprang from my throat when he added another digit. I clenched on his finger as he sunk in to his knuckles. "Fuck, you're hot." He hooked his fingers just right to find my G-spot, and he kept his eyes locked on mine all the while. He watched my face, as if he was reading every shift in my expression to figure out which movements and positions rubbed the most involuntary pleasure through me.

He kept rubbing in that perfect position, seeming to revel in the way my heartbeat was climbing as I soaked his palm.

Then he upped the ante. His thumb followed a line up my center until the tip was up against my clit. He rubbed small circles in a way that communicated he knew exactly what he was doing with me. He had my whole body shaking, and I was near drawing blood from biting my lip harder and harder in my efforts to avoid audible moans. But *fuck*, he was good. Really fucking good. "If you could see your face right now... You're so responsive, little fireball."

He continued inching pleasure up my spine, adding in a third finger, while varying the pressure on my clit. Two fingers was usually more than enough, but three was a new kind of thickness and pressure. I opened my legs for him, and he leaned in and flicked my nipple with his tongue. My whole body was hot and blushing at the way he was working me, and I'd lost any desire to protest. I'm not sure I ever had any. Why I closed my eyes and let myself focus on how good it felt, I couldn't explain. Why I let myself start to express that heady orgasm through my moans, I also couldn't explain. Maybe it'd been too long since someone other than my own hand and a vibrator had been able to make me come like this. Maybe it had been too long since I'd been with a man who sought my pleasure instead of his own.

Or maybe I was just a cheap whore like all those men told me I was, and I just wanted to feel something that was purely sex without strings attached.

There wasn't a transaction out of this. There was no *"get on your knees, and you can have any role you want."* He wasn't taking pictures to blackmail me with. He was simply pleasuring me. Was it okay to like it?

I don't know when that sense of fear slipped into fantasy, or when abduction turned into a willing one-night stand, but when he grazed my breasts with his teeth, I couldn't take it anymore. I was losing myself on his fingers. A rush of perfect adrenaline and ecstasy drove through my core, rippling through my every muscle until I was practically seeing stars. I writhed on him shamelessly, and I felt every ounce of tension in my body slipping away.

He stilled, watching me through the whole ride, just savoring the way he'd played me all the way off the edge. With a slow and controlled motion, he withdrew his fingers, and he sucked them into his mouth.

He closed his eyes and groaned as he indulged in my flavor. "You even taste good."

I was at a loss for words. I just stared at him as I inhaled deeply and exhaled slowly, trying to gather my wits. "W-why did you…"

"Did you like that?" He asked in a measured way that somehow still made me feel more a specimen than a sex object.

"I… I didn't hate it." I heard myself say. Honest. I shouldn't be so honest, but orgasms seemed to function as truth serums for me.

"Good. Because I think I want to keep you." He made a show of biting his lip until blood bloomed on his skin. Then he leaned in again, and this time he pressed his teeth into the inside of my breast. I yelped as he sucked the sensitive skin with a punishing bite—more than hard enough for his fangs to penetrate my flesh. He skated his lips over the wound, fluttering soft kisses to my nipple, then he returned to his bite and licked me languidly.

With the eyes of a hungry beast, he withdrew and smiled lovingly at the first traces of a bruise that appeared in my cleavage. I hesitated to look down, but my curiosity got the best of me. That bruise settled in the shape of a fang, and the flesh darkened as if it was a sharp tattoo. Like some sort of magic, he'd left a mark.

He was claiming me, yet I was such a disheveled mess, still so high on orgasm, that I didn't even try to argue.

He cupped both of my breasts again, then he met my gaze. "Have you ever been fucked by a lion, *my fireball?*"

I bit my lip and drew a long breath through my nose. "Bigger ones than you." I said calmly. A taunt. Though I couldn't say if it was mockery out of spite or if I wanted him to do it.

This was crazy. He was a wild and dangerous stranger who just fingered fucked me without my consent. Sure, he had the body of a god and the face of a Viking, but he'd kidnapped me. I... I couldn't let some monster inside me just because he was hot and good with his fingers. I couldn't let him mark me and make me his, just because he'd sent my soul flying. I... I needed to get back to my friends. My mission. My home. Right I... had a home.

His laugh interrupted my moral dilemma. "Good answer. I like that." He tightened his grip on my breasts. "It's not true, but I like your spunk." Then he released me and sat up straight, making distance between us.

"Is that what you are? A lion?" I managed as his new, more casual position subsided any remaining tension in my gut.

He frowned. "That's what I was. I was Alpha of the Lion Shifters until Gwen sealed my ability to shift." His eyes fell back down my body, then he carefully and delicately returned my dress to my shoulders.

"Gwen?"

"The Wicked Witch of the West." He clarified.

"Oh, so you're…" another cursed puppet. I hesitated to say it. Who would want to be reminded that they were little more than someone else's toy? I'd lived that life, and I still held that shame so deeply that it slowly killed me every day.

"A discarded fuck boy." He finished the sentence for me completely unironically. "But I'd prefer if you'd just call me Leon if you're deciding between the two."

Leon. I liked that name. It suited him. "I'm Dorothy." It was suddenly so casual between us. He had a charisma about him that was completely disarming. It was almost disturbing how quickly I was finding empathy and common ground with each of these fucked up men. I should have been livid. I should have been angry. I should have punched him in the face.

But… I didn't want to. There was no fear left in my system. From the moment he marked me, all I felt was calm. A trauma bond.

"Dor-o-thy." He pronounced each syllable like he was turning it around on his tongue, tasting it as it settled in his mouth. "Such a pretty name for my warm little fireball."

That little tick, however… I couldn't help but notice the way he now kept referring to me by possessives. "What do you mean by—"

My words were immediately cut off as a hard fist connected with the side of Leon's face. In a flash of black and gold, Tobias had Leon against the wall, held by his neck, with his thumb ready to press down on his pulse and cut off his consciousness.

"Get the fuck away from Dorothy." He growled with a viciousness I'd never seen from my gentle friend.

Chapter 15

"TOTO"

TOBIAS

His head hit the stone wall, and I squeezed his windpipe until his face started turning purple.

Good. So he needs to breathe. He wasn't some inhuman doll like the others. I took that as my confirmation to clamp down harder. He clawed at my arm with dagger sharp nails that effortlessly tore through skin, but I didn't give a fuck.

I could smell it. I could smell it on him, I could smell it on her, I could smell everything he'd fucking done, and I wasn't going to let it slide. "I'll fucking kill you." All I could see was red. My blood boiled so hot, I hoped my contact would burn his fucking flesh.

I'd tracked them here as quickly as I could, delayed by nearly losing the scent amidst the rain soaked ferns of the woods, but I was determined to find her before she'd become a feast for some monster. For her to be snatched right in front of me, and I wasn't able to stop it… I wouldn't let that stand. My only respite was that she was still alive, but I couldn't forgive myself for such egregious failure.

"Tobias!" She shouted from behind me. "It's okay!"

Okay? It's not o-fucking-kay. I pulled him from the wall and slammed his head back into the rocks. I loosened my grip only long enough to let him take a single breath.

"Did he hurt you?" I forced myself to ask the question despite the absolute rage and adrenaline coursing through me. As much as I wanted to protect her, I also wasn't going to be one of the many men who took her voice. Still, I was going to keep him pinned until she told me otherwise. And I'd break his neck without hesitation if my assumptions were correct.

"No. No, it's okay, Tobias." Her voice was soft and pleading. I loosened my hold a touch. "I'm okay. He wasn't going to eat me after all."

"*After all?*" And I tightened it again. I glanced back at her, while his fight was fading with the lack of oxygen. She shook her head rapidly.

"He eats munchkins and—" Another shake. "That's not the point. He's like Crowe and Talos, Tobias. He's just trying to break his curse."

I nodded to her in understanding, then I released him so suddenly, he had no chance of finding his footing without ending up a crumpled mess on the floor. I glared down at him as he choked air back into his lungs and rubbed his neck.

"Holy fuck, you're strong," he managed through a coughing fit. The tattoos, the piercings, the muscles—He was completely her type. Of course she would defend him. As much as I adored Dorothy, it wasn't the first time her judge of character was horribly misguided. I wanted to trust her, but her choices in men were frustrating at best, and traumatizing at their worst. "I was completely overpowered. How the hell..." Disbelief dripped from every word, while his catlike eyes were wide. "You're lucky that damn witch took my power—"

"Leon." She interrupted him with a stern look. He stopped speaking immediately. *Strange.*

He cleared his throat when he finally managed to stop coughing. "What I meant to say was I'm so happy to

115

know that this little firecracker has such a big, strong protector." The bullshit of the statement wasn't lost on me. "My mate should only have strong men around her."

"Your *what?*" That red filled my sight again, and I hoisted him back upright by his neck. Though this time, he didn't fight me on it. Dorothy looked just as confused.

"Show him your mark, Dorothy." The grin on his lips was abhorrent. I contemplated pounding his head into the wall until it disappeared.

"What's he talking about?"

Dorothy blinked repeatedly, "I don't know." She squeaked in that way that told me she absolutely knew. I could hear her heart rate pick up. I could sense her growing anxiety. I couldn't understand why she would even try to hide something from me. It was my job to read her emotions.

And then it dawned on me. Was that spike due to this bastard, or was *I* the one flaring her anxiety right now?

I eased off my grip on Leon, and that heart beat slowed a touch. She dropped her gaze with embarrassment.

Leon glanced between us, then he addressed me once more. "You're a dog shifter, and you can't sense her mating bond? It's strange enough that you can overpower a lion, but how are your senses that broken?"

"I'm a what?" I shook my head, certain I'd misheard him, but also knowing my ears were too good for any such mistake.

"A dog shifter." Leon repeated while his body language was that of someone completely taken aback. "A beast man? A wolf in a man's clothing? What witch cursed you to the point you don't even recognize your own kind?" He squinted, inspecting me in disbelief. His strong hand

116

fell on my shoulder, then he leaned in and sniffed me along the neck. I remained still, too stunned to react or protest. He nudged my ear forward. "Eloise of the North. The stench of her magic is hard to mistake, and that mark, even more so." He spoke definitively then added with the utmost contempt. "To think they call her a good witch. I suppose if you rob your cursed puppets of their memory, it makes it easier to keep a clean reputation. Vile bitch."

"What do you mean I'm a shifter?" I repeated the title, not caring about some witches or their grudges. Though the word sounded wrong on my lips. "I think you're mistaken. I'm from the human world…"

"The human world?" Leon scrunched his nose. "She banished you to an entirely different dimension? That's brutal."

"No." Dorothy stepped in to explain when words were failing me. "Tobias was my dog back home. It wasn't until we arrived here that he ended up trapped in this body."

"Are you fucking kidding me right now? Do I have to spell this out for you when it's your own damn body?" Leon balked as he looked back and forth between us as though we were completely insane. "So you were banished to the *'human world'* where you were trapped in animal form, then when you returned to Oz, you ended up in your true form." Not a question but an explanation. Leon threw up his hands as both of us stared at him dumbstruck. "Look, I'm a Lion Shifter and I'm an Alpha. I know what fellow shifters smell like. The Witches of Oz have been running about unchecked for a long, long time, so it doesn't totally surprise me that you were a victim without even knowing it. But no matter what your body looks like, *as a shifter,*" he emphasized heavily, "your beast lives inside you when you're a man, and your humanity lives inside

117

you when you're a beast. If anything, the way you nearly strangled me to save this girl tells me that your beast still very much lives in you."

I remained still, shocked, and paralyzed.

A shifter. A dog shifter? If what he was saying was true, this form here had always been myself. Even if we found the Wizard and he broke everyone's curses and sent us home, I would still be able to exist like this.

I could still be this man for Dorothy.

Despite the confusion, this revelation was… a good thing. I wasn't certain what that meant for who I was— things like, how old was I? Was my past all a lie? Did I have some deep seeded memories I'd blocked out? Did it even matter if I did?

But ultimately. I didn't care about that. All I cared was that there was a chance that this change was permanent.

Dorothy grabbed my hand and drew small circles on the back with her thumb. A calming technique I'd performed for her many times since we'd arrived here. She was trying to be my rock this time, but I didn't need her to be. If anything, this was the most free I'd ever felt with her.

My whole stance softened, and I met Leon's eyes squarely. He tipped back his chin and placed a hand on his belt of furs. "I'm gathering, since this is such a revelation to you, that you can't shift anymore either?" A question and a statement.

"I… no. If I can, I don't know how." So many revelations bombarding me at once made it difficult to process any of them.

"You would know. Your instincts are clearly intact regardless of your memories." He rubbed his neck, soothing the marks I'd left from my grip. "To get back to my original point…" He motioned with his chin towards Dorothy. "That mark on your chest means you belong to me, my little fireball." Then those words had me tensing again. Dorothy flushed but didn't deny any such mark. "But there's no reason you have to limit yourself to a single mate, you know."

With that, Leon stepped in close. His height matched mine, making it an easy task for him to touch his lips to the collar around my neck. I didn't pull back. Dorothy just watched us curiously. Then he whispered in my ear, words so soft that only an animal could hear: "You should mark her, too. I have a feeling she might like it." A soft chuckle, "That's the privilege of an Alpha after all."

He pulled away, and he beamed at us with an uncharacteristic and surely false gentleness. "Since we're all a cute little team now, where are you two headed?"

CHAPTER 16

"THE SCARECROW"

CROWE

"It seems we lost them somewhere." I exaggerated a shrug, while Talos glanced back into the dark veil of forest behind us. I might admit that I did hear her adorable, helpless little squeak when she got kidnapped. But I also heard Tobias don his super hero cape and rush off after her, so I figured it wouldn't be long before they caught up.

<*"Should we return to the forest to find them?"*> A verbal frown. He was a bit of a softy it seemed. Probably for the best that I was in control of what he could communicate to the others. I wouldn't want his sympathy flaring up and telling Dorothy I didn't care if she died out here. As long as I had her shoes, the Wizard would give me audience, and it was easier to plunder a corpse than it was to entertain an ordinary, albeit pretty and curious, little human. As it stood, the shoes could only be removed of her own will, and as the shoes held my curse, I was incapable of killing her, so overpowering her and stealing them was the only option I didn't have.

Well, she'd probably already assumed as much anyway. She didn't strike me as particularly daft, after all. More just sweet and oversensitive and a bit over trusting. If I was capable of caring about her, maybe that would be charming, but in a place like Oz it was a hindrance more than a positive.

I'd liked *'scared and bleeding on a post Dorothy'* much more than *'sunshine and gratitude Dorothy.'* At least one of them made me feel something other than boredom.

"I'm sure the dog has her covered." I rolled my eyes. Considering Tobias was completely and obviously in love with her, it's not like there was any need for either of us to pretend to be knights in shining armor anyway. He'd probably get offended if I even tried. He needed her to see him as something beyond a puppy, and coming to his aid would only infantilize him further. It was really a favor to stand back and let them get into life-threatening danger.

<*"Perhaps."*> Another stray glance over his shoulder.

"Are you that worried about her? Really?" I raised an eyebrow.

<*"Both of them. Tobias appears strong, but he doesn't seem to be a fighter. And Dorothy is rather delicate, don't you think?"*>

Cute. "Yes on both accounts. But I didn't take you for the type to bond with others so quickly."

<*"Strange. I had you in the palm of my hand within moments. Or to be literal, I suppose you had me in the palm of your hand."*>

Unexpectedly cheeky...

"What can I say—Hard is my favorite look on a man." With a smirk, I shoved my hands in my pockets and strolled over to my only remaining companion. "Out of curiosity, after having endured Sasha..." I lifted his chin with my forefinger, while I slid my thumb along his muzzle where his lips would be. "Are you really interested in getting involved with some girl wearing a witch's shoes? What will you do if she turns on us once we get to the Wizard for an audience?"

<*"She won't."*> His eye contact was firm and unrelenting. <*"Though I'm surprised you're so scared of a little girl."*>

121

My gaze narrowed in genuine irritation. "The last *'little girl'* I went home with lobotomized me and hung me on a cross until I bled out, so pardon my distrust." *Why did that get under my skin so deeply?*

< *"I'm sure your charming personality had nothing to do with that."*> He rolled his eyes in smug. Who the hell was this asshole? He seemed so gentle and caring when he met the girl, but now he was full of nothing but snark and mockery.

... I have to say, I rather like it.

"And I'm sure your sarcasm had nothing to do with the fact that *your* 'little girl' ripped your tongue out, eh?" I effortlessly switched back to the offensive.

< *"No, my fault was simply the way that tongue showed her far too good a time, until she wanted to keep it all to herself."*> Perfectly deadpan and so matter-of-fact, it was as though he was reading a history tome as he said that.

I nodded along. "I *have* heard she has a thing for blades and dismemberment. We should have traded places. She could have cut me into as many pieces as she wanted without ever worrying about lasting consequences. I would be the toy that kept on giving."

< *"I think that might have taken some fun out of it for her."*> Talos shrugged. < *"It was the blood and the tears that lubricated her miserable cunt."*>

I couldn't help but laugh at that. *Fuck, I DID like him.* "Grunhilda was more about manipulation. Her only joy came from turning people against each other and watching them fight. She had the munchkins wrapped around her wart covered fingers."

< *"I think I might have preferred that. Though it's a shame..."*> A ghost of a smile reflected in the tin man's

122

eyes as he lightly brushed my arm with his fingertips. <*"I won't ever be able to show you how good I was whole. Unless we make it to the Wizard with Dorothy in one piece, anyway."*>

"Speaking of manipulative…" We shared a silent laugh between us. "Fine, you win. We'll check on the girl." I sighed, though the grin on my face betrayed the sentiment.

<*"Is that a conscience speaking?"*>

"Weird name for my dick, but sure." One last roll of my eyes, and I turned my attention back to the woods that blackened the yellow brick road. I supposed that, whether I cared about her wellbeing or not, I *would* have to find her to retrieve her shoes if she did get murdered in there. It was inevitable that I'd have to go back for her, so no reason to overthink it. I would stay by her side until the exact moment I didn't have to, and not a moment more.

The gentle hum of the jungle resonated from the darkness like it was a record player projecting nature's melody. The soft chirps of birdsong, the rustling of leaves, and the trickle of flowing streams was deceptively peaceful. Though I hadn't picked up on any Kalidah while we traversed the road, so I couldn't imagine that was what got her. Their growl was rather distinct in its wavering pitches to the point it would be impossible to mistake them for any other creature. I wouldn't profess to know all the beasts that roam Oz, but I certainly knew all the deadly ones.

I'd resolved to take my first step when a hint of gold appeared in the nearby shadows. A wild animal of a man, wearing furs and patterns of tribal ink, paced into clear view. He had the presence of a shifter, but… there hadn't been any beast men around the Eastern lands in decades as far as I was aware. If there had been, Hildy would have surely sent me to fetch one. *Curious.*

Behind him was that familiar glint of black—the dog, of course—and in Tobias' arms was Dorothy, nestled comfortably against his chest like a newlywed bride.

Adorable. So precious I might gag.

I settled on Dorothy, who despite resting so peacefully in his arms, looked like she'd just been mud wrestling in a hurricane. She was a mess of dirt and twigs and scratches, and her hair was frayed and disheveled, even despite her braids. Perhaps I should have stopped to help after all, even if just for the fact that I'd missed out on the show of it. Being a complete disaster was a good look on her, I'll admit. The clean and polite Dorothy didn't interest me much, but the messy Dorothy who smelled of sex and dirt was...

No, I had no interest in the girl beyond her shoes. She was a means to an end.

I tore my eyes from the ever sweet and bonding couple, not wanting to think on that further, in favor of this new face in our band of fucked up men. "A beast man?" I asked with a tip of my chin.

"Did you figure that out just by my handsome face?" He nodded and extended a hand in introduction. An absurd gesture that I ignored. He seemed unbothered, however. "Leon. Former Alpha of the Lion Shifters at your service. Crowe and Talos, right? I've heard a lot about you in the last couple hours."

"There are no Lion Shifters left in Oz." I stared him down with no interest in his niceties.

"Correct. There are no Lion Shifters left in Oz." The way his eye twitched as he said it was a tell all its own. "That's why we're all going to see the Wizard."

124

"I see." *One of us. I should have known.* "Well, hopefully you're less of a burden than these two."

His glance back at Dorothy and the dog was rather curious. "You won't even notice I'm here."

With that, he continued past me, and Talos gave me a nod before he followed suit. When Tobias neared, I met his eyes first. "Good work." I said blandly. Then I shifted to Dorothy. "Why don't we camp by a stream tonight so you two can get washed up? You'll want to look your best before we meet the Wizard." I motioned toward the very distant horizon, where the first glimpse of the Emerald City had hazily come into view.

"That would be wonderful." The sweet girl flashed me that perfectly polite, well-mannered smile. Tobias remained stoic, however. Quite unusually so. He was much more of an '*honest and true*' type from prior dealings, so I couldn't imagine why he seemed so rattled. If the Lion had been rough with her, they'd obviously come to some point of forgiveness. I considered making a jab that would rile him up enough to get that information out of him, but I thought better of it. He didn't seem in the mood, and I didn't have the patience for sour whining.

He kept walking, and I followed behind, where I could easily catch the occasional glances between the Dog and the Lion.

Most curious indeed.

CHAPTER 17

ⓞ DOROTHY ⓞ

Tobias didn't put me down until we found a suitable camp spot. I couldn't tell if he was upset or confused or simply emotionally drained. Oz had been a strange place for both of us so far, after all. Every day was such a whirlwind of new things and questionable characters that it was easy to become overwhelmed. I made a point to help him build the tent, while Crowe and Talos created a perimeter of sorts, and Leon went off to fetch some firewood.

The apples had given me quite a bit of energy, still lasting through dusk as we finished setting up camp. That confirmed all my fears about their calorie content, but it also meant our small supply would be adequate to sustain the eating and sleeping among us until we could find some more libations. Finally everything was starting to work out.

With a heavy exhale, I reached for my braids that were still caked in mud. I started undoing each side, struggling to get the frazzled hair free of itself without it knotting further. The corners of my lips drooped, thinking what a mess I must be. I couldn't imagine how prominent my naturally brown hair was in my roots by now, and I had scratches and bite marks and bruises on my skin. A nice bath did sound lovely. What I wouldn't do for some candles and a lavender bath bomb in an oversized tub full of water that was hot enough to burn the lesser men. Oh, and with jets. And bubbles. And some rose petals on the side. That's the only heaven I wanted to go to right now.

But out here, I didn't even have the luxury of soap. At best, I would just be splashing muddy water on my face from a cold stream.

I used to love doing that as a kid. I don't know how many lakes I cannonballed into growing up. Back then, I didn't care if the water was dirty, or if there might be moss or frogs or bugs or even leeches or snakes. It was part of the danger and excitement of it, and joking with my friends that every oddly shaped branch floating in the water was going to bite them was half the fun.

When did I lose touch with that carefree, happy girl? I spent so much of my adult life trying to erase the Midwestern country girl from my personality, that I forgot I didn't used to need anything but a net for lightning bugs and some familiar faces to feel content.

But that was probably how all children felt, wasn't it? Being an adult was complicated. I wanted so much more than that now. I wanted financial freedom so I'd never struggle and worry about putting food on the table like my aunt and uncle did. I wanted to be a success they could be proud of, and I wanted to prove I was more than just an orphan from a small town who would be forgotten by history. I could have stayed in Kansas after all. I could have found a good, stable blue collar man who would provide for me while I raised his children. I could have taken over the farm from Aunty Em and Uncle Henry and scraped by, always worrying if this year would be a good one or a bad one, but never worrying if a casting director would reject me for my boobs not being perky enough. I could have had any of those lifestyles. They were simple, but everyone I knew back home was happy in that simplicity. Happier than I was these days, at the very least.

Why couldn't *I* be happy like that? Why did I need so much excess and grandeur, that I was willing to do *anything*, even sacrificing my pride and dignity and self-respect in order to get it? What was it inside me that drove me to that?

Ambition? Desperation? Dreams? Greed? Or maybe I just wanted the attention. Maybe I just wanted people to notice me for the first time in my life. How great it would have been to stand out and be the popular girl that everyone covets. Be something other than *Dorothy from Kansas.*

A tear dripped down my cheek, and I was quick to turn away from my companions in hope that no one would see it. I thanked the mud that was caked on so heavily it could hide my tears, and I used the back of my hand to rub the salty liquid into my skin. Though I only smudged the dirt around even more as a result. Cold stream or no, I needed to clean up, even if just for my mental health.

Tobias was still gathering leaves to soften the bed, Leon had started to assemble the firewood, and Crowe and Talos were talking amongst themselves, so I took that as a good time to excuse myself to the creek for some privacy. Camp wasn't far from the water, but there were enough trees and rocks between us to give me a sense of privacy. I followed the sound of rushing water, then I climbed over a large boulder, and I hiked down to a beautiful, crystalline pool at the base of a small waterfall. It was deep enough to submerge in completely, but clear and clean enough that you could easily see the rocks on the bottom. A perfect oasis.

I dipped a finger into the water to mentally prepare myself for the temperature, only to find it was pleasantly neutral, far removed from the frigid streams I was used to. I crouched down and splashed some water on my face, enjoying how refreshing it felt, then after looking over my shoulder to verify I was still alone, I undressed completely, and I sunk into the perfect piece of paradise.

The water was just shallow enough that I could touch the ground if I stayed on my tip toes, though I was a good enough swimmer that it wouldn't have been an issue anyway. I dunked my head underwater, and I wildly ruffled my hair, doing my best to clear some of the clumps from each individual strand. The mud came off in clouds of brown, before it dissipated and settled on the floor of the pool.

Next I took the time to rub my face clean until my reflection showed only the soft pink hue of my skin, and I got to work on cleaning the rest of my body. I rubbed my shoulders first. I contortioned my arms to wash my back best I could, then I bent a knee, one at a time, to work the dirt from my legs.

It felt so nice. The enchanting rush of the waterfall paired with the perfect temperature, the clean water, and the bright green foliage that surrounded dark, wet rocks was like an image of paradise. A feast for the eyes and a gift for my skin.

I cleaned my torso next, rubbing at my sides and my belly and my lower back. Yet in all my enthusiasm, I was still avoiding touching certain… other places. The spots that were perhaps the dirtiest of all.

I flushed at the memory of Leon's skillful hands, then I dipped down, submerging myself all the way past my lips as I listened for movements. No sounds beyond the water and the crickets. I scanned the trees again. No one was approaching. I was still alone. I still had privacy.

I waited for several seconds, as if someone might walk in on me at any moment, but no one did. This pool was all mine. Still, silent, private.

Staying on guard, I let my hands drift up from my naval until they were just beneath my breasts. Another moment of quiet survey, and I let those hands move upward. Traces of Leon's rough handprints still remained on my skin, and I used those as a guide, mimicking the way he'd squeezed me, while lying to myself that I was simply being thorough rather than touching myself with intent. I winced when my thumb brushed the mark he'd left in my cleavage.

My clit throbbed just thinking about it. His *"mate."* Like a werewolf taking a bride, he'd picked me as his lover just on instincts. He'd touched me, he'd played in my pussy, and he marked me, never once asking if I was okay with it, using only body language to decide I'd liked it. I wanted to detest him, get mad, and say he was wrong.

I rolled my perked nipples between my thumb and forefingers. I wanted to say all of that, but I wasn't much of a liar. My heart had never raced like that for a guy before. And fuck, I'd never come like that for anyone before. The men I rolled with never cared if I got off, and I was often so distracted that I couldn't have even if they'd tried.

Still quiet, still calm, I slid my hands back down to my stomach. I took one more peek at my surroundings before I let them explore a bit lower. My clit was already incredibly sensitive by the time I was dancing light pressure around it. I swallowed, held my breath, and sunk a little deeper into the water. Someone could walk in at any moment. It could be Tobias or Leon or Crowe or Talos. The water was so clear, they'd see me without even having to hike down. They'd know exactly what I was doing. I didn't want them to see me like this. I shouldn't be touching myself at the thought of being pinned down and pleasured.

I definitely shouldn't be getting off on the thought of one of them catching me. All of them catching me.

I nudged my finger into my pussy, and I rubbed shallow circles just barely inside myself. Then I slipped in a second finger and pushed in a bit deeper, until I found the spot I was looking for.

It was a wonder that the water around me wasn't turning to steam with the way my body heated under my own movements. With my other hand, I pinched my nipple, sending signals of pleasure up from between my legs, and back down from my breasts. I'd always been sensitive, but it was different when I was touching myself, and a whole different world when someone I was attracted to was testing my limits.

Leon may have made me his, but if Tobias was also a shifter, couldn't he claim me too?

That was insane. I couldn't think that way about him just because he was tall and dark and strong now. I rubbed at my clit with my thumb. I couldn't admit that it made me wet watching a guy like that slam someone into a wall for me. Threaten to kill them for touching me. That would be so fucked up to be turned on by something like that. Almost as fucked up as being turned on by my powerlessness.

I came up for air, no longer able to contain myself. *Gotta clean everything*, I told myself. *I'm just cleaning up.*

As if I was possessed, my fingers effortlessly found the perfect tempo to flick my clit. I tugged at my nipples one more time before I joined my other hand down below. I imagined how it might feel to be rubbing that same spot against Talos' hard body. It was awful that something as silly as a man finding me food was enough to make my heart skip a beat. A simple gesture that made me feel loved and cared for. I'd never had a total stranger do something like that for me. Not without expecting something in return.

Maybe that was what made it so much better: He *was* a total stranger, and he was still interested in looking out for me.

I threw my head back to take another breath. I was so close to orgasm, I might drown if I continued. Maybe I'd be okay with that if it could feel this good. Maybe despite myself, I still wanted it a bit rough and dangerous. Someone like Crowe, who would kill me in an instant if I let him, shouldn't make my heart race. I knew he didn't honestly like me. It was obvious in every bit of his body language. He was completely incapable of emotion, after all, and he'd told me as much.

132

Yet that stupid, immature girl, still so driven by that need to make the world acknowledge her, wanted that. I *wanted* to take a guy like him and break down his walls with my pussy. I'd *revel* in making a sociopath who couldn't feel anything become desperate to keep me.

My moan was involuntary as my shaking knees clenched together. I could barely keep my head above water while maintaining this high, and I barely cared if I couldn't.

"Missed a spot." My eyes shot open at the sound of Crowe's voice bouncing off the water. The resulting gasp filled my lungs, and I held that air there as my heart stopped completely. I immediately removed my hands from my nethers and wrapped my arms around my chest. That only added an extra crookedness to his smile. "A little late to be modest, Dorothy."

"C-Crowe. What are you doing here?" I clenched my knees together and pulled them to my chest, using the little air I was managing to keep in my lungs to help me float. Though drowning might be preferable right now.

"Just thought I'd clean up a bit. I never got all the munchkin off me after my stay on the pike, after all." He cocked his head to the side with a curiosity, though that wicked grin never vanished. "Here I've gone all this time thinking you were such a sweet girl, but I may have misjudged you."

My cheeks were absolutely on fire. I couldn't get out. I couldn't keep my body covered without sinking. I *definitely* couldn't explain that I was touching myself to the thought of all four of them having their way with me. And above all, I could absolutely *not* tell him that I was throbbing even harder the second he caught me doing it. I now cursed the perfectly clear water that let him so effortlessly enjoy the whole show.

"I-I—" I was at a complete loss for words. It didn't matter how hyper aware of sound and movement I was when I was dealing with someone who could move as silently and stealthily as our resident scarecrow.

"Don't stop on my account." He dipped his fingers into the water and drew languid circles in the surface tension. His dark eyes practically burned into me. "The last thing I want is for a woman to ever have to walk away from me still unfinished."

I backed up, inching toward the opposite edge of the pool, away from him and all of my clothing. There, I found a spot where I had better footing and could more easily keep my head above water. I scooted back a little more, until I found a rock I could sit on. If I was mortified, my clit didn't seem to get the memo.

"This pool is big enough for two people." I somehow said without shaking any words. "I mean if you want to clean up, too."

Crowe kept that gaze locked in mine. His sights didn't wander down to my completely exposed breasts, nor did he so much as glance at the way I was clenching my legs together, trying to keep some amount of low key friction. "Is that right." His demeanor was no longer playful. He spoke in a serious and probing tone, while those fingers just kept drawing those taunting circles.

His eyes stayed on me as he picked up my dress from the pile of clothes beside him. He dipped the material into the water, and he started wringing out the dirt and muck. I watched as he took care to assure every stain was fully and clearly dissolved.

Then he spoke, deep and severe: "Keep going." He cocked his head back. "Show me how you like to be fucked, Dorothy."

"What?" My eyes were so wide they were straining.

He didn't repeat himself. He narrowed his own gaze and continued. "If I don't see you orgasm by the time I'm done washing your clothes, I'll come over there and finish you myself."

My heart jumped into my throat, my blood scorched through my body, and I near came just at the threat of it. Yet still, I listened. I was shaking like a leaf as I slowly spread my knees again. My whole body was trembling as I placed my hand back down between my legs. His eye contact was unyielding, even as I slipped my first finger back inside. It seemed he was more interested in watching my expressions than anything else. I leaned back, supporting my shoulders on a large rock, I squeezed my tits in clear view, and then I demonstrated for him, *exactly*, how I like to be fucked.

He laid out my clean dress on a rock, letting it dry in what sunlight remained, then he picked up my panties and dipped them into the pool. He washed the thin lace with extra care, then he set them beside my dress, and he picked up the first of my silver shoes.

I don't know if I'd ever been more painfully aroused than I was with Crowe's vicious eyes watching me while his strong biceps flexed and softened as he washed my clothing for me. Is it possible to have a chores kink? Because it was triggering something deep and domestic in my soul that was hard to put into words.

I bit into my lip and let myself make some noise as I pressed on that perfect spot again. And again. And again.

Crowe took extra care to clean any traces of dirt from the shining silver surface of my shoes. He scrubbed gently, then paused for an extended second as he admired its sheen. He picked up the second shoe. Careful again, he began cleaning that last piece of my outfit. I knew I was running out of time, and a rebelliousness in my gut almost wanted to fail on purpose. See if he'd really come over here. See how someone like him makes love to a woman.

Love?

No. Crowe was the type to fuck a woman senseless. He didn't know what love was.

Maybe I didn't either. We were all broken puppets here.

"Crowe— "A sharp gasp filled the air between us as I found the edge. I lost myself to that feeling. It was a struggle to keep my eyes open as that perfect wave hit, but I didn't want him to miss any part of me. If he wanted to watch, I wanted him to see all the way into my soul when I was riding the top of the world.

I sat against that rock, panting heavily, with eyes glazed over, and overflowing with too many endorphins to remember to be ashamed of what I just did for him. Crowe's expression remained attentive and calm as he finished cleaning my last shoe.

Then with the utmost care, he placed my silver shoes beside my dress on the opposite bank, he stood up, and he placed his hands in his pockets.

"Interesting." He said. "I'll keep that in mind for later."

Without another word, he took a silent step back. He turned on his heel. And he left me alone to get dressed in my wet but clean clothing.

In a way, I was glad he hadn't said anything more, because I never would have been able to find words to explain myself in that moment.

I waited until my heart stopped racing before I swam back to shore and sat down to put on my little silver shoes. I stroked the shiny leather and remained there on the edge of the water in silence, trying to process what the hell had gotten into me since I arrived in this strange place.

Chapter 18

"THE SCARECROW"

CROWE

Pacing. I was pacing through the woods, hesitating to go back to camp at all now. I'd had them in my hands. *In my fucking hands.* The silver shoes I needed, so carelessly and neglectfully discarded where anyone could come up and steal them, and she left them there without a second thought. It would have been effortless to steal them. Such a careless girl she was.

A careless *woman*. I should have taken them. I could have left her there, so vulnerable and defenseless, and taken back the object that cursed me. That's all I'd need to free my mind of its damage, then I'd never have to bother with her again. So why…

The way she'd said my name as she came was fucking *ringing* in my head, and I couldn't un-hear it. That look on her face, the hard nipples, the whimpers and the trembling and that prim little package looking so completely undone—

I clenched my hand in a fist, and I turned back towards my chosen guard station.

Talos stared at me with pronounced suspicion in those heavy silver eyes as I returned to our position just out of sight and earshot from the rest of the group.

"What is it?" I spat with a sudden unexplained burst of irritation.

His expression remained steady and unmoved. <*"Nothing. I just couldn't help but notice…"*>

"What '*couldn't you help but notice?*'" I scoffed. Why I was so annoyed right now, I wasn't about to try and dissect. I didn't have feelings anyway. Not real feelings. So really, there would have been no point in reading into any such thoughts.

I attempted to storm passed him, not remotely interested in confessing what I just did with—no, did *to* Dorothy, but he was having none of it. Talos placed a wide palm on my chest, and he used that accursed strength of his to shove me back against a tree. He held me there firmly, trapping me against the trunk with his rock hard chest, and his over built biceps.

I glared at him, while amusement filled his eyes. This total reversal of our usual dynamic only irritated me more. <*"Well, since you asked. Two things."*> I attempted to push him off me, but Talos only pressed me harder into the bark. <*"First, you're a bit empty handed, aren't you?"*>

"What should I be holding exactly?" I hated how sharp he was right now. I hadn't told him why I was going down to the watering hole, but I was sure he noticed the way I'd waited and watched for Dorothy to take her leave of the camp.

<*"A pair of silver shoes that your sweet girl took off so she could bathe, perhaps."*> So nonchalant. I was glad I was the only one who could hear him. It was difficult to discern whether that was an accusation of my ill intent or if he'd simply come to understand me all too well in our casual conversations.

"Ah, I should have thought of that." A weak lie he'd see right through. If the words weren't unconvincing enough, his ability to sense what was going through my mind would be. I'd disclosed entirely too much about my plans to him, I was starting to find. Trusting a mute as my

139

confidante would have been fine if he couldn't both overpower me and shove that information back in my face.

<*"Oh, but you* did *think of that. That's the whole reason you went down there."*> His voice was stern and accusing in my head.

I swallowed, but I didn't give away anything in my expression. "It was bad timing, so I changed my mind."

<*"Bad timing, huh. Is that why you're so* frustrated *right now?"*>

"Tch." More mockery. I turned my head to the side, stealing his view directly into my mind. Though the physical contact meant I couldn't block his communication even if I wanted to. "Yes, that's why I'm so frustrated. There are your two questions. Can I go now?" It hadn't ever occurred to me that Talos was the dominant one between the two of us, and I was not fond of this development. I'd taken our unspoken camaraderie as an alliance. I'd never expected him to use that strength against me. Perhaps I'd been too quick to let my guard down around him. After all, just like me, he couldn't be killed, but unlike me, while I was built from evil, he was built from physical pain and endurance.

<*"Don't worry. This last one isn't a question. It's a statement."*> He kept me caged in with his body as he slid the hand on my chest downward. I refused to flinch as he made it down to my very hard cock. <*"I'm just glad to see you don't hate Dorothy as much as you pretend to."*>

He drummed his fingers on the underside of my balls, while the heel of his hand pressed into my length, and I resented the way it made my whole body tense. "You're wrong. It's more like so long as she's the living owner of those shoes, she's got me by the balls more securely than you do right now." I finally spat the words. He loosened his hold. He gave me space. I relaxed against the tree, while grateful it was there to hold me up. "So I couldn't do it. I had her shoes in my hands, and I couldn't do it."

I said it as though Dorothy had me under a spell, but if I was being honest with myself, I'd not been enchanted by anything other than the way she unraveled for me. But I was absolutely not going to be honest with either of us if I could avoid it.

< *"Interesting. "*> He stepped back a full step, and he seemed to be studying my tone and expression, rolling them around in his mind as if he didn't know if it was a plausible statement. But by my luck and his weak heart, his empathy won out. < *"So was it magic then? "*>

"I don't know." And that *was* honest. The first honest words I'd said to him tonight.

< *"I see. "*> He continued to study me, then his tone shifted to something resolute and reassuring. < *"In that case, until we know what kind of power she had, we'll both stay by her side until we get what we're after. If your assumptions that she has dominion over you are wrong, we'll go our separate ways peacefully. If she should turn on you and prove to be the evil witch you fear, I'll kill her myself to free you of her curse. Fair? "*>

I nodded subtly. He accepted that as enough. Then he turned on his heel and took a seat back at our makeshift guard station.

And I used that moment of privacy to step back into the woods and take my own release under the silent moonlight.

I wasn't going to fall for another woman in silver shoes. I fucked my own hand, trying not to imagine it was her tight cunt. I should have asked Talos to do it for me, just so I wouldn't be picturing her face in orgasm.

Too intimate.

I froze on that notion. *Why would the thought of Talos jerking me off be* intimate *to me?*

Fuck! I thought in a silent and aggravated scream.

I'd never had any issue enjoying sex. I was happy to indulge in pleasure just so I could feel *something.* This was normal for me. Before Grunhilda had broken my mind, I'd indulged in every pleasure under the sun.

So why did it feel so different when that person was her. Was *him.* When there were…

Feelings? I slammed my fist into a tree as I came on my hand. The tension that left my body both muddled and cleared my head in the same hard jerks. No, there were no *feelings* here at all. Not from me. This was just a passing game to ease my boredom.

A game. That's right.

Monsters don't fucking feel.

CHAPTER 19

"THE LION"

LEON

With enough friction, the moss and twigs ignited effortlessly. The resulting heat was quick to catch the smallest sticks, which radiated nicely to the larger tinder, before it burned into the broken up branches of my teepee camp fire. The warmth was pleasant and comfortable, and I relaxed into the gentle glow. I'd built so many fires for myself since I'd escaped the Western Castle. Once something I'd enjoyed with my entire Pride of lion shifters, now it was just something to keep me alive for one more day.

One more day of a pointless existence as an Alpha without a Pride and a shifter who couldn't shift.

I lifted my gaze to Tobias who had dressed the tent with a leaf pile built for a wild princess. I preferred to sleep outside, but it was cute the way he doted on my mate so much. *My* mate. I'd never felt compelled to mark someone, but I couldn't seem to resist that pretty little human. I was sure this dog shifter had an interest in her in the same way, so I could only imagine how heartbroken he must be. It probably sounded to him much like he'd lost her to another man at the altar.

His deep brown eyes met mine, and I tipped my chin in a gesture to suggest he sit with me. His uncertainty was easy to read in his body language, but after sorting through some manner of internal battle, he listened.

"Don't look so down. Lions are naturally polyamorous. Everyone in my old den had multiple

143

partners, official or otherwise." I started with the elephant in the camp, hoping to clear the tension between us as quickly as possible. Well, I *hoped* that was all he was stewing about anyway.

Tobias kept his eyes forward, locked on the flickering flames. The gentle orange glow reflected in the shine of his black hair and the moisture in his equally dark eyes. "Do Lion's usually give their mates a choice to be a part of that dynamic?" There was a hint of venom in his words. I'd gathered he understood life as an animal now better than he understood life as a man, so I had to keep that in mind when addressing this… delicate situation. I didn't want the only other shifter I'd met in years to hate me, even if he *was* of the canine variety.

"It's hit or miss, honestly." I pursed my lips. I considered adding *'I wouldn't have marked her if she wasn't drenching my fingers in pure ecstasy,'* but that probably wasn't what he wanted to hear. So instead I opted for "but when you know you've found the right person, you *know*, and Dorothy struck me as quite special. I immediately knew I couldn't let her go."

"I can understand that." That softened his expression. *Thank the Devil I read that right.* "Dorothy is much more special than she'll ever treat herself."

I was completely taken aback by his candidness. He was sincere in his melancholy, but also in his devotion and admiration for the woman. It would have been easy for him to make a dig at me in that statement—call me out for being rough or cruel—but instead he was effortlessly standing on the high road of compliments and empathy.

"If that's how you feel, why don't you show her that?" I prodded with the lightest poke.

"What do you mean?" Finally he met my gaze.

"You don't share an official mate connection, yet you're clearly bonded to her. Have you considered that your instincts are telling you she's also supposed to be *your* mate?" As much as I wanted to tease him for his obliviousness right now, the reality was that he was mentally new to being a shifter. He likely didn't understand anything about how this worked. I'd been a leader long enough to know this was an opportunity to create an alliance more than it was an opportunity to stake dominance, and I'd been a slave to a Witch long enough to have sympathy for another victim. Especially considering that he was an Alpha too. We were more the same than we were different, and I wasn't going to ruin this friendship before it began.

The slight widening of his eyes told me I was on the right track. We didn't have to hate each other just because we both had taken an interest in the same girl. I would actually prefer that we didn't.

"She doesn't see me that way." His tone was distant. He paused for several moments before he spoke again. "But if…" several moments more, "if I did mark her one day—hypothetically—"

"Hypothetically." I nodded along.

"What does a mate mark do?"

The question made me smile. His struggle to be honest with himself was almost adorable. "Well, first and foremost, it allows you to sense your mate wherever they are. If they're in danger, you can feel it in your gut. If they're lost, you'll be able to find them." I started with the things I knew would appeal most to his sensibilities. "Sexually…" The word made his breathing hitch. *So innocent.* "It will amplify every touch and sensation. You'll feel each other's pleasure and emotions and thoughts deep in your gut, and you'll be perfectly in tune with their needs

145

without having to say a word. It increases the power of an orgasm tenfold." I waited long enough for him to fully picture Dorothy in orgasm, because I *knew* he was, and then I continued. "But in its most basic essence, a mark is simply a way of showing that this person is under your protection. It's a subtle threat to those who would consider harming someone who has a mate. Or mates. The more marks, the more untouchable that person appears."

"I see." Those wheels in his head were turning at full speed. He chewed on his lip, then he addressed me again. The look alone told me he was starting to see potential perks. "But I... I won't force her. If she doesn't want me then I don't want to trap her."

"Fair enough." I shrugged. *That's the difference between a lion and a puppy, I suppose.* "Then just show her why she *should* see you that way, and I'm sure she'll choose you." He nodded absently, and for some reason, that disheartened look on his face made me frown. So I stood up and I placed a hand on his shoulder. I squeezed it with a friendly familiarity while gazing out at the darkening horizon line. Only the vaguest residual sunlight was left, draping a dark green hue over the trees, the grasses, and the Yellow Brick Road. "I think I'm going to go for a hunt. Care to join me?"

CHAPTER 20

"TOTO"

TOBIAS

Leon and I ran side by side through the grass and the leaves and the trees. Even in this human body, it felt good to just *run*. The strain of my muscles, the wind against my face, the heavy breaths refreshing my lungs, and the adrenaline of my speeding heart. It was the most wild and free I'd felt since I'd lost my canine body.

A shifter. The notion still seemed so strange. Not to mention the idea that Oz was my true home. *That's not true.* My true home was wherever Dorothy was, even if I may have been born here.

I made these internal declarations confidently, but I couldn't help but wonder what kind of memories I'd lost. Had I had my own mate before my past was taken from me? Had I had a family? I didn't know. All of the men we'd met since arriving here had nothing but trauma and tragedy at the hands of these witches, so why would I be any different? How much had I lost when I was sent to the human world as a dog, and what had I done to deserve it?

I shuddered at the thought and tried to shift my focus back to the hunt.

Leon was fast and graceful, and he truly resembled a lion in the way he dressed and the way he ran. I envied his knowledge of who he was and what he wanted, and the confidence that let him take it without question. He was fierce, and he was secure.

Could I be like that one day? I thought I'd ask the Wizard to return home with Dorothy and reclaim my place in her life as her emotional support pet, but… was that really what I wanted? Even if it was, that wasn't my curse. My curse was suppressed memories and losing the ability to switch back and forth between a canine and human body. So if I did get my old self back, what if I found that my old life was better? What if I didn't want to be with Dorothy anymore, because I had someone else?

The thought alone made me sad. So long as I retained who I was now, I couldn't even imagine a world without Dorothy at its center, and I didn't want to. I needed some way to assure that my curse could be broken without losing that connection.

Like marking her.

I chewed on my lip. Marking her as my mate sounded like a good way to keep her safe, so even if we never did anything… I forcefully held that thought… in a *sexual* way, there were plenty of other benefits. It may be worth proposing to her in the morning.

I splashed through a stream, fanning water up to my knees from the impact of my boots. My step was always sure and stable, and I had no problem keeping up. My senses and instincts were firing on all cylinders as we heard a slight rustle in the bushes. I caught a flash of movement in the dense foliage, and any other thoughts fell away in favor of pure, unbridled instinct.

If I truly was what they call a beast man, this would be my moment of truth.

The moon was high in the dark sky by the time we returned. My body still shook with adrenaline and endorphins, while my stomach was sated and full in a way that apples and plants could never provide.

I felt alive. So *fucking* alive. My pulse was absolutely pounding, while the flavor of blood still so pleasantly coated my taste buds. It was unlike anything I'd ever experienced in any lifetime. Not as a dog and not as a man. To be so wild and animalistic and powerful—I was drunk on that aggression, and I didn't want to let it go. *What a fucking rush.*

Leon gave me a pat on the back and a knowing smile. "There's nothing like the first hunt. Once you've tasted blood like that, you'll never want anything else." With a soft chuckle, he squeezed my shoulder, then he whispered in my ear, "Don't ever let go of this feeling." His hand drifted to my bicep, where his fingers slid through the still wet traces of crimson on my skin. He dragged his claw downward, scraping a clean line through the blood spatter, then the lion licked the blood from his nails with steady, satisfied strokes. He addressed me again with one last wink. "Good night, little black wolf. Don't let your princess wait too long for your warmth."

Leon sauntered off and found a comfortable spot to rest beneath a tree. I turned my sights on my tent. The small privacy door I'd woven from leaves and vines had been closed but not secured, and I could hear Dorothy's steady breathing of sleep from here. Her natural scent filled my nostrils. She was giving off so many natural scents.

I was too charged to think. I got down onto my knees, and I undid the door cover. Dorothy stirred, lifting her chin as if to verify the right person was joining her in her bed. The slight skip in her heartbeat immediately calmed to easy and comfortable levels, just as it always did when I was with her. The perfect contentment and safety a person experiences around a most trusted friend.

A most trusted *friend*.

When I crawled in with her, her eyes widened when she caught sight of the blood on my skin. "Toto, are you hurt?" She asked with so much concern it was smothering.

"Tobias." I corrected her, before I pulled her back against my chest with an aggressive tug. I didn't want to hear that cute little nickname right now. I didn't need to be treated like a defenseless puppy. Maybe it was the near drunken surge of adrenaline that was still pumping through me, but I wasn't able to hold myself back right now. "Toto was your puppy. I'm not a frail little black dog anymore, Dorothy."

"N-no, of course not." She snuggled back against me of her own will, and she rolled over in my arms, until she was resting her head on my bicep and staring directly into my eyes. The look on her face was one of confusion, worry, and curiosity. "But then… Whose blood is this?"

That delicate concern did something to me. I responded before I gave myself even one more moment to overthink it.

"Not mine." I said, before I leaned in and pressed my lips against hers. She jerked back with a slight hint of surprise, but only for a second before she relaxed into the kiss. When she nibbled at my lip, I took that as mutual interest, and when she placed a hand on my cheek to pull me down further and deepen the contact, I lost any restraint I had left. I shoved her hand back down to the leaves, and I repositioned myself on top of her. I pinned her body beneath my weight, and I slipped her my tongue, just wanting to taste more of her warm and perfect lips.

She sucked on me before she slipped me hers. She dug her fingers into my hands that had hers locked against the ground, and I shifted my hips to grind against her pelvis. I know she could feel how hard I was, and I wanted her too. The moan that she shared directly in my mouth told me she didn't mind it.

I released her hands so I could better brace my weight above her, then I pulled away so both of us could catch our breath, Her chest heaved while I fluttered kisses down her jaw line, and she lifted her chin to give me access to her neck. I sniffed along her skin, savoring her natural scent while relishing in her taste as I fluttered soft pecks downward. When I reached her collarbone, I paused and breathed so many possibilities over that sensitive skin. I hadn't seen Leon's mark yet. It was somewhere invisible while she wore her clothes, and I suddenly had an overwhelming urge to find it. Taste it. Share that same spot.

I can mark her too. She can be mine. She likes being taken like this.

The thoughts all flashed through my mind at once, and I clenched my fists in the leaves below us to try and get a handle on this animalistic need bubbling up in me.

No. Absolutely not.

I pulled back, and I instead placed a single soft, delicate peck on her lips again. "Good night, Dorothy." I said, as if it was the most casual night in the world. She stared at me in surprise but was at a complete loss for words.

Words weren't necessary right now anyway. I rolled off her, got into a comfortable position at her side, and I wrapped an arm around her again. I secured my lady up against my chest, and she rested her forehead against my shirt without protest.

151

Her body was trembling, her heartbeat was racing, and she was exhaling short breaths through her still open mouth. But I knew what fear smelled like, and that was not the scent she gave off now.

Her stress signals calmed, and she snuggled up more tightly against me of her own accord. Then she whispered three simple words that meant more than an entire novel:

"Good night, *Tobias*."

She was asleep shortly after, while my adrenaline had only just started to subside I stared at the wall of our tent, wide-eyed, horrified, and processing that I'd really just done that. Without even asking, I just kissed Dorothy.

I rested my chin on top of her head, and I swallowed down my mortification.

Fuck fuck fuck fuck fuck. Would she forgive me for this? Had I ruined our relationship?

Maybe I really am a beast.

CHAPTER 21

DOROTHY

Black filled my vision as I awoke, still cuddled against Tobias' chest. The rise and fall of his muscles implied he was still asleep, and I held firmly, not wanting to wake him. The blood that was smeared on his body had fully dried, and he looked so intense against his usual soft and collected demeanor.

"Not mine." He'd said, but… whose was it? He and Leon had been nowhere to be found when I'd come back from the waterfall, and I could taste the blood on his tongue when he kissed me. Maybe they'd gone hunting together. But Toto was such a sweet little dog. He wasn't a killer. He wasn't rough and aggressive like this. I'd never seen him like that before at all.

I'd never… *felt* him like that before. Whatever synapse in his brain snapped last night, I was fairly certain he was ready to wreck me from the inside out, and with how sexually frustrated I'd been lately, I was ready to let him.

Focus, Dorothy! I admonished myself. Just because I was suddenly surrounded by a bunch of hot guys with issues, didn't mean I needed to ride all of their dicks. I'd have been way more successful in Hollywood if I had this kind of desire for old, creepy narcissists. Stupid picky hormones.

I was already in too deep with Leon and playing exhibitionist with Crowe. The last thing I needed was to corrupt Tobias. The only guy I hadn't crossed a line with

153

yet was Talos, and now I almost felt like I owed it to him to at least sit on his face or something.

These last twenty-four hours—or however long a day was in Oz—had been a whirlwind and a half.

When I sighed, that was just enough stimulation to wake up Tobias. He tightened his arms around me in a good morning hug, then he released me enough to let me pull away.

"Good morning." He said, as if nothing had happened.

"Good morning." I returned the greeting with an involuntary smile despite myself. As easy as it would be to freak out some more, it was as if his whole existence was crafted to bring me calm, and it was hard to stay riled up and in a tizzy when he looked at me with those friendly morning eyes. I supposed that was why he was my emotional support for so long. Last night didn't have to change that. Right. Act normal. "I'm going to start making breakfast if you want any." I said.

"I'd like that." He hugged me one more time, and I crawled out of the tent without a single word about what happened between us.

We didn't need to talk about it really. We could just sweep everything under the rug. No need to just come out and say *"oh wow, I never expected you had such an appealing cock, Toto!"* or *"nothing like a little making out and dry humping between friends!"*

No, no reason to talk about any of that at all. *Instead, let's talk about apples. I love apples. Who doesn't love apples!*

I laughed to myself like the crazy person I was, then I resolved to go find Talos for some apples, and absolutely not to sit on his face.

154

When I approached, he and Crowe were seated back to back, and despite the fact that they could silently communicate, I could tell that they weren't currently speaking. Crowe noticed me first, and just the way he made eye contact had me blushing and replaying bath time in the woods.

"Oh good. The humans are fully charged again." He said with his patent sarcasm. *I guess we're all just talking to each other like nothing at all happened and everything is not awkward or tense or weird.*

I raised an eyebrow and corrected him in an attempt to be as cool a cucumber as everyone else. "Not without breakfast we're not."

"Sweet fucking Lucifer, seriously?" He groaned, and I laughed.

"You'll get used to it someday, I promise." With a pronounced roll of my eyes, I approached Talos. In immediate understanding, he handed me some apples from his satchel. I curtsied for my immortal companions as an equally sarcastic thank you, and I headed back to the campfire without doing any further sex things with any of them.

And I sat across from Leon, who already had the fire crackling and ready to go. His eyes crawled over my body, the least subtle of all my men, apparently.

Then he frowned. "No new marks? Shame."

My whole entire body turned red. "Y-you—"

"You're both welcome." He interrupted me so obnoxiously and smugly and singsong. "What fun this is going to be."

So *he* knew what happened already. He probably took Tobias on a hunt with him just to get him riled up.

155

Maybe he even slipped him something. Tobias could have been the Oz equivalent of drunk for all I knew. Maybe he didn't even remember last night at all.

I opened my mouth to say… something. Anything at all. But I was absolutely speechless.

Before I could figure out how to make my brain or mouth work, Tobias sat down by the fire with us, carrying a fresh pot of water and a conveniently shaped rock that I could use to bake the apples. He took a sip and handed me the pot, and my mouth was so dry in my new state of what-the-fuckery that I guess I downed the whole thing in a series of desperate and not very ladylike gulps. They both stared at me for several moments.

Then Tobias patted me on the shoulder. Leon shook his head. And we all laughed.

It was possible I was over thinking this. Maybe it didn't have to be weird or awkward at all.

After an eventful morning—for me anyway—we were back to walking the Yellow Road to Nowhere. Every step took us closer and closer to the dark green monument in the distance, and I was finally starting to feel like we had some hope of making it to the Wizard and having all of our issues fixed. *Ah, who needs therapy when you have magic?*

The guys all seemed to be getting along well enough. Crowe tended to walk with Talos, while Tobias had somehow turned animosity into friendship with Leon. It was kind of cute, honestly, and I was starting to like the chaos of juggling so many different personalities. All of the camping and struggles had been a nice way to bond, even if I was starting to question the wholesomeness of my own bonds with everyone.

But my interest in them was different, too. I hated how often I was supposed to pay for roles with my body, but I also hated that I'd started to view sex as something to give to others in barter instead of something to enjoy for myself. If I got nothing else from this interruption of my life, I hoped it could be that.

The day's walk wasn't without its obstacles, but with everyone's unique talents, nothing felt terribly bothersome. When we came across a gushing river where the road had been washed out, a very hard hit from Talos' fist was all it took to down a tree to create a bridge. Tobias carried me across to make sure I didn't trip. When overgrowth blocked the path, Leon's claws made quick work of the vines, and Crowe made quick work of any beasts or munchkins that crossed our path.

The sun was just drifting past high noon when the Emerald City appeared close enough to feel obtainable. All that stood between us and our goal was a field of soft yellow flowers, both lining the road and spouting up between every gap and break in the brick construction. My heart felt lighter looking at the enchanting contrast of bright and cheerful with deep greens. Pair that with the vibrant path and the clear blue sky and Oz was truly a beautiful place.

"We're so close!" I shouted with excitement. My silver shoes clacked as I started to run through this last stretch of open road. It felt so good to have finally made it. The journey had felt far longer than the handful of days it had taken. "Finally." I spun on my heel to face my companions behind me. I took a pronounced inhale, reveling in the fragrance of the flowers.

An overwhelming sense of dizziness surged through my brain. I might have puked if not for the fact that, the very next moment, my whole world went black.

Fuck. So close. So fucking close…

CHAPTER 22

"THE TIN MAN"

TALOS

Crowe moved swiftly and immediately, almost as if he'd expected the sudden loss of consciousness. He had Dorothy in his arms before her knees had finished buckling, while I saved Tobias and Leon from a concussion or broken tail bone by only the narrowest of margins. All three of our eating and sleeping companions were completely limp and silent in an instant.

< *"What happened?"* > I asked as I lowered the men gently to the floor. Crowe, conversely, hoisted Dorothy over his shoulder like an old sack of potatoes.

"Mandragora is what happened." Crowe scoffed. "The Aurora Mandragora Blossoms only grow here in the Eastern fields, but Hildy was fond of them. Ingesting the root, they're hallucinogenic poison. *If* you survive, you'll go mad in the process." He glanced at the woman on his arm. "But the smell of the flowers works more as a powerful tranquilizer. We nicknamed the plant the *Assassin Root*, as it's a perfect tool for disabling and finishing a target, and can only be used by someone like you or I, who has no need to breathe or smell. As an added perk, the fibers of the plant are digested cleanly and can't be detected even under magical analytics." He paused for several moments, though his expression returned to something much more neutral and emotionless now. "Excellent way to hold onto power for someone who's as weak as they are universally hated and needs some hands off weapons." He added with a shake of his head. "You can ask me how I know, but you seem like a sharp enough guy."

< *"Yes, I don't need to ask."*> An assassination plant. I'd never seen such a thing in the South. < *"How long do the effects of the tranquilizer last?"*>

"Not sure. I always made sure they were dead before they woke up." Crowe shrugged.

< *"So how do you know they* ever *wake up?"*>

With a purse of his lips, Crowe tapped his chin with his index finger. "I suppose I don't. That's just what the witch told me. But she *did* like to make me kill for her amusement, so it could have been a well thought out lie to force me to finish the job faster. I had more of a conscience back then, and it took a minute for her to convince me to murder indiscriminately." He shrugged, then he motioned towards Dorothy again. "The woman seems pretty tough. I'm sure her body can fight it."

She's 'the woman' instead of 'the girl' now, huh? Another vote of confidence. I wondered if he even noticed how often he subtly complimented her. Though I opted not to bring it up again. He was so sensitive sometimes. < *"Is there an antidote in case she can't?"*>

Crowe turned toward the Emerald City, that was so incredibly close now, then he returned his gaze to me with a frown. "Our best bet would be to get them out of the fields so they stop breathing in the pollen. Hopefully they'll recover on their own from there." With that, he patted Dorothy on the ass and motioned towards our beast men. "I've got this one. Do you think you can—"

I had both men hoisted over opposing shoulders before he could even finish the sentence. < *"Yep."*>

"Strong man." Crowe smirked, then he turned towards the city and began making his way to the other side of the field. I followed behind him, taking note of the very delicate way he cradled her on his shoulder. His walk was steady, assuring she didn't get jostled too much. Small gestures, but calculated and pointed ones. It was marginally adorable.

<"You don't strike me as someone who has ever been bothered by death."> I made small talk as the flowers passed us by.

"We've all had our flaws. I worked on it." His dark red eyes met mine as we walked side by side. "You?"

<"Part of pleasing Sasha involved indulging in a lot of pain play, and the goal post always moved. Sometimes the pain was on me, and other times it was me inflicting pain on others. Not everyone could take it."> Such a strange thing to bond over, yet it felt natural with Crowe. It was hard to convey these sorts of things without fear of judgment to anyone else. Speaking to fellow puppets within the kingdom had been not simply frowned upon, but punishable, and having once been her favorite toy, I certainly wasn't allowed to fraternize with anyone she deemed lesser men. I hadn't realized how lonely being a witch's fuck doll truly was until I'd met Crowe and found this refuge in casual conversation.

"That's not what I asked." He lifted an eyebrow. "Did it *bother* you?"

<"Murder? No."> The words surprised me as I said them. *<"I took comfort in knowing I couldn't feel the same pain I'd dealt. Slicing someone open felt as natural as breathing.">*

Crowe raised an eyebrow. "Here I thought *I* was the fucked up one."

<"I was sold to Sasha by my clan from the Naraka Mesas. The east is a tropical paradise compared to the southern sector.">

That ordinarily unmoved expression of his faltered at the realization. "You're from the Naraka Mesas. So you're…"

<*"From a clan of cannibals, yes."*>

"So cutting people for pleasure was…"

<*"My birthright, yes."*>

"Do you still—"

<*"Absolutely not."*> I didn't want him to finish that question. I resented my origins nearly as much as I resented the witches themselves. <*"All of Sasha's favorites are granted immortality so they can survive long enough to get her off. Setting aside that I don't eat anymore, making human butchering an ordinary punishment changed my view of the practice. When the sight of blood stopped getting me hard, she was done with me."*>

Crowe frowned. *Empathy?* "I guess I'm glad she bought you then."

<*"What?"*> Stunned, I stopped walking, while Crowe continued several more steps. He turned to face me, Dorothy still cradled so gently on his shoulder.

"Don't the Naraka sacrifice their men after their first son is born?"

<*"Yes. It's said that if a son should eat his father's heart, their souls will join and their strength will amplify. We've done it for generations, and I was not exempt. It's much of where our power comes from."*> I'll admit I was impressed he knew so much about my clan. Though we were rather infamous in Oz, so it should have been expected.

His gaze drifted casually down my muscles, then they climbed back up to my face. "How old are you now? Thirty? Fifty? Two hundred? Five?"

162

< "I lost count so long ago, I couldn't begin to guess.">

"Exactly." He nodded. "So if not for the witch, you'd have already been a heart sandwich, and you wouldn't be having this conversation with me right now. Which means I'd be stuck carrying all three of these buffoons myself."

That elicited an involuntary laugh from deep in my chest. He tried to make it sound like he was being so burdened, but the compliment wasn't lost on me. *< "I suppose so.">*

"Funny though—I don't recall much of who I was before Grunhilda, but somewhere vaguely in my gut, I know I was terribly ordinary and soft. But where I had to forget ingrown compassion, you had to learn it. Amazing how our journeys are the exact opposite, yet the end results are very much the same."

I didn't need to ask him to clarify, because I knew exactly what he meant. *< "The duality in our souls, you mean?">*

Crowe was unexpectedly poignant at times. He was right though. Our lives had granted us an unusual understanding of both extremes. To know the heart of a killer who could slaughter innocents mercilessly, while also holding the heart of a man with desire to love and protect and feel emotion for others. We'd held and lost both feelings, and were now creating our balance with the pieces we could get a hold on. Our souls were like coins that spun on their side for infinity—both faces always present, yet so long as that coin spun fast enough, it was impossible to know which you were looking at.

The softness of Crowe's resulting smile didn't suit his face, yet I liked it on him. "The duality of our souls. You should be a poet, Tin Man.

I chuckled. < *"And you should be a jester, Scarecrow."*>

"I'll talk to the Wizard about it and see what he thinks."

We continued on in quiet conversation until the Emerald City was near enough to dwarf us with its grandeur. With the flowers behind us, it wasn't long before I felt the men in my arms starting to stir. I took a few more steps before placing them gently in the grass beside the yellow bricks, and I waited patiently for them both to fully wake.

I was glad I could help them. While I was closest with Crowe, I enjoyed the continued presence of friendly company. It was hard to believe I'd been allowed to exist among good people. At times, I felt unworthy of being part of their travels at all. Once they knew who I was, I wondered if they would still let me stay. I could only hope that this time, my companions might see me as a savior more than a monster.

While Leon slowly blinked his way into consciousness and Tobias began to stretch, a commotion up ahead drew my attention back to the other two in our party.

"I'm awake okay. You can put me down now." Dorothy whined while she hit Crowe in the back with her balled fists.

"Nope." Crowe tightened his hold around her waist, and he secured her with a hand very firmly on her ass. I think I could guess which portion she was drawing objection to. "Can't risk you carelessly passing out again and hurting yourself."

"Then how come Tobias and Leon get to walk?" Her protests had a bite of playfulness.

"Because they're built from meat and metal, and you're built from glass and marshmallows." He said, knowing exactly how much that would rile her up.

"What?! I am not. You'd take that back if you ever saw me chop a whole cord of wood in an afternoon. You have no idea the kind of things I've endured." She hit him a few more times before she harrumphed and resolved to her fate.

"Hmmm, you're right. I guess I'll have to test those limits later."

Her face burned red, and I caught myself smirking behind my mask at the exchange. I liked their dynamic, too.

I hoped when all was said and done, we could still keep these simple moments.

CHAPTER 23

DOROTHY

The Emerald City was spectacular beyond anything I ever imagined. The castle spires towered over the high masonry walls built from sparkling green gemstones that encased the city, while even the yellow brick road turned to sage as we approached the entrance. A tall but human sized man in heavy plated armor stood guard at an ornate gate—a welcome sight compared to the munchkins and monsters I'd encountered thus far. I took some amount of relief in the knowledge that there were, in fact, other people at least sort of like me here. I didn't know how far off the humans of Oz were from the humans of my home, but being among the munchkins, the witch, and the "cursed puppets," I was starting to feel like a total outlier these days. In Hollywood I was a dime a dozen, and here, I was something unique and special. This might be the first time in my entire life that I'd been able to feel that way about myself.

The guard remained stiff as we approached. "State your purpose." He demanded, though never making eye contact.

"We've come to see the Wizard." I stated confidently.

The guard didn't relax in the slightest, but he did take a moment to scan over the lot of us. We must have been quite a sight, between myself: the cute, nonthreatening, normal one (in my opinion), Tobias: the regal and soft looking one, Talos: the rock hard body builder with a metal muzzle, Leon: the tattooed Viking in nondescript animal furs, and Crowe: the red eyed demon of a man whose skin was only one stage warmer than an undead grey.

He opened his mouth in a shape that told me he was about to say no, but then his sights caught on my shoes. He paused and changed those rounded *'no'* lips, to a sharper *'right this way.'*

The gates creaked loudly on unoiled hinges, and we were escorted through the emerald streets.

I took the time to observe the city around me on the way to that massive central palace. The townsfolk had taken the emerald moniker to an extreme, decorating literally every inch of the space with the deepest green. Even things that shouldn't be green at all—cats and meat and hair, for example—were dyed or painted. Or maybe cats and hair were naturally green in Oz. *Fuck if I know.*

My silver shoes tapped on the green cobblestone, past small market stalls and medieval blacksmith shops and shoe cobblers and bakers and leather smiths. Men pulling green rickshaws shuffled past us, hauling around important looking people in olive petticoats, while an armorer fitted a soldier with jade plate mail. In some ways, Oz felt like a dreamlike version of the world I came from, and in others, it was distinctly clear I'd been spirited away to magical fantasy land.

When we arrived at the castle, we were left in a carpeted entryway to be received by another servant of the Wizard. She was a young and very beautiful woman with an updo that resembled a cinnamon roll, while dressed in a long, silky gown. The shimmering fabric cascaded down her body, leaving no part of her shape to the imagination.

"Welcome to the Emerald Castle." The woman said with a curtsy. I'd gotten used to the way everyone gawked at my silver shoes the second I stepped into the room, so I said nothing as she paused for a bit longer than a standard blink when her gaze reached my feet. I didn't know why these shoes were so special, but whatever they meant to that witch and these people, I'd continue to use it to my advantage. "The Wizard will be happy to receive you. But first, you must be exhausted from your travels. Please follow me, and I'll show you to your rooms. You may rest and freshen up, and your audience will be scheduled for the morning." A judgmental look hopped to each and every one of us. "Appropriate clothing will also be provided."

I bowed my head and offered a simple thank you, then we followed the attendant to the hall. Everyone was given their own room. I was going to inform her that Crowe and Talos didn't sleep, but it didn't do much harm to just let them have a private space all to themselves for the night. I bid goodnight to each of my friends, then I entered my own room at the end of the hall.

Now I might believe I'd died and gone to heaven. The bedroom was everything I missed and everything I'd needed after days on the road. I hopped onto the bed and practically giggled as the soft mattress bounced me off its soft and springy surface, then I ran straight to my own private bathroom, where the water in the shower got hot enough to steam up this entire castle wing, and the water pressure was strong enough to blast the mud off a tractor. I was naked and covered in soap as fast as I could get my dress off, then I doubled down with a hot bubble bath in the Jacuzzi tub. I felt like the princess I always dreamed of being, and I was going to savor that comfort as long as I could get away with it. I didn't even care that the bubbles were as green as everything else. It felt good on my joints, and I so needed this.

It was worth it to travel all the way to the Emerald City just for this alone. *Fuck going home. I'm just going to wish to stay in here forever.*

I closed my eyes and inhaled a lovely aroma akin to rosemary and cherry blossoms. It was nearly two hours before I willed myself to dry off and get dressed.

When I returned to the bedroom, a couple different outfits had been left on my bed. I set aside the dress for my audience with the Wizard and went straight for the comfortable pajamas. Also made from a shimmering satin, the pajamas were cool and smooth on my skin. The top was a small tank top of bright jade, with thin spaghetti straps that barely held the material high enough to cover my chest, and the bottom was a pair of loose short shorts that just reached the bottom of the curve of my ass. Small slits lined with lace on each side of the shorts made the ensemble feel more like comfortable lingerie than a royal set of PJs, but I wasn't about to complain. I'd missed sleeping naked or near naked since coming here and spending every night in mixed company, so I was going to savor every minute.

Pleased, I wormed my way under the weighted covers, and I settled in to enjoy some quality sleep.

Three hours later, I was still wide awake.

I stared at the green ceiling in frustration. I'd barely ever slept alone in the last decade, whether I was with a boyfriend, a date, a producer I was trying to impress, or just snuggling Toto. Though I was borderline sweating from the heavy comforter, the bed still felt so... cold. Cold and empty.

I frowned and rolled over again, hoping a new position would make it easier to sleep, but another hour passed and all I'd accomplished was staring at the backs of my eyelids.

I sighed and I huffed and I jumped when I heard the light tapping on my door.

"Dorothy, are you still awake?" *Tobias*. My heart sped, not out of nerves, but out of thankful excitement that my snuggle buddy had come to my rescue.

I got out of bed and answered the door as quietly as I could.

There, on the other side, Tobias was freshly bathed and smelled like almonds. His black hair was clean and messy, and it just begged to have fingers run through its softness to straighten it out, while his pajama pants were slung low on his hips. The way the satin hugged every shape and curve of his body left little to the imagination, and I'll just say that "grey sweatpants season" has nothing on "satin pajama season."

All things I absolutely should not be noticing about my most trusted friend and emotional support.

"I couldn't sleep." He said as he nervously rubbed the back of his head, ruffling that soft hair through his long fingers. Another thing I was not trying to notice.

"I couldn't either." I admitted.

"I've never slept alone, and I don't really think I like it. S-so…" He glanced away, and the light blush to his cheeks was even visible in the low light of the hallway's torches. "So I just thought I'd see if you were struggling too. Since you don't usually sleep alone either."

"Oh." Was all I said.

"I mean, I understand if you don't want to sleep in the same bed as me after last night." His tone sped up to a panicked level. "Sorry, I didn't mean to—"

"No." I stopped him with a shake of my head and a grateful smile. "I would sleep a lot better if you slept with me."

His whole body relaxed, from his expression to his tense shoulders. I motioned back towards my bed, and he followed me into the room.

I was glad he was here, but… my heart was also racing to see him. I'd been doing my best not to betray his trust and platonic, genuine love for me with an unwanted shift in physical attraction, but when he looked like that, it was difficult not to. And when *he* looked at *me* like that, eyes accidentally brushing over my visible headlights under this top, I wondered if he was struggling with the same thoughts, or if the other night was just an adrenaline-drunk mistake…

I swallowed as I climbed back into bed now with his strong warm body at my back. I nudged up into him, and he squeezed me with a palm on my stomach to close any remaining gap between our bodies. His firm chest pressed into my back, while he kept the slightest distance between my ass and his hips.

Strategic. Or just polite. My mind wanted the former, but it was likely more about the latter.

"That's much better." His deep voice in my ear had me immediately on fire. I was grateful for the darkness that hid any visible confessions.

"Yeah. Much better." I squeaked. I was very experienced in sharing beds with men. *This shouldn't be freaking me out so much.*

Well, I was used to sharing beds with men I had no interest in. It wasn't hard to sleep next to a guy I had happily in my friend zone, or a guy who'd passed out from alcohol after a long party, or a boyfriend who'd I expected to roll around with. But sleeping with my hot, emotionally secure confidante who I had no sort of sexual relationship with was dangerous. I just kept telling myself we'd done this for many nights now. It had become normal for us, and I slept like heaven, so I shouldn't be reacting so strongly. This should be fine.

I pressed my cheek into the pillow, trying to distract myself from the feeling of his warm, firm bicep cradling my neck. I squeezed my eyes shut when he rested his other arm on my waist, letting his hand dangle on the bed in front of my chest. He kept respectful distance, just as he should.

"Goodnight, Dorothy." Tobias whispered.

"Goodnight." But now I couldn't sleep for a different reason. So I placed my hand on top of his knuckles, and I interlaced our fingers. He answered by closing his fist, securing my grip there.

I smiled silently. My heart rate slowed. Calm and peace filmed me. Calm, peace, and an urge to…

I pulled his hand closer, and I placed it against my breast.

He accepted the invite. He opened his palm, and he cupped me gently. No pressure, just his warm palm touching me through my tank top. He held me there, and he idly stroked the inside of my breast with his thumb through the material. Back and forth, back and forth. He drew electric lines over my night gown, while his palm cradled me like I was a delicate treasure. I was sure he felt how perked my nipples were against his palm, but he didn't say

172

anything. He didn't react. He just kept absentmindedly drawing small shapes on me.

I nudged back my hips, wanting to feel a bit more of him, while he got to feel a bit more of me, and Tobias placed his chin on my shoulder. His warm breaths buzzed my ear, when he spoke very, very softly.

"Careful." The strain in his voice made me not want to be careful at all. The rebel in me only wanted to test those limits.

"Careful about what?" I played naïve, while I squirmed until my hips were just a little closer to his. "I'm just trying to get comfortable." A little closer. Just a little more.

His grip tightened on my breast, and he squeezed me to try and keep me in place. As much as I liked it, and as disappointed as I was, I took the hint that he didn't want to go any further. I stopped moving and tried to settle down the thump in my chest.

"I said, *careful*." He muttered more softly now. But *he* wasn't careful. He drew slow lines of pressure across my chest until he reached my other breast. He pinched my pert nipple between his fingers, the fabric creating very little barrier to the sensation, and I moaned softly on accident. "Do you like that?" He asked, and I nodded in immediate confirmation.

Tobias drifted his hand down to my stomach, and he hooked his fingers under the hem of my top. I'm sure he could hear the absolute pounding of my heart as he started to drag that material upward. The satin slid over my skin, and that delicate touch was so absolutely erotic. I took a deep breath, puffing out my chest as his fingers reached my rib cage. I held that breath as they lifted higher. The slick fabric passed my nipples without a hitch, and Tobias left that material by my neck as he replaced his hand on my now completely exposed chest.

His hands were rough and hot when there was nothing between our skin. "You're so soft, Dorothy." He lifted his chin until his lips were touching my ear. Then he spoke with an unexpected harshness. "You feel really fucking nice in my hand."

If those words weren't enough to take me over the edge, the way he fondled, pinched, and explored me might. I clenched my thighs, trying to get ahold of myself, but that need in me only had me sinking my hips lower. I pressed back until I could feel him against my ass. Hard, thick, long.

"Fuck." He was the one unable to hold in a moan this time, and hearing him directly in my ear did something to me.

So I pushed further. I rubbed my ass on his cock. Feeling bolder now, I taunted him back. "I know somewhere that feels even better."

He traced circles around my nipple, trailing powerful sensations despite the subtlety. "Lead the way, Dorothy."

I loved how my name sounded in his unraveling tone. I did as I was told, taking his hand in mine, and directing it downward. I kept his hand over my shorts as I placed it between my legs. "Can you feel that?" I asked, not at all innocently now. I was so wet, it took only the slightest pressure to communicate that even through my clothes.

He drew a line up my center, then he slipped that hand back down and sank the material further into my arousal. "I think I prefer the feel of your skin."

A compliment. A dare. I hooked a finger under the waist band of my shorts, and I nudged them down. I pushed my shorts down to my thighs, then I lifted my knees so I wouldn't have to sever the connection between our bodies. With a little effort, I managed to get my shorts all the way off, then I grabbed his hand, and I placed it back where I'd left it, directly skin to skin on my pussy.

"Is that better?" I asked coyly, though my body was still on fire. I was still nervous, still doubting myself, but I couldn't seem to stop.

Tobias pressed his elegant fingers between my folds. He brushed my clit before dipping down to play in my wetness. He slipped a finger inside, then he drew a line back up my body. My voice was completely unashamed this time.

He nipped at my ear before dipping into me again. "You're right. This is better." Deeper. "Spread your legs for me."

If Tobias wasn't hot enough as it was, him telling me what to do while he played with my pussy had me desperate to have more of him inside me.

"What will you give me if I do?" More boldness. Fuck, I was so turned on.

He nudged his clothed cock more fully against my ass, giving me a preview of the size of him, and I was prepared to beg for it before I'd leave this room without feeling its full length.

"What do you want, Dorothy?" The question was explicit, demanding my verbal consent, and I had to psyche myself up to put such a thing into words. He kept ghosting the lightest touch on my clit, which only made clear, logical thought more difficult. When he dipped into my core again,

I started fucking myself on his fingers, hoping he would take me without making me say it out loud.

My breathing hitched. My heart skipped a beat. He removed his fingers, and he smeared my arousal up my stomach. He continued upwards, then he slipped his fingers between my lips. I whimpered as I licked and sucked on each digit, tasting how he made me feel.

Then he jerked his hand away suddenly. He shoved his pajamas down. And he placed the head of his cock at my entrance. "I need you to tell me, Dorothy." He growled into my ear, my name now sounding even hotter in his rough and deep voice.

I sunk my hips down, drawing the head of his cock into me. That first inch of pressure, as he made room for himself in my body, elicited a filthy sound from my throat.

He clamped down his hands around my hips, and with strained commitment, he pulled away again, leaving me empty and wanting.

Tobias shook his head against my shoulder. "I need to hear it, Dorothy. Tell me exactly what you want."

"Fuck me." I breathed out in desperation. "Please Tobias. Please just... I want you to take me."

He pressed the head back in, and I clenched on the little bit of ecstasy that he offered. I sank down, pulling him in another inch, then he met my efforts to give me two more. I kept going, taking him a little at a time, until he was buried in to his base.

"Is this what you want?" His words were strained as I fully embraced his cock. He remained completely still as I adjusted to his size, and he kept that harsh hold on my hips to prevent me from moving for him.

Friction. I *needed* friction. But he wouldn't give it to me without verbal consent.

"Y-yes. God, yes." I grabbed his hands, and I put them back on my breasts. He obliged me with another tug on each sensitive bead. "Tobias." My voice was so breathy. His stillness was driving me mad. "Please. Show me how you want me, Tobias."

Those seemed to be the key words he needed. Immediately Tobias grabbed my hips. He unsheathed himself, pushed me onto my stomach, shoved my legs apart with his knees, and he lifted my hips, forcing me up on all fours. To assure I couldn't reposition, he hooked his shins over my calves, so he had all of the control over how wide I was spread for him.

And then he inched back in at an excruciatingly slow pace. His cock hit different at this angle, and I was bunching the sheets in my fists as he reached full depth.

With the heel of his hand, Tobias drew a line of pressure down my spine, then he held my hips and massaged the small of my back with his thumbs. He said nothing as he withdrew to his tip, and I cried out when he slammed back in so hard he nearly sent me back down on my stomach.

He braced my hips as he drove his perfect cock in and out of me, again and again and again.

"Let's have no more confusion between us, Dorothy. This is how I want you." He kept going until I was falling off the cliff of pleasure. When I clenched on his cock, that only goaded him on more. "This is how I've wanted you since the moment I got my human body back." I was still rolling as he continued to fuck me. "This is how I'll always want you." I was bordering on a compounding orgasm as he hit that spot relentlessly. "And I'll show you that as many times as you need me to."

"Then mark me." I must have been losing my mind. "I want you to mark me just like Leon did."

I knew those words hit him right when his cock tensed, his fingers dug into my hips, and he filled me with a guttural groan. He drew in a sharp breath, and he was frozen by his own release. It was slow that he pulled out. It was tender that he moved down my body. I kept still as he pressed his lips to my pussy, and as he dipped in his tongue, tasting our mixed orgasms. I was shaking when he fluttered kisses to my ass cheeks, and I let him do as he pleased when he grabbed me roughly again, flipped me onto my back, and shoved my legs wide.

Tobias blew softly on my throbbing and sensitive clit. He kissed my folds, then the apex of my thighs.

And he bit down hard, leaving his mark where only a lover would ever see it. He sucked, he nipped, and he made me his.

While his claim slowly formed on my skin, Tobias crawled back up my body, and he connected our lips with painful gentleness. I could taste both of our blood and both of our come mixed on his tongue. I don't know why I liked that so much.

I laced my fingers through his silky hair, and I kept us connected as long as he'd let me. And as that gentle friction between our bodies got him hard again, I wrapped my legs around his waist.

Tobias was so much more than my emotional support. So, so much more, and I might have never met the true him if I'd not ended up in Oz.

Once we were both sated, I drifted off into the best sleep I'd ever experienced that night with that thought heavy on my mind.

When I met the Wizard tomorrow to ask for my wish, did I truly want to go back to that old life?

CHAPTER 24

"THE SCARECROW"

CROWE

Arms crossed, I leaned against the wall of the hallway, escaping the suffocating confines of our assigned spaces. The puppy had slipped into Dorothy's room, the lion was asleep, and Talos was likely as annoyed by these nights as I was. I considered slipping into his room for company, but I'd had a touch too much *company* lately, and it was starting to make me question myself.

In the morning, we'd speak to the Wizard, and in theory, we'd all have our curses reversed. I'd go back to having normal human feelings, Talos would be able to speak to everyone, the beast man would be able to shift, and Dorothy and her mutt would go home to wherever the fuck Kansas was.

The thought made me frown, and *that* reaction annoyed me. Why would any of that be a bad thing? I was the one who'd instigated this journey to begin with. I once felt everything so vividly, from love to lust to happiness, and I wanted that back. The way the dog's heart beat for his master was once how I felt about Grunhilda, after all—the stolen glances and desperate need to have affection returned. Misguided infatuation, sure, and I very quickly learned my lesson, but that didn't negate that there was once a time where that was exhilarating and tense and visceral and terrifying. I missed that chaos.

I chuckled at the thought. Was I jealous of Tobias, or did I pity him? These idle thoughts were difficult to navigate as my brain battled with itself, one side enjoying the freedom of being dead inside, and one side envying the butterflies and heart flutters that I'd lost. Physical pain and the ripples of orgasm were all I had left, while my idle smiles and laughs and taunting was little more than act to appear more human. I'd integrated myself well in this group, as we all made allowances for each other's quirks, but did I deserve their friendship when the protection I offered was a lie?

Maybe that was what I saw in Dorothy. An actress, she'd called herself: someone who fakes a personality to win over an audience of strangers. *We* were the same just like Talos and I were the same. Yet in my soulless existence, what was that pang in my chest whenever I thought about these things? I didn't have a heart anymore, so it wasn't care. I didn't have the portions of my brain that could muster empathy or compassion, so it *certainly* wasn't love. It was more like a dull discomfort. An illness, perhaps.

I rolled my head to the side, absently fixating my gaze on her door, then I rubbed my neck where the barbed wire scars still lingered.

Once everything changes tomorrow, and we all go our separate ways, these thoughts will go away. The kind and honest Crowe would live again, and the immortal demon scarecrow would die the death he deserved.

That was what I wanted, right?

CHAPTER 25

DOROTHY

I showered again first thing in the morning, while Tobias returned to his own room to wash up and get changed. I was sorry to see him go, but I was also bubbling with happiness as I brushed out my hair and stared at my reflection in the mirror. There were no blow dryers or styling tools available, so I let it dry naturally into its normal loose, uneven curls. My roots were a couple inches long now, and I didn't have my makeup, but there was a glow to my face that radiated something beautiful.

I dressed in the emerald gown that the attendant had left for me, and my expression sunk back down. It was a combination of shimmering silk and soft, sheer chiffon, designed in a way that was so revealing, I wasn't sure I could reasonably wear it in public. The silk crisscrossed my chest, pushing up my boobs for maximum cleavage, while the shape of my nipples was not remotely hidden under that thin, unforgiving bodice. The fabric continued downward in two opposing spirals that were strategically spaced to cover my nethers, while every gap between the crossing strips of silk was filled with the see-through chiffon. Gemstones of jade and emerald directed the eye where I would prefer it wasn't, and every movement I made risked total exposure. My marks, even in their intimate placements, were barely covered.

It would be a beautiful dress for the bedroom if the goal was to seduce and entice, but it left me wondering if the Wizard was some kind of creepy pervert if he expected women he didn't know to meet him in this. The only good thing I could say about it was that it went well with my silver shoes.

I mustered up the courage to step into the hallway despite myself. Almost all of my companions had seen far more of me than this, so I should be okay with them by my side, but I didn't feel like I wanted anyone else to see this much of my body anymore. I should have been used to it, yet the memories only made me feel gross instead of confident.

"Dorothy." Crowe greeted me first with a tip of his chin. Dressed in a suit of green that covered all of his scars, he looked unusually clean cut and high class, even despite his always demonic eyes. He pushed himself off the wall he'd been leaning on to approach me. His gaze fluttered down my body then returned to my face. "Breathtaking." He said in a way that almost seemed idle and subconscious in its softness.

I flushed and wrapped my arms around my chest to give a hint of modesty. "I feel a bit silly, to be honest."

"You shouldn't." Crowe shook his head and reached out to run his fingers through my loose hair. His expression softened at the simple touch. "Your real, natural state is perfection." And that had me completely taken aback. Was he… complimenting me? With my roots? My visible blemishes? My lips that looked too thin without carefully applied lipstick, my dull, shapeless eyebrows, and my ordinary eye lashes that were barely visible? "The Wizard will definitely do anything you want if you show up looking like that."

Okay that was definitely a compliment.

It was so simple, yet it made my heart race. He placed a hand on my cheek with unusual tenderness, and he drew a line beneath my eye with his thumb. Then he leaned in and whispered softly in my ear: "But just let him *try* and touch you, sweet girl, and I'll drench those shoes with his blood."

And a smirk. Violent threats of murder weren't supposed to make my clit throb, but with the thoughts that had been swirling through my head, and the flash backs I'd been having since I'd wriggled into this dress, I'd almost think Crowe had just read my mind and knew I needed to hear that.

He... He was just teasing, I told myself, while the proclamation had me red as a beet.

Talos emerged from his room next, and I tried to get my composure back so he wouldn't ask why I was blushing so hard. If he said anything, Crowe chose not to share it with me.

Talos was also dressed in a perfectly tailored suit, though the material strained against his muscles every time he moved. I couldn't help but notice all of the men's outfits seemed to be classy and well structured, while mine was a green smoke show. I rolled my eyes. *Typical.*

Next was Leon. He didn't bother to wear a shirt under his suit jacket, and he seemed to be rather uncomfortable having anything touching his upper body. He paid me a similar compliment before he offered me a place on his arm. Tobias emerged last, and my eyes widened at the dark haired prince charming who stood across the hall from us.

He flushed when he saw me, and it was by impressive willpower that he'd kept his sightline up with mine. I confirmed nor denied nothing when Leon and Tobias shared a silent knowing look between them. I didn't know how the senses of shifters worked, but it was as if they could smell that they'd each put their teeth on me. My only respite was that they still seemed to be friends regardless.

With everyone together and a bunch of conversations and feelings that I didn't want to talk about, I was grateful when Crowe nodded to the group. "Shall we?"

An attendant walked us down a long stretch of hallway that served no purpose beyond building anticipation. The Wizard struck me as arrogant before we'd even met, but I did my best to withhold judgment until he could give an honest first impression. For all I knew, this was just Oz custom. It wouldn't be the strangest thing I'd heard about this place.

At the end of a quarter mile, the woman opened the door, and we were ushered into the audience chamber. The door slammed behind us with a violent thud, and the tick of a lock echoed in the silence.

A throne of dark velvet punctuated the center of the room, while torches and ornate swirls of gold and green decorated every visible surface of the walls, the furniture, the tiles, and the carpet that directed visitors to the Wizard's royal perch.

The room began to fill with smoke. Tobias acted quickly to cover my nose and mouth with his sleeve to prevent me from fully inhaling, just in case this was some sort of trap, but it was only a few brief moments before the cloud dissipated, and a phantom took form on the seat. My most trusted protector eased off with a nod.

The phantom manifested in the shape of a man, but its features were otherwise vague and nondescript. "Speak." Said a voice that boomed off the high ceilings and gaudy walls.

I swallowed, I stepped forward, and I put on my bravest and most unflinching 'audition' face. "Great Wizard." I said confidently. I puffed out my chest and crossed my arms to cover anything he had no business seeing. "We've traveled far from the eastern lands, through trial and hardship, to ask for your aid. Each of my companions has befallen the horrible curses of Oz's witches, and I'd like to clear this wretched magic and set them free." That sounded good. Official even. I channeled that time I auditioned for the role of a dragon princess, so I might latch on to someone else's strength to get me through this. I won't say I was a brilliant actress, but I was still a more than competent one.

The neon particles of phantom essence surveyed each of us. Imagine my complete lack of surprise when his gaze lingered very obviously where it didn't need to be. *So classy. My eyes are up here, bud.* I raised my brows, while I waited for a response.

"I see. It can be done. A witch's magic is very powerful, but it isn't unbreakable." A brief pause as that gaze finally returned to my face. "But you are not cursed. What do *you* desire, my lady?" He asked. I exhaled and relaxed at the response that was so amicable and positive. Here I thought there was going to be a fight on my hands.

I glanced at my friends, and I chewed on my lip. The wizard's demeanor was a relief, but the question was not. After all, what *did* I want? Did I want to go back to the farm? Go back to LA and become an A-List Celebrity? Get revenge on everyone who hurt me? There were so many latent desires inside me, some ambitious, some petty, some vicious, and some charitable, yet with only one wish, what was I supposed to pick? The most fantastic or the most simple?

No, that was all too specific. What I *really* wanted was to actually succeed at something I set out to do. For once, maybe even reach the goal I'd set. I wanted to help everyone, because I'd said I would. I couldn't be selfish and betray Tobias' needs by staying here, nor could I expect to intrude on Leon or Crowe or Talos once they got their lives back. I had to ask to go back to the homestead and face whatever my normal human life had in store for me, right? Aunty Em needed me, and someone had to take over the family business. All my hopes and dreams were just silly fantasies of grandeur—not necessities. Goals for people who were more special, more talented, and prettier than I was.

I could do this. I could keep to my word.

"I want to return to…" My voice hitched, so I forced the last words through a cough. "To my home. In uh…" *Where was home again? Oh right. Kansas. Yeah, Definitely Kansas.* "Kansas. In the United States. That's what I want." *Well, so much for that confidence.* To be fair, when presented with an opportunity to be granted any wish my heart desired and wasting it on a trip to Kansas was a bit hard for me to process. I could have at least said I wanted a trip to Cancun with a stiff margarita and then worked my way back to Kansas from there.

"You're from Kansas?" Was that… curiosity I was hearing?

"Yes." I nodded. "Do you know it?"

"I do." *Wait, what? Why?* "I know it very well." *Is he fucking with me?* "I can grant that wish as well." *Great. Woohoo. Err, I mean great! Woohoo!* "But in order to give

187

you what you seek…" *Ah, there it is. I was waiting for that.* "You must first do something for me." *Of course we must.* It's not like I thought there was ever such thing as a free lunch.

"Anything." I said, despite not being remotely willing to do *anything* anything. Not for *that* prize anyway.

"As I've said, the Witches of Oz are powerful, and their curses cannot be easily broken. To break these spells, I'll need a piece of each woman's soul."

"A piece of their souls?" I scrunched my nose.

The phantom particles confirmed with a jerk of its chin. "Each witch will keep an artifact that channels their powers. If you can steal this enchanted object, you can deliver me their magic, and I can combine them with rituals that will undo the curses they've dealt."

"I see." I frowned. I figured it was safe to say that the witches wouldn't be voluntarily handing over these artifacts. This was probably going to get a bit violent if they were anywhere near as heartless as my companions implied. But then, it's not like I could say no, either. I'd promised to help them, and I couldn't get home to the safe and sane world of humans again without doing this. I just had to hope, when push came to shove, if a witch had to die, my friends could do the dirty work for me. They deserved to have that revenge personally anyway. "And what about my wish?" I asked, just to confirm this was non-negotiable.

"Once I've broken each of their curses, only then will I be able to help you return to the Kansas of your heart's desire." When he put it that way, I'll admit I cringed a little.

"Thank you, Wizard." I said with a bow of my head.

"I have spoken. You will take your leave now." No sooner had those words boomed off the walls did five attendants appear to shove us from the throne room.

"I was going to leave of my own free will." I protested, as a brute of a man threw me over his shoulder and hauled me back to the guest rooms. We were all returned our old, though now clean, clothes, and the moment we were changed, we were kicked out onto the street.

I turned to each of my companions, befuddled by this whirlwind of an audience, and I asked: "Alright, well, who wants to go first?"

The Wicked Witch of the West

CHAPTER 26

"THE LION"

LEON

Gwen, the Wicked Witch of the West. She was the twin sister of Grunhilda, Crowe's favorite witch, and cousin to Tobias' Eloise, and Talos' Sasha. It was a brief debate as to who we would face first.

The fact that the Wicked Witch of the East was already dead meant that Crowe could have his curse cleared on the spot if Dorothy gave up her silver shoes. There were a number of cobblers in the Emerald City who could have made her new footwear, after all, so the sacrifice wouldn't hinder our travels.

But Crowe was quick to dismiss the idea, figuring he might need his callousness for the task at hand. Emotion and understanding were enemies of indiscriminate slaughter, after all. Dorothy wasn't dumb, so I knew she understood as well as the rest of us that our real task was to *murder* the witches, and not to just barter for magic wands. There would be no other way to get these objects. A witch always kept her power close. And Gwen's magical artifact? Well, I'll just say I knew it closer than I wanted to think about.

I was willing to wait my turn in favor of the more pressing afflictions, honestly, but Tobias wasn't terribly interested in regaining his memories or his ability to shift— which I couldn't blame him considering he'd just gotten his first taste of Dorothy's pussy—and Talos felt we should have a trial run before Sasha. As Crowe had explained for the class, the "Good" Witch of the South was not for the faint of heart, and we may need to be a touch stronger and more desensitized before we stood to raid her kingdom.

I couldn't say if Talos had actually said that, or if Crowe had spoken in his place. I didn't trust the scarecrow in the slightest, quite frankly. He had motive to keep the big guy all to himself. I suspected they had a bit of a bond, and I also suspected Crowe had some possessive tendencies, despite how much he pretended he didn't care about anyone or anything.

Talos hadn't visibly protested, however, and I'd heard enough about Sasha to feel he was likely right either way. I couldn't imagine that Dorothy was particularly ready for what we were about to put her through for us, so to start with a mild psychopath like Gwen was a good starter murder.

Plus, the sooner I could regain my lion form, the easier it would be to tear the other witches limb from limb. It was a service to all of us for me to get my strength back.

"Gwen's Castle is approximately…" I pointed to the dark mountains in the distance that were permanently cloaked in black clouds. I waved my finger about until I landed on a small, narrow crevasse in between the two peaks. "There-ish."

It was a good and strategic position. Her throne room was not only perched high enough that she could easily see over the tall pines and evergreens, but it was surrounded by incredibly challenging terrain that made an ambush near impossible. Not only would she see us coming, but she would have the element of surprise if she chose to attack first.

The only advantage we might have in this assault was that she didn't know we were coming for her. Witches never expected anyone to challenge them, and when they did, well… that's how a shifter loses his Pride, a hulk loses his tongue, and a zombie gets a lobotomy.

I lead the way as we entered the heavy forests of pine. The Blue Brick Road in the west was barely stitched together. Much of the continuous path had been lost to frost heaves, fissures, and wash outs from the heavy rains over the years, and Gwen never bothered to make repairs. She could have fixed them with a snap of her fingers, but much like her sister and *her* cobbled together mess that was the Yellow Brick Road, these two didn't care much for infrastructure. Not the least of which because they travelled via flying broomstick. If it didn't hurt them, the rest of us be damned.

Besides that, giving her subjects an easy escape route to the Emerald City, where they might seek a better life, was counterintuitive to being a soulless wench.

"So what do we know about Gwen?" Crowe walked beside me and was first to ask the important questions. "I can tell you a lot about her sister, but she never spoke much about family. Nothing useful anyway."

I met his red eyes and contemplated in silence for a moment. He likely wasn't interested in hearing about the kinds of toys she enjoyed. Her love of whips, chains, and phallic objects weren't terribly relevant to taking off her head, and he probably didn't care about that eye twitch she had when she orgasmed. "She's playful." That would suffice for that part. "And she has a fairly large collection of beast men at her disposal. My Pride is dead, but the monkey shifters she enslaved were painfully loyal. She's not terribly powerful herself, but she keeps strong company."

"She sounds a lot like Grunhilda then." Crowe looked to be reminiscing. "Mortal strength with an undying army that makes her appear stronger than she is."

"It should be easy if we can get close to her." I said in confirmation of that assessment.

"More like if we can get *to* her." Tobias said as he was helping Dorothy over a large fallen log. He lifted his chin toward the distant mountains.

"I didn't think it was possible to build a pathway even shittier than the Yellow Brick Road," Dorothy frowned as she was placed softly on the ground by her doting dog.

I grinned at the sight. So cute it was sickening. "Oh just wait, it gets worse."

And it got worse. So much worse. Fallen logs and streams were manageable, but even I wasn't prepared for the fifteen foot wide chasm that cut across the road. Blue bricks were scattered about the rocks below, while the cliffs dipped down a solid two hundred feet, disappearing beneath a rushing river that split the earth.

I stared down into the impassable canyon in disappointment. It was hard to say whether this was due to poor management or if it was a strategic decision. I would put neither past her. But then, unless she knew someone might be coming for her, why would she have seen a need for this much effort?

A bolt of lightning lit up the dark mountains, and the expected thundering boom followed shortly thereafter. I turned to my companions. "It's getting late, and we can't go much further today. Let's make camp, and we can figure out our plan going forward."

I caught Dorothy's vision lingering on that storm up ahead, and I saw this as a good opportunity to demonstrate the advantages of this mate bond. Sinking into the flurry of her racing mind, I couldn't hear her explicit thoughts, but I could feel the way they piqued her stress. Her fear and her nerves sunk into me, and only my own courage was enough to prevent them from overtaking my psyche. Was a monsoon a trigger for her? That seemed such a mild thing to instill such a reaction. "The storms never leave the mountains. You'll be safe here." I said. She jumped at the realization that I'd noticed.

"Oh, I wasn't worried." She lied, and I felt that too. I'm sure Tobias noticed as well, though he had a good read on her even without the magic of shifter ritual.

"Well, *I'm* a bit afraid of storms, so I thought I'd mention it." I also lied, but the solidarity put her at ease. I knew she could sense I was only telling half-truths, but the gesture was more powerful for her than the reality. As a shifter, we didn't need the ability to communicate words across the bond when our feelings were so vivid. It would be a treat when I got to introduce her to my favorite perks of that arrangement.

The usual hustle of setting up camp ensued, with makeshift tents and wood gathering and water procurement. We'd stocked up on more nutritious food in the Emerald City, so dinner was a pleasant affair of meat and vegetables. I didn't have to pretend to enjoy apples anymore, nor did I have to sneak out after everyone was asleep to hunt, which freed up my time for if I might need to protect the camp alongside Crowe and Talos tonight. We'd not encountered beasts yet, but the chances of a dangerous encounter were much higher in these woods. I was far from the only shifter species in the West.

Once Dorothy and Tobias settled into bed, and the feast of sensations—ranging from warmth to cuddling to safety to orgasm—subsided from the mate bond, I settled against a tree and stared listlessly into the darkness. It was calm tonight, save the occasional rumble of lightning strikes. The winds didn't howl down here in the trees, and the crickets were…

Wait, where were the crickets? This should have been prime toad and newt territory. Not to mention the owl shifters who feasted on all three. Their gentle hoots were the true music of the woods.

A sick feeling settled in my gut. I scrambled to my feet and approached Crowe and Talos, who both seemed unusually on edge.

"Crowe—" I began, only to have him lift a hand to silence me. His body was tense, while his gaze was darting through the trees. Talos responded by taking a single step, pivoting behind his comrade so they were back to back. The perfect sync of warriors.

I sniffed the air, searching for that first hint of danger. Nothing. Were their senses sharper than mine?

Of course they were. Fucking Gwen. My beast instincts were barely a shadow of what they once were.

Crowe rotated his wrist, then with a brutal chop, he broke his own forearm so the bone was jutting through the skin in a sharp, splintered point. He drew his own radius from his flesh, and he twirled it in his free hand as a weapon. He didn't so much as wince.

Of all the things I'd witnessed in Oz, I'd never seen anything like him. That moment of absolute shock was the one thing I couldn't afford, however.

I caught the scent of apes only a split second before I watched Crowe plunge the weapon of his own body through the chest of a large winged monkey. He skewered the beast, and the shifter immediately returned to human form as he lost his soul to the scarecrow's violent dance.

Talos followed suit in his own way, using his chiseled muscles to brutalize the flying monsters under his fists. For the first time, I watched the both of them fighting with intent to kill, and it was near impossible to rip my attention away from the spectacle of blood and bone and flesh.

But that was hardly the most significant surprise of this assault. No, what truly had me stunned were the beasts themselves. They weren't just ape shifters. They were winged monkeys. *Owl* winged monkeys.

Chimeras.

Fuck. What kind of experiments has Gwen been running since I escaped?

"Pay attention!" Crowe hissed, while he grappled a wiry haired, feathered hybrid. He sliced clean across its neck with the edge of his bone blade, and I took that as my cue to get to work.

I extended my claws and joined the fray, scratching and slicing and biting at the demons. But they just kept coming. If I was at my full strength and could shift, it wouldn't have mattered, but today I was being reminded exactly how steep the toll of the witch's curse truly was.

Two chimeras struck me at once, and I was barely able to get my claws into one of them before I was being snatched backwards into the sky. "Let go, fucker!" I bit into his arm, but drawing blood did little to slow it down. Nearly too high in the air to safely escape, I made a last ditch effort. I reached behind my head until I managed to get my claws into his neck, then I ripped forward, severing his jugular on both sides.

His hold loosened as his muscles gave in to death, and under the rain of his blood, I managed to break my fall on a nearby tree branch. I hopped down from one branch to the next to rejoin my companions, but the fight had only escalated.

Crowe was now fending off three chimeras at once, while it was everything Talos could do to keep the things from grabbing him. I ran to their aid, but before I could reach them, a violent ping of terror struck through my heart.

Fuck fuck fuck!

"Dorothy!" I sprinted for the tent, only to see both of my mortal teammates getting whisked into the sky. Tobias thrashed, but he didn't have my claws to free himself with. Dorothy sobbed, squirming without hope. There was nothing *her* human body could do, cursed or not.

"Help! Leon!" The fear and hopelessness in Dorothy's cry gutted me, and the emotions rippling through the bond near paralyzed me. My gaze darted around the trees, mapping out the quickest route upward, then I sprinted for the first tree trunk and started bolting up the branches. I spread my claws, and I leaped at the winged ape holding Dorothy, daggers primed and ready to swipe.

And but inches away from success, my breath was slammed from my lungs as another ape caught me midair. His thick, hairy biceps hoisted me upward, immediately too high to survive a fall. I'd not even gotten to take another swing at him before he had my neck in a headlock, and I was out completely.

CHAPTER 27

DOROTHY

The sound of a constant drip can be soothing. Like the ticking of a clock, it's something you only truly notice in the moments of the most intense silence. It's in that environment that something so simple becomes the most significant and prominent feature in the room.

As I laid on the cold stone floor of the Wicked Witch of the West's dungeon, that constant drip felt like my only proof that I was still alive.

My body ached. The monsters had been rough, and they didn't seem to care how viciously they brutalized me. I envied my companions who were so strong, physically and mentally, while I was on the floor clutching my sides, sobbing because I was too weak to bear it. Crowe could decapitate himself and keep fighting. Talos could blush and care for others despite having had his tongue cut out. And I was over here feeling sorry for myself because I was a little bruised and battered?

Weak.

So weak.

I'd come to depend on these guys to protect me, but what could I do to protect them? Crowe and Talos and Leon and Tobias had fought tooth and nail, while I'd folded like a dime store camp chair in a hurricane. I knew these missions would likely end in a fight, yet I'd not even bothered to prepare. Somewhere in my mind, I'd decided it wouldn't be my problem. I'd just be the sweet, friendly glue that held the team together, while they did all the work.

Weak.

Weak.

Weak.

I remained on the floor, my cheek damp with a contrast of my warm tears and the cold rain water that dripped into my dungeon cell. I didn't know what they'd done with Tobias. I didn't know where they took Leon. I couldn't say if Talos or Crowe had been captured. All I knew was that I could vaguely sense my mates from somewhere deep in my heart. They were still alive, but who knew for how long. It's not like I'd be able to save them even if I had months before their executions.

I hugged my knees to my chest, and I fixated on that singular, consistent water drop that formed from some unsealed crack in the masonry. My only respite was that they hadn't taken my silver shoes.

Chapter 28

"TOTO"

TOBIAS

My consciousness crawled back to me slowly, but a sense of urgency yanked it closer with a jolt. I shot upright and took in my surroundings as quickly as I could. Blue, thick blankets, with a hefty weight for comfortable sleep in a cold mountain climate, cocooned me in a bed, while the rest of the room gave off the image of a cozy manor. It was not unlike the guest rooms we'd been offered in the Emerald City, only the prevalence of green was now replaced with a deep cobalt.

Dorothy wasn't here. We'd been separated at some point. I knew she was alive—I could feel her life force radiating through me. But she wasn't *here*. All I could sense was her sadness pressing heavy on my chest.

I nudged the blanket off to test my limbs, only to find a ladder of leather bands climbing up my arms. Each band was clipped in to a chain, and each chain kept me locked to the bed. I could barely move enough to sit up, and the chains kept my arms far enough apart to prevent me from undoing either side. My shirt was gone, and my boots were missing.

I nudged myself as far back against the headboard as I could, though my restraints had been strategically placed to assure no position gave me enough slack to free myself. All I could do was sit here and wait.

I placed my head against the hard wood backing, and I rolled back until I was staring at the ceiling.

Dorothy must be so scared right now. I ground my teeth together at the thought.

This witch is as good as dead.

Chapter 29

"THE SCARECROW"

CROWE

I sheathed my broken bone back in the flesh of my forearm, and a roll of my shoulder was enough to will my arm to heal itself. My bone reattached and my flesh reassembled. I flexed each digit on my left hand just to verify the connection was complete.

"So I'd always heard that Kalidahs were the most powerful creatures in Oz," I began aloud, "but I'd never known much about where they came from."

Talos rubbed an open wound on his abdomen where one of those wretched bird monkeys had managed to gore him through. The only laughter I'd gotten to indulge in last night was at the look on that monkey's face when Talos reached out, grabbed his neck, and broke it in two without so much as slowing down. My immortal companion couldn't be disassembled and healed as easily as I could, but he also couldn't be killed by pathetic attempts at disembowelment. You had to still have organs for their removal to kill you, turns out, and our witches had both been kind enough to give us undying empty shells to live in.

The ignorance was to our advantage, but the results still hadn't left me particularly satisfied. After all, we'd both still failed. We were at this useless camp, while all of our lesser allies were spirited away as food for monsters and magical cunts.

< *"A beast with the head of a tiger and the body of a bear. I'd always accepted Kalidah as an unusual evolution*

of crossbreeding, but in hindsight, it makes more sense that they were an experiment gone wrong.">

"Or gone right." I frowned. "So Grunhilda was a manipulator, Sasha has a mayhem kink, and Gwenny over here likes to sew her toys together. I don't even want to ask what Eloise gets up to."

< *"I can't say I've even heard rumors."*> Talos rubbed the last of his wounds until they vanished completely, then he looked at the flattened tent. His Adam's apple bobbed with an unexpected air of worry. < *"If she were to take Dorothy and—"*>

"We'll fucking kill her before that happens." I caught myself when I'd realized how severe my tone had been. With a quick shake of my head, I added. "The last thing I'm going to allow is the silver shoes falling into the hands of another witch. There won't be a house big enough to crush a monster with that kind of power."

Talos nodded without another word, while thunder crashed through our camp again. I fixated on that eyesore of a palace, marring what would otherwise be a majestic mountain range. Dorothy was in there somewhere, and it would be near impossible for us to get there within the day.

Tobias and Leon had better keep her safe, or I'll have their heads on a pike right next to Gwen's.

Chapter 30

"THE LION"

LEON

"Get the fuck in here, Gwen!" I roared into the dark room, yanking on my restraints until they rubbed my wrists raw. My arms were splayed above my head, a metal clasp locked my neck to the wall, and every jerk and movement scraped the rough stone texture against my back. "Don't be such a fucking coward!"

I should have fucking known. From the first time she forced me into her bed, and she got off to an audience of stuffed animals that had been torn in half and sewed back together with mismatched parts, it was obvious that she was sick. When she'd started collecting living animals and playing with alchemy to create the Kalidahs, it was inevitable that she'd eventually want to try out her chimera obsession on shifters. For all I knew, maybe the current crop of Kalidahs *were* shifters. Yet in all the nights I'd spent with her, and with all the horrors I'd seen, I had still somehow never imagined she'd go this far.

I jerked again, but there was little I could do with my neck trapped in steel.

"Oh calm down, Pussy Cat." That voice dripped with more viciousness than the devil, even as she raised her pitch to sound like a demented child. My heart rate spiked, and my pulse was loud and vivid in my neck. Panic. Pure panic surged in my chest. My mouth went dry. My lungs had forgotten how to hold air for more than a fraction of a second. "Here I thought you'd never come back here after you put soooo much effort into running away." The Wicked

Witch of the West's laugh was something between a banshee's scream and a hag's cackle.

She snapped her fingers, and the torches lining the walls blazed to life. She knew what she was doing. Her voice in the darkness could have been transmitted remotely, but the image of her physical body, indisputably standing in front of me, assured I didn't leave any terror on the table.

She was only a few feet away, standing with a hand on her hip and a patchwork teddy bear in her arms. Her short, black, lacey skirt flared out wide, and her thigh high stockings, accented with cat ears at the top, made her appear youthful and childlike. Conversely, the ten inch heels, the unforgiving corset, and her large bust dispelled any such illusions that she was anything but a very sexual being. Her black and blue streaked hair was tightly curled in the kind of ringlets that could only be obtained with styling magic, and that heavy dark lipstick gave her smile the likeness of a deadly rip in the fabric of space.

"So imagine my delight when one of my little pets spotted a lost kitty in my woods." She took one step forward. I pressed myself back into the wall, wishing I could get even an inch more space. No matter how tough I felt when coming here, no amount of resolve had prepared me for being bound in chains while we were face to face. "I'm surprised you fought so hard though. I lost at least fifteen of my little monkeys. You and your friends wiped out a whole family."

She giggled at that. "Speaking of friends…" Another step, and she was up against me. Gwen pressed her cold, hard chest fully on mine as she connected our torsos at every possible inch. In bed, she was nearly a full foot shorter than me, but with those heels, she easily tapped the tips of our noses together. Her deep navy eyes were large and close. I held perfectly still. "Who's the girl, kitty cat?"

I jerk my head to the side, which she dealt with by tossing her plush toy away and grabbing my cheeks with her dainty gloved hands. She forced my face forward again. "You know I can get it out of you if you try to hide it. Or better yet..." She slid her grip down to my neck, and she pressed softly on my throat with her thumbs. "I can get it out of *her*."

"She's just a girl I ran into on the way. She's nothing." I resented the way she pressed her chest harder against mine just to revel in my increasing hyperventilation.

"Just a girl, just a girl." The Western Witch repeated in a singsong tone. She punctuated her amusement by pressing her lips to mine. I knew better than to bite when I was in this position. I'd already learned that lesson. She shoved her thumbs harder into my neck, and the resulting gasp forced my mouth open so she could lay further claim to me. My fangs were practically quivering with the desperate desire to take that invading tongue from her. Then she withdrew sharply, and she pounded her fist into the stone wall beside my head. Her otherwise cute and innocent expression warped into something unhinged. "*Just a girl* wearing my dead sister's shoes."

With that, Gwen stepped back and she regarded me with an animosity she'd never shown me before. I was used to her amusement, her cruelty, and her sociopathic tendencies, but... I wasn't used to genuine expression of anger. *That... That can't be good.*

"But really, Leon..."

My eyes widened. *Her using my real name really can't be good.*

"I'm glad you found her. I've had this idea swirling around in my head *forever*, but I didn't know where I could find a good, fresh human heart. Why, this may just be my masterpiece!" A sickening smile graced her vile face again. "I can't *wait* to show you."

With that, Gwen straightened out her skirt and turned on her high heel. But before she left, she glanced over her shoulder and lifted a single finger in the air. "Now don't you go running away again. I have so many plans for us that you won't want to miss."

The torches went out the second she shut the door, and I was left in darkness again.

I didn't know when I'd started crying, but now that I was alone, I couldn't help but notice the warm streams running down my cheeks. I stilled my quivering lip with my teeth, and I fought to slow my breathing. I didn't want to transfer these feelings to Dorothy. Her life was about to become terrifying enough without needing my weakness pulling her down.

There was a reason I was the only living member of my Pride. I'd felt empowered when I met the other witch's slaves, and I thought things might be different this time with all of them behind me. But I should have known better. I shouldn't have underestimated the one and only Wicked Witch of the West.

Chapter 31

DOROTHY

Who were the wicked witches, anyway? I wondered. Were they born in Oz, like the munchkins and shifters and scarecrows of the world? Were they a species separate from conventional humans? Or were they people like myself who were unexpectedly thrown into another world and ended up with magic?

I didn't have magic though. I tapped my shoes together, while I stared at the ceiling. We were supposed to collect each witch's magical artifact, but how significant were these items to their actual power? Were they compliments to these women's innate enchantments, or were the objects the source of what made them witches?

Maybe it didn't matter, but maybe I was just subtly hoping that these shoes on my feet might give me the ability to defend myself for once.

Who was I kidding? I couldn't even defend myself against regular people. I was pushed around by men whose only "power" was in their connections. Hell, that one director literally broke his hip when I rode him too hard. And now I was pretending I could fight back against the mighty, magical rulers of fantasy kingdoms?

Girl, please.

I sighed, but was soon interrupted by the sound of footsteps echoing off the stone walls. I turned my attention to the stairway that led out of this depressing dungeon. Two men emerged from the dark doorway, both dressed in what I assumed was the Wicked Witch's guard uniforms.

Otherwise, there was no way multiple people would *choose* to dress in leather harnesses over black leather pants, with a necklace of some unknown predator's teeth, piercings in their nipples, and black leather sleeves that extended to their shoulders. Their heeled combat boots clacked loudly as they approached my cell.

"What are you going to do to me?" I'd barely finished asking before the barred door flew open, and I was being hoisted to my feet by my arms. Neither man bothered to answer my query. They just locked their arms in tightly with mine and forced me to walk up the stairs. It was no use to keep asking. I just hung my head and let them take me.

At the top of the stairs, we reached a long hallway. A navy blue carpet extended down its length, while picture frames accented in sapphire lined the walls. In every painting was a different animal. I couldn't say if they were true beasts or shifters, though considering that this was Leon's witch, I could assume that she had a thing for beast men.

At the end of the hall, the guards opened a door and threw me into another dark room. I stumbled in, and by luck alone, I caught my footing before making a complete fool of myself.

Steady on my feet now, I lifted my gaze to the center of the room. And slowly I processed the display before me.

A simple alter of stone sat prominently atop a pentagram-like pattern that glowed with a gentle sapphire light. The same pattern reflected on the ceiling, casting a cool light back down onto the slab. It illuminated the features of the man who was resting on that table, naked and unconscious, and the woman who was squatting over

210

him, working a needle and thread through the large incision that rounded his chest and shoulders.

She was a gothic Lolita bondage princess in black and blue and traces of blood red, with a pout that would make a baby doll jealous, and punk rock highlights that gave her an edge. She was perched over him, stitching him together with thread that appeared like a translucent rope of magic, while perfectly balanced on a towering pair of ten inch heels. Her attention remained transfixed on her subject, while she hummed a simple and childlike melody. The blood on her hooked needle caught in the light of the pentagram every time she lifted her arm high to tug the thread taut, then she returned to his flesh to plunge metal into muscle again.

When she reached the end of the incision, she banished her tools with a twist of her wrist, and she placed a hand on her victim's chest.

"Won't you be beautiful for me, Freddy?" Her voice was soft and sweet.

With a tap of her fingers, the pentagrams glowed brighter, completely filling the room with their cold light. The body beneath her shook and spasmed, while her eyes never left her handiwork. The room warmed, and then it turned frigid. I hugged my arms to try to still my own shivering, when the light completely overwhelmed this small stone space.

Then it was dim and dark again. The woman stood upright now, a heel on each side of his waist, and the man convulsed between her feet. He jerked and choked a wet, gurgling cough, and his body started to transform. Dark brown fur sprang from his arms and legs and chest. Bones broke audibly, while his muscles tensed and doubled—no tripled—in size. From the stitch up, the fur was more orange, broken up only by tiger stripes that decorated his neck. The transformation was violent and slow. When it was done, there on the alter, strapped to a table beneath a gothic queen, was a beast with the body of a bear and the head of a tiger, clawing at the stone, growling at the ceiling, and moving like a creature discovering how to use its limbs for the first time.

"You're perfect." She cooed over him. "A work of art." With a lift of her heel, she hopped down from the altar, and she placed a hand on her monster's heart. She ruffled the fur, and those pouty lips twisted in a smile. That was when she at long last met my gaze. "What do you think, Dorothy? Isn't he just adorable?"

I froze in place, though I couldn't say if it was because of fear or magic. It went without needing to be said that this must have been Gwen, the infamous Wicked Witch herself.

"How do you know my name?" A silly question, but I needed to form some sort of words.

"How?" She looked up at the ceiling. "Why, my kitty cat has told me a lot about you. Of course I wanted to know the name of his *mate*." Her voice was high pitched and sweet, while her walk conveyed the energy of a no nonsense femme domme. She approached slowly, then she lifted my chin with her finger. Dark blue eyes examined me as if appraising my worth. "I'm guessing he's told *you* even more about *me*, though."

"Only lies, I'm sure." I attempted to laugh, but my acting skills weren't winning any Oscars right now.

Gwen chuckled, more genuinely amused, as she had no reason to fear me. She was well aware of her power in the current situation. "I'd be curious to know what praises he sings me in private, but I have a feeling he's missing all the best parts of the story." She released my chin, then she waved for me to follow her. She directed me to the slab, where the half bear, half tiger creature had slowed his convulsing. Now it just breathed erratically. "Do you know much about alchemy, Dorothy?"

I shook my head, and that made her smile. I had a feeling she was hoping for the chance to make a speech, and it was probably best I obliged her.

"It's the art of equivalent exchange." Gwen paced around the table until she was at the beast's head, then she placed a hand on each edge and leaned over it. Her substantial bust threatened to spill from her corset. "Much like laws of conservation of mass, where energy and matter can neither be created nor destroyed, Alchemy is a sort of magic that takes that principle to the next level."

I dared not touch the animal on the altar. I swallowed and attempted to keep my nerves down. "So is this alchemy?"

"Mmmhmm." She smirked at his strained breathing. "You're from the human world, correct?"

I nodded absently in response, so she continued. "I've heard a bit about your world. My cousin goes their often, and she just *loves* dumping old, used-up toys over there to die, since your realm doesn't support immortality like ours does. I can't imagine what it's like to be so weak and easy to kill." A statement that shouldn't have been followed by a giggle. My heart panged knowing she was at least possibly referring to Tobias. "For example, in your world, if you cut two creatures in half and sew them back together, they would die. But here—the possibilities are endless! You can take any two beast men and come up with something so much better than the way the Devil made them."

I bit my lip, knowing it would be pointless to ask if consent ever factored into these experiments. She was so thrilled to talk about herself, however, that it wasn't long before she was waxing again. "Maybe that's hard for you to understand," she began with a pout. After a moment of pondering, she lifted her finger in an aha. "Think of it like cooking. You must have cooking in your world, yes? You take a number of ingredients that make up what you want to create, you combine them with heat, motion, energy, and a splash of love, then you come up with something new that's so much better, even though it's still only a sum of its parts. It's thrilling isn't it? Do you like cooking, Dorothy?"

I once liked cooking, up until this moment where I'll never be able to look at it the same again... But I definitely didn't say that out loud. Instead, I went with "I never really thought of cooking as a form of magic."

"Oh, but it is." Her whole face lit up as she clapped. "Here in Oz, in *my* kingdom, we *love* cooking." With a snap of her fingers, four of her guards entered the room, and like brainwashed puppets, they began to transform. In an instant, four hulking beasts with the head of a tiger and the body of a bear stood in an orderly line, blocking the only door in or out of the room. "I've named these beautiful masterpieces '*Kalidahs*.' They were my first success, and now they live throughout Oz as a new, thriving species. You've already met my flying monkeys—those were my…" She tapped her finger to her lips in thought. "Fifth big success, I think? I've achieved so much, it's hard to keep track sometimes."

"Were all of these Kalidahs once shifters?" I knew the answer in my gut, and I felt queasy just asking it. All I could do was imagine someone like Leon or Tobias being cut up and reassembled, and I hated the mental image.

"Yes! You're sharp Dorothy! No wonder Leon chose you. He always did have a thing for clever women." Her smirk made it clear she was complimenting herself more than she was complimenting me, while the bite in her voice clearly conveyed her bitterness towards Leon's misplaced attention.

Gwen approached me again, this time she settled in behind my back. She placed her hands on my biceps and leaned over my shoulder. With the superior height she'd gained from her high, high heels, she easily towered over me. "Though it's amazing how much of my kitty cat I can smell on you…" She spoke ever so softly into my ear. I froze as she began playing with the straps of my dress. Literally froze, as though a magical paralytic had taken me. I couldn't speak. I could barely breathe. "Offensive even." Her voice lost much of its cheer when she nudged the straps down. She took her time inching the material off my chest. My breathing hitched as she exposed me to her monster on the table. Her hands rounded the outside of my breasts, then she continued down to my waist, over my hips, and at last she released my dress, letting it pool at my feet. "Is this what my pet's mate scar looks like?" She lifted my breast, so she could examine Leon's mark from over my shoulder.

"Or is it this one?" She slipped her hand beneath the band of my panties, and she slid down the lace until Tobias' mark was in clear view. She rubbed the mark at the top of my inner thigh.

Gwen's poking and prodding felt more clinical than sexual, but knowing the eyes of her guards were all on me only spiked my anxiety. She chuckled softly as she felt my pulse pounding under her touch. She examined me like a surgeon determining the best place for an incision, while the way she undressed me was a clear tactic of humiliation.

"You're not turned on at all. Do you not find me attractive, Dorothy?" Gwen's eyes narrowed, and her expression contorted with wickedness. "I suppose you do seem to have a thing for beasts. Maybe I should let my Kalidahs fuck that disgusting mark off you. Would you like that?" Then a playful smile. "Or maybe I'll just see what I can create from all three of you as punishment."

All three of us? That was the best confirmation I had that Crowe and Talos hadn't been captured. Though I couldn't say if they'd have any chance of reaching us in time if that was the case. Not with how rough the terrain was and how many beasts Gwen had under her employ.

Gwen lifted her attention to her guards, and she nodded to each of them. "Make some room on the table will you please? Then strap her down in his place."

Like an army of robots, the Kalidah immediately complied. Three of them took to removing the new guard, while one of them hoisted me up and dropped me onto the stone surface. I regained my ability to move the second Gwen stopped touching me, but even as I started fighting and thrashing, it was immediately obvious that it was pointless. Still I hit and bit and screamed and struggled, because I wanted to feel like I'd at least tried.

Tried? No, all I'd done was fail.

The monster stepped away when I was fully and completely secured by wrists, ankles, waist, and neck. Tied down to a table in a room full of candles, on an altar with magic circles of sacrifice above and below me, the reality of my predicament sunk in hard and deep and fast.

Breathing became difficult. My heart was in my ears. My whole body broke out in a cold sweat. I was verging on a panic attack, and I could feel my insides

216

shutting down as my terror lassoed me and dangled me off a cliff. I really, *really* wished Tobias was here right now.

It'll be fine, I told myself in a blatant lie that my racing mind didn't even pretend to entertain. My only respite was that maybe, if I was to be part of her next experiment, she might accidentally splice me with someone strong enough to kill her.

I'd never thought about taking someone's life before. No matter how mad at the world I was, the idea of actual cold-blooded, intentional murder wasn't even something I liked to joke about in the safety of my own head.

But today, I wished honest death on someone I'd just met, and I wondered if that was the true evil of this place.

No, I wouldn't let myself think that way. I wouldn't be a killer like she was. I couldn't be that person. We were here to get her artifact, but that didn't mean I would give up my humanity. I wouldn't let her truly win.

Yet that grin on her lips didn't help. "Excellent. Now fetch the puppy and my little kitty cat, will you please? I want to play a game."

The Kalidah disappeared and the door slammed behind them. That was when I realized I was now truly alone with the Wicked Witch of the West.

"Now that the boys are gone, why don't we have some girl talk time, Dorothy?" Her smile was terrifying. "I've just been dying to tell you that I *love* your shoes. Where did you get them?"

There it is. I knew she knew. That wasn't even a clever trick. *Deep breath*.

"I got them when I murdered the Witch of the East." I spoke steadily, trying to sound bold. She already hated me and being the meek person she expected wasn't going to help. She knew too much for me to lie to her anyway, and I needed to throw her off and let her think we might be more alike than she realized—that I was a touch wicked, too. I wouldn't show the fear I was feeling if I could help it, even if my voice was shaking as I spoke.

"Oh?" The surprise in her eyes was satisfying. I knew the honesty would take her aback. "You mean my *twin sister*?" The harshness returned to her voice, but I was going to gamble on the likelihood that I knew her type already just by how possessive, demeaning, and selfish she was. I'd met *lots* of her type, after all.

"Oh, was she your twin? You're so much prettier than her though*." Learned this little technique from a bad reality show script.* If I was guessing right, even her own twin was her enemy if she could be perceived, in any way, as better than her.

Her expression brightened, and it appeared to be genuine and on accident. "You think so? I always told her that, but Hildy was *such* a narcissist." *Unlike you, of course*. "I'm more powerful than her too, you know. She could barely keep her puppets alive, while I perfected the pentagrams of temporary immortality, so my puppets could actually live through play time."

Gwen rolled her eyes and continued. "Conversely, she had to figure out revival spells, and those just about always go wrong. I don't fuck with that kind of black magic. When we celebrated our four hundredth birthday, for example, she would *not* shut up about her new necromancy magic and some *human* she'd murdered and reanimated. *'You've not lived until you've experienced big, thick rigor mortis between your legs, then had him come back to life just in time to finish in you,'* she'd said." *Wait…* "She was so proud, only to have that same lowly human turn on her the following month, because how can anyone keep a damn zombie in line? She strung him up on a cross, only to discover that once you *un*kill someone, you can't *re*kill them. So stupid!" Gwen scoffed, while my mind was racing. *She had to be talking about Crowe. No one else fit the bill. But was he really once human? Like me? From my world?* "Not to mention absolutely disgusting. Can you even imagine being attracted to such a thing? My men are works of art. Hers are works of failure."

Her laugh was harrowing as she took a step back from me. "Almost as disgusting as being attracted to something like you." With a slight cock of her chin, her expression shifted, and she looked at me with daggers in her eyes. "If I have to share my Lion with you, I need you to be much, much prettier. And I have just the thing to fix you."

"How are you going to fix me?" I asked through a breaking voice.

"Oh, don't you worry about the details. Just lay back, relax, and you'll thank me when I'm done." Gwen caressed my cheek. "I promise this won't hurt too badly. I'm not a monster after all. I always numb my toys before I make them better."

She tapped me on my cheek as two of her guards shoved a bound and gagged Tobias into the room. The Kalidah gripped the back of his neck and shoved him onto his knees. Two others manhandled Leon.

Leon thrashed in their grip, which served to brighten the witch's smile. "Oh calm down, Pussy Cat." She paced over to her old slave with her heels tapping loudly on the stone. Her guards shoved him onto his knees, and he hung his head in defeat. Though the look in his eyes was one of pure malice.

With a small clap of Gwen's hands, two new pentagrams appeared under my shifter companions. She crouched down to Leon's level, and she fluttered a kiss on his forehead. The unbridled hate in his eyes could not be overstated.

"I was a little jealous to see that you'd marked her. I begged you to bite me for years, and you never ever listened." That pout again. "If you'd just given me what I wanted, you could have been my king." She nodded to her guards. One gripped his hair and yanked his head back, exposing his neck to her. The other held him down by his shoulders. With a flick of her wrist, a dark blue marker appeared in her hand. She bit the cap of the marker and popped it off between her teeth. With one hand gingerly on his cheek, and the other wielding her writing instrument, she started drawing a line around the base of Leon's neck.

"Do you regret it yet? Don't you wish you'd stayed, my sweet little kitty cat?"

Leon dug his teeth into his black ball gag so hard I thought he might break it. Gwen giggled, then she started dotting the line down his chest. She reached the waistband of his pants, then she paused playfully. "Your face is so handsome. I think I'll keep that. I've always liked your arms, too. The tattoos, the muscle definition—just divine." She purred. "But that ugly heart that left me so cold and alone? I think we can do better, don't you?"

A growl vibrated through the gag, and Gwen lit up at his anger.

"Don't you worry, Leon." Gwen placed her hand on his chest and absentmindedly traced his tattoos. She slid her hands down his skin, then started undoing the laces of his pants. "Your perfect cock isn't going anywhere. I'll keep your body alive forever, my little kitty cat. She leaned in and whispered something out of earshot. With the softest of kisses on his collarbone, she stood tall and grinned at me from over her shoulder.

"So what do you think, Dorothy? A lion with puppy dog ears and that gentle little heart of yours?"

CHAPTER 32

"THE SCARECROW"

CROWE

I'd never run faster than I had in that moment. The thunder struck, and I increased my pace until it hurt. Until my immortal muscles strained, wind whipped in my eyes, and the sting made them water. Talos and I had split up, hoping one of us would make the better guess on the fastest route. If we were lucky, being lone targets might attract those flying beasts again, and I could use them as unwitting transport.

A stray Kalidah popped up in between me and the castle, and I didn't waste more than twelve seconds ripping open his ribcage with my bare hands to create a pathway straight through him.

Gwen may be a mad scientist, but magic like this was nowhere near as black as Hildy's. Hybrid beast men with beating hearts were a comedy compared to the demons her sister once manifested. She'd created me, after all.

Though *my* strength wasn't the problem. *Dorothy* was the problem. She was mortal, frail, and easily extinguished. Though she'd murdered a witch, it was by lucky accident that she skewered Grunhilda, and the more time I spent tolerating our little traveler, the more obvious it was that she would never intentionally kill anything.

It didn't matter. So long as Dorothy was alive and wearing *my* witch's shoes, I could find her. If it cost me my own undying soul, I'd make a murderer out of her yet. And if Gwen were to kill her before I arrived, I'd change my request to the Wizard and find a way to make Dorothy like me. I wouldn't lose her like this.

I shook my head, not even wanting to entertain such a thought any further than that. My curse didn't need to be anyone else's.

The base of the mountain came up quickly, and I scaled a tree to launch myself up the first high ledge. The rock walls were built of sharp crags that cut at my palms and tore into my flesh as I propelled myself upwards with high impact leaps. Pain had stopped slowing me down a long, long time ago.

As I bounded upward and that fortress came into reachable view, a piercing scream shot straight through my gut, and the sheer terror of it nearly knocked me off my rhythm. I was much too far still to hear any such thing, but something told me it was a telepathic cry for help that had hit me. It was the kind of anguish that resonated through your entire soul.

Fuck!

Stay alive just a little longer for me, Dorothy.

CHAPTER 33

"THE LION"

LEON

"When I gut her and make you eat her fucking heart, you can live with the warm and fuzzy knowledge that your 'mate' will always and forever be a part of you."

Gwen used that large blue marker to start drawing on Dorothy's skin. She made dotted lines around the small part of her breast that I'd marked, then she drew a straight line vertically over her heart. Her next target was the apex of her thighs where Tobias had placed his bond. She drew a targeted circle, then she put the cap back on her pen.

I dug my fangs into my ball gag when she touched the cold plastic head of the marker to Dorothy's vagina and started pushing it in as far as it would go. The way Dorothy squirmed, I could tell how much that friction hurt as Gwen forced the tool through dryness until she hit her cervix with a merciless thrust. "Keep that handy for me, won't you?" She grinned, while Dorothy made an obvious effort not to cry out.

I extended my claws as far as they would go in pure rage, and I shifted in my restraints in an attempt to reach the binding on my wrists. It was tight, but I managed to just barely graze the surface. Just enough that I could make it through if I kept working at it.

It's going to be okay. Don't be scared. I did my best to communicate confidence and fighting spirit down the bond, but I couldn't say if it gave her much comfort. Her shaking and nervousness was still echoing back to me loud and clear.

224

Gwen's next target was Tobias. She paced over to the dog, and she indicated to her guards to grab him by the chin. They lifted his head and moved it about so she could inspect his face.

"Her other mate is pretty too." She ruffled his hair. "And so silky. I think I'll enjoy your company in my bed, puppy dog. My Leon could learn a thing or two about loyalty after all, and where better to find that than with the brain," she began as she tightened her grip in his hair, "of an Alpha dog shifter."

She jerked his head back roughly, and he growled through his gag. As always, that only amused the bitch.

"Oh, but would you look at this…" She circled his ear with her fingertips, then she pulled the lobe forward to reveal a small mark. "My cousin already branded you as hers. That's unfortunate." Her lips pursed in disappointment.

Gwen frowned then stood up straight. "I suppose if I just take your brain and discard the rest, she won't ever know I have you, but you can never be too careful around Eloise, you know." The wicked witch giggled. "Actually, you probably *don't* know. I'm sure your memories were delicious."

She manifested a new marking pen then started drawing a line across his forehead. "I used to cut up my men free hand, but I mixed up a few of my experiments and ended up with one too many legs and one too few cocks the last time, so I do want to make sure I do right by you." She touched her lips to the ink on his face, and his eyes flashed with a viciousness I was only vaguely familiar with. She drank in his hate lovingly. "You're so handsome after all."

With a dismissive wave of her hand, her guards responded by shoving Tobias face down on the ground. A heavy foot on his back and another on his head forced his cheek into the pentagram.

If I knew *anything* about her magic, I knew that these symbols could keep someone alive no matter what was done to them, and so long as we stayed within their confines, we would have to be awake to witness her fucked up slicing, dicing, and restructuring of our bodies from beginning to end. I had no idea that she had gotten this deep into chimera magic, but I'd seen her use these pentagrams to test out her sharpest and most painful toys in her early days of alchemy. Most of those experiments being a part of my own Pride, and none of them survived once she withdrew the circles. I didn't want to think about how many shifters had to die before she figured out how to make viable hybrids.

So fucking close. Keep calm, keep calm, keep calm, Dorothy. I did my best to communicate that hope through the bond again. I needed her to know I was going to save her, no matter how bleak it may have felt. All I could do for her now was to ease her worry the slightest bit.

"Do you remember when you used to partially shift just so you could share that rough kitten tongue with me, Leon?" She returned to my side and caressed my cheek like I was still her docile slave. Like I was still the coward who ran away without ripping her heart out. The man who had nothing left to live for but himself, who didn't care where I ended up as long as I was away from here, even if my friends were left behind to die. Her guards held me as she straddled my lap and placed her arms on my shoulders.

"How jealous would she be if she saw you buried inside me, Pussy Cat?" She rubbed her cold cunt against my lap. "Why don't you show her who you really are? Show her the fierce lion who turned into a house cat for his master."

I tensed at the reminder, and I resented the deep pang of humiliation that near paralyzed me. When she and her minions captured my entire Pride, I'd been much too weak to fight back. I'd done everything she said when she'd threatened their lives. I'd rolled over when I thought all was lost, and I'd disgraced myself, time and again, just so I could live another worthless day. Pathetic. I was so pathetic then. Selfish, empty, and weak.

I would not be that man anymore.

I kept grazing those restraints, scraping across the fibers as they tore under each pass of my nail.

"I might have to remove your gag just so I can hear you cry." She kept grinding on my lap, but when my body wasn't reacting how she thought it should, she only pushed further. "I do love it when you play hard to get."

Just a little more. Her biggest mistake would be her arrogance. She expected a beaten down and defeated shifter, but she was about to get the king of lions who had something to protect.

She kept rubbing, and when she couldn't get me hard, she tried pouting. "I'm not above using my magic to make your body do what I want you know. Make it easier on yourself, Leon."

There! I yanked hard on my partially severed restraints until the fibers tore under my strength.

Before I so much as stretched my fingers, I was drenched with a scalding gush of blood from the beast men behind me, and crimson coated the both of us like a tidal wave. Gwen was knocked from my lap as two massive Kalidahs smashed down, face first, on each side of me. Their hearts followed, hitting the ground with a sickening thunk.

Two more thunks and two more thuds, and Tobias was also standing free.

And there, in the wake of it all, stood the scarecrow, sharp teeth bared, eyes narrowed, drenched in death, and

absolutely.

Fucking.

Seething.

CHAPTER 34

"THE SCARECROW"

CROWE

Her neck was in my vice grip, and her head hit the wall with every cursed ounce of strength in my body. I squeezed, then I banged her head on the stone, not once, not twice, but ten. *FUCKING*. Times. I counted every instance of stars flashing through her detestable fucking brain.

"You must be Gwen. I hear your sister misses you." I snarled. "How about I send you to see her?"

When she smiled through the blood that poured from her nostrils and ran down her lips, I wasn't surprised. A witch couldn't be killed this easily—otherwise there wouldn't be any left. If anything, being treated like this probably had her sopping fucking wet.

"I have a feeling she misses *you* even more." She said so softly and sweetly, it made me want to slam her head into the rocks again. I might have, if she didn't take that moment to wrap her legs around my waist, then her hands around my pinning forearm. "But your dirty talk is working for me. Keep going."

With the sleight of hand of a martial artist and the gravity manipulation of a demon, she twisted us around, then pinned me on the floor with a knee on my back, and my arm jerked past the point of dislocation. I felt my shoulder leave its socket when she gave it a hard twist. My muscle fibers strained to stay connected.

"Plot twist, little puppet. I rule the beast men because I'm the real muscle in this castle. Not the other way around." She giggled while her glare contradicted her feigned amusement. "You puppets are all the same. You think you're *so* powerful, only because *we* made you this way. You would be a fucking corpse if my sister hadn't been desperate enough to come on your dick. Don't forget that what's been given can always, *always* be taken away." Another twist, until the muscle and tendon started to tear fully. That was her first mistake. "And all you'll be able to do is watch as I take everything from you."

As she sat atop me thinking she'd won, I just laughed. *Oh how I fucking HOWLED.* Then I jerked hard and tore myself free, leaving her to hold my severed arm in confusion. With the element of surprise, I threw her onto her back, pinned her under my weight, a knee on each arm, and I held her down by her neck.

"Dorothy. Now." I snapped at my companions, who were taking entirely too long to get all of the restraints undone. I tensed my fingers around Gwen's neck as I watched Leon pull a writing instrument out of our girl before making her decent again. When magic snapped my lost arm back in place, the lion tossed the pen over, and I caught it with my free hand. "Hildy always told me you were an artist, but I can't say I'm impressed." I twirled the marker between my fingers. "Your penmanship couldn't even get her wet, and I've watched her jerk off to the fucking devil."

The puppy helped Dorothy from the table, steadying her shaky legs, and Leon started fixing her clothing. Though the material couldn't totally hide the ink on her chest. All the places this bitch would have cut into her. All the places I would happily carve into Gwen of the Wicked West.

Gwen stared up at me, still smiling. The witches were always *smiling*. A bullshit strategy to make it appear that they might still win. "At least my magic actually works." Her attempt at laughter shook convulsions through her neck, and I responded by tightening my palm. Still she managed to speak. She must have had a barrier that protected her windpipe. "Because she told me *her* puppet had no feelings left at all, yet here you are, losing your mind over a plain, ordinary, boring human who will grow old and die in the blink of an eye. What comedy that her heartless warrior is acting like little more than a sensitive, love sick puppy. So I wonder, big, scary monster, are you doing this because you truly hate us, or have those shoes on Dorothy's feet turned you into *her* little puppet—" I slammed that marker down into her open mouth until it was hitting the back of her throat. She choked and gagged and she shut the fuck up.

"Dorothy." I growled. I covered Gwen's mouth so she couldn't dislodge the marker, then I lifted my gaze to meet Dorothy's, and she lowered hers to match mine. "Finish her."

"What?" Dorothy's eyes widened, still processing everything that was happening, yet not processing what I was saying.

"*You* are the only one here who has the power to kill a witch. Don't make me tell you again." I annunciated each word very, very carefully. But Dorothy faltered. She looked to Tobias. She looked to Leon. I shook my head. "Eyes on me, Dorothy."

A nod. And her eyes were on mine. She took one nervous step forward, then another. Gwen started to squirm beneath me, but I knew enough about witch magic to know that disabling her hands and her mouth took all of her conjuring ability away.

I also knew enough about witch magic to know that breaking her neck, taking her head, or stabbing her through

231

the heart was impossible for a cursed puppet. That was the power they held over us. It was a safeguard, where no matter how strong and angry and motivated we were, we would never be able to truly fight back. As much as I wanted to yell at the lion for failing to protect Dorothy, I understood the magic that bound him perhaps even better than he did.

Gwen wasn't my witch, but *my witch* would be the one to end her life.

And then Dorothy would be Leon's witch too.

When Dorothy neared enough, I watched Gwen's eyes bug out of her head as she took in the sight of Grunhilda's shoes. She knew what was coming, and she knew exactly how easy it would be.

The two of them seemed to be having a non-verbal conversation of shared shock, fear, and uncertainty.

"Do it." I demanded.

Tobias, who I expected to look mortified at what I was forcing his sweet girl to do, surprised me when he stepped forward and placed a reassuring hand on her shoulder. Dorothy's heart rate slowed to a level that could be called comfortable, calm, and content. Leon stepped forward next, with a hand on her back, and an unflinching stoicism. He'd locked in on Gwen, and I was certain he was savoring every flash of hopelessness in her eyes.

How couldn't he be, after all? *I* certainly was.

"I… I can't." She bit her lip and looked me in the eye, as though she was pleading me to help. Tears welled in her eyes, and I knew that the terror I was seeing was too real—too deep and visceral—to even be calmed by her precious little dog. "I've never killed someone. I'm not like you. I'm sorry. I just… I can't, Crowe."

I should have been mad, but that desperation softened every muscle in my face. I closed my eyes, took a three count, then returned every bit of my attention to Dorothy. "You really are weak."

Those words hit her in the gut like a crowbar, and it was obvious from the tears that built in the corner of her eyes. Gwen smirked against my palm despite herself, but Gwen didn't know what game I was about to play with this sweet, sensitive, and powerful woman.

My witch was a vile manipulator, and no matter what her stupid sister may think, she most certainly created a demon. If I was to be drawn to whatever woman wore Grunhilda's silver shoes, then that woman was going to do my bidding, and not the other way around. I just had to push the right buttons.

CHAPTER 35

DOROTHY

Murder. I really had to murder her? What did he want me to do? Stomp on her head until she died? At least if I had a gun or a sword, the distance might help me detach from the act, but I had no weapons other than my shoes, and that was such a horrifying mental image, I couldn't even fully conjure it in my mind's eye.

That battle raged inside me. I didn't want to disappoint Crowe. No, I wanted to help everyone. With everything in my heart and soul, I *had* to set them free. But we didn't need to actually murder her to do that. Now that she was disabled, we could just steal her artifact, couldn't we? If I stooped to her level, I may as well be a wicked witch myself.

"I'm not like you, Crowe. I'm not from this world. This isn't normal for me. I don't want to be as despicable as she is. Let's just take her artifact, break your curses, and leave her here to rot. Taking her head isn't necessary."

It sounded good in my ears, but when Crowe nodded, his agreeableness was only more unnerving. "You're right, Dorothy. You're not like me. You always try to take the easy way out. You won't do anything to protect the people you care about."

Those words struck like a javelin, and my eyes widened as it truly dawned on me what he'd just done. He was heartless, sure, and it was easy for him to brutalize someone he didn't like, but...

234

He'd just shown me that he was good to his word, and whether he realized it or not, he just grouped me in as a person he 'cares about.' While I, on the other hand, was about to fail everyone who was counting on me because of my weakness.

"Crowe. Stop." Tobias snapped in my defense, but Crowe was having none of it. The worst part was: I couldn't blame him. He was right.

"Tobias would kill for you, yet here we are, the tables turned, her head on a platter, and you can't do the same. She would have carved him out, and you would have let her." Crowe pushed. Tobias tensed, but he didn't lash out again. How could he? Crowe was right on that too. "And Leon here—this woman has destroyed everything he ever had. She took his family, his dignity, and she was about to do it all again. If I'd not stepped in, she'd be force feeding him your fucking heart while he cried. Yet *still* you'd rather us leave her alive. Instead of punishing her crimes, you would slap her on the wrist, and let her continue to torture countless innocent beast men in Oz. Is *that* the girl we've all been following around all this time? Is this who I promised to protect?"

"I-I—" Even though he said it—even though I couldn't argue, my body was shaking at the thought.

"You're better than that, Dorothy." He said. And in that moment, I believed him.

I was better than this. I was better than taking the high road that only meant evil people didn't have to suffer consequences for the pain they caused. And I was better than being the weakling who was so worried about my own selfish morals, I wouldn't inconvenience myself the slightest bit to save the people who loved me most.

This was Oz, after all. She was a witch. These weren't real people. I'd go back to my own world, and the consequences wouldn't matter. *It was just like Hollywood.* I thought to myself with an internal mocking laugh. When the curtain dropped, the cameras cut off, and when I limped away from another man's bed, disgusted, defiled, and doubting myself, I just had to remember that it was all just a silly little story along the way of becoming something great. And today, I wanted to be something great for the people who already thought I was.

And today, I wanted Crowe to be one of those people too.

"It's okay, Dorothy." Tobias said. When even he wouldn't talk me down, that was my sign. His comforting aura radiated through me, and it shooed the first of the angels on my shoulder that told me not to give in to cruel temptation.

Good riddance. The angels never gave me what I wanted. It was the devil that got me every role I'd ever landed.

"Just lean on me, Dorothy." Leon whispered next. He placed an arm around my shoulder, and he pulled me close. Then he kissed me, slowly and fully. He placed his hand on my breast, and he pressed his thumb into his mate scar. "Use my strength."

A surge of killer instinct flooded through my entire body the second Leon placed his hand against my skin. It was as though his will and his soul were taking control of mine, and I had no power to deny them. Every ounce of hate, hurt, pain, and resentment came pouring into my muscles so fast and hard, I had to close my eyes and hold my breath to take them.

I became his vessel, real or imagined, and I used that mental trick to disown whatever actions came next.

The rush was overwhelming, and my muscles committed for me. Or at least that's what I told myself.

"Be my sword, Dorothy." He spoke low so only I could hear. Crowe never took his eyes off mine, and I channeled his viciousness and his unapologetic courage as I lifted my knee to a height that gave me maximum power and momentum.

I hovered that shining silver shoe above her head, while her big, navy blue eyes stared up at me with real, visceral, honest terror.

And I stomped down hard.

I stomped again, and again, and again until I heard the loud crack of bones. I felt the force of every stomp and the give of the breaking skull beneath me. Cold liquid gushed and splashed all over me.

I couldn't look, but I also couldn't stop myself. This was wrong. It was so wrong, but I had to do it. I had to.

Had.

To.

Another hard stomp and I squeezed my eyelids tighter. I didn't want to see what I'd done. I didn't want to know the color of her ice cold blood or the expression on her lifeless face. I could feel her death under my feet, and that was already more than enough to make me shake.

When the world fell silent, I knew she was gone. I covered my face with my hands, and I stepped away. Slow inhale. Slower exhale.

Several counts. Several breaths. If I was lucky, she might shrivel up and disappear like Grunhilda had.

A violent jolt of guilt hit me—did I really just do that? Did I really just kill someone? With intent. With free will. With nothing but peer pressure urging me forward—

Tears didn't come, but my blood was as cold as the witch's death spray in my horror and self-admonishment.

The frigid liquid ceased when Leon engulfed me in the heat of a tight hug. He squeezed me so fiercely, my pieces started to reconnect slowly and completely, while his warm embrace gave me new life.

I didn't deserve this kind of affection after doing such a thing, yet the rush of his feelings was like a gentle thank you. I buried my face in his chest, and he stroked my hair before nuzzling his nose in my roots. He pressed a kiss to the top of my head, and I felt a warm strength starting to fill me.

"It's done." He whispered, and I was shattered. It's done? I killed her. I killed someone. The thoughts consumed my head until I was sobbing freely. Leon rubbed my back. Then quietly, so only I could hear, he said, "I'll never be able to repay you for this, Dorothy. I know you didn't want to do this, but you'll never understand how many people you just saved from the same pain I lived with for so long." He was completely burrowed in my locks, and I could feel the tears dripping down his cheeks now too. It was a sob of joy and relief, like a thousand pound cross had been removed from his shoulders.

And that thousand pound cross instead rested on mine.

Slow inhale. Slower exhale.

When I opened my eyes, the body had already vanished, though a stain of crimson still coated the floor.

Then... the stain moved. The blood began to draw towards me. I stepped back, but it followed. "What's going on?" I asked in alarm. Neither Crowe, Leon, nor Tobias were able to answer me. The blood caught my shoes, and it started to climb the silver. "Guys, what's going on?" I stepped back again, and I nearly rolled my ankle when I put my weight down on my heel. An inch tall block extended from the sole of my shoe, and the blood continued to draw into the slippers, swirling the red with silver until it took on a shimmering pink. When all the blood had been absorbed, my little metallic flats were rose gold pumps.

A shiver radiated up through my body, and I glanced between my companions in utter confusion.

I recalled the moment the Wicked Witch of the East had died, and her red stilettos had fallen from her feet. I'd watched them shrink, retract, and ooze out their color. Only, at the time, I didn't know what that had meant, and I'd been so overwhelmed, I hadn't thought on it since.

The blood of her enemies. It was no wonder her heels had been so high if this was how the magic functioned. How tall would my heels be when we'd encountered the final witch?

How dark would my heart be when I committed to killing four strangers in a fantasy world of horrors...

Tobias' comforting hand pulled me back into the present, and the gentle happiness that radiated off Leon engulfed me in a place of ease. It was only Crowe who offered no comfort here. He'd backed away from the witch, and he now leaned against the opposite wall where he watched us quietly. He watched *me* quietly. Though his expression betrayed no emotion. I didn't know if he was disappointed, proud, or if he simply didn't care. He'd gotten what he wanted, but what did he think of me now?

I didn't entirely understand Crowe. At times he was empty and callous. At others, he felt normal and friendly.

He'd lost his ability to feel and love, yet he showed so many faces that I wanted to truly believe were genuine.

He *had* protected me, after all.

If he didn't actually care about any of us and was simply an actor, he was the best I'd ever seen.

Talos met us in the castle entryway with a pile of dead Kalidahs. With the death of the witch, all of the remaining beast men had been freed. The castle guards had been too deeply brainwashed to rescue, but the flying ape men that were left had awakened like they'd all come out of a lifelong coma. One half of their soul mourned the loss of their monkey troops, the other lamented the loss of their parliament of owls, but all they could do now was move forward as a new species.

It should have been satisfying to know I'd been the hero to save the day, but I still couldn't help but worry. Gwen had truly been a monster of a Wicked Witch, yet she was supposed to be the *least* dangerous of the remaining witches. What did the southern witch have in store for us? Or the northern witch for that matter. My friends jokingly called them "good" witches, but I'd gathered that was a bit of a misnomer. News of my having killed their cousins probably wasn't going to help matters. All I could hope was that collecting these artifacts and freeing each of my companions from their curses would be enough to keep us all safe.

Just the same, the monkeys had agreed to give us a lift back to Oz as a thank you for their newfound freedom, so I wouldn't have long to think on it. But before we left this kingdom for good, there was one more little loose end I needed to tie up.

"So we've defeated the witch and all, but the Wizard had said she should have an enchanted artifact, no? Don't we need to find that in order to break your curse, Leon?"

"Oh... right..." Leon's whole face turned red, which completely took me aback. He never seemed the bashful type.

"Should I be... worried?"

"No. I know where it is. Follow me." He grumbled, then he led the way. We all followed him to a large bedroom that could only have belonged to the wicked Gwen herself. It was her same style of childlike toys juxtaposed with leather spiked collars. Chains and whips and dildos were displayed prominently on the shelves, while the bed was a large, comfortable California King covered in twisted stuffed animals.

Leon located a key under one of the shelves, then he opened a locked drawer with a hard hit of his fist. He reached in and tossed me the enchanted object without making even the briefest eye contact.

I caught it and held the thing in my hand, where I stared at it for several very long blinks to process that I was really seeing what I thought I was seeing.

"This is..."

"A dildo. Yes." Leon said with a somewhat embarrassed and nervous shrug of his shoulders. My mind, however, was now racing to all sorts of places it shouldn't. *But fuck it.*

241

"I'm sorry, but I have to ask. Leon… Did she ever…"

"Pleasure herself with it? Yes." He rolled his eyes, and I shook my head. I couldn't let this go. I *had* to know.

"No, I was going to ask if she ever… uh… used it to…" *How can I say this nicely?*

"What?"

"Did she ever peg you with it?"

Tobias started choking on his saliva, and Crowe straight up cackled. Talos turned away to stifle his own reaction.

Leon, however, just stared at me with his mouth agape. "Y-you mean like… did she…" The way he stammered was definitely, *definitely* not a no. "Are… Are you into that?" Absolutely flabbergasted. He was completely and utterly stunned.

Tobias choked louder and more pronounced, and I glared in his general direction. My sweet little dog had maybe seen me in one too many compromising positions over the years. If I'd known he was secretly a man who I'd be inviting into my bed one day, I'd probably have been a little more careful about keeping him out of the room…

"Wait, you *are* into that?!" Leon was shooting looks between the two of us with abject horror written in every line of his face.

"No, not normally—"

"NOT NORMALLY?!"

I cleared my throat. Now *I* was the embarrassed one. "It was just one—" Tobias raised an eyebrow. "Okay, two—it was two times." I shook my head. "I mean, no, I don't know much about it or anything. It's just that the way it's flared…" I ran my hand down the length of it to the end that was clearly made to be affixed to a harness. A fact I probably shouldn't explain why I recognized so easily. "I-I mean, all of the witch's objects are something wearable, right?" *That. Explain it with a reasonable, logical jump to conclusions instead of a deviant one.* "I was just curious… You're a cat, so you know how curiosity is." I nervously chuckled, while not convincingly feigning innocence as I rubbed the back of my neck.

"I marked a woman who is going to peg me…" Leon's tone was distant and hollow.

Tobias gave him a hard pat on the shoulder. "This is why you get to know someone before you claim them forever. Consent is fun, eh?" He turned to me. "Good job on killing the witch, Dorothy. Let's get back to Oz and drop this off so we can head off to the next one."

"Sounds good to me." Crowe said while stretching his arms to the sky. Talos nodded. And I turned on my pink one-inch heels.

"Whelp, off to see the Wizard." I said in a singsong voice.

Leon just stood there, dumbstruck. We all got a much needed laugh that day.

CHAPTER 36

◎ DOROTHY ◎

The monkeys dropped us off back at the Emerald City, and just like last time, we were given nice rooms, and I went straight for a shower. While much of the witch's blood had absorbed into my shoes, there was still stray spatter and ink marks all over me, and I felt cold, sticky, and gross.

I scrubbed at the dotted line over my heart with a wash cloth, not wanting to register that it was there because I was about to be butchered like livestock, and I watched as the blue ink swirled down the drain. There were so many things I still had to process.

I wasn't a cold blooded killer, for one. I wasn't supposed to be, and I didn't want to be. But was what I'd done really so wrong? What was the difference between this and self-defense? The fact that she had been defense*less* when I dealt the blow probably didn't help my opinion of myself, but then if she hadn't been defenseless, she would have killed me with no reservations. Repeating these things was the only way I could cope, so I just had to keep reminding myself that she deserved it.

As I cleaned the ink around my mate scar, I recalled the way Leon had poured his emotions into me, from the blood lust to the relief, and it was also prudent to note that she'd tortured thousands—if not millions—of shifters throughout her long life. No one cried when dictators fell, did they? I did a good thing. I saved and avenged countless people from oppression and torture.

If I'm a hero, why do I feel like a monster?

I sighed as I turned off the shower, then I started the bath to help myself relax. The bubbles frothed, and the scent of rosemary calmed me. I stepped into the scalding water and relaxed into its soothing embrace.

A light tapping on my door caught in my ear. Tobias, I assumed. "Come in." I said quietly, knowing all of my companions had practical super human hearing. The door creaked and shut, then in the doorway to the bathroom stood Leon, dressed in comfortable pajama bottoms and little else.

"I wanted to see how you were doing." He said, both concern and feigned casualness in his voice.

I smiled at that. His gentle but handsome face put me at ease. "I'm not dead, so better than Gwen at least." My attempt to make light of the situation was strained, but it was the only way I knew to push through my current complicated emotions.

"I'm sorry you had to go through that." His expression sank. He approached the tub and crouched down beside me. "All of it. Not just killing her, but I should have been able to protect you. It never should have gone that far." Leon chewed his lip for a moment. I swallowed but couldn't find words. "You're my mate, and when you needed me most, I was powerless. I've always been powerless around Gwen I guess."

It dawned on me in that moment that the only one more broken about this than me right now was… Leon. Gwen's abused toy who lost everything—the person I protected when I ended her life. It made me feel loved when someone would risk everything for me, yet I was harboring guilt because I put myself on the line for someone *I* cared about?

I shifted in the tub, repositioning with my arms on the edge closest to him, and placing my chin on top my forearms. My face was only a few inches from his. "Maybe you're looking at this backwards." I placed a hand on his cheek and spread bubbles over his skin. The little spheres of soap fizzled, leaving a sheen on his face. "I'm your mate, just like you're mine. The burden of keeping a partner safe isn't only on you."

A gloss shined in those golden, slitted eyes, and I realized how deeply I believed my own words. I wasn't just here to be some helpless damsel in distress surrounded by capable men. I wanted to be strong and worthy, too. I couldn't reasonably stand up to the magic in Oz as a human, but when I *could* step up and do my part, I would regret being a coward more than I would regret the damage I'd done.

I'd always shown kindness to people, even when they only hurt me in return, living on that idea of treating others how I hoped to be treated. But all that had done was make me a doormat for people who never had to experience consequences for their bad behavior. Perhaps being good sometimes meant stopping those who weren't, instead of enabling a narcissist with unearned compassion.

Aunty Em always told me I'd catch more flies with honey than I would with vinegar, but why the fuck did I keep working so hard to be covered in flies? At least with vinegar, I could make a great potato salad.

"Dorothy…" Leon said my name in a way that was genuinely surprised. The corners of his lips upticked, while tears threatened to spill down his cheeks. He laced his fingers through my wet hair, he leaned in, and he feathered the lightest, most innocent kiss on my lips.

I returned the gesture and rose out of the bath to deepen the kiss. Bubbles covered my naked body, and they

246

popped in random, sporadic threats of exposure. It wasn't long before we were both lost in each other's rhythm. I didn't want to stop. I wanted to share this comfort with him after so much pain and fear and trauma.

Leon took the hint. Still kissing me, still rubbing slick bubbles all over my bare skin, He lifted me out of the bath, and he carried me back to the bed. He didn't care how wet I was when he dropped me on the covers. He loosened his pajama pants and let them fall to the floor, banishing any thoughts that I'd ever been fucked by a bigger lion, and he climbed on top of me to reconnect us by our tongues.

The soap still on my skin slickened his touch. His ordinarily rough touch glided smoothly along my inner thighs, up my stomach, and over my breasts. Wet hands squeezed me, popping a few more bubbles in the process.

"Let me show you what else it means to be my mate." He whispered against my lips.

"Show me." I traced the tattoos on his chest, and I nibbled on his lips. He grinned against my teeth, then he pressed his thumb into the mate scar he'd left.

Like lightning, an overwhelming sense of arousal shot through me, and I gasped in pure shock. He caught my lips again, taking advantage of my open mouth to pin my tongue. Then he drew back and simply watched me shiver beneath him.

"When we're apart, we can communicate our feelings only vaguely. I can feel when you're sad or when you're angry or scared, but I can't feel what you're physically experiencing." He dropped back on his haunches, and he nudged my knees wide. I was still quivering with an overwhelming need to have him. "But when we're together…" He brushed his thumb over my clit on the way to lining himself up to enter me. I saw him shudder and hold a breath in time with my own. "We can share every sensation that goes through the other's body."

He pressed in, and my eyes shot open. I could feel the blissful stretch as he reshaped my pussy for him, while my clit throbbed with a perfect bliss. I'd never felt anything like it, and I might burst in seconds if it continued.

"Do you feel that?" Leon asked, low and husky and smug, just *knowing* I could. His breathing hitched as he started to move in me. Sweat was quickly forming on his brow, while his expression was strained and his breathing was heavy. The fucking electricity through my clit was filling me with heat and intensity and an exquisite high.

"W-what is that?" A full body shudder hit me with every pump of his cock. "G-god, Leon." My words were a breathy cry. Pressure, bliss, magic, pleasure—I was feeling all of it all at once.

"You're feeling what I'm feeling, little fireball." His words seemed every bit as strained. "And you feel so fucking good." He ran me through again, tagging my G-spot, while also communicating that warm, snug embrace straight to my clit. I was over the edge in seconds, faster than I knew possible, and I was clawing at his arms as my orgasm took me. He groaned, his eyes closed and his body shaking in elation, but he didn't come with me, not yet.

He started fucking me again, this time with measured strokes, increasing his pace while I was still lost on high. The pleasure pounding through me was more than I knew how to bear, and his own orgasm was starting to build to a head. My eyes were watering, and I was holding onto his shoulders for dear life.

He covered my mouth with his, and I loved the way it felt when he sucked on my tongue, when he drank in my voice, and I tasted his roar. He dug his fingers into my hips as he found that tipping point of his own, and I was damn near sobbing when he gave. That tense pulse of his cock inside me had me clenching around him, and that powerful release was pure fire in my soul.

I came again while he did too, and I was pounded by the crashing wave of both of our pleasure at once. He clawed into me for dear life, drinking in my kisses like a drowning man trying to breath, and dragging his grip down my waist liked he was thrown a life raft in a storm.

Our breaths were heavy as we came down together, and my pussy ached as I felt the dual sensations of him pulling out. There were no words that could express how that had just felt. Even the sweetest praise wouldn't capture the relief and peace and power surging through me thanks to his magic fucking dick.

But our bond meant we didn't need words to express ourselves anymore. He laid down beside me, and I rolled over and nuzzled my face on his chest. He wrapped an arm around me and hugged me closer in response. It was then that I felt that protective, warm feeling that could only be coming from his own heart.

And I knew I'd done the right thing. I'd killed his devils, and he'd shown me heaven. This was where I was meant to be.

Tobias came to my room a couple hours later. Leon taught him exactly how a mate scar worked. Sandwiched between the two of them, I'd never felt more safe and secure and loved. Sleep was its own pleasure that night.

Dressed in our stupid green clothing again, we were escorted to the Wizard's throne. The servants chattered and pointed as we passed them, and I could understand why. This was only the second time in the history of Oz that a witch had been murdered, I was told. Considering the first time was also my fault, I wasn't sure if I should have been proud or ashamed. I didn't mind being treated like the celebrity I never was though, and I'll admit I actually kind of liked it. We deserved *some* kind of recognition for what she'd put us through.

When we entered the throne room, this time, the Wizard's magic particles took the shape of a house cat. He laid on the throne lazily, and I felt a little bit like he was making a fool of us. But maybe it was symbolic somehow. I might never understand Oz custom.

"I've heard stories of your success, travelers. Please, present me with the enchantment of the Western Kingdom. Let me see proof of your exploits." His voice still boomed despite his docile appearance. It was impossible to tell from where the sound came, but I knew it wasn't from the glowing plasma house cat.

I hesitated, only out of awkwardness and second hand embarrassment, then I came up with Gwen's strap-on dildo for the Wizard to… uh… evaluate. "This was the source of the Wicked Witch of the West's power." I said, trying not to be as immature as my internal monologue wanted to be.

The phantom cat nodded with acknowledgement. "You've done well." He said. "That is, indeed, Gwen's cursed artifact." *Not gonna ask how he knew that.* "You've proven yourself a worthy warrior. Keep this prize with you and channel its power, for you may need it for the coming

250

trials. Once you return to me with the remaining artifacts, I can grant you your freedoms."

"Wait what—" With that, we were once again hauled out of the audience chamber and tossed into the streets without any sort of prize or respect. I pursed my lips in irritation.

Leon frowned. "I guess I'll have to continue without my Lion form for a little longer."

"Ugh, this is so unfair." I huffed. "We went through all that and walked away with nothing."

"Don't look at it that way. I was able to witness justice against the person who'd hurt me the worst. By comparison, this is a small inconvenience." With a reassuring pat on the shoulder, Leon added. "I've gone this long without my ability to shift, and it hasn't slowed me down. A couple more weeks won't kill me."

I appreciated the sentiment. There was no point in wasting time with idle wishes anyway, and it made me feel less guilty that we hadn't used the shoes to free Crowe yet, either. So I nodded to Leon, then I turned to my companions and shared a wide smile. "Well, who wants to go next?"

The Sadistic Witch of the South

CHAPTER 37

"THE TIN MAN"

TALOS

Mixed feelings. A torrential and wild mix that couldn't be easily reduced to a simple soliloquy, so I kept my thoughts to myself. Crowe was the only one I could share them with anyway, and with the way he'd been unusually distant and quiet since the encounter with his witch's sister, he likely already understood what kind of conflicts that were swirling around in my head.

In our misguided and traumatized brains, we all still had some vague affection for our witches at one point in time. And while all that remained was bitterness, animosity, and unbridled hatred, I'd be lying if I said I wasn't unnerved by the prospect of seeing Sasha again. At times, I considered that I would rather remain silent forever than climb this mountain, but it wouldn't be fair to the others to deny them freedom for fear of facing my demon.

I shook my head at my own reservations. *How emotional of me.* But then, as I spent more and more time with Crowe as my closest friend—a title he would scoff at—was it any surprise that I had an unreasonable affinity for psychopaths? I was born in a clan who had normalized human sacrifice and cannibalizing our kin, after all. Sasha seemed tame by comparison. *Crowe* seemed tame by comparison.

So many thoughts that drifted through my head as I walked the Orange Brick Road to the South. Here, the ordinarily lush greenery of Oz quickly fell off into yucca trees, sage brush, and a variety of cacti. Grass and mud gave way to deep red clay before fading to the tanned dunes of the Southern desert. The road, however, was meticulously maintained, with perfectly even cut stone, flush cement work, and smooth finishing.

Sasha took great pride in her aesthetic. While rain was rare in this region, she still made a point to constantly survey her infrastructure for cracks that might reflect poorly on her. Image was everything to the Sadistic Bitch of the South.

Witch of the South, I meant. *Only not really.*

I'd warned the others as much as Crowe allowed before we left the Emerald City, and we were adequately packed with food and fluids for the mortals. The lion had been in good spirits despite still wearing his curse on his shoulders, though the disappointment of our last meeting with the Wizard didn't give me much hope. At best, I could get my mask removed on this quest, but I wouldn't get my tongue back. I couldn't help but think we were little more than errand boys, doing the Wizard's bidding, rather than earning any sort of prize. It was a discussion I'd like to have with Dorothy one day if I could.

"You know you can always just fuck her if you want to talk to her so badly." Crowe interrupted my thoughts through our silent channel. Though he was right, the crass way he'd said it knocked me off guard.

< *"Projecting?"* > I asked with a rise of my eyebrows.

That got under his skin. I could tell by the forced nonchalance he employed when he shot back with *"I just want to see her scream when she feels the first piercing on your cock."*

< *"Definitely projecting."* > I taunted him again. His denial of his affinity for Dorothy made him such an easy target. I'd not yet raised the point of how distraught he was

when she'd been captured in the West, but it was fine ammo for later.

Crowe flattened his lips in a rather perturbed looking line. *"On second thought, I'm not sure I want you to be able to talk to anyone else..."*

I shook my head with an internal chuckle, when Dorothy turned to face us. Her new heels clacked into place when she spun around. "Can you tell us a bit about this witch?" She asked. A question for me, but her attention was on Crowe instead. I did mildly resent that part of the arrangement. But as much as I wanted to be able to communicate with Dorothy directly, I didn't feel confident she could survive a night in my bed. Killing one witch on accident, and another while channeling her mate, was well and good, but it certainly didn't make her hardened or tough. She was still such a terribly delicate little flower. The type who would cry and break if you tied her up, put a knife to her neck, and threatened to slit her throat if she so much as breathed too heavily while you fucked her.

I cleared my throat to dismiss the memory. In my youth, such a thing was exciting, but that was a very different point in my life. The idea of keeping disconnected body parts in jars for later pleasure now appalled me instead of getting me hard.

Cultural differences and all.

Crowe said nothing, but I could tell by his micro-expressions that he'd picked up on far more of those thoughts than I'd meant to share. Instead, he was kind enough to translate something much less savage. "She likes blades and buckles and blood, and her dildos aren't made of silicone. But unlike Gwen, her intent is more to kill than to create." *As nice as anyone could have phrased it, really.*

"I see." Dorothy processed that with an unfortunate amount of understanding. I supposed that with all she'd seen now, that was par for the course. "What are the chances we'll be attacked by her cronies when we stop to rest?"

Crowe looked to me then looked to her. "Damn near zero. No one likes that bitch."

If I could have snorted in pure amusement, that did it for me. Accurate. Where Gwen had enslaved and brainwashed beast men, Sasha's sex toys didn't typically survive long enough to be beaten into loyalty. The only reason *I* made it this long was because I'd shown such unbreakable promise early on that she granted me everlasting life. Yes, Crowe was a fine translator.

"Then would it be reasonable if we started doing our traveling at night for this one?" Dorothy fanned herself with her hand under the brutal desert sun. Sweat was blooming from every pore, while the sunlight reflected off the shine of her soft but drenched skin.

"Soft skin, huh?" Crowe invaded my thoughts again. This time I was the one whose expression flattened in annoyance.

< *"An observation of fact."* >

"It's important to verify facts, you know."

I ignored him to nod in her general direction. She lit up at the confirmation. It was likely much safer to travel at night anyway. Though many creatures could hide in darkness, the worst of the south were not in the form of bats or lizards.

"Don't you think it'll be more dangerous at night?" Crowe pecked at my consciousness again.

< *"Possibly, but you get off on putting Dorothy in danger, no?"* >

Crowe hesitated just long enough to prove me right. *"I didn't realize you cared about getting me off, Talos."*

< *"Really? Even in all of our flirtations? I suppose I need to do better at making my priorities clear."* >

Crowe shook his head, though the smirk that slipped was rather telling, then he communicated for me a simple "He knows a good spot, but we can stop as soon as you're tired, and we'll reconvene after dark."

We walked on only a couple miles further before I directed the group's attention to an oasis of shade and water. Palms surrounded the pool loosely, while a large rock face on one edge of the springs created a natural privacy shade from the main trail. This was a popular destination on the Orange Brick Road. Sasha had taken me here many times to relax and fuck outdoors. The abundance of cacti were great for her brand of sexual acupuncture.

"This seems as good a spot as any." Leon said with a tip of his chin towards Dorothy. Her resulting smile was as bright and vibrant as her soul.

"I could definitely go for a swim." She approached the beach and crouched down to dip her fingers in. "It's so warm. It's like a natural hot tub."

"You don't have to sell it to me." The lion was already getting out of his clothing as she spoke. He hopped on one foot to get off his shoes and out of his pants, then he tossed his abundance of furs to the side. In a full blown naked sprint, he cannonballed into the center of the springs, splashing all of us with the explosion that followed.

Tobias was next to disrobe. He hesitated for only a moment, but a shake of his head dispelled any discomfort before he committed to stripping himself bare and plunging in. Leon seemed to be a good influence on him. He'd become a touch bolder and less serious since we'd started traveling with the shifter.

"This is incredible." His words were a practical moan.

"You never liked baths this much when you were a dog." Dorothy teased with a puff of her cheeks. The beast men laughed in response. She motioned towards the strap on her dress to remove it, then immediately she withdrew her hand. Her expression sank. "I suppose I don't have a swimsuit. Or even a bra for that matter." Her face flushed with sudden shyness, and she took a step back from the beach. "I'll just dip my feet in."

Standing on one leg, she started to remove her shoe, and I couldn't help but notice the way Crowe's eyes fixated on the little pink pump. Offering no further communication with me, he walked up to Dorothy and placed an open palm on her back. He leaned in and he whispered something in her ear.

His hand drifted down to her lower back. She blushed an even darker red, then much to my surprise, Crowe tossed away his hat, pulled off his shirt, and approached the water.

Dorothy pawed at the hem of her skirt, but still hesitated to undress.

"Curious?" Crowe's taunting nearly made me jump. *"You're the only one who hasn't seen her naked, so no wonder you haven't taken your eyes off her."*

I flinched at that realization. But I wasn't interested in sexual encounters with any women these days. Let alone such a delicate one. *<What did you say to her?>*

"I told her she should relax and recover before we meet the next witch. That's all."

<Why do I somehow doubt that's ALL you said?>

"Because your mind can't stop thinking about all the things you would be saying to her once you get her naked, Tin Man." Crowe swam backwards, where Tobias and Leon were enjoying the soothing, healing waters. And now I stood even more tense on the shore.

Yet my eyes were still on Dorothy, who was, indeed, still hesitating to undress beyond removing her shoes.

She turned to look at me, her face painted with uncertainty and insecurity, and I approached her with a sigh. Crowe was right about some things, but terribly wrong about others. I wouldn't currently determine which category *'getting her naked'* fell into.

"Are you getting in too, Talos?" She asked. And I answered, silently and without warning, by hoisting her up into my arms like a princess, and walking us straight into the oasis. "Hey hey hey—what are you doing?!" She squirmed half-heartedly, but the smile on her face dispelled any illusion of distress. I was comically stronger than her anyway. I dropped us both into the deep center, still fully clothed, and now soaking wet.

I released Dorothy, and she thrashed about in a pool that couldn't be more than a few feet deep. When she realized it was barely up to her waist, she stood up, dripping and drenched and with a glare on her face. "How could you?" Her whine barely made those three words before she started laughing. Everyone else followed suit.

"I'm sure it'll dry quick." Leon said as he swam up behind her. He hooked his arms under hers and pulled her backwards into the water. She screamed playfully as she splashed down again. Her skirt flowed in the weightlessness of the pool, while her top clung tightly to

259

every curve of her body, leaving very little to the imagination.

She truly did look fragile and breakable, and such thoughts had me constantly looking away as she splashed our companions and enjoyed a brief moment of simple joy. Despite their shared curses, Leon and Tobias were ordinary, somewhat well-adjusted mortals, capable of acting light and happy. Even Crowe could feign normalcy around Dorothy. Whether due to her possession of Grunhilda's shoes, or by his own changing soul, he picked up on her energy and adapted to her mannerisms in a way I think made her genuinely like and respect him, no matter how cruel he pretended to be in our silent confidence.

But who was *I* in this group? I didn't fit in with this kind of ease. While everyone else was getting to know each other through words and touch, I was the outlier, condemned to silence, who could never truly relate to anyone. I held a sad and lonely existence even in a group. That was the truth of my curse. I was never much for casual conversation, and I was more inconvenienced and upset by Sasha's initial petrification spell than I was the loss of my voice. Not until I'd met these people had I realized how much I *wanted* to be able to speak again.

Friends: a word I knew but had never spoken.

A blessing and a curse. What was that old saying? A little taste of happiness was worse than none at all? I might have felt less complicated if I could go back to my cold and heartless and singular existence. Maybe after all was said and done, that's what I would do.

Some more playful splashing, and the water settled with Leon's lips locked in Dorothy's. His hand was over her clothing, but comfortably gripping her breast, and their laughter was replaced with a much heavier atmosphere. She bowed her back, pressing her chest more firmly into his palm, and he dipped her low, so her hair was in the water, and her balance was completely dependent on his support. "I'll never be able to thank you enough, my little fireball."

She smiled into their kiss, when a jealous Tobias grabbed her shoulders from behind. He pulled her back into his embrace, and planted his lips on her shoulder. He nudged the strap of her wet dress down to her bicep, so he could continue his kisses down her collar bone. "Let me help you relax," Tobias whispered against her skin.

Crowe made eye contact with me, then as if he wanted to taunt me—see what I'd do—he swept Dorothy away from both of them. "You still have bloodstains all over your clothes, you know."

"Do I?" She batted her eyelashes back at him. Clear flirtation. I didn't entirely expect that. "Can you wash it for me again?"

"Only because you've been such a good girl." Crowe reached into the water to locate the bottom of her dress, and she lifted her arms to let him pull it off of her. I refused to take my eyes off his, no matter how nice the view. I knew what he was doing, and as much as I wanted to be able to communicate with Dorothy, I wasn't prepared to hurt her. My cock would definitely hurt her.

Though as brash as Crowe may be, I couldn't believe he was ready to commit to sticking his dick in her either. If he was worried about being enslaved to her shoes, swapping fluids wasn't going to help that. He wouldn't give into that risk no matter how badly his instincts were begging him to.

So I kept watching him, my eyes narrowed, and I silently dared him to keep going. I wanted to see how far he would go to provoke me.

"How long can you hold back, Talos?" He nudged through our silent channel. *"It's okay if you like her."* Naked in his arms, she let him follow the shape of her body with his fingertips. *"It's even okay if you want to fuck her. She's not the witch you're so afraid of, and her skin is every bit as soft as you thought it would be."*

I cocked back my chin, unfazed. <*"I have a better question, Crowe. How long can you hold back?"*> Still I kept eye contact, ignoring the way she was being displayed and played in my periphery. <*"You pretend you do this out of teasing, but how hard does it get you every time* you *so much as think about her?"*> I smirked beneath my mask, and I knew he could see it in my eyes. <*"And how much harder does it make you when you do it with your eyes on me?"*>

The slightest spasm and twitch of his muscles told me I hit the right nerve. Crowe seamlessly handed her off to Leon, who pulled her into an embrace from behind. Tobias rejoined in the space between her parted legs. He lifted her hips, and she wrapped her thighs around his waist. He supported her weight as he started nibbling his way down her chest. He lapped the water off her body with his tongue. It wouldn't be long before he was dipping into a different flavor.

I might not have minded being an idle spectator as Tobias forced her moans into Leon's mouth. I'll admit that she was beautifully erotic when she was being pleasured. But Crowe had other plans.

"Do you really want to know how hard that makes me?" He hissed aloud in my ear as he flattened his palm on my chest. He was no longer in my silent channel. He shoved me until my back was against a rock. I could overpower him easily, but I didn't bother.

<*"Her or me?"*>

He put his hand on my neck and squeezed. A pointless threat against someone who didn't need to breathe. *So angry.* Crowe got *so* terribly angry whenever he was called out on his emotions. The beautiful irony of it being *that* was an emotion too. His lack of self-awareness was adorable.

With a chuckle, he returned to internal communication. *"Just because my dick still works, doesn't mean either of you are special."* A weak attempt to take the upper hand, but I'd let him feel like he'd won this time. I couldn't help but think the real reason he wanted me to take Dorothy was simply because he wanted to share her with me more directly. It sounded far more *'Crowe'* to pretend it was to hurt her, but the longer we travelled together, the more he struck me as being just as desperate to relate to someone as I was, and he was finding that ability in the two of us. I would trust him with Dorothy's life and well-being on that basis alone.

The scarecrow jerked away suddenly, splashed some water through his hair, then he exited the oasis in a huff. I crossed my arms and smiled to myself as he left. Even when the sound of Dorothy unabashedly reaching climax on Tobias' lips bounced off the water, I still kept my attention on my immortal confidante. A man of so many secrets and so many lies. Once we killed Sasha and I regained my voice, I looked forward to exposing them all.

Chapter 38

DOROTHY

I'd lost myself on Tobias twice, barely able to breathe when he grazed his teeth over the mark he placed on my inner thigh. Shifter sex was ecstasy that I might never be able to get enough of.

Leon decided it was his turn next, hard and straining under the feel of the same orgasms Tobias had just given me. He bent me over a rock with urgency, putting my ass fully out of the water and in his view. He slid into my still trembling and sensitive pussy, and he exhaled shakily as he sunk to his base inside me.

"I'll never get tired of this heat, my little fireball." He growled in my ear. He retracted his claws enough to safely drag them down my sides, then he pumped into me. I braced myself against the rocks with my hands to lessen the friction each time his hips hit into my ass. Leon's hold on my hips was forceful and demanding, and the way that made me feel used and desired and needed and cherished at the same time was all it took to have me on high again. His thick cock rubbed over my G-spot relentlessly, while his own pleasure radiated through my nethers until he was filling me with his come, and I was drenching him in mine.

I was still catching my breath and still quivering when Leon grabbed my hair and yanked me back upright. He pressed his lips to my neck, then he gripped my thighs and hoisted me upwards. My back was against his chest for support, while he had my legs open and my body on display again for my companions.

Tobias took his position in front of me. He drew a line up my center with his hand, smearing some of my own fluids on my clit, then he shoved his own hard cock in, pushing any of Leon's spilling semen right back into my depths. Tobias took my mouth and my pussy, while Leon played with my nipples and nipped at my neck. I was an unraveled mess for both of my mates, and the following orgasms were impossibly satisfying.

But as much as I enjoyed being wanted like this, I couldn't help the way my thoughts drifted off to the two men I'd never had.

Crowe had teased me so many times. When he undressed me in the water, I thought that was the moment he meant it. I thought he was going to take me right then and there, and make good on his threats to fuck me to completion. Some sick part of me wanted to know how rough he might be. How demanding he might be. How vicious and punishing and satisfying he might be.

I could feel how hard he was—how big and thick and ready he was, but still he wouldn't go all the way with me. He'd touch me, he'd tease me, he'd kill for me and corrupt me, but... he still wouldn't kiss me. He wouldn't fuck me. He wouldn't even let me touch him.

I shouldn't have wanted him to want me, but something about him kept drawing me in. Tobias loved me in a pure way. Leon loved me in an animalistic way. But how would Crowe love me if he could?

Sometimes I thought Crowe cared more about Talos than anything else, though I had to keep reminding myself that Crowe had no feelings. He wasn't capable of love or humanity or compassion anymore, so all of these thoughts, in all my machinations, where entirely invented in my mind. None of them were based in reality. They were just a hope that he was more complex than the sociopathic puppet he tried to portray himself as.

Speaking of that silent giant...

While I was in the pool, enjoying two cocks at sunset, Talos and Crowe were both back on land. Though today they stood apart from each other, not appearing to be speaking. I wished I could know what went on in Talos' head. I didn't know how Crowe had come to open that telepathic channel between them, but at times, I was jealous I couldn't truly know him like Crowe did.

Talos seemed kind at times. Playful at others. He was interesting and dark and I could only imagine the trauma he'd suffered. When he threw me in the water today, I thought we'd had some slight connection, but how could I connect to someone who I couldn't truly speak to? Was body language and touch really enough to get to know someone? I didn't think so. I hoped that when we met his witch and I freed him from his curse, he might stick around long enough that I could get to know him in earnest.

I hugged Tobias as his cock tensed and released his own orgasm inside me. I should have been more embarrassed to be on display like this for them, but some deep desire to perform made me like it. And maybe I hoped it might entice Crowe and Talos to give me a chance too.

When we were all three sated, I pulled my wet dress back on, and we settled on the shore of this beautiful little oasis in the sand. I laid back and stared at the hazy orange dusk through heavy eyelids. A good orgasm almost always made me sleepy, and I was quick to give into rest under the trailing desert sun. Once the moon was high in the sky, we'd continue our journey. I hoped this witch would be a bit less violent. I didn't know if I could repeat the last encounter. Not without Leon's killer instincts radiating through me anyway.

I might need to channel Talos' grudges this time,
but how could I make that connection with him?

Chapter 39

"THE SCARECROW"

CROWE

The perishable travelers among us took a cat nap in the shade while they waited for more manageable temperatures, and the Tin Man and I remained in a bit of a stand-off. Had I been pushing him to make a connection with Dorothy lately? Yes. Frankly, it would be easier for me if they could talk among themselves, and I didn't always have to play translator. Furthermore, I would prefer he have a genuine connection with her before we faced off against his witch. That would only be to our advantage.

Everyone else was much too soft on her to force her to become a murderer, so the onus of corruption always fell on me, and I would like Talos to join my efforts. Tobias was as much a puppy dog as his former life implied, and Leon was annoyingly good natured and honorable for someone who called himself a beast. The Wicked Witch of the West would still be alive if they had been her only company, and I wouldn't travel with someone who didn't at least *consider* murder as a reasonable way to exit a social situation.

But how could I convince Talos to just make her bleed on his pierced cock already? He had the discipline of a fucking rock. Maybe Sasha could loosen him up where I couldn't.

I was appalled at the thought, though I'd admit it could be my only real bet. If I wanted those two to have a connection outside me, I needed to be the one to facilitate it somehow. All I had to work with was the fact that Dorothy seemed to fantasize about monster cock, and that hot, dangerous men made her wet. A really convenient combination, really, but entirely too one sided to help me right now.

The sliver of the moon rose in the sky, not providing much lighting. A recipe for disaster, to be sure. *'Hey guys, it's hot out. Why don't we just travel in the dark, so we have more chances of being ambushed?'* I mocked in my head.

Fucking humans. If it's not food or water or sleep, it's temperature and being killable by minor flesh wounds. If I got separated from the group again because of this, I was going to just let them all die this time.

My peripheral vision caught a glimpse of Dorothy stirring from her nap. I wandered over to entertain myself, since Talos was being boring and all.

"Have a nice nap?" I asked as I crouched down beside her.

She rubbed her eyes then blinked several times before she acknowledged me. Her cheeks were pink with blush. "Too nice, maybe." She laughed nervously, before glancing between her two partners. "How long was I out?"

I shrugged. "A few hours. We should have about eight hours of darkness left before the sun is fully bearing down on us again."

Dorothy nodded. I offered her a hand to get her to her feet. She straightened out her dress, which had dried easily in the hot, arid climate, then she stared at me for several moments, as if studying my expression to find some hidden story. I had no clue what was going through her head right then, and I found myself preferring Talos' company on principle. Emotions were hard enough to understand as it was. I wasn't a fan of having to guess what someone was feeling. I just about always got it wrong.

"Since it's just the two of us, can I ask you a question, Crowe?" *Why did she sound so nervous?*

I rolled my eyes at the irony of the request. "Asking permission while also committing the crime. You're a human after my own heart, Dorothy."

Another chuckle of nervousness instead of amusement. *Confusing.* "How did you know how to find me when the Wicked Witch kidnapped me?"

That question had me completely taken aback. "The castle was rather prominent. It didn't take much guessing to figure out that's where she took you."

Dorothy shook her head. "The castle was also gigantic. There must have been a thousand rooms in that thing, but you knew exactly where to go. You never would have made it in time if you didn't."

Now *I* was the one blinking in confusion. I opened my mouth to speak, but I wasn't sure how to answer that.

No, I did know the answer. I could sense her. I could feel her scream in my gut, and it was obvious where she was. It hadn't even occurred to me that I would have to search. "You screamed, and I followed the noise." A dismissive answer felt least damning. Though what I was damning myself for, I couldn't quite explain.

"I didn't scream." Those big blue eyes felt invasive as she looked at me. "I could only speak by the permission of her spells. I wanted to, but I couldn't make a sound."

I paused. *I know I heard her scream. It vibrated through my fucking bones.* "Curious." Was all I managed.

"So you could feel my internal screaming. Is that because I have the Wicked Witch of the East's shoes?" The conclusion she'd reached was logical—which she often was, I'd admit—but I didn't like it. The last connection I needed her to make was that she'd taken on some of Hildy's power. On the list of revelations she didn't need, that was just ahead of the fact that I would let her die as soon as it served me.

"Perhaps it was just a lucky guess. Gwen was Grunhilda's twin, after all. I was likely just drawn towards the similar magic signature of my old witch." *A better explanation.*

Again her chin swung back and forth, and again I was annoyed by her observational skills. "I see." She said, dropping the subject, but it still felt as though she was seeing something in me that wasn't supposed to be on display. It made my fucking skin crawl.

"I said I'd protect you until I got my wish from the Wizard. You don't need to read any further into it than that." I took a step back. I wasn't scared of her. She didn't throw me off. I simply didn't want to risk what else she might spy if she kept staring into me. "Sasha likely won't be as docile as Gwen. Don't let yourself get distracted by nonsense."

"I'll have to kill her too, won't I?" Dorothy hung her head as she asked.

I nodded. "Are you scared?"

"Yes." She confessed immediately. *Honesty. Refreshing honesty.* "I don't think I can do that again. I understand that she deserved it, and that far more people— good, innocent people—would have been hurt if I'd left her, but that doesn't mean I'm so bold as to be able to dole out the death penalty myself."

"Then keep your eyes on me." I lifted my chin and spoke with a deathly calm. "Stare into the eyes of the devil long enough, and you'll be amazed the evil you can commit."

"Crowe…" A pang of sympathy punctuated my name. There was no need for such sentiments. I wasn't ashamed to be who I was. Perhaps that was the lobotomy talking, but I'd gotten comfortable in this mind and body. Perhaps even more so since I met her.

"The four witches of Oz have earned their executions. If you'd feel better calling yourself a vigilante or a savior, take whatever title you need to get the job done." I grinned despite myself. "But for me, sweet girl, I would be happy to stroke your black wings if you're strong enough to be my fallen angel."

The expression she shared with me was complex and conflicted, but I meant every word I'd said. In all my own inner conflict over my opinions on Dorothy, it was that small, corruptible part of her soul that spoke to me, and it was that same piece that gave her the power to put a stop to the witches.

If I was little more than a witch's scarecrow, then I would make her the raven who unabashedly landed on my shoulder.

CHAPTER 40

"THE TIN MAN"

TALOS

The orange bricks glowed at night, making the path an easy trek to Sasha's castle. A few more stops for rest, and we were practically on her doorstep.

It was exactly as I remembered: a massive and beautiful palace of decorative gold, bronze, and tans, with towers that ended in points that scraped the sky. It was sharp in construction, with shapes that resembled shards of shattered glass and splintered wood, and the architecture was distinctly menacing despite the luxury within. A palace befitting of a psychopath.

"Do we know what her object is?" Leon turned to me first. I looked to Crowe, hoping he might be willing to be my voice, despite our recent conflicts.

"A bronze knife. More like a scalpel, really." The Scarecrow said for me. I thanked him with a nod. "She keeps it in her garter belt."

"This place seems unusually empty though, don't you think?" Dorothy frowned as she surveyed the small desert town at the base of her castle. An astute observation. This was normally a bustling town full of trade and entertainment. Street performers and merchants made up a majority of the economy in the South, and their absence was rather suspect.

Though the more violent Sasha got, the more her people were running for refuge wherever they could find it, so I couldn't be entirely surprised. There were likely more southern merchants in the Emerald City than there were here.

That still didn't explain this complete and utter silence, however. Night was often the most lively time here, and this scene gave me a sinking feeling deep in my gut. No guards, not even children playing in the streets. Were they all hiding in their homes? Or was there something more going on?

A dark shadow crept across the orange cobblestone streets before us, until the little moonlight we had was no longer visible. I looked to my companions when I heard a rustle from the rooftops.

Then I craned my neck, and my eyes bulged.

Eight long, powerful legs, with seven joints along their spindly length, supported the bulbous body of the desert's most vicious predator. The Sa-Nakht Spider was colored in black hair with orange stripes up and down its body. A lock shaped mark that glowed neon decorated its underbelly, announcing its presence while also making it difficult for its prey to hide. The paralyzing poison in its fangs was one I was all too well acquainted with.

She'd always had a predilection for spiders, but I'd not realized how much she'd allowed her pets to grow. There was no longer any question as to why the streets were empty. If there was anyone left alive at all, their only hope was to stay hidden until the nightly hunts passed.

I could hear Dorothy's pounding heartbeat from here, and I wanted to tell Tobias to calm her down. But there was no way to convey that without noise, and any movement at all would get its attention. This would have been a prime moment for me to exercise the advantage of silent communication, but I'd kept my distance from everyone, and now we would all pay the price.

Crowe was right, as much as I hated to admit it. Even if I asked him to speak for me now, it was too late to hide the slightest vibration of even the faintest sound waves from the creature stalking the rooftops.

Dorothy took one single step back. Just one. The near inaudible tap of her heel on stone was all it took. The spider stopped in its tracks. It shifted its attention downward.

Fuck…

Fuck!

<*"Grab Dorothy!"*> I shouted to Crowe, but he was already ahead of me. She squeaked as he swept her up around the waist, and he sprung out of the way of a large glob of projectile poison splashing down on the cobblestone.

Leon and Tobias moved quickly on their own, dodging to the best of their abilities. Though the poison would only stun them temporarily, that would be all the Sa-Nakht needed to capture them. It was only my body that was subject to a more permanent paralysis—an unfortunate side effect of my metal bones and Sasha's brand of immortality.

We split up, sprinting in different directions, hoping the narrowness of the streets might make it difficult for such a large arachnid to give chase, but the Sa-Nakht was fast and it was clever. These spiders were bred in the distant mountains, and they were adept hunters that thrived on large prey. Their long, thin legs gave them both agility and maneuverability that far exceeded even the beast men's nimble feet, and the chances of any one of us escaping was near zero once it started binding.

I juked down an alleyway, barely wide enough for the food carts that traveled these routes, and I banged my fist along the wall in steady beats, trying to draw the spider to me. I knew the frequencies they looked for. I just had to draw it away from the others long enough for them to find refuge. If I was captured, I could deal with Sasha and her pets, but the others…

The shadow followed me much quicker than I could run. It got ahead, and I came to a skidding stop when it jumped from the roof and blocked my path.

Immediately I turned on my heel and started in the other direction. And that was when another shadow dropped between the walls and stood in my way.

Two.

There are two?!

Dorothy's distant scream was the last thing I heard before the venom hit me square in the chest. My body began to freeze, one muscle at a time.

And then the webs. I was wrapped in a white sticky mess in an instant, and the battle had truly been lost.

Though I couldn't move, I knew I was being carried somewhere. Next would be the darkness of a beast's belly, and I mentally prepared myself for the pain of it. My consciousness wouldn't die, but that didn't mean I couldn't be torn apart and digested alive.

I did my best to channel Crowe, hoping to find his consciousness somewhere in the night, but our connection was silent. Perhaps they'd been carried off elsewhere. He was in my same boat, but Leon, Tobias, and Dorothy wouldn't stand a chance against arachnid stomach bile.

I attempted to wiggle my fingers, but I was fully paralyzed, from the crown of my head to my feet. A familiar feeling. Too familiar.

The arachnid's bindings began to retract, and I found myself standing in a dark room like a statue. A flicker of light caught in the corner of my eye. It illuminated the spider webs in the corners and down the walls. Sandstone was coated in silk string so thick, the once softly colored tans and deep red iron ores vanished behind its veil. I couldn't move my neck to get a better survey of the area, but as the spider at my feet was withdrawing its webs, I knew full well I was simply being stored for later in the Sa-Nakht's feeding room.

How many of these spiders did she have now? I should have expected as much. Without me to play muscle for the dainty little witch, of course she would ramp up her guard.

Though it was ironic—comically so—that the only reason I knew where she was holding me was because I'd once been the man who put people here. I'd brutalized Sasha's prisoners, her enemies, and even her friends, and I'd locked them in this room to be digested by monsters. At times, I'd been tasked with holding her victims still so Sasha could play her games in their flesh, and at others, I'd fed them personally to her young Sa-Nakht. It took magic to hold me when the roles reversed, and I'd angered her enough to reach the feeding block. But up until that point, I was Sasha's muscle and marionette.

The heavy iron door opened, and the room filled with more gentle orange fire light. Soft light... and the ginger from hell.

Sasha entered the room, carrying herself on soundless steps. She looked exactly as I remembered her, not a single day aged despite having been alive for well over half a millennium. Her hair was perfectly straight, tinted with the color of a flickering flame. It streamed down her back, almost reaching her waist, while long bangs framed her citrine eyes. Her stature was slight, but her posture was proper, and she looked nearly harmless in her sensible flats, her silk button up, and the knee length pencil skirt that hid the top of her dark thigh high stockings,

A beauty with a devil's heart: that had been my first impression of her all those years ago. At one point, I even thought myself lucky to get to bed such a woman. My tribesmen and women were simple and primitive— something I'd not appreciated back then—and this woman was sophisticated, careful, and astute. To leave a world of cannibals to a world of red wine had felt like great fortune, up until I learned that the red wine was blood, and her affinities were of the same violence. At least the Naraka had ritual to justify our kills.

"If you love him, let him go, for if he returns, he was always yours. And if he doesn't, he never was. That's what they say, isn't it Talos?" She blinked up at me with her near invisible strawberry blond eyelashes. "And here I thought you hated me after all those awful words you said. I suppose removing your tongue was all I had to do to remove that hate from your heart." A delighted smile graced her pink, softly painted lips. "And you brought a friend. Several even. Imagine you, of all people, having *friends*. That would have been impossible for the Naraka man who feasted on his own bone marrow with me, before I gave him immortal flesh and turned his skeleton to tin. It's almost like I've fixed you with every cut and break I've made."

She placed a single finger on my chest and drew a line down my sternum. "I've missed you truly, my big, strong mountain." Her touch freed my nerves, not needing magic ointments or lotions when the source of the antidote shared skin-to-skin contact. She continued downward to my waistband, then she dropped to her knees. She grinned up at me while she traced the outline of my cock. "We have so much to catch up on, Talos."

I'm sure we do.

I knew she had access to my mental channel, so I made a point to regulate my thoughts carefully. I revealed nothing, and I remained as still and quiet as the statue she'd wanted me to be.

She undid my pants and nudged them down. Her face lit up as she traced the barbells that pierced a metal ladder along the underside of my full length. "I'm so sorry about the paralysis, but this will be much more enjoyable if you don't move. I just can't trust you to hold back anymore, so we can save the rough play for your little entourage." She lifted the edge of her skirt until her garter belt was visible. She pulled a small knife from the lace and ribbon. "When's the last time someone was able to make you come, Talos?" Her grin could only be described as cat like. She touched the perfectly sharpened scalpel to my leg. "I wonder if you even can anymore."

Sasha slipped her tongue on the underside of my cock, and she pulled the tip into her mouth. When her touch freed my body from paralysis, any illusions of arousal were completely shattered. She pulled away from my flaccid dick with a huff.

"Did someone borrow my toy and break it?" She pouted with more animosity than sadness. "Oh, no no no, that won't do." She stood, drawing a line up my torso with her blade. The pain from being sliced so shallow barely registered. I kept my mind blank as I felt her clawing at my thoughts. "That won't do at all. It sounds like you need a reminder of who you are and who you belong to, my Tin Man."

CHAPTER 41

DOROTHY

Again, I found myself in a cell. So unoriginal. Kidnap the enemy, put them in a dark room, tie them up. The only difference was that this time, I had company, and I couldn't help but think that the witch of the South had already made an egregious mistake.

Spider webs tightly bound my wrists to Crowe's, who sat back to back with me on the dungeon floor. Tobias, Talos, and Leon were nowhere to be seen, but while I could never be certain that Crowe liked *me*, I was extremely certain that Crowe did *not* like the witches, so between his immortality, his strength, his eternal grudge, and the fact that I was apparently the only one who could actually end a witch's life, I was in a pretty safe position, all things considered. It was almost a little comical to think that the more heartless brutality he showed me, the more I trusted him.

Be that as it may, being alone with him with no one else to rely on or keep him in check still had me feeling unexplainably tense. I'd had Tobias with me from the first time I'd met the scarecrow on his crucifix, and even throughout our travels, there was never someone far away. That shouldn't have made me so nervous, but it did.

Crowe shifted in our bindings, as if testing the strength of the webs. "These ropes must be enchanted." He grumbled when there wasn't the slightest give. "Do all your limbs work?"

I wiggled my fingers that were tingling from the tightness, then I nodded. "Circulation isn't completely cut off, but it's close. Everything else works though." I squirmed against him, creating friction between our skin, but doing nothing to the threads. "Can't you, like, dislocate your wrist or pull your arm off or something to get out of this?"

Crowe sighed. "Doesn't work like that. I need some sort of tearing leverage or sharpness to sever a limb, just like you would. The only actual difference between our bodies is that yours will bleed out and die after, while mine is magically forced to reassemble."

Well, so much for that idea. I sank back against him, accepting the hopelessness, but still trying to keep myself from panicking. "Do you feel pain when you come apart like that?" I asked, wanting to both distract my mind and to take advantage of this rare moment to better get to know him.

"Of course I feel pain. I still have all my nerve endings. Did you spend this whole journey thinking every time I touched you, I was just numbly feeling around?" A scoff. Maybe even genuine offense. "Rich." He chuckled darkly. "So when I threatened to fuck you, you thought I would do such a thing for only *your* pleasure?"

Memories of that evening at the waterfall rushed back to me, and I was embarrassed knowing he could now, in fact, feel the heat filling my body just from the recollection. I wondered if watching me had made him hard. "I-I suppose I just don't totally understand how the witch's magic works." I fought the urge to point out the way his phrasing implied he would still be doing it for *my* pleasure as much as his, but I thought better of it, and just stored that little admission in my heart for later.

"It works in a way that the witch's themselves are always satisfied, but despite their often twisted predilections, it's also to their advantage that their victims bond to them to some degree. When she took my ability to feel love or empathy, she made sure my brain still retained its reward center and endorphins. Someone like Grunhilda needed an enthusiastic pounding, and never an empty one." Crowe was unusually forthright. But then, I supposed he never seemed to hide much from me when I thought about it. Most of what I'd learned about Oz thus far had been thanks to him, even if he struggled with understanding human needs.

"Do you ever miss her?" The question had been on my mind for a while. In all the drama, these women who they claimed to despise so much still seemed to be the most central focus of their minds. While Leon and Tobias were sweet as vanilla, I couldn't help thinking Crowe and Talos needed something more than I could provide as a plain, unspectacular human.

Crowe paused for a few moments more than an extended blink. His body tensed when I asked the question, and it didn't relax until he spoke again. "No." Unconvincing. His head dropped to his chest, and I wondered if I'd hit some sort of forgotten emotion deep inside him. Something the Wicked Witch of the East had failed to take. "There was no honest affection between us, but I don't know who or what I was before her, so in some strange way, she was like my first love."

I was completely taken aback by that answer. "You never forget your first love, I guess." I actually felt bad for him. But then, it's not like I couldn't relate at all.

"Would be nice to though." Crowe laughed. "Nothing like the first person to give you lifelong trauma and emotional baggage, you know?"

"Preach." I shook my head. "Mine was a little less extreme, but the first guy I ever fell for—like, *really* fell for—used to treat me so badly, it was almost comical looking back. He would pay just enough attention to me, feed me *just* enough hope that he might be interested in me too, then he would use that to get me to do things for him. Sometimes just little errands or chores, like getting him food or paying for everything, and sometimes it was sexual favors. I still think about all the times I jumped through hoops to make him happy, never even noticing—maybe never even caring—that he wouldn't lift a finger in the reverse. If he was nice enough to simply take time out of his day to text me back, that was all it took to make me feel special enough to keep trying. Keep believing I mattered and just had to put in a *little more* work to deserve to be seen."

Crowe was quiet as I told my story. I don't know why I was telling him this at all, honestly. It must seem so trivial and low stakes compared to his experience. But I wanted to relate this to someone. It was a dumb story I'd always been too embarrassed to speak of.

"The worst part was, when he finally got a girlfriend who wasn't me, that didn't even snap me out of my trance. I just thought *'I didn't try hard enough. I didn't please him well enough. She's better and prettier than me, so of course he chose her instead.'* God it was so stupid." I almost wanted to laugh at how pathetic this must sound. "I should have learned from that relationship, but even when I opened my eyes and saw it for what it was, I still ended up repeating the same cycle over and over again. I fucked anyone who promised me the slightest acknowledgments. I thought I could turn the tables and use *them* for once, and instead I found myself taking bigger risks with even shittier men. I was 'beating' them by being a toy who never argued, so long as they promised to give me what I wanted.

Yet still I left with nothing. I don't know how I ended up so deeply in that mindset of low self-esteem, but I couldn't get out of it."

A ping of shame struck me as I spoke. That was stupid too. "Even as I talk about it now, I still don't know that I'm out of it. If anything, you're probably a testament that I'm still in that toxic cycle. A guy like you is probably worst of all." My laugh was ironic.

Bound at our wrists and still silent, Crowe pressed his palm to mine. He slipped his fingers in between each of my digits, and he squeezed softly. He leaned back and the crowns of our heads touched. Quiet affections that sent a jolt through my heart.

"He was an idiot." An extended pause. "But you're right. I feel nothing for you." He said, stoic and measured. A direct contradiction to every little gesture, which only made those words sting more. "That's reality, Dorothy. If you die, I'll feel nothing. If you succeed, I'll feel nothing. I'm with you because I'm using you. It's not personal, but I don't have a choice to feel differently. So if you're confused, don't be. I am exactly who I said I am, and nothing more. If I'm someone you're feeling misguided affection for, I suggest squashing that right now."

And that reminded me that I was the one being unfair in wanting something more from Crowe. The way he lost it when I was in danger sometimes made me think he cared about me, but then I had to remember that he was simply with me to *fix* the fact that he couldn't care about me—or anyone else for that matter. My death would also be the end of his hope, not the end of someone who mattered on a deeper level. Being a Sociopath by choice was one thing. Being unfeeling by magic and lobotomy was another. "I know—"

"I'm not finished." He interrupted and gave another squeeze of my hand. "But when I said I'd protect you, I meant it. Not holding emotions does not mean I'm not a man of my word." He turned his head to the side, and I followed suit, meeting his cheek with my own. I felt his muscles shift as his lips dropped into a frown. "But for your sake, reserve that hope in that sweet little heart of yours for men like Tobias or Leon or Talos. You deserve men who will place the world at your feet, not a heartless monster who will light that world on fire. I'm not willing to be another mistake that makes you cry behind closed doors." The graveness in his tone was uncharacteristically serious for Crowe. Maybe that's why my heart sunk so deeply from his words. Because I *was* falling into that same trap again, entirely of my own unfair invention.

I faced forward again, not wanting him to see or feel my own expressions. The strangest part about the battle now raging in my mind was that his words hurt while also making me trust him even more, and maybe that was the most fucked up part about me.

"Gwen had said that you were human once." I uttered next. "She told me her sister stole you from my world. I know you don't recall that, but I felt like it wasn't fair to keep that information from you."

"Is that right?" Still so measured and still so unreadable. "Maybe I don't want to go back to what I used to be then." His chuckle shook us both, and that made me laugh too.

"I'm not sure I would want to go back to being someone like me either if I'd had a taste of the freedom you have." I spoke much more cheerfully now. He squeezed my hand again.

"There is a freedom to it for sure, but don't cut yourself short. If feeling nothing was fully satisfying, I

286

wouldn't be tied up in spider shit with a pretty girl from Kansas in a far off witch's dungeon waiting to be digested alive right now."

"Fair point." I squeezed *his* hand this time. I relaxed against his back, and he relaxed against mine. Harsh as he was, this softer version of Crowe that he let me see in private was comforting. "So then, how are we getting out of here? I don't think your heroics of the West are going to work with you being tied up and all."

"You're stronger now with Gwen's blood in your shoes, no? I'm expecting *you* to save *me*." He said with a teasing smirk.

"Well in that case, I can be a woman of my word, too." I hugged my knees to my chest, giving myself a better view of my little pink heels. Did these shoes really have the power of a witch in them? That would be helpful if I had any clue how to utilize it. Assuming a regular human even *could* tap into magic.

We sat in the quiet dungeon for minute after minute, hour after hour—idly chatting like we were actually friends. I couldn't guess how long had passed, but I savored this calm before the storm for as long as I could. The tornados were rarely forgiving, and I'd learned to cling to the good until it was time to deal with the bad.

"So why is it that you can hear Talos when the rest of us can't?" I asked idly.

"How indeed." Crowe seemed more amused by the question than anything. "It's a ritual that he has to initiate. I'd prefer he show you rather than I try and explain." I couldn't help but think he was being a bit tongue in cheek.

"Does it… hurt?"

Crowe snorted. "What fun would it be if it didn't?" *Not very reassuring.* "I tried to talk him into it, but he's soft on you. I don't know why though. As human as your flesh and morality may be, you strike me as pretty hearty."

"Is that a compliment?" I smiled quietly to myself.

"Depends on what face you want the world to see. A person who wants to appear delicate might be bothered by that statement, but a woman who wants to feel equal might be proud. Which one are you, Dorothy?" His tone was casual, but his words bordered on philosophical.

"As an actress, I've pretended to be so many different people, I honestly don't know what I want anymore. Sometimes I'm not sure who 'Dorothy' is myself." My answer came from deep in my gut, and I was surprised by my own words. Equally obtuse but... honest. "Do you ever feel that way? Like you're putting on an act to be accepted, to the point you can barely discern what's you and what's a persona for everyone else?"

"I wonder..." was the only words Crowe managed when the door to our cell opened noiselessly on well-maintained hinges. In the new light that filled the room, the silhouette of a petite woman blocked the orange glow, offering only darkness in a pathway of hope.

Though much to my surprise, this wicked witch wasn't alone. Sasha, who gave off the energy of a killer librarian, stood with a mountain of a man at her back.

Talos held position behind her like a patient, mindless bodyguard. His hands were folded in front, and his expression was empty and vacant. I couldn't say if he was a prisoner or a willing subordinate.

A glimpse of new wounds traced the contours of his pecs, like a checkerboard of cuts, yet he wasn't healing as quickly as I would have expected for a man with immortal flesh. That must have been from Sasha's magical knife.

Yet Talos seemed so unbothered. Was he into that? Maybe that was the kind of thing Crowe was referring to when he said the ritual that let them communicate would hurt. I was sure the witch could speak to him, so she must have performed that ritual, too.

Crowe helped leverage both of us to our feet, and he rotated our positions so he could stand between me and this incoming threat. He offered only the quietest "stay close to me" and I envied that unrelenting confidence he had no matter the situation. As sad as it must be to lose his emotions, the ability to fearlessly walk into any fight was something I'd never be able to do with my body of flesh and blood.

"Dorothy and Crowe, correct? Welcome to the South." Sasha spoke sweetly. "I have to give you two my gratitude. Talos has told me it was you who I can thank for his return. I feared my punishment was too severe when I found myself suffering months and months and *months* without him, and I'm over the moon that he's found such good friends to help bring him back to me."

Crowe remained silent. I didn't know if he was speaking internally to Talos or not, but I felt it was in our best interest to acknowledge her praise. "We should be thanking you for the privilege of having met him." I spoke over Crowe's shoulder.

Sasha nodded, accepting the compliment, then she snapped her fingers. Our bindings loosed, and I rubbed my wrists under the rush of blood returning to my cold, tingling fingers.

"Your other friends are already being escorted to the dining hall. Won't you come with us for a celebratory dinner? It's the least I can do."

Crowe still said nothing, but he did well to hide the skepticism from his expression, so I continued to be the polite one. "O-of course." I said.

My stomach was full of nothing but nerves, but still, we followed the Wicked Witch of the South right into whatever trap she might be setting. Crowe didn't protest, and Talos remained stoic, so when she turned on her heel, I answered her call.

Talos and Crowe followed behind us, while Sasha walked beside me in a long hallway carpeted in burnt orange. Long, corridor length shelves lined the walls, and what must have been thousands of jars covered the entire walk. Each jar was filled with fluid, and each batch of fluid contained different… pieces. Eyes, hands, ears, tongues. It was a collection of victims, displaying the only remaining piece of their bodies like trophies.

I wanted to puke, but I had to keep up the act best I could as long as I could. She paid her trophies no mind, as if they were the most ordinary thing in Oz, and she kept a pleasant smile on her friendly face while she engaged me in small talk. "Please don't judge me for how you found him," she began. There were so many things to judge her for, and the fact that she'd paralyzed Talos almost seemed like the least significant now. "I know the paralysis looks bad, but it was a bit of a test. I wanted him to find a good soul who was willing to help a total stranger in need, and I wanted that soul to lead him back to me. Somehow, I'm not surprised that person happened to be a woman like you."

"Like me?" I asked, assuring my tone remained non-confrontational lest I end up on the shelves beside us.

"Kind hearted, pretty, and put together." She elaborated without missing a beat. *Unexpectedly nice compliments.* "Talos needs a woman like that in his life. He would go off the rails if he was left to his own devices."

290

Talos sent me no visible signals, and Crowe continued to say nothing, so all I could do was accept her kind words and continue to keep peace.

"Thank you. You seem like a good soul too." I attempted despite myself. Sasha laughed. Talos furrowed his brow, Crowe legitimately covered his mouth to hide his amusement. I wanted to ask questions like *"so want to explain the whole 'cutting out his tongue' thing then?"* Or *"Do you think someone is missing that brain?"* or *"So who did that toe belong to?"* but until Talos made a move, I'd just take my best guess at what the plan might be.

"Here we are." She said in the most upbeat voice when we reached a large entryway. She nudged open the door, and she ushered us into a high vaulted chamber.

A long table extended down the center, with candles in between bronze centerpieces filled with vibrant poppies. The table was already set with an extravagant dinner, and each placemat had a fine china plate with portioned servings. A butler wearing a blindfold was pouring wine in the chalices at each place setting, while a maid with a wooden leg placed a bread basket in the center of the feast.

"This looks incredible." I said, even as my eyes followed the blind butler who poured wine entirely too red. I was starving, in all honesty, but knowing that the blindfold around his face likely hid empty eye sockets negated any appetite I might have had.

"You've come such a long way. I figured you must be hungry." Sasha paced over to the head of the table, and the butler scurried over to pull out her seat. She sat down with exaggerated daintiness, while I surveyed the room as subtly as I could. The spider webs that created a loose canopy on the ceiling did not go unnoticed.

Talos stepped forward first, taking his place behind the tall backed seat occupied by his witch. It was a terrible of me to think this, having received so many hints about the Southern Witch's predilections, but when I saw the cute, polite, scholarly looking red head standing with the muscular god that was Talos, I couldn't help but notice they looked really cute together. Gwen had been shameless about who she was, and her eccentricities were broadcast from miles away, but Sasha seemed so put together and classy.

It would have been so nice to be able to judge this book by her cover, but the décor wasn't helping. If I'd learned anything in my stay in La La Land, it should probably have been that fine clothes and good public relations didn't make a devil any closer to a saint.

Still, not being able to talk with Talos and gauge *his* character outside of superficial interactions had been frustrating, even more so now that I felt so in the dark about what we were dealing with. The fact that he and Crowe were so close wasn't really indicative of being a good person either, considering Crowe joked about slaughtering munchkins.

I tried to shake the thought as I took my seat at the table. Leon and Tobias were already seated across from me, but aside from nonverbal check ins for our collective well-being, we kept up this eerily quiet façade. Crowe stepped in behind my seat, mimicking Talos. Being similarly immortal and uneating, it would have been suspect for him to take a seat, and I'm sure he knew the witch would notice such a thing.

The food in front of me looked good though. Something that resembled ham covered in a glaze took up a third of the plate, while some vegetables and potatoes took up the rest. I didn't trust any of it, don't get me wrong, but by pure outward appearances, it looked entirely edible. Appetizing even. Another testament to strong appearances for vile packages.

Of course, I had to consider that she may have just liked cutting people up, and didn't *necessarily* also eat them. But questions like *'is this a leg of pork or a leg of your unfortunate maid over there?'* were still circling in my head. I sat stiffly, eyes forward, and I waited patiently for her to say grace or pray to the god of death and spiders or whoever it was that witch's in Oz thanked for their meals.

As my eyes held forward, a small spider, dangling from a near invisible web, began lowering in front of me. It dropped to eye level, hovered for a moment, then continued down to my plate. I swallowed, but still said nothing as it crawled all over the mystery meat.

"Eat, eat!" Sasha said. "Please, I want everyone to get their strength up."

I stared down at the unwelcome eight legged guest now moving on to my vegetables. The last remnants of my appetite fluttered away into oblivion. I wasn't planning to touch the meat, but I kind of wanted to eat the broccoli at least…

I stuck my fork into the potatoes, so it at least looked like I was going to try the food, while Sasha began cutting her pork/maid/whatever steak cheerfully. Leon sniffed the air subtly, using his beast senses to figure out what we were eating, I imagined, and Tobias, played with his vegetables.

I just watched the spider crawling about my plate with irritation.

I lifted my fork and committed to putting it into a piece of sautéed summer squash, when the little pest went darting for my veggies without any mind for where I was trying to eat. Before I could stop myself, my prongs plunged into the little black body, and the spider stilled. Its legs curled into itself.

Mortified, and now definitely not touching this food, I made my best effort to appear outwardly normal. Sasha had already half finished her meal however, and she was too distracted by her wine to notice the rest of us just pushing the food in circles on the plate.

Sasha swallowed the last bite of her meat, then she stood up and grabbed her goblet of wine. She clanged a knife on its side three times to get everyone's attention. "So how about a toast? To my Mountain's new friends!"

We all mimicked her, standing with our metal cups. I lifted my chalice into the air to be agreeable, and I tried not to think about what the sloshing red liquid might actually be.

She clanged her knife against the cup one last time, and I swear the whole entire room started to shake.

Tapping. Rapid tapping of spider legs on stone began echoing through the chamber, and all of the blood drained from my face.

Fuck.

Sasha tilted her head to the side and smiled widely. "I hope you've all left room for dessert."

Six massive spiders surrounded the dining table on the ceiling, the walls, and in the corners of the room. I'd not even had time to shout before Crowe was pinned to a wall in webs, and Tobias and Leon were bound in white cocoons. I pushed back the large, heavy seat behind me, ready to run, but my legs didn't move fast enough. In an instant, a rope of webbing had my wrists, my ankles, and my neck. I was thrown into the wall beside Crowe, completely trapped in sticky webs.

There's No Place Like Oz by Leann Belle

Chapter 42

"THE SCARECROW"

CROWE

The spiders did a great job of securing me, and Talos was doing an even better job of appearing loyal to his witch.

Complicated.

This was a perfect moment to use Talos' silent channel to communicate behind her back, but then, chances were likely, Sasha could hear his thoughts as easily as I could. Possibly more easily considering she'd ridden his dick before. She couldn't hear *my* thoughts, but he wouldn't be able to respond.

So the question then was: Would it be best to help navigate this situation *with* him, sharing information one way, or would it be best to keep our channel closed so he wouldn't risk blowing his cover from an accidental, idle response? All we had to do was get Sasha into a vulnerable enough position that Dorothy could land a finishing blow, but currently having the majority of us bound to a wall wasn't making that particularly manageable.

I met Talos' gaze, and the look he returned was impressively unflinching. I'm not sure *I* could even feign loyalty that well. My mask had slipped a few times over my years with Hildy. Though Talos did strike me as someone with impressive discipline, whereas I wasn't much for caring about consequences.

When Sasha approached Dorothy, he followed behind in perfect step, like the good little soldier he was.

The giant spider crawled down the wall above us. It poked and prodded my shoulders then felt around my chest and face, as if gauging my size and digestibility. Next it crawled over to Dorothy. I tensed as it followed the line of her neck with its sensors. I couldn't do anything while trapped in its webbing, and as much as I trusted the Tin Man, I would prefer to know I could step in if needed.

Sasha walked the perimeter of the room, inspecting each of us like she was evaluating a painting. She started with Leon, looking him over while her spiders continued prodding. She moved over to Tobias, who was still testing his binding despite the furry, striped arachnid poking at his face. She watched them struggle for a few moments until she was satisfied, then she continued on without even a taunt or a jab. Next she was in front of me, looking up at me from her diminutive height. She was even shorter than Dorothy, if that could be believed. She placed a hand on my cheek and tilted her head back as she inspected me.

"You're similar to my Talos." She said, measured and matter of fact.

"Barely. I promise the ride is entirely different." I smirked down at her, and that elicited a pleasant smile. Her soft touch moved down to my chest, where she traced the spider's ropes, then with a raised brow, she lifted her skirt and removed a small knife from a garter belt. Her enchanted item.

She drew a line along my bicep with her blade. She watched as my body healed itself near immediately. "You must have been Hildy's toy. Gwen and Eloise prefer their men more… killable." Her face was much too sweet for her words. "I wonder…" She shoved the knife in until she'd gone completely through the muscles and was hitting the wall behind me. When she'd not gotten so much as a flinch from me, she leveraged the knife downward, and it cut through my bone with impressive ease. A flick of the wrist, and my arm was severed completely. And a second later, it had reattached. Sasha frowned. "How boring." She pouted. "No flinching, no crying, no screaming. Either my cousin took your nerves, or you're simply too tough. Neither is a quality I want in my bed."

"What a loss for me." I rolled my eyes.

Sasha returned a glare, then she continued on to Dorothy. Talos still stood idly by.

"You, however…" She touched her knife to Dorothy's neck, and every muscle in my body tensed. She started to draw a shallow line to her collarbone—enough to draw blood but not enough to cause real damage. Dorothy swallowed. Her eyes were moist with the threat of tears, and her heartbeat was pounding with unbridled fear. A shiver shook the witch like a chill down her spine, and the corners of her lips ticked up slightly. "You're my favorite flavor of vanilla."

She withdrew her knife and replaced it in her garter. "Talos, baby. Won't you give me a show. I've been so bored lately."

She stepped back, heading back to her seat like a queen waiting for the court jester to make her laugh. Talos took her place in front of Dorothy. His muscles flexed as he tore the webs binding her there, his superior strength on full display. He still communicated nothing, and his acting was starting to make *me* nervous.

"T-Talos, what are you doing?" There was panic in her voice and anger in the surrounding eyes. Tobias upped his effort to free himself, while a spider was pressing its fangs to his neck, and Leon was jerking roughly in his webs, while venom was dripping down his shoulder.

He hauled her over to the table and used one hand to sweep away Sasha's place setting. Porcelain shattered and metal utensils clanged when they hit the floor. Talos slammed Dorothy onto the table, and she cried out at the pain of the blow.

"Talos, please—" Her voice trembled. Not an act. Honest fear.

I bit my lip as he climbed on top of her. He held her down with his weight channeled through his hands on her wrists. His expression was empty, while Dorothy was starting to panic. Sasha sat back in her chair with crossed legs and her hands folded in her lap, watching the scene like she was in the theatre.

"If you hurt her before we've killed them all…"

Talos closed his eyes and opened them again. No words flowed between us, but that was all the communication I needed. I relaxed in my restraints, unbothered by the Sa-Nakht that was feeling its way down my leg, and I kept my gaze locked in his.

"No need to be gentle, my Mountain. Tear her clothes off." Sasha directed her own show. "If she fights too much, knock her out and keep going."

A flicker of anger reflected in his silver eyes, but so long as Sasha was behind him, she wouldn't pick up on his micro-expressions. He was safe to express himself to my eyes.

Dorothy, realizing she couldn't stand up to the strength of either one of them, stopped thrashing, but tears still flowed freely down her cheeks. Neither of us could communicate anything to her, and I could only imagine what was going through her head in that moment. She didn't know Talos like I did. She didn't understand what was happening. If anything, she may have even truly believed he was back under the witch's control. It's not like she understood how we truly worked—that a slave doll's free will was stolen via manipulation, but not by literal puppetry. And Talos had shirked off Sasha's lies long ago.

Dorothy squeezed her eyes shut as Talos firmly grabbed her dress. He tore the material like it was a tissue. He removed her lacey panties with the same ease. Though he left her shoes. He couldn't have taken them off her if he tried, and I was certain Sasha was well aware of that. She'd not said anything about them yet, but all of the witches knew exactly what they were looking at. Which was probably why Dorothy was the one specifically placed on the chopping block right now instead of making Talos dominate Leon or Tobias.

Sasha giggled. "I don't think she's going to be able to take you, Talos. But I look forward to watching her try."

Dorothy looked up into Talos' eyes, while a whimper escaped her lips. I should be enjoying her fear, but the fact that Talos was going to do this because Sasha told him to, yet wouldn't when *I* had made the same request, bothered me. It would be advantageous to open the channel of communication between them, so why couldn't I shake the bad taste in my mouth.

<*"This is what you wanted, isn't it?"*> Talos communicated with me directly. I didn't know if Sasha could hear those thoughts or not, but they were vague enough that it wouldn't matter if she could.

"If you really want to piss off your witch, make Dorothy come until those whimpers are from begging for more instead of fear."

<*"I didn't expect to get this hard just seeing her beneath me. She's beautiful when she's a mess. Imagine something so delicate unraveling on my rough cock."*> His

phrasing stayed vague, answering me, while not making it obvious he was in conversation. The implication that he wanted and felt no such way with Sasha was clearly understood considering the annoyed expression that flashed across her face.

Still, Sasha stayed in her chair. "Don't hold back." She requested coldly. "If you like her so much, why don't you just fuck her 'til she dies." The words were pouty disguised by sadistic harshness.

Talos swallowed while Dorothy so subtly nodded her head in submission. His acting wasn't as good as I'd initially thought, and it was obvious the little cues of body language were starting to give him away. Though I couldn't say if Dorothy was fully picking up on them all, but she didn't really know him either. As long as she figured out the big ones—that he was still her ally—it would be fine.

Talos shoved Dorothy's legs apart, and he pushed her knees up, so her pussy was in clear view for his witch. He placed her shins on his shoulders then drew his grip down her thighs. His fingertips pressed into her soft muscles, trailing red marks downward until he reached her ass.

He *was* fucking hard. It was clearly visible through his clothing, and he was way too big to hide it. There was a shift in his expression that went from restrained mortification to honest lust. He gripped her ass. He squeezed. Then he started tracing circles around her opening. Dorothy's eyes popped open when he entered her with his forefinger. He sank in as deep as he could, and he started working her until his whole hand was glistening. A second finger. Slow, careful, gentle.

I swallowed when he started teasing a third.

Talos sunk in those three fingers, inching carefully until Dorothy could take them all. She'd need at least that much stretching to fit him without tearing. *He was so much nicer than I would be.*

Her eyes were locked on his now, their own form of silent communication, and the sound of her heart rate was elevated in a way that started to beget arousal more than fear. She'd started to understand he wasn't trying to hurt her. That he was still on her side. That this was an act.

They held that contact in a way that felt genuinely intimate. Caring. *A way she'd never be able to look at me...*

Where the fuck did that thought come from?

I wanted to see him hurt her on his dick, then I wanted to see the witch die at her hands. That look of horror as she was forced to commit murder was the only one I ever wanted to see reflecting in her eyes.

Right.

Her chest heaved, and her small, soft breasts shifted up slightly towards her collarbone. Her nipples were hard as fuck, and Talos had her wet enough to start dampening the table cloth. He drew those three fingers out of her then threaded his fingers between her folds. She gasped aloud.

< *"Do you think she can take four?"* > He thought for all of us to hear.

Sasha looked more perturbed than pleased by the question. There was a comedy in the fact that she was starting to get annoyed by the same act she'd wanted him to commit. "Enough with the foreplay." She demanded. "Fuck her, Talos."

<*"Forgive me for this, Dorothy."*> slipped through his mind next, and I knew he'd not meant for Sasha to hear that one.

I jerked in my restraints again when I saw the witch stand up. But she remained still, as though just wanting a better view. I knew this wouldn't end well, but then, I was counting on that fact.

Talos kept playing with her clit, assuring she stayed drenched and aroused, and he started undoing his pants with the other hand. She looked so fucking hot in his hands, it was starting to get to me. She was too scared to move, yet ready and wanting in the same breath. A beautiful contradiction.

He freed himself, revealing his thick cock, barbell piercings and all, to her widening eyes. Her surprise only made me want to join him.

Her breasts shifted as she leveraged her ankles on his shoulders to lift her hips, pressing into his hand and reveling in the way he was playing her. Her little gasps and moans had me straining to get free.

Talos watched her body with such interest. Even without the lower half of his face being visible, his expressions were divine.

This was rather unfair. All the times we could have both fucked her, he'd not given in, and the one time I was forced to be a spectator, he was ready to pound her until she screamed. Maybe he just liked it when I watched him get off.

Dorothy's gaze was transfixed on those barbells that reflected the soft light of the dining hall torches. She bit her lip in such an appealing way as he lined up his cock with her soaked pussy.

"Ready to admit you've always wanted to fuck her?" I forced his attention back on my words. Back on me.

<*"No."*> He entered her slowly, filling her with his tip, and only stopping as the first rung of his metal ladder was against her opening. His eyes rolled back in his head, as if he was near ready to come just from the feel of her around his head. It would take some force to push the metal in, and I'd near forgotten about the witch entirely in that anticipation.

"Would it help if I admitted watching you makes me *want to fuck her, too?"*

<*"Yes."*> Short answers. Still nothing revealing. Not to Sasha anyway. That admission was perfectly vivid to me though.

Talos forced the first piercing into her, then he stopped briefly at the second step. Dorothy winced as he continued slowly to the third. He was stretching her but also testing her, making sure she could feel his ridges without it being vicious. *I wish he'd make it more vicious.*

"Look at her taking you like a champ." I jerked in my webs again, but it was pointless. *"Imagine if you didn't have to hold back."*

<*"She's a good fucking girl. She could take it."*> Even Talos' thoughts were starting to sound ragged and undone. He sunk in all the way, then he drew out again slowly. The piercings tugged at his rock hard cock as he drew out and pushed in again. <*"You would like her."*> He slid in and out of her again. <*"You would fucking revel in her."*>

Dorothy squeezed her eyes shut, "Oh fuck." She moaned. She was trying not to visibly enjoy it, but they were both starting to lose themselves to the other. Acting was a chamber in their brain that had been locked shut and forgotten.

Talos lifted her hips to change his angle, and he started moving faster. <*"Fuck, Crowe. You were right."*>

Sasha's brow twitched at that. Any illusion that he was speaking in idle thoughts as he fucked her, rather than having a conversation with one of his companions, was lost. I glared at the spiders crawling on my body, hoping I could free myself before this escalated. These were unwanted pests just like me. Just like the crows. She didn't deserve dominion over these monsters.

"Enough." Sasha spat with animosity and jealousy. She paced around to one side of the table, then she took two tall steps to place herself atop the platform. In a swift motion, she pulled her knife from her garter again, and she crouched down by Dorothy's head. She placed the blade firmly against Dorothy's windpipe. Both of them froze solid. The slightest shift would be enough to slit Dorothy's throat. "Now harder, Talos."

Dorothy's heart rate climbed again, and it seemed loud in my ears. Neither of them had been satisfied yet when Talos started to pull out. I couldn't tell if he was terrified of the way his thrusts could now kill her, or if he was even harder at the possibility.

And I'd never wanted to fuck the both of them more than I did in that moment.

CHAPTER 43

"THE TIN MAN"

TALOS

Fucking Lucifer. I'd been doing everything in my power to keep up this act of loyalty and not hurt her, but her cunt was so hot and wet, it was unlike anything I'd ever felt. Sasha had been cold and rough inside. If I had any clue how otherworldly it would feel to sink into Dorothy, I'd have fucked her in the tent with Tobias, and these communication challenges wouldn't be an issue.

And now I had to find a way to control how hard my thrusts shook through her, lest I be an accomplice in slitting her throat. I couldn't kill Sasha no matter how rough I'd been, but humans were so fragile. The fact that such a thought only stirred my arousal was a problem I'd address another time.

I drew out of her slowly, savoring the tug of each bar, and the way she tensed on the ridges was exquisite. My gaze fell on the girl who looked at me with undeserved gentleness, even with a knife to her throat, even through the small winces of pain while I fucked her, and even when my piercings risked tearing her apart. I didn't know how much time we had before Sasha got angry enough to finish the job and start putting Dorothy's pieces in jars and on the dinner table. If I came in her now, I could still forge the connection I needed to talk to her, but the chances of Sasha letting me get off without killing Dorothy for having the audacity to take my seed was less than zero.

If I treated her more roughly, I could calm Sasha, but I might scare Dorothy again. If I pounded into her the way I would a witch, I might permanently wreck her pussy.

I hated myself for even thinking such a barbaric thing—even more so for the fact that the thought of breaking her on my dick edged me closer to orgasm. Becoming her villain would save her life, and it would cost me all of the humanity I'd fought for.

If I was Crowe, would I be able to do it? Would I like the sound of her cries? I shook my head, not wanting to answer that question for her sake or mine.

Crowe wasn't the heartless bastard he thought he was. But me? I absolutely could be.

CHAPTER 44

DOROTHY

My blood was trickling down my neck as the blade broke skin, while my arousal was dripping down Talos' pelvis. I was trembling but trying to stay still at the same time. I kept my eyes on Talos and far from the witch's gaze. His cock was so thick, and those ridges were hitting all the right places, and I don't know that I could have figured out how to care about the danger of it all anyway. Any pain had long since turned to pleasure, and I wanted that orgasm more than I'd ever wanted to come in my life. So long as he was filling me with confidence as strong as his dick, I'd keep up that trust.

I couldn't speak to Talos, but he'd made it abundantly clear how good he wanted me to feel. We were all actors here, but I was finally getting to see who he was under his mask.

I shuddered when he drew out again.

"You heard me, Talos." Sasha snapped. She moved her knife up to my chin. She pressed the flat side against my check then placed the blade behind my ear. "Every time either one of you orgasms, I'll take one piece of her." She twirled the blade on its tip, puncturing the skin. The little bites of pain under each poke and slice heightened the sensation of my ride on Talos' ladder, and I wouldn't admit that she was only making it more satisfying. "An ear, her nose, her legs, her breasts. If you want to go out into the world and bring home another woman, I'll show you exactly what the consequences are for betraying me."

Shit. That, however, made my blood run cold. The threat was one thing, but knowing it was about to be reality was an entirely different one. I could see the glaze in his eyes, and he was as close as I was. I found myself desperate to think of anything but how good his pierced cock felt.

Which was impossible with the way he was using it. What was wrong with me that I was staring death and dismemberment in the face and I was still shaking on him?

"If you hold back, I'll notice." She glared at him, and I could feel the way that made him tense inside me.

Talos listened. He slammed in hard, and I cried out when her knife nicked me deeply. He pulled out, and he started to move with an unfair, dangerous, yet intoxicating rhythm.

"F-fuck, Talos." My eyes were watering both with tears and heady orgasm. He braced me with one hand on my hips, and he leaned down over me to grab my hand and place it between my legs. My eyes widened as he pressed my own fingers against my clit, as if urging me to help get myself off.

He was urging me towards that corridor of pain and death, and I was too terrified to second guess him. He must know something I didn't. I wanted to believe that. I had to.

My only respite was that the fear might distract me from how good he felt, but that was barely enough to save this situation.

Sasha twirled the knife in her fingers like a baton, while she watched me, waiting for my expression to give me away. I closed my eyes, trying to fight it, while a pressure was building.

"Look at this girl, so hot and bothered even when she's being torn up and cut up. See Talos Baby, she wants to be treated this way. She wants to bleed for us." Sasha purred. She drew a line down my neck with the blade, cutting a shallow scratch to my shoulder, then she drew back up to my ear

Talos reacted to her languid knife strokes by placing his hand on my neck. He squeezed without fully cutting off my air or circulation. A protective move to keep Sasha's blade off me, disguised cleverly as escalating roughness.

Fuck, I wish I didn't like this kind of roughness so much.

Talos came first, and it was hot and intense and powerful between my legs. He squeezed me harder as he filled me, while his eyes started to water—though I couldn't say if it was more from tearful apology or pleasure.

Sasha cackled when she watched him give in, and I was fighting to not double my penalty. I stilled my hand as the only way I could save myself from following him off the cliff.

"Humans feel good, don't they, my Mountain." She smirked as she pressed that scalpel against my earlobe. She drew a thin line from the bottom of my ear to the top to announce her intention. "*This* won't feel so good though."

<*"Don't flinch. You'll be okay, Dorothy."*> A voice I'd never heard entered my head as Sasha bore down with the knife. I felt it sink into my nerves, and I cried out.

The pressure ceased. The knife dropped to the table and bounced beside my head. I looked up to see the wicked witch of the south in a head lock, Crowe choking her out from behind, while keeping her arm pinned behind her back. Severe anger reflected in every tensing of his muscles, while she fucking thrashed.

"How did you get free—"

310

Crowe tightened his lock, cutting off her words abruptly, then he flexed, and the spiders swarmed her. Sasha shrieked as the arachnids tied and gagged her with webs, and they left her helpless on the table. The centerpieces clattered, and the place settings were knocked onto the ground as she struggled to get free.

Crowe's critters scurried off to start on Tobias and Leon's bindings with another nudge of Crowe's chin. It was like he'd taken control of her spiders just as he had control of the birds he was meant to scare away. Maybe the scarecrow had more power than I knew.

Crowe locked eyes with Talos, who was still inside me. His eyes narrowed. "I hope you weren't planning to pull out, Tin Man."

< *"Of course not."*> That voice again, this time followed by a cruel chuckle. *That… that's Talos? This is what Crowe hears?* < *"I was just waiting for you to join me, Scarecrow."*>

"Why can I hear his voice directly in my mind?" I thought idly, only to get an immediate response.

< *"Because you're mine now, Dorothy."*> Talos spoke as if he was reading my thoughts. Perhaps he was. < *"And this connection will never break."*>

Crowe smirked. Could he hear the things Talos said to me, too? "Is that right?" He said aloud with a cock of his head.

A laugh reverberated through my mind. < *"This contract is binding, didn't you know?"*> Wait, had Crowe and Talos… < *"I've long had immortal flesh, but you didn't realize it's been your power I've been drawing from when I heal? Sasha built me to hurt me, not to be unbreakable."*> Talos was completely fixated on Crowe. < *"But you were*

311

always going to be mine too, Crowe. I was just waiting for you to realize it.">

Crowe smirked his deceptively unfazed smirk, then he turned his attention to me. "I guess we really are the same, you and I." He crouched down and he slipped a hand under each of my shoulders. I gazed up at him, and he lowered his face down to mine. He brushed my lips with his in a way so tender it made my heart skip a beat, then in immediate contrast, he grabbed me roughly and jerked me upright. He gave me a hard shove, and Talos caught me and hugged me into his chest. He was still inside me, and I could feel him starting to grow and harden again.

Talos placed a hand on each side of my waist, and Crowe took a position behind me.

<*"Enough denial.">* He looked at Crowe as if they were sharing some untold secret.

"Enough denial." Crowe repeated as he drew a massaging line of pressure down my spine. He settled his hands on my ass, and he spread my cheeks. Then he put his mouth on my neck and touched his sharp teeth to my skin. Fangs pierced flesh as he bit down just enough to make me bleed. I moaned involuntarily as he sucked on my neck. His otherwise low body temperature warmed just slightly when he drew my fluids into his throat. "I can't wait to hear you cry on my cock, sweet girl."

"Crowe…" Even knowing he'd seen me naked and freshly fucked and having pushed myself to completion right in front of him before, those words still made me blush.

He fluttered kisses up my jawline, then he licked the blood off my earlobe. He sucked on me as a distraction as he subsequently slipped a finger into my ass. I tensed at the sudden intrusion, and I felt his lips pull into a smile before he whispered, ever so softly, "Don't worry, Dorothy. I won't fuck you dry."

Chapter 45

"THE SCARECROW"

CROWE

Talos' balls were already tightening again as I lifted Dorothy's hips off his cock. With his full length a mess of his come and hers, she unsheathed him smoothly and easily. I was gentle at first, letting her think me a lover and a friend, then I balled her hair in my fist and jerked her backwards, sending her stumbling over to the bound and tied "Good" Witch of the South.

The spiders had been a quick ally. Their simple minds made them much easier to manipulate than the sharp and intelligent crows in the field. Which was good, because I couldn't stand watching that scene for another minute. I wouldn't have Dorothy turned into a dismembered corpse, but I also couldn't stand watching Talos having his way with her without me. The Tin Man might mistake that for affection, but it was more a selfish drive.

But first, I needed her drenched in witch's blood.

Dorothy caught herself on all fours, and she hovered over Sasha while naked, with Talos' release dripping down her thigh, wearing nothing but her pink heels. It was a fucking gorgeous view.

"You know the rules." I stated steadily. "Kill her, and you'll be rewarded." I picked up the witch's knife, and I handed it to our girl.

She accepted the instrument absently, then she sat back on her haunches and stared at the blade.

"If I have the magic artifact, I don't need to kill her, do I? I know we need to stop her, but can't we put her in a prison?" She looked up at me with pleading eyes. Pathetic. I would *not* have her be pathetic.

"You think a cell would hold her? That she'll let you walk out of here and never seek revenge?" A cock of my brows seemed to set her straight.

She glanced at Sasha, who was squirming in her bindings, then back to the knife. "I-I just—"

"You've done it once. Do it again. For your sake." My tone dropped to something severe and harsh. "You can do this, Dorothy." I spoke slow.

"I can do this." She parroted back to me.

Dorothy played with the knife in her hand, before she gripped the handle and pointed the blade downwards. She lifted it over her head, as if she was about to plunge it straight into her heart... then she froze in place.

"I can't do this while she's looking me in the eye though. I can't—"

"Then cut her eyes out." No quarter. Offering her an easy solution would only breed weakness. "Help her, Tin Man."

Talos positioned behind her and massaged her shoulders, while he spoke directly into her mind. < *"Relax, Dorothy. Drive in the blade straight and true."* > He pressed his chest to her back, grabbed the hand holding the knife, and balled his fist firmly around hers.

With a quick squeeze of her weapon hand, Talos released her and bent her over again, placing our girl eye to eye with Sasha. He moved back down her body, sliding that grip down the sides of her waist, then he pushed his fingers into her wet little cunt. His knuckles tensed as he hooked

315

his digits and dragged it over a spot that made her clench her thighs together. <*"Let me help ease your nerves Dorothy."*> Talos muttered into both our minds. He drew leisurely lines over her clit that had her white knuckling that blade, trying to keep it together.

Sasha looked delightfully livid all wrapped up, being forced to watch her dearest *'Mountain'* bring a girl to orgasm right on top of her. It was twisted and cruel in the most delicious way.

Dorothy was panting to keep it together, but still she wasn't ready to kill the witch. Murder with her eyes closed and looking away was one thing, but stabbing someone to death while close, intimate, eyes locked and naked was another.

So I lowered down to Dorothy's level, I lifted her chin so she was facing me, then I kissed her. I tangled my tongue with hers, and I took every moan Talos worked through her into my throat.

She tasted good on my lips, and she fit just right against me. I was only doing this to help her confidence. That was all. But her soft touch was delicious. She let me control her through my kiss, angling whatever way I nudged her, parting her lips more when I flicked them with my tongue. She rose up as I rose, and she followed when I pulled away, gripping my shirt to keep me from retreating too far. I coaxed her tongue into my mouth, then I sucked on her to keep it.

Talos withdrew his fingers, then he repositioned to fuck her properly from behind. She gasped as he shoved in hard, so I nipped her tongue before she could take it back.

"What are you so afraid of?" I whispered against her lips, while Talos' thrusts knocked her forward. Our lips tapped each time he slammed in, and they parted each time he pulled back.

"I'm afraid of being like her." She breathed the words, while her eyes were closed, and her expression relaxed into that feeling.

"Then be like me instead." I fisted her hair and I took her mouth forcefully, assuring our lips didn't part again. She met my intensity, and I couldn't help wanting to take more and more. She tasted of honey and all the flavors I'd lost. Like an angel I didn't deserve.

She cried into my throat as Talos pumped into her, but I wasn't ready to release her mouth and let her breathe. She was sweet indulgence, and I'd denied myself long enough.

Dorothy pulled away suddenly, pushing back into Talos' hips, and immediately I missed her flavor. She bit her lip so attractively, as she lifted that knife in an unsteady hand. Her other hand supported her on the table, as she positioned the point of the blade over Sasha's heart.

"Can I really be like you?" She was pleading for me to tell her it was okay. That we wouldn't judge her, think less of her, or shun her for her crimes. But her innocence wasn't why I loved—

I crushed that pathetic thought before it could fully manifest. A misnomer. False words due to the limits of language. A tightness took my throat.

"Do it." I said, betraying those confused thoughts that bubbled in my head. A conscience. Did I... have a conscience? Where were these foolish thoughts coming from? *No. Fuck that.* "Keep your eyes on me and channel my devil if you need to, but fucking do it, and I'll make you my queen."

317

Dorothy's grip tightened with resolve, and Sasha's eyes bugged in her head. The witch tried to wriggle away, but Talos held her still.

I shoved my tongue back in her mouth as she lifted that knife, and using my demons for strength, she plunged it downwards directly into the witch's heart.

Instantly, the thrashing stopped, and death spilled from the wound, staining the table cloth and the webs that wrapped around her body. Life faded rapidly from her eyes, and the gag of webs didn't even offer her the mercy of last words.

Dorothy, however—she kept kissing me, now taking control of our dance of tongues. She was shaking with the orgasm dampening her thighs as she slid off Talos' dick, and moved closer to me.

Had she just reached climax from killing the witch?

I couldn't help chuckling through our locked lips, and I grabbed her waist to pull her closer to me, not wanting to share any inch of her for at least a few brief moments. I returned to tongue fucking her perfect little mouth, while Sasha's body returned to Oz.

The blood climbed into Dorothy's shoes. The pink hit a new shade of light red, while her blocks turned to a more narrow two-inch heel. She shivered when that power hit her, and the surge had her grinding herself against my lap. She looked fucking gorgeous in death.

Dorothy was determined. She pushed me down until my back hit the table, and she straddled my waist. Naked and writhing on my lap, I couldn't begin to refuse her when she begged, with a simple and succinct "Fuck me, Crowe." She was undoing my fly with an urgency. "I've been a good girl, so let me know what your power feels like."

"Now, now." I grabbed Sasha's knife from the table, and I tapped the back of it playfully on her naval. "I'll let you be on top, but don't think for a second you're in control." With a flip of the knife, I cut a surface scratch down her abdomen.

"Take her from behind," I nodded to Talos, and he smirked back.

<*"Crowe, Crowe, Crowe."*> He chuckled through our shared channel. He took position behind her, and she lifted her hips so he could remove my jeans. <*I have a better idea."*> Talos grabbed her waist, and he lifted her up. She leaned back into him, using his rock hard chest for support as he lowered her down on to my cock. I shuddered as that wet heat wrapped around me. There was no chance of disguising that surprise in my expression as perfection hugged my entire length. Her warmth was unexpected. And fucking divine.

A flash of delight filled her when she saw mine.

Talos, on the other hand, had his own game he wanted to play. <*"Why don't you fuck her..."*> He dug his fingers into her breasts, squeezing them up as she rose on me again, then he released her as she dropped back down to my base. That hard hit rippled fucking ecstasy through me. Then he pressed those same iron grips into my thighs, and he lifted my hips. He lined up with my ass, and he grinned down at me. <*"And I'll fuck you."*>

I swallowed hard, my composure suddenly shaken to its core. Talos' cock still so slick with their shared fluids pressed into me, creating a whole new pressure and pleasure I'd never quite felt. The ridges of his piercings dug in, and I thanked my body's healing ability. Though the shots of pain only made it so much fucking better.

Dorothy on top of me, and Talos buried inside me, I was experiencing more sensations than I had in my known existence. She started to take control of the tempo, fucking herself on my cock exactly how she'd showed me she liked it. As much as I wanted to throw her down and take control, watching her breasts bouncing, her fingers on her clit, and her pussy clenching on me was a masterpiece too breathtaking to ruin. There would be plenty of time later to take her however I wanted. For now, I was content to watch her chase her sole pleasure to her heart's content.

Once I filled her, she'd have the first traces of my immortality, after all. Dorothy would be mine now, too, and she would be mine forever.

CHAPTER 46

DOROTHY

Ice, fire, lightning, drowning, flying, and falling. When Crowe filled me with his fluids, a parade of extremes hit my system all at once. I was dizzy, I was hot, I was shivering, I was about ready to throw up, and I was shaking with adrenaline. The last thing I remembered was the compounding elation of multiple orgasms ripping through me a moment before I blacked out.

I opened my eyes what felt like only seconds later, only to wake up wrapped in emerald silk sheets. I shot upright in bed, and I felt around my body, assuring all my limbs were intact. I was still alive. I couldn't have imagined it all.

I peeked under the sheets to see my shoes still on my feet. They had changed again. I removed each small red high heel, now two inches tall, and I placed them on the night stand beside me. I was still naked, but a new outfit rested on the table for me. A pretty sundress with flowers and vines. It was bright and sunny and made me smile.

It was then that I noticed in my periphery that I wasn't alone in this room in the Emerald Castle.

Crowe stood against the wall, his arms crossed, as if he was waiting impatiently for me to wake up. He met my gaze with an unreadable interest.

"Where are the others?" I asked. "And how did we get here?"

Crowe cocked a smile. "I appreciate that I was the first and only person you noticed."

Taken aback, I looked around the room. Tobias was in a chair at my bedside, just now stirring to consciousness. Leon was sitting on the floor shaking his head. Talos was guarding the door like a good soldier.

Tobias spoke first, "You're awake." His smile was like a puppy wagging its tail, and my heart melted at the sight of it. "How are you feeling? You passed out so suddenly, I didn't know what to think."

"I'm fine, I guess." I returned the expression, always feeling more at ease when I was with him. "If anything, I feel better than I ever have." And that was true. I felt strong, energized, and healthy.

"I'm surprised you didn't tear." Leon was up on his feet and looking me over next.

< *"Don't listen to him. I know how to use my cock for good* and *evil. You only would have torn if I wanted you to."*> Talos rolled his eyes. He still wore the mask, and I was a bit sad the Wizard couldn't save him yet.

"With all your experience, the next witch will be a breeze. She's the *nice* one after all." Crowe added with a mocking cock of his head. "Ready to finish the job, my Devil Princess?"

I flushed at my new nickname that by no means should have struck me as cute or endearing. Yet, from Crowe, I knew it was only a compliment.

The grin that took my face was completely involuntary as I looked at the four men in my room, all here because they were worried about me.

"I'm ready." I said with confidence.

Unearned ego. It would surely be put to the test as we entered the realm of the fourth and final witch: Eloise, the Witch of the North.

Tobias' witch.

I could only hope she was less vile than the last.

The Nice Witch of the North

Chapter 47

"TOTO"

TOBIAS

My witch. Eloise of the North was supposedly the one who banished me to earth and stole my memory and ability to shift, and I had mixed feelings on the whole thing.

Seeing my punishment through everyone else's lenses of trauma, it was easy to only see the bad in what the witch had done. I'd lost who I was and a fundamental part of my being, technically. Yet, for me, I just kept thinking if I hadn't ended up in the human world, trapped in the form of a dog, I might have never met Dorothy at all. I might be alone or running with some pack of Oz's beast men. I may have never met Leon and experienced the thrill of the hunt, and I wouldn't have the heart and warmth that calmed her soul.

I might never know what it's like to love a girl like Dorothy.

So I was grateful for what Eloise had done. If she'd tortured me or abused me, I didn't remember and didn't want to. There was no value in recalling those memories now that I was happy and content. All that could come of it was pain and regret.

But… for the sake of breaking everyone else's curses, I forged on with the team with the intent of putting an end to the last witch, even if I didn't know if I wanted my own curse reversed. I could only hope that was a choice I would get to make.

The brick road leading north was colored in a purple so dark, it swallowed any light that touched it. The landscape itself wasn't far off of what I recalled of Kansas. Open plains, big fields, and the occasional rift or rolling hill to break up the monotony of it all. I didn't mind it, to be honest. Maybe some part of my soul sensed it was familiar.

I walked quietly behind my companions, unable to offer any insights into what to expect. I felt useless. All of the others had known their witch's intimately, while I couldn't even remember what my witch looked like. I was a foreign mind in a foreign body in a foreign place here to challenge a foreign enemy. None of them knew any more than I did, beyond having been told the Northern witch was one of the so called "good" witches. Considering Sasha was a "good" witch, and she ate people, I couldn't understand where the claim had come from, unless the witches had run some sort of PR campaign. That was the kind of strangeness I'd only expect in a place like Oz.

Dorothy fell back to match my step. She looked at me with concern. "Is any of this jogging your memory, Tobias?"

"Not remotely." I frowned. "If Leon wasn't convinced I've been cursed by a witch, I still don't know that I would believe it."

"Well, whatever happens, you've got me now. As long as you don't forget that, I think we'll be just fine." A melancholy smile graced her lips, while she interlaced our fingers and swung our hands with her step. I wondered if Dorothy had some of the same worries I did. I was content with my life now, regardless of my past, and I wasn't interested in how green the grass could have been on the other side.

We were only doing this to get the last magical object and for nothing more. I didn't want to put any doubts in her head, though. I'd talk to Dorothy about it further once we returned victorious.

CHAPTER 48

DOROTHY

Tobias looked so conflicted. He was the type of person who had his heart so unabashedly displayed on his sleeve, that I would have to be blind or a total narcissist to not notice his discomfort. I understood where it came from after all, since I had a feeling I was thinking something very similar.

If Tobias really was a shifter who had his memory erased, would he be the same person when he got it back? Or would he want to go back to whatever life was stolen from him?

Selfishly, I didn't want to risk losing him, but as his friend, I would be there for him every step of the way, even if it meant handing him off to another woman, to children—whatever that life entailed. The thought made me sad, and I was trying not to think on it for the greater good.

We shuffled along a nice enough road of the deepest violet, and I distracted myself with the view of the beautiful spring flowers scattered about the fields. It brought me back to when I was a child and used to get so excited about spring. I would wake up every morning with the sun just to see how many new wild flowers had bloomed, and I would spend hours picking the perfect bouquet or tying together the stems to make myself a flower crown. Then, when the late summer months started to turn the grasses brown again, I would sob and sob as the last petals disappeared, and the beauty went into hibernation for the year.

In some ways, I could relate to those flowers. When life was good and full of sunshine, I was vibrant and excited and full of life. I laughed freely and felt the whole world could be mine. But when the winter settled, and the light and warmth was blocked by the darkest clouds, there was often nothing I could do to force a smile. Part of what had enticed me to move to sunny Los Angeles was to escape those sad, sad winters, but little did I know that eternal sunshine casted its own shadows, and some were far darker than any rain cloud or snow storm.

I was doing better now, right? My new heels clacked on the brick, and I stared at the cloudless sky. A breeze swept across the road, catching my hair and my skirt in its gentle flow. Oz was changing who I was, to some extent, but in others, I was simply fitting in. I'd found my place among the dysfunctional and abused, but none of us were truly coming out better at the end of this journey. We were just feeling more heard and less like outcasts.

Maybe that *was* a form of healing. Or maybe it was just a rebrand of our trauma.

I'd come here a sad and broken girl, and I was going to leave a murderer after all. A lonely murderer, considering I couldn't imagine someone like Crowe or Talos would be coming with me back to Kansas. What value would they find in my old, normal, ordinary, boring life?

Hell, I didn't even know if I found value in it anymore.

"This road is just as long as the others, but it feels so much shorter and easier when it's this flat." Leon said casually over his shoulder.

I nodded, appreciating the reprieve from my own dark thoughts. "The nice weather helps, too." I lifted my chin and closed my eyes to savor another comfortable flutter of wind caressing my face. Small talk on a big day. The one time I didn't mind just chatting about the weather. After the heat of the desert, it was a welcome change.

We walked on for ages, while the castle in the distance got ever closer. Our nights were calm, and our days were like a pleasant stroll. There were no chimera's coming to kidnap us and no spiders threatening to eat us. It was almost eerie in the emptiness of it all, if I was being honest. The occasional village we'd pass had been little more than ghost towns, with abandoned houses and empty yet pristine store fronts. No one and nothing appeared to live in the North, and our passage was easy and safe. It was *so* pleasant that I began to wonder if this nice witch of the north really might be exactly that.

On the other side of an uneventful journey through the northern prairies, the landscape started to sparkle. It was subtle at first, with glimpses of a crystalline shine off in the tall grasses, but then the crystals started to multiply. The grass, the flowers, the weeds—eventually the entire field was made of unbending glass that chimed and clinked when the gusts hit their stems together. A distorted image of our passing was reflected in every blade and petal. While beautiful in its own way, something about that ambiance of chimes and whistling wind made me uneasy. There were no bird songs or chirps of insects. Only the music of complete and utter solitude in a strange place.

I tried to shake it off as we at last reached the kingdom on the other side.

It was a castle that could have been taken from any fairytale, with its tall lavender towers built from smooth stone. White accents added a softness to the fortified walls, while glass and crystals sparkled in the sunlight, and the soft song of wind chimes tinkled in the breeze. It was the kind of place that Cinderella fell in love with before a prince swept her off her feet.

"This is it." Crowe said upon stepping up beside me. He placed a hand on the small of my back, and his eyes drifted down to my red heels. "The last castle with the last witch. Are you ready for this, Dorothy?"

I chewed my lip at the question. My head said no—I could never be *ready* to take a life, but my body almost craved it. If it was side effect of the magic shoes on my feet, or genuine corruption reaching my soul, I truly couldn't say. "If I'm not, can we go home?" I smirked back at him with my tongue in my cheek.

"Sure." Crowe shrugged. "Rip her heart out and steal her enchanted object, and we can go wherever you want." My expression flattened, and Crowe responded with a pat on the back and a chuckle. "Try keeping your eyes open as you kill the witch this time. You might find you enjoy it more when you have the full visual."

Crowe walked ahead, and I tried not to think about the fact that the last time I killed someone, it literally triggered a full body orgasm. Or the fact that it made me so horny, I was *begging* him for his dick. There were a lot of things happening here that I probably shouldn't think on too hard.

So, so many things…

When we arrived at the gate, a wide moat and a towering drawbridge stood between us at the entrance. I pursed my lips at the realization that this was the first time we had to actually figure out how to get into the castle. All of the other times started out nice and easy with kidnappings and dungeons. I suddenly lamented not having another unoriginal, blatantly evil witch to count on.

"So how do we get in?" I frowned. "Can we just knock or something?"

Tobias took his place by my side, and we stared up at the massive door. Just then, the draw bridge started to creak. It slowly lowered, making a plume of dirt and glass shards when it hit the ground. A sweet scent of bergamot and lavender wafted from the entrance, and immediately it relaxed my nerves and drew me in. I looked to my companions, then I looked to the wide open door. With a shrug, I took my first steady step onto the violet wood.

"I guess that's an invite." I said.

Crowe followed, then Talos and Leon. Tobias stayed behind, staring at the castle for several moments. He heaved a heavy inhale, release a long exhale, then he took his first step.

Chapter 49

"TOTO"

TOBIAS

Nothing about this castle was familiar, yet I could feel its significance in my life in my very bones. Obscure and foreign furniture with deep purple upholstery sparked memories that were purely physical, radiating unexplainable tingles through my skin, while portraits of men and women on the walls had my stomach tight and queasy. Had I slept with these women? These men? Had I napped on these chairs or couches?

I knew nothing about who I was, and the deeper we trekked into this eerily empty, yet luxurious and plush, kingdom, the more I was certain I didn't want to know.

No one greeted us at any point. I couldn't even guess who had dropped the draw bridge. We were given free rein to explore, and yet, like we were being drawn in by magic, all of our steps followed a very specific path towards a very specific room.

We climbed the stairs of a foyer into a long corridor colored in a soft lilac. The rooms that lined the passage were all enclosed with locked doors of glass, trapping in a variety of prisoners. Each room had bowls of food and water in the corner, not far off the shelter Dorothy had rescued me from. Some held women in priceless gowns or men in fine suits—they appeared to be human, and the way they pounded on the doors as we passed only confirmed that fact for me. But still we walked, unable to break the pull of magic.

In the next set of rooms, I saw an eagle shift into a beast man as soon as he saw us. On the opposite side of the corridor was a snake who did the same. The next set had some munchkins who appeared to be shouting, but the glass had sound proofed their words away.

Every room held people of different races, species, shapes, and sizes—some young, some old. Some magical, some ordinary. My chest was tight and my stomach was sick just imagining what this witch might use her subjects for. If Grunhilda reanimated corpses, Gwen stitched people together, and Sasha feasted on flesh, what horror would the northern witch bring?

Dorothy's face was green, likely on the verge of vomiting, and I couldn't blame her. This explained the ghost towns along the way. Eloise must have been kidnapping people from every region for whatever sick kink she had. I placed a hand on her shoulder to try and calm her down.

The end of the hall housed a door of silver and white. Dorothy tried to open the door first, then Crowe, then Talos, then Leon. No amount of force made that knob budge. It had to have a key.

I stepped forward and placed my hand on the knob. With the slightest turn of my wrist, the door fell away, melting into the ground like it had been liquefied. I didn't want to speak my suspicions that my body had free passage to traverse this place. I think they'd all come to that conclusion without it needing to be said.

Our band of misfits entered the room that followed—a massive chamber made of pure glass and mirrors. Crystals dangled on the walls like wind chimes, and dark purple carpets reflected in every surface, visually shrinking an otherwise large space.

Sparkles of lavender fairy dust twirled through the air around us, then they collected in the center of the room. The particles formed together until they crafted a breathtaking beauty of the fairest complexion. Soft violet waves of hair framed an innocent and rounded face, and a lightweight dress of lace and tulle cascaded loosely down her body. A full figure of large breasts, pert nipples, and soft curves was clearly visible through the sheer fabric of her dress. If someone had told me she was an angel, I would have believed them. My heart was pounding just looking at her. Dorothy was the only woman I wanted, but my body was having a visceral reaction to this new figure, like I had been branded by her memory regardless of how badly I wanted to forget.

Eloise, the Good Witch of the North, shared an enchanting and twinkling smile with the room, then she spoke in her soft, endearing, and nurturing voice. "Welcome travelers, to my Kingdom of the North. I'm always pleased to make new acquaintances."

Dorothy stepped forward on her red heels, and she spoke as confidently as she could. "My name's Dorothy." She responded, that hint of confusion and awkwardness echoing in her tone. After the shock of the other witches, I was as uneasy as she was. None of us had so much as a guess as to what her game might be.

"What a beautiful name." She approached, and there was a tension across our party. Eloise' dress swayed with every shift of her hips. As was always the case, her eyes caught on Dorothy's red shoes. "To what do I owe the pleasure, Dorothy?"

My mate hesitated, and I couldn't blame her. The other witches felt innately sinister, but just because she feigned sweetness, that didn't mean Eloise wasn't simply a better liar.

Dorothy worked up her courage, then she spoke calmly. "We've come on a quest to gather the four enchanted objects of Oz, so I might free my friends of the curses they've suffered." Though the words were a threat when aimed at the others, I could tell by her breathing and heart rate that Dorothy was speaking with the vague hope that Eloise might just hand over the object for the sake of charity and good will.

"What curses have befallen your comrades?" She asked with concern. Genuine or fake, I couldn't say, but my instincts tilted towards fake.

Her eyes lifted to mine for only a second, and her eyelashes fluttered with in an unspoken flirtation. Another uncomfortably familiar gesture.

"Talos lost his tongue to Sasha of the South. He can no longer speak and his mask is permanently fixed on his face. Leon lost his Pride and his ability to shift into a Lion at the hands of Gwen in the West. Crowe lost his humanity and compassion to Grunhilda in the East..." Dorothy paused, while my nerves were radiating through my chest. I could have used my *own* emotional support animal right now, even if I couldn't quite explain why I felt so anxious.

"And him?" Eloise motioned towards me. "What has befallen the dark haired one?" A question that felt distinctly nefarious in nature—not simply because I knew she was my witch, but because there was the slightest hint of a dare to her tone. Pretending not to know who I was either meant she'd cursed so many that she didn't recall my face, or she was a liar and wanted an excuse to punish someone who spoke out against her.

Either way, this line of questioning was definitely putting Dorothy in danger, and I wouldn't let her speak for me now.

After all, the longer we lingered in the witch's presence, the more I *knew* she'd had me before. I could feel her in my bones and on my skin, and I could *taste* her now, lingering on my tongue like a taunt.

"Eloise, my Queen." I said with a bow. The words came from somewhere deep inside that I couldn't locate or identify. My lips moved without my control. "Just as I promised, I found my way back to you." *What?* I was a puppet, speaking thoughts I couldn't locate anywhere in my head. *Why couldn't I stop myself?* "I have brought you a woman whose soul is kind and true, so you may take it for your own, and live ever after in goodness and purity."

I jerked back, horrified by my own voice. Was *that* my task? Is that what I was to Eloise? Some sort of retriever? *Who better than a dog to fetch things for her...*

Her grin flashed an invisible wickedness—one that could be felt more than it could be seen. Dorothy stared at me with wide eyes, and I stared back with the same degree of confusion. I wanted to tell her this wasn't me speaking, but my mouth no longer seemed to be my own. No part of my body felt mine anymore. If she'd casted some sort of spell on me in our brief moments of eye contact, I was completely in its clutches now.

"Tobias, my prince, I knew you would come through for me." Eloise fixated on me, and that gaze wrapped a fist around my heart and my mind. "You've always been such a good hunter. It's incredible to see all of the fruits of your labor gathered together in a single room." Dorothy stepped back as a defense mechanism. I wanted— *needed* to step in and protect her, but try as I might, I couldn't go to her. I had to trust Leon and Crowe and Talos to take care of her for me. Eloise continued. "I adored that my cousins all had their own signatures for their art, but they were also so very closed off and selfish. They never shared their men with me, even as we'd worked so hard to pick them out. So to finally see their puppets in person— it's delightful. Each of my cousin's unique personalities are so prominently represented, it truly feels like my family's souls are going to live on forever through each of you." Her pleasant waxing sounded far more positive than the dark undertones actually were. "I was worried I might never see them again after this pretty little thing murdered them, after all, so it's truly such a relief."

"What is she talking about, Tobias?" Dorothy tried to look at me, but Eloise was quick to grab her face, and pull her attention back towards her.

"Yes, what the fuck is she talking about, Tobias?" Leon, however, had no problem looking my way.

I held up my hands, at a loss for words. "I… I don't know." I managed, finally in control of my speech and body again. Her fixation on Dorothy seemed to have set me free for the moment.

"Oh, of course. I'd nearly forgotten. I had to wipe your memory before I sent you to the human world, otherwise, you may not have found someone with a good enough soul." Eloise snapped her fingers, and my whole body was on fire. "Let me fix that for you, Love. I would hate for you to be trapped in that innocent little puppy mind forever."

My head pounded like a sledge hammer hitting stone, and I was on my knees, clenching my temples, and screaming despite myself.

I never saw her move, but I was hearing colors and seeing sounds amidst the migraine ripping through my brain, so I couldn't have identified when she'd come to crouch down beside me. I barely felt when she'd started

337

rubbing my shoulders through it all. "There, there, my prince. Don't fight it."

Don't fight it. I heard those same words in my own voice, as memories came flooding back to me. Memories of teeth, of claws, of hard blows to the stomach. Memories of brawls I'd fought in and blood I'd shed and prisoners I'd captured from their homes.

Memories of the day Eloise had claimed me as her prince and filled me with her magic.

Crowe. I saw his face in the human realm, tanned and full of life. He was a gentle farmer in a distant field, somewhere in Central California. He'd been kind enough to buy me a drink at the local bar. I'd roofied him, I'd taken him back to Oz, and I'd delivered him to Eloise, who'd prepared him for sale to her cousin, Grunhilda.

I watched, stone faced, as Grunhilda brought him home to groom her perfect sex toy. She'd laughed when she'd placed the rope around his neck that she'd later use to strangle him in the act. The man she'd kill and reanimate for her own sick fantasies.

Crowe's energy radiated through me, and I knew we were sharing that memory.

Talos was a child in a distant mountain tribe, and I'd bolstered the deal to sell him to Sasha. I'd delivered him personally to her bed chamber, where she had her last toy still bleeding and in pieces on the wall. I'd turned my back on the boy, not worried what happened to him. As long as my queen was pleased and her wallet was fat, I'd been good for her.

Talos' intensity hit me like a gut punch as that shared story flowed through both our minds.

Leon was the king of his Pride. A mighty Alpha, so tough and so dignified.

Exactly the kind of animal Gwen wanted for her collection.

The satisfaction of breaking him radiated through my chest, while I used my witch's magic to paralyze his entire Pride and capture them for sale. As a lowly dog, I'd gotten off on dominating a lion. I was so pleased with myself when I delivered the beasts to the western she-devil, wrapped in chains and heads hung low. I fucked Eloise senseless after, absolutely buzzing on that adrenaline.

The thrill of the hunt. That same surge that had convinced me to kiss Dorothy for the first time, and that I'd shared with Leon in the jungle. I was sharing it with him again now, through detestable memory.

Then I saw Dorothy, so downtrodden and sad. The actress who needed an animal for emotional support, because she couldn't bear the pain of her day to day anymore. The girl who chose me and brought me home, who I was evaluating unconsciously as a viable candidate to sell to my witch.

The girl I'd fallen in love with completely, despite the undercurrent of nefarious intent.

Dorothy was someone I'd chosen as a weak, easy to manipulate, and perfect target to feed to my most deserving and gracious queen.

I choked on that hurt and betrayal I'd committed as the reality was fed to my lady.

Then I watched myself, so desperate to be the man Dorothy deserved, falling away in the cloud of my old memories. Every moment of peace and happiness was washed from my mind in favor of memories of Eloise: the queen who chose me as her right hand. I wasn't a loyal protector at all. I was the man who kidnapped, sold, and brutalized the Cursed Puppets of Oz.

Reality snapped me into the present with a jolt, and I came back sobbing. Tears stung my eyes and poured down my cheeks, before they dripped from my chin to my open palms below. Every evil I'd committed—unknown creatures and souls and bodies I'd destroyed—projected against the walls of my brain in a vivid montage of cruelty.

"It's funny the way trauma works." Eloise began, not remotely interested in keeping facades anymore. "All of you traveled together for so long, killing my sweet cousins to get back your past selves, while not even recognizing the true evil who walked beside you the entire time. You've actively fought for and defended the same man who captured and sold you, and you got off on doing it." She stood and patted me on the head like the disappointment I was. "This is why we treat our little dolls as less than human. You're so easy to fool, you're hardly more than a toy in our play chests."

I kept my head down, not wanting to see the expressions on my companions' faces. She was right. I… I'd judged Crowe, I didn't trust Talos, I questioned Leon, and all the while, I was the one who deserved to be shunned. Not them.

I hated myself. I wasn't worthy to stand among these people, and I wasn't worthy of Dorothy. That was the most devastating realization of all.

I repeated that statement to infinity, echoing off every chamber within my mind. *I'm not worthy of Dorothy.*

Getting my memories back should have endeared me back to Eloise, who I now recalled so intensely I could practically feel the ice cold walls of her vagina wrapped around my dick, but the only thought my heart was pumping through me now was that I'd let Dorothy down.

"I'm sorry." I covered my face and sobbed into my palms. "I'm so, so sorry."

Chapter 50

"THE LION"

LEON

It was Tobias. He… he was the one who captured my Pride? Had I blocked it out? Had Eloise taken fragments of *my* memories, too? I recalled that there had been a dark warrior among the people who attacked us, but… it was *him*?

I couldn't believe it. I didn't want to believe it. I liked Tobias. We were shifters in arms. We shared each other's pain. We'd become like brothers. How… how could it have been him?

The man I met in that cave was fierce, strong, and dedicated. He had the heart of a loyal dog who would do anything to protect the people he cared about, and the soul of a gentle friend and lover who put other's pleasure before his own. *That* was Tobias. Not this.

I didn't understand where his superior strength had come from before, but now it made sense. He was Eloise of the North's pet, so of course he was strong—stronger than a king of lions even. A cursed puppet just like me. Still… True or not, I wouldn't let her turn me against him so easily.

We'd all done awful things for our witches, and if I judged him on his past service and ignored his present person, I'd be a hypocrite. Dorothy had given all of us a clean slate, despite our mistakes. She'd forgiven our sins, and as Tobias was the most important person in her life, I could do the same for him. So long as he was still the man I knew today and not the man he'd been forced to be under a witch's rule, we would be allies and friends until the very end.

I wouldn't be manipulated that easily.

Chapter 51

"THE TIN MAN"

TALOS

Eyes fixed on the witch and her puppet, my mind was glazed over by the realization. Though not in shock or anger, but in genuine sympathy for the guilt that Tobias must be feeling.

Eloise wanted me to blame him for having been sold to Sasha, but the reality was, it was my own mother who had accepted the deal. The middle man was hardly my biggest enemy.

And who was I to judge? For my witch, with full working knowledge and free will, I'd held down a man while a spider ate him alive, and I'd fucked a woman while Sasha removed her fingers with a knife, *and* I'd gotten off doing it. If I were to list my crimes and depravities for the room, I'd look like a worse monster than the witches themselves. We were all broken and vicious things in this twisted world of Oz. If anything, his sins were the softest of us all.

If I could have laughed out loud, I would have. If her strategy was to turn us against each other, she was going to be sorely disappointed.

CHAPTER 52

"THE SCARECROW"

CROWE

I practically snorted at the *'how do you like him now'* look on Eloise' face. As much as I wanted to feel again, if she thought I'd be angry to have been taken from a mundane life as a human and turned into an immortal demon from hell, she had no concept of how my brain worked.

Not surprising. The witches loved to call us stupid, when they couldn't even read their own subordinates. If anything, this revelation made me want to shake his hand and thank him for the eternal life.

There was a reason Hildy was the manipulator and Eloise was not. Pathetic. Comical even. And best of all, she was so convinced this reveal would paralyze us with division and hatred, that she hadn't bothered to prepare bindings or protection to keep herself safe.

If she was depending on Tobias to be her knight and protector right now—oh, I'd *delight* in that battle. If there was one, single person in this troupe who would never, ever even *dream* of betraying Dorothy, it was him.

I was the first to step forward. Eloise grinned at me smugly, practically wetting herself with the anticipation of satisfying fallout, and I returned a wide smile of razor sharp teeth.

< *"Ready?"* > Talos asked me through our connection. Dorothy glanced in his direction, looking mildly confused by what he might mean, but *I* wasn't

confused. I nodded to Talos, I tipped my chin to Leon, then I returned my gaze to Eloise.

"So sweet little Toto is a fuck puppet trafficker. Who'd have thought?" I kept my expression neutral as I approached our comrade who remained on his knees. He was still sobbing in shame. Sentimental bullshit that only proved how soft his heart actually was. "He must be the strongest of all of us then." Another step. Eloise placed a hand on her hip. That confidence was as unwavering as it was unearned.

"I'm much more picky about the company I keep than my cousins. Only the best and the most powerful are allowed to remain in my glass castle."

Oh, what a burn. I didn't roll my eyes only because I didn't want to ruin the surprise. He could have been stronger than me, but that didn't matter. I'd never be on the receiving end of his wrath.

"Is that right?" I looked down at Tobias, who continued to be absolutely pitiful. That wouldn't do. I needed all that alleged power, and I needed it *fucking angry*. "On your feet, Puppy Dog." I spoke harshly, implying anger, but mostly for my own amusement. I could play this role in the show one more time for one more witch.

Tobias stilled, and his sobbing quieted.

"Stand up and look me in the fucking eye." I demanded again.

Tobias drew his hands from his face slowly. His nose and eyes were red with his tears, while those past atrocities flooded his annoyingly soft heart. "Crowe... I'm so sorry." He muttered again.

"Stand. Up." I repeated. And this time he listened. He lifted his chin, and he looked me in the eye. His gaze darted to Leon, to Talos, back to me. He didn't look at Dorothy. He was likely much too scared to see her disappointment. "Tobias." I annunciated every syllable carefully. "You heard the woman. You're the most powerful person in the room." I swept my hands across the open space. "Why don't you fucking prove it."

Tobias' eyes widened. Eloise lit up, like I'd just challenged him to a fight to the death.

Idiot.

That lightning fast movement, where Tobias turned around, tensed his grip, and grabbed his witch by the neck with a violent swing, made me fucking cackle. He had her pinned to the wall faster than she knew what was happening, with his teeth bared in a growl, and his face possessed with pure, unbridled, hard-earned loathing.

"M-my prince, what are you doing?' She choked out through the vice grip on her throat. "I'm your witch— your queen. You can't—" He dug his fingers into her with unforgiving rage.

I knew he'd get my meaning. The witches mistook magical limiters that kept us from killing them with genuine weakness and simplicity, and time and again, that would be their undoing. Even if Dorothy had to be the one to drop the blade, it would be their victims who put their head into the guillotine.

I clapped a soft and delicate golf clap, then I turned to Dorothy. "Go on now. You know the drill. Kill that bitch."

Chapter 53

DOROTHY

"A-aren't you mad that he—"

"No." Crowe interrupted me with a raise of his eyebrows. "You've seen enough of Oz to know that light kidnapping barely registers as violent. I've done way worse shit than that, and I did it for fun." He punctuated with a chuckle. "Hell, I still do."

I thought they'd take it more personally, but Leon shrugged next. He walked over to the wall, where crystals dangled like rodeo fringe across the glass surface. He ran his hand along the surface, creating a piercing and chaotic song of chiming glass. "I was the one who failed my Pride, not him. Let's put an end to this nightmare once and for all, and we can start to rebuild again."

"Leon…" I clutched my hands to my heart, grateful that his bond with Tobias was true.

< *"The day a witch's crimes are enough to turn me against a comrade who stood with me despite my demons, is the day I'm not worthy of my immortal soul."* > Talos reaffirmed for all of them. < *"Kill her, Dorothy, so we can all start to heal."* >

I nodded to all three of them, then I took my first step towards Tobias and Eloise. "Tobias." I said softly. He looked back at me and tipped his chin.

"Dorothy." The way he said my name sent chills down my spine. I pulled Sasha's knife from my pack, and Tobias manhandled Eloise into an arm lock. He held her from behind, and he kept his eyes on me. Strength and calm filled me, just as it always did when I was with him, and I took steady steps towards the fourth and final Witch of Oz.

"How can you forgive him so easily?" Eloise squirmed. They always thrashed about, like a fish on a hook. *Pathetic*, I thought. "He kidnapped you all! He sold you!" She screamed.

"The enemy of my enemy is my friend." Leon said.

"I actually like him better knowing he's not so pure and perfect." Crowe noted with a shrug.

< *"I've rolled with monsters long enough to recognize the difference."*> Talos added so casually through our bond.

As reassuring as their forgiveness was, I knew it was me who Tobias wanted to hear from most. I readied my blade, and I looked to my former emotional support dog, my best friend, and my lover.

"We've all made mistakes." I spoke boldly. "I'm nowhere near as pure and perfect as Tobias believes me to be, yet no matter how much I've messed up, how many bad choices I've made, he still stuck by my side, through thick and thin, always, *always* believing me to be worthy. If I were to walk away from a man who can only see the good in me, even when I've showed him my ugliest tears and my most shameful imperfections, who loves me so fiercely, he would risk his own goodness and turn into a killer to keep me safe, just because he'd once given himself to someone evil, that's the only thing that would truly make me a failure."

"Dorothy…" I saw the tears of relief in his eyes, and I was glad I could put them there.

I drew back my knife, and I plunged it straight into her heart without another second to let her bargain. Blood splashed back, staining my dress and spattering all over my face. "This is for Tobias." I pulled back again, and I slammed in even harder. More crimson drenched me. "This is for Leon." Another stab. "For Talos." One more. "And for Crowe. This is for everything you put them through."

Eloise choked and gurgled. I watched the light rapidly fading from her eyes, and if I was being honest, *I liked it.*

Not enough.

Crowe reached down and took my hand. He lifted my fist back to eye level, then he whispered in my ear. "Once more, Dorothy. You're missing the most important strike of all." He squeezed my hand gently. "This one is for *you.*"

I looked at him wide eyed, and my whole heart warmed at the notion. *For me? Yes. This is for me.* Not to go back to Kansas or find my old life, nor to become a movie star or get revenge. It was for me to put an end to everyone's pain and to stand up for myself for once. It was succeeding at something and being the hero of my story instead of the victim. It was for every dream and hope I'd ever had that had been trampled by cynics and fucking assholes.

I slammed the blade in again, again, again, again, AGAIN. I was covered in her blood, and I didn't remotely fucking care.

"This is for telling me I was nothing when I poured my heart and soul into every word of the performance. This is for making me the quirky best friend because I wasn't hot enough to be the main character. This is for every rejection, every *'not good enough,'* every *'not pretty enough,'* not skinny enough, not smart enough or strong enough or talented enough. Every time I got cheated on, cast aside, and forgotten by the people who centered my whole world." I don't know when I started crying. I could barely discern the difference between my tears and the blood pouring down my cheeks. "This is for every goddamn time I wasn't *enough*."

I'm enough. I repeated for myself, while I was ugly crying in the middle of the room. Silly affirmations that felt so important now. "I won't ever let someone tell me how to feel again—not about my friends, my lovers, my dreams, or myself."

The witch started to shrivel in Tobias' arms, long dead from the repeated stabbing. The blood started draining down to my shoes, and I could feel my heels getting taller. But my eyes were too blurred by my frustrations to see them darken in color again. I drew back my hand for another swing, and someone caught me mid-air.

"Enough." Tobias said, sending that word back to me. "Enough, Dorothy." He held my face between his hands and he pressed his lips to mine, not caring that we both tasted of the vague, cold, metallic flavor of death. "You're okay." I dropped the knife, and I closed my eyes. Then I gave myself completely to Tobias.

He pulled away only long enough to drop a fine necklace over my head. The purple gemstones sparkled. The Northern Witch's magical artifact. "I'm sorry, Dorothy. It's my fault that you're here. You never would have had to endure this if not for me." He kept kissing me. Kept apologizing.

I wrapped my arms around his neck and didn't let him pull away again.

"No." I shook my head, then I nibbled at his lower lip. "You're the reason I never have to feel like a failure again."

He hugged me tight, and my soul felt lighter. We stayed for moments that could have been hours as my friends coaxed me down from that violent high.

When we started the long journey back to the Emerald City, I was still processing everything that had happened, from my life before Oz, to my arrival in the East, to my journey to all four corners.

It was hard to wrap my head around the fact that the most unpredictable, terrifying, and ruthless place I'd ever existed was where I found the most calm from the anxiety and depression and pain that used to taint my everyday life.

The only fear I held now was knowing, once we made it back to the Wizard, I was going to have to go home.

The Wonderful Wizard of Oz

Chapter 54

DOROTHY

We returned to the Emerald City and the attendants eagerly accepted us into the castle. Just like every other time, we were given nice rooms, warm showers, and fine clothing. I stared at the little green slip of an outfit—the ridiculous dress that was more lingerie than day wear—and I threw it back on the dresser to put on my own clothes. Red and green didn't go together as it was, and I wasn't going to perform for anyone who didn't deserve my respect anymore. The Wizard was going to receive the real and true Dorothy, and if that was a problem, we could take our magic trophies and go.

On the day of our audience, I walked proudly into the green throne room, my misfit group of demons at my back, and I waited for the holographic wizard to appear.

"I see you've defeated all four witches and returned with all four artifacts." The voice boomed, while a fireball manifested on the throne. "It is now that I can grant your wishes, fine travelers. Each of you: step forward, and tell me what you desire."

I nodded to my companions, feeling so proud to have gotten them this far. I hadn't cowered and given up when they needed me, and now they would all get their ultimate reward.

Leon stepped forward first. "I've lost my ability to tap into my beast form. I want my inner lion back."

"Take your witch's artifact in hand, and it shall be done." The flame crackled.

I absolutely did not smirk as I handed Leon Gwen's old pegging dildo, and he absolutely did not shake his head at my immaturity. He gripped it firmly at the base, while it flopped around in his hand.

"Tap it three times, and chant the line 'There's no courage like a lion's.'" The Wizard insisted.

I tried not to snicker as Leon tapped on the silicone cock, while repeating the phrase "There's no courage like a lion's" three times.

The sex toy started to vanish in pearls of light. The magic swirled around him, and his whole body glowed blue. The sparkles absorbed into the Wizard's holographic flame, and with one final blinding flash of light, Leon was gone, and a lion took his place. He checked his paws, one at a time. He sniffed them. He licked them. He ran around the room, feeling his muscles flex and move.

Then he shifted back into the man I knew with a shit eating grin on his face. "Thank you, Wizard." Leon could barely speak through his overjoyed tears. "Thank you, Dorothy." My lion whisked me up into his arms and squeezed me tight with his newly returned strength. He was warm and bursting with joy and vigor, and I loved seeing him like that. His happiness was the kind that radiated into anyone who saw it, and I took in as much as he'd let me.

Talos stepped forward next. I handed him Sasha's knife, and he looked to the Wizard for his spell.

< *"I'd like to be able to speak again. I want to be free of this mask and restore my tongue."*> I heard him say, and the Wizard heard him, too.

"It shall be done. Tap your knife three times and repeat the phrase 'There's no power like voice.'"

Talos nodded, then he repeated in his mind:
< *"There's no power like voice."*>

Under an orange surge, he got his wish. The unbreakable clasps on his mask fell apart, revealing the half of his face that I'd never seen in our entire time together. I saw the strong jaw, the full lips lined in piercings, and the soft smile on Talos' gentle expression. Pure relief sparkled in those silver eyes, and tears welled up in their corners. He licked his lips, playing with the ring piercing on the bottom, before he returned his tongue to his mouth. Then he asked through the strain of a neglected voice box: "Can you all hear me?" The sound was familiar, yet completely different when projected aloud for the first time. "I almost forgot what having a tongue felt like." He laughed. Such a blissful sound. I liked his laugh.

He had me in his hands in no time, and he hoisted me into the air and spun me around. My skirt flowed in the small whirlwind he created, and that elation flowed freely into my heart.

Before he put me down, he kissed me hard, letting me feel the tongue he'd lost first hand. I was crying happy tears for both of my freed companions.

Tobias took the next turn, and I gave him Eloise's necklace. "I want my beast form returned," he said. No talk of going home or re-wiping his memories. I respected the fact that he wouldn't turn a blind eye to his mistakes. Instead, he chose to stand tall, own who he was, and be better going forward.

Again the Wizard's fireball blazed, and again he offered a spell. "An easy task. Tap the gemstone on the necklace three times, and chant the phrase 'There's no love like a dog's,'"

Without hesitation, Tobias obliged. He tapped that gemstone, just as commanded, and thrice he spoke the words, "There's no love like a dog's."

His purple glow dispersed in a small explosion of light and magic, and when it faded into the fireball, I had my little Scotty dog back in my arms, licking my face, wagging his tail, and whining happily.

Then in a lightning fast shift, I was in Tobias' arms, and he was squeezing me tight, claiming my face with his tongue in a completely different way.

Once the thrill of it all started to die down, Crowe looked at me, and I looked at him. We stared at each other with the *'you go first'* look, as we both struggled with what we truly wished for.

Did Crowe really want his emotions back? Was it selfish and unfair to say I liked the vicious scarecrow I'd gotten to know over all these months? In all his emotional unavailability and threats, I felt like he was special as he was. We had bonded and come to understand each other in all of our broken, unacceptable traits, and I loved him for it. How much would he change once he became a normal man again? Would I even recognize him anymore?

Unfair thoughts. Leon, Tobias, and Talos had all had physical wishes, and I didn't bat an eye at the idea of them ending their curses, but I expected Crowe to remain an emotionless monster just because of the misguided idea that we were similar in his current state.

I wanted to relate to him so badly, I was willing to let him suffer so he'd be as broken as me? No. He deserved happiness just like everyone else, even if that meant we may no longer be compatible.

When he stepped forward, I wouldn't say a word to stop him.

Beside that, the other conflict swirling in my gut was 'what am *I* going to wish for'? To go home? Was that random homestead in an open prairie really my home at all? I'd found my strength here in Oz in all its wildness, and maybe, just maybe, I loved that too.

Plus, if I did leave, what would become of Leon, Tobias, Crowe, and Talos? Would they just go their separate ways? Would they all rule their witch's old castles, or find new wives or lovers? Who would they talk to, who would be their confidante and friend, and who would they find pleasure in?

Surely they would move on from me. Even if I stayed, with my mortal body, they'd have to forget me eventually. Was it selfish to not want to even imagine such a thing? Was it fair to expect an immortal zombie, a man with bones of tin, a lion shifter, and a dog shifter to be bound to an ordinary, unspectacular human?

No… I couldn't back out now. I had to go back home, just like Crowe deserved his emotions again, Leon deserved to build a new Pride, Tobias deserved to figure out who he was amongst his own kind, and Talos deserved to speak and make friends, regardless of how I felt about them. Their whole lives didn't have to center me, even if I couldn't imagine my life not centering them anymore.

"Two shoes mean two wishes." The Wizard said. "Step forward, young Dorothy, and tell me what you truly desire."

I stepped forward on my three inch ruby red heels. I looked over my shoulder at Crowe, whose unexplained frown had me questioning everything I was about to do. I tipped my head to ask him to stand beside me so we could make this wish together.

"You should go first. I can't wish to return home before you've all gotten what you fought for." I spoke inaudibly to the rest of the room, but Crowe heard me. He always did.

He laced his fingers between mine and he pierced my soul with those dark eyes of demonic red. "What I fought for?" He was every bit as quiet. "Think back, my devil princess—what *did* I spend all these months fighting for?"

I swallowed as my heartbeat reached my ears. There were a lot of possibilities that I wanted to be the right answer, but Crowe had no emotions or compassion in his soul, so they were all unfair and absurd. "Your humanity?" I attempted the right answer.

He bore a hint of his sharp smile, and gave my hand a little squeeze. "Not at all." A chuckle. "I could have taken your shoes at any time if that was all I wanted. Why would I have stuck around just to help a group of strangers if I had no reason to stay?"

I was taken aback by that. I chewed my lip, and he squeezed my palm again.

"My wish was never to have my soul back. I simply wanted to end the rule of vicious tyrants."

Surprise hit me, only for a second, then I settled into a growing confidence. Those were exactly the words I needed to hear to commit to what I'd really wanted since we returned to this castle.

I nodded with shared understanding, then I faced the ruler of Oz.

"Dear Wizard." I began with a curtsey. "I thought long and hard on this, and I finally understand exactly what I want."

The little fireball surged in anticipation.

I inhaled deeply. *Tap the shoes together and chant a phrase that goes like, 'there's no blank like blank,'* I told myself. It was simple enough to replicate without needing to ask the wizard for my own set of words. For Crowe, it might have been something like 'there's no joy like compassion,' and for me, a simple 'there's no place like home.' It was obvious, and it was easy, and... *I hope I understood Crowe right, because I'm about to take his one wish from him.*

"Over the long journey through these lands, it's become obvious that this is where I was always supposed to be. Because of that, I've decided that I want this place for my home." Maybe being surrounded by psychopaths had made me one myself, because I wasn't going to take no for an answer anymore. "More than that, I've decided I want *this castle* to be my own."

"What?" The voice boomed at my audacity, but I wouldn't be intimidated.

"It's obvious to me now that you could have reversed these curses at any time once we had the objects, yet you did nothing until we limped back, bathed in blood, and thoroughly traumatized. Because you needed us to do the dirty work for you. You let the witches run free, terrorizing the land, and yet you still did nothing, year after year, because you weren't strong enough to stand up to them."

"You know not of what you speak." The voice growled, but I shook my head, undeterred.

"Then correct me!" I shouted back. I could feel everyone's eyes on me. I could feel Crowe's hand in mine, radiating with the strength I needed. I had to take this gamble. For all of them.

When the Wizard only fumed in response, not providing even the lamest of excuses, I knew I was right, so I kept on the offensive. "And the best part of all is, it was still the *witch's* power that we've drawn upon here today. It was their objects that banished our curses, while you're taking all the credit like you're some great and mighty magician. But you're not, are you? If you're so fucking strong, show me! Make me shut up."

Nothing. Still nothing. I fucking knew it.

I had the shoes, so *I* had the power. "That's what I thought." I laughed. "I'm not going to go back to Kansas and leave my friends here under the rule of a man who never made any effort to protect them. A man so cowardly, he can't even show his fucking face to the people he'd throw into danger, even as we've done everything you asked."

"Dorothy." Tobias uttered, surprised but not alarmed.

Leon nodded to me with a smirk.

Talos covered his laugh with his hand, perhaps not ready to share that much emotion openly, even if he was still supporting me silently.

Crowe simply studied me with the most quiet and gentle and honest smile. He said nothing, not in protest or support. He stood by my side as I stood up for myself for once—for all of us.

The Wizard was a pompous ruler in a castle built purely for his ego anyway, and I was sick of men like that being in charge. If there was one single thing I wanted to leave behind, it was this kind of bullshit, and that was what I could grant them. If I had to return to Kansas, at least they wouldn't have to be subject to a new evil in a different cloak.

The blaze ignited to ten times its size when I tapped those shoes together for the first time in pure provocation.

"There's no place like Oz." I said.

"Stop this." The Wizard shouted again. "You don't understand what you're doing."

I wanted to laugh at the irony of his panic. Confirmation that he couldn't stop a damn thing. I'd been thrown out of this castle so many times now, I wasn't about to give him dignity he'd never offered me.

Another tap. "There's no place like Oz."

"Wait!" There was no heat radiating from that hologram. He didn't really exist here at all. I was about to tap my shoes together the third time, when a voice of normal pitch and volume sounded from behind the royal chair. "Don't you tap those shoes again!"

The fireball vanished, and in its place was a small, angry, ordinary blond haired man with hate in his eyes scrambling into view. He had plastic looking hair, high cheek bones, and a wizard robe ripped out of dungeons and dragons. He looked like a Hollywood reject—which I knew all too well, being one myself—and he whined like a child.

"Wait, who are you?" I was laughing through my disbelief.

"I'm the Wizard of Oz, who the fuck do you think I am." He hissed. *Livid.* "Stupid bitch. Do you have any fucking clue what you're doing?" He screeched. "When my balloon hauled me to Oz, this place was a bigger shit hole than my trailer in Nebraska. The beast men terrorized the land, the monsters roamed free, the munchkins governed their miserable little villages. They made me ruler because they thought my falling from the sky made me a Wizard," *sounds consistent,* "but you have no idea the hard calls I've had to make figuring out how to fulfill that role. Without the witches, this whole continent would have crumbled into disorder. Sick as they may have been, they kept their regions in line. They paid their taxes, and they made the Emerald City flourish."

I shifted on the red shoes still on my feet. Nebraska? *No wonder he knew Kansas. I guess I wasn't the only one who had accidentally stepped through a storm portal to Oz.*

"You've done enough by eliminating the witches. You saved the world. Be proud. Good fucking job." He clapped mockingly. "But Oz is mine, and it's time for you to go home to Kansas, Dorothy."

Crowe took the initiative, stepping forward into the center of the room with unrelenting confidence.

"No, I think she has a point, Wizard. You've done a shit job of keeping us safe and happy. If it's so hard to rule, then why would you want to when there's a perfectly strong candidate to replace you right here." He spoke strong and firm. Crowe rolled his shoulders, and stretched his lips into a grin. "She killed the witches that you were too afraid to keep in check, and as such, it's about time you stepped down. We can use the last wish to send you back to wherever the fuck Nebraska is. Oz belongs to my devil princess now."

His words and support warmed my whole heart. I let him talk for me now, because I knew he understood what I wanted, and I needed to hear his voice, loud and clear, saying that he wanted that too. Deep in *his* soul, he reflected *my* soul, and I trusted any words he shared.

The whole throne room went dark, and the building started to shake. "How dare you. After I've extended my magic to help you." The Wizard bellowed. *His magic? Bullshit.* "I am the great and powerful Wizard of Oz. You can't—"

"Can't what?" The lights returned once more to reveal Crowe dragging the Wizard down the stairs by his ankle. "Go on. Tell me more about what I can't do." He threw the man onto the floor at my feet, and he immediately scrambled to make distance. But Crowe was having none of it. He placed a foot on his chest, and the Wizard stilled. "How old are you, Wizard? A few decades? All that talk of working with the witches, yet you never bartered for real immortality?"

He gasped in terror. "How did you know—"

"That you were a weak fucking mortal with a barely-enchanted wizard's robe?" Crowe rolled his eyes. "What kind of monsters do you think you're dealing with? You think I can't sense body heat in a room full of fake lights and holograms? Maybe you've been locked in your little room too long if you don't even know how the denizens of Oz work. Here *I'm* just impressed that you figured out how to use the witch's magical artifacts at all, so we could have whatever we wanted without any effort from you, while still appearing like you had a hand in it." Crowe narrowed his gaze. "And when those artifacts were caught in your magic traps and absorbed into your stupid cloak, you would have the power of all four witches and finally be worth a damn. What a fucking hero."

The Wizard backpedalled ten miles, as he threw up his hands in desperate bargaining. "Wait, wait, please— hear me out. You're right, okay? I was placed here by the witches, because I wasn't powerful enough to stand against them. I may not have real magic, but it was my command that inspired you to defeat them. I'm a good ruler to the people, so please—"

His story changed, but I couldn't help but think that was much more honest than whatever treaty he was pretending he'd formed. Being little more than a powerless, unchallenging figurehead sounded more accurate than him taking real charge.

"Well, then please grant me my wish, great ruler." Crowe ground his heel into the Wizard's chest. "Leave the coat, and give us the castle."

"I... I can't. I won't." The Wizard's robe started to glow green. Then his previously sympathetic expression warped into a snarl. "I have the magic of the witch's items you've used thus far. I may not have them all, but you aren't strong enough to take this from me anymore."

He threw a small blast of plasma, trying to throw Crowe into a wall, but the impact did nothing. It was like someone had thrown a sock at the scarecrow.

"That's it? That's your power combined with three of Oz's witches?" Crowe continued to mock him, while the display gave me a new understanding of my own magic object. The shoes that absorbed the blood and magic of every witch I killed.

"Why didn't that work?" He whined in panic. Weak as he was, that attack killed any sympathy I may have had. He was as bad as the rest of them, and just as much a burden to Oz as the witches themselves.

Crowe was right. I did want this castle, and I did want power for once. Why should I have to choose to go home for good at the expense of my friends, when I could have everything I wanted right now? This unhelpful, sleazy wizard was the only one standing in my way.

So I walked over, to my trusted friend, who kept the wizard pinned on the floor, and to the song of begging and horror, I stomped down on the Wizard's neck and dug in my sharp red heel until I felt the tile on the other side of flesh.

"Enough." I said. The mortal wizard had no further words for me.

I yanked my red shoe from his worthless body, where his blood drew into the heel until I was comfortably mounted atop four inch stilettos of the darkest crimson.

I didn't flinch as he bled at my feet. Death had taken on a new meaning for me now. My whole body surged as his magic drew into me. I placed my foot on the ground, and the new height put me in a satisfying position, towering over the Wizard of fucking Oz.

"I'm your Wizard now." I said with a nod to each of my men. And for the first time, I knew that was the real wish that I'd wanted to have. Finally, I was in control. I was the person in power who everyone would have to listen to.

I was the Queen of Oz, and my men, who had been abused and battered and beaten down, would never have to suffer again.

Because that was what power was supposed to be. Tobias, Leon, Talos, and even Crowe had all showed me what real strength was. It was protecting those you love from anyone who might hurt them, and it was creating a safe and loving place for them to live in.

So long as I sat on this throne, that was exactly what Oz was going to be.

CHAPTER 55

DOROTHY

Oz was a bustling and beautiful place, and that was never more true than when the Wizard breathed his last breath, and everyone who had been under his false rule at last got to relax.

In the East, the munchkin's crops had at last begun to grow—no sorceress blood required. The death of the witches and the wizard had broken the curse that made the land infertile for edible plants, and with my agricultural know-how, it was easy to get them steered in the right direction on successful harvesting.

In the west, the beast men had slowly been replenishing their clans. Species who had once been in hiding had begun to emerge, while Gwen's chimeras were beginning to form new societies of their own. The Flying Monkeys and the remaining Kalidah were going to be permanent fixtures in Oz, but without a witch to command them for evil, they were a normal and peaceful people. The damage couldn't be undone, but what remained didn't have to be a nightmare.

I dared not venture to the south, but Talos assured me that order had been restored. While I didn't agree with the ways of his original tribe, it wasn't my place to dictate whether their beliefs were right or wrong, unless I was asked to intervene. He came from a land that coveted strength and brutality above all, and that was simply what the South would be.

In the North, we'd found that the thousands of rooms throughout Eloise' castle had all contained cells and cages for the various creatures she would buy and sell into various forms of slavery. Some were sold as pets, some for sex, some as servants or workers. The entire staff of the Emerald Castle were all little more than products the Wizard had purchased, and it felt good to set them free. The people returned to their homes, and the only staff I retained were those who chose to stay.

But best of all, at the end of the restructuring, the people of each sector started to mingle. Open trade meant new produce, new inventions, mixed colors, and cultural sharing, and it filled my heart to watch a people once so limited to their little green world opening their hearts and homes to blue shirts, yellow apples, or purple flowers. I was happy, and I hoped that the peace would prosper for years and years to come.

Though how many years I would be able to stand at the head of Oz, I couldn't say. I was in my late twenties now—not far off thirty—and as a human, I was likely only looking at 50 or 60 more years of life. It sounded impossibly long when I was in Los Angeles or Kansas, but now in Oz, it felt like the blink of an eye. I envied my companions who could live forever. Crowe and Talos would never die, and even Leon and Tobias had no actual time clock to their years. As it was explained to me, much like Oz's witches, beast men could live as long as they could survive, and the only way to end their lives was through murder or starvation.

When I aged and they were still young and beautiful, would they still love and want me? When my short life reached its end, and their eternal lives continued on without me, would they miss me? Replace me?

No, I couldn't think about things like that. Anxiety was such an unfair plague to happiness, it was important to focus on the *now* instead of the *someday* that was still so distant in the future. I didn't even know how the passage of time worked in Oz, after all. Many things about this place mirrored the real world, but did time? *Who knows?* I was still new here. I had time to learn it all.

Though that thought didn't bring me much calm, despite my wishes, and I found myself under an extra-long and extra hot shower, trying to calm my thoughts. I'd moved into the Wizard's old room—a massive yet comfortable bed chamber with a mattress that was more than double the size of a king bed, and a bath tub that was practically a swimming pool. Why the Wizard had needed such large things, I couldn't say, but… when you occasionally wanted to take a bath with five people, there were definite perks.

I turned off the water then started drying off with green towels soft as velvet. I pulled on a satin robe—a pink one that I'd had commissioned by a local seamstress learning about new types of non-green dye—and I returned to my room for some much needed rest.

The lights were off and the shades were drawn when I entered. I scanned the darkness suspiciously, knowing I'd not left it that way. I took an uneasy step towards the first torch, when a hand covered my mouth, and my arm was twisted behind my back to the point of pain. I attempted to scream, but it was lost in the muzzle of my assailant's heavy mitt.

I'd only been ruler of Oz for a few months now. I hadn't made enemies yet, had I? The witches were dead—did they have family? Was this an assassin? So many thoughts swirled through my mind, all of them bad.

I struggled until I was bent over the bed, wishing I could see who'd grabbed me. My attacker bent over me, pressed his chest to my back, then he whispered into my ear: "You're looking rather melancholy, Sorceress of Oz." Crowe said mockingly. My heart rate immediately began to slow, and my expression flattened. He'd taken to calling me the Sorceress of Oz as a teasing blend of my time with the munchkins, who once thought me magical, and for my new status at the head of the Emerald City. I didn't entirely hate it. "What worries are swimming around that silly little head of yours, sweet girl?"

His hand rounded the curve of my ass, dragging up my thin robe in the process. He kept his weight pinning me, while he caressed my rear.

"Have you ever considered knocking before attacking me in my own room, Crowe?" I snapped, only mildly, and somewhat dishonestly, annoyed.

"That sounds like a terrible strategy." He cocked an eyebrow, while still rubbing me with a massaging pressure. "Imagine if I knocked and announced myself before an assassination. Just tell everyone I'm coming and give them adequate time to fight back." He paused. "Actually, you have a point. That might be somewhat entertaining."

I drew my lips into a line. "Are you here to assassinate me then?"

"Perhaps." He pressed the firmness in his pants against me. "Impaling you would be my greatest pleasure." I jerked when he slipped a finger in my ass. "But I'll give you a chance to fight for your life first."

"You'd like that, wouldn't you?" I pressed back into him, taking his finger in deeper. "Or would you be too scared to hurt me?"

"Heh." Crowe forced a second finger in. I winced at his rough, dry entry. "The best part of having no conscience is getting to revel in those selfish, cruel pleasures." He withdrew his fingers, then he pulled back and flipped me over on the bed. With a gentle kneading, he began working his palms down my shins, before he retrieved my red shoes from my bedside. He slipped a high heel onto my right foot, then he massaged my left shin before placing the other on my left foot. "The real question is: Are *you* afraid of me hurting you?"

The way that question hit me must have reflected prominently in my eyes, because Crowe frowned as he looked down at me from between my legs. An expression I'd never seen from him when he had me in bed and on full display.

"Kind of." I said, near inaudibly, before I bit my lip to prevent any further words from slipping out.

"Really?" Crowe seemed genuinely hurt by that, and I couldn't wrap my head around how that was possible. He had never asked me to return his emotions. He seemed content with whatever it was he could already feel, and he didn't want to give up who he was in favor of a past self that he didn't even know.

I understood his reasoning. There was no guarantee that returning to the past would result in happiness, though I still felt guilty he'd not gotten anything from our trials. Everyone else got their wishes, but Crowe remained the same—just as broken and just as detached. Still, no matter how heartless he was when he stood up against those who threatened me, these moments where his mask slipped often made me wonder if he *did* have more feelings than he knew.

"It's hard to explain." I looked away, only to have Crowe reach down and grab my chin. He forced my eyes back on his.

"Try me."

I bit my lip again, then I decided to just come out with it. Crowe had always been a good confidante. Whether he understood my struggles or not, he always listened and he never judged. A strangely nice side effect of not caring, I suppose. "You're immortal, Crowe. Pain means nothing to you because you can't be permanently hurt. You can't die or suffer lifelong injuries. Whereas I—" I stopped myself, not wanting to get too emotional in front of him.

"Whereas you're a fragile human who can be extinguished with the slightest twist of the wrist." He raised an eyebrow. One side of his lips upticked. "Is that what you think, sweet girl?" With a sudden jerk, Crowe tugged me closer until my bare pussy hit the front of his jeans. "Well, I guess I'll have to fix that for you."

"What?"

He started undoing his belt. "You heard me." That smugness on his face was more worrying than I realized. He gripped my ankles again, and he placed a kiss on the tops of each of my feet before he tugged free the tie on my robe. The satin slid off my body, leaving me completely vulnerable and exposed. But I trusted Crowe, and he was a good distraction. "Let me fix that little mortality problem for you."

"What do you mean—" His hand was on my throat, stealing my ability to speak. He tightened his grip as he entered me, rough, hard, and sudden. He plunged in deeply, and my body was forced to compensate faster than it knew how.

Crowe stayed still inside me as he loosened his hold on my neck. He slowly and languidly drew that hand down to my chest, over my breast, down my abdomen, my naval, and settling the heel of his hand on my mound. He held me there, not moving in the slightest. "To think I've always thought you so very sweet, when you are so very, very dirty." He began tracing lines up and down with the backs of his nails. He'd reach my naval, then drifted back down and back up, teasing the sensitive skin with the lightest feather touch. "Do you want me to fill you, Dorothy?" He drew out then slid back in, slow and agonizing and perfect. "Fill you with my come until it's dripping out of you, then shove it back in until you're mine forever?"

I swallowed while maintaining eye contact. His red, demonic irises burned into me, and my body heated at the implication. I didn't think he could get me pregnant. None of these men were human—not anymore at least—yet, with the way he spoke, all I could imagine was him possessing me through that connection.

His forever.

But forever was such a short time for me.

He kept dancing that soft touch across my lower abdomen, while he continued to rest inside me. He was hard as all hell, and I could feel the little twitches as he resisted his own urges to fuck me properly, but he didn't give in.

So I wrapped my legs around his waist, and I locked my ruby red heels behind him. I wordlessly held his gaze, as I clenched on him. His eyes popped just slightly when I did it again. Teasing kegels. I tightened again, and I smirked at the way he couldn't keep a straight face no matter how much of a soulless puppet he thought he was.

"Go on then. Make me yours."

"Fuck, Dorothy." He shook his head, but I was reveling in how I could effortlessly affect him. "You truly are the Devil's princess."

"The Devil's queen." I corrected and I clenched again. "And you're my Devil."

"The Devil's queen." He repeated with a dark laugh. Then he grabbed my hips, withdrew to the tip, and slammed back into me. "You have no idea what that truly means, sweet girl, but I'll be happy to show you."

I squeezed my thighs on his waist, and he held nothing back. It was the kind of hard fuck that made you forget your problems and all the day's worries.

"Crowe—" I damn near sobbed his name when he started to vary his rhythm. The way his cock filled me, he hit every spot I wanted, and he did it with such exquisite precision.

He dug his nails into me as he got closer. "Tell me how much you want it, Dorothy." His voice was raspy and rough. "Tell me you want me to fill you."

"I want it all." I moaned shamelessly for him. "Give me all of you, Crowe."

A cruel smile danced on his lips and his grip shifted to my thighs with a bruising strength. I couldn't concentrate enough to clench on him anymore, but it felt so fucking good, I didn't care what his intentions might be. He could fuck me, fill me, impregnate me, call me his—as long as he didn't pull out. I'd live on this cock forever if he'd let me.

I threw my hands over my head, giving him a perfect view of the way his thrusts rippled through me, and that only goaded him further.

My bed suddenly dipped under weight. A strong, rough hand lifted my chin, and Talos pressed his lips onto mine. He slipped me his tongue, and the ball piercing on its tip grazed my taste buds. I reveled in the flavor and feel of his freedom. < *"So much noise. Do you need help keeping her mouth occupied, Scarecrow?"* >

Though he could speak in earnest now, Talos still exercised his silent channel whenever he saw fit. I loved the way he could whisper sweet, dirty nothings even when our mouths were tangled together and his tongue was down my throat. His soft lips moved down my cheek, my jaw, my neck, 'til he was fluttering and nipping at my collar bone. The cold metal hoop on his lower lip pressed into my skin, while the heat of his mouth sucked on the nape of my neck.

"I was wondering when you'd show up." Crowe wasn't the slightest bit surprised.

"I heard your calls loud and clear." Talos chuckled, and I shook my head. I should have suspected Crowe had used their connection to call him over.

With sudden force, Talos dragged me backwards, unsheathing Crowe's softening cock, and sitting me upright, so my back pressed into his muscular chest. I could feel Crowe's release inside me, and a curious warmth spread through me. The last few times he'd fucked me, I'd about blacked out, but this time, it felt like a surge of power.

Talos fondled my breasts, and he claimed my mouth, never seeming to tire of kisses. I pressed back into him as he snaked a hand down to my nethers. He pressed two fingers into my pussy, pushing Crowe's seed back into me, while I was squeezing my eyes shut, letting myself feel every sensation.

He exited my depths, and drew a line up my center, before returning to play with my breasts. I was supporting myself completely on his chest, leaning into that feeling, as rough hands pushed my legs further apart, and small love bites started climbing my inner thigh. When those nips reached Tobias' mark, it was pure electricity through me. I shuddered and moaned into Talos' mouth, while a wet, hot tongue slipped between my folds.

"T-Tobias?" My voice was little more than a shuddering squeak. He sucked on my clit, and my gasp hit a new octave.

"Your heartbeat's been out of control. I thought I'd help calm you down." Tobias grinned up at me through his dark eyelashes, while he so mischievously flicked my clit again. He climbed those kisses up my body, and I could feel his arousal as intensely as my own. Talos held me, while Tobias started sucking on my nipples. He grazed each side with his teeth and ran a broad lick over Leon's mark. I shivered, just knowing what was coming next.

The weight of the bed dipped again, and Talos handed me off to Tobias. Tobias leaned back onto the bed, pulling me down on top of him, so I was on all fours with him beneath me. He directed my hips in line with his cock, and he lowered me down onto it. I'd taken him in completely when a second pair of hands grabbed my hips.

"Naughty, naughty having so much fun without me." Leon's voice was a purr. One shifter's tongue on another shifter's mark was like a dinner bell, and I was happy to be devoured.

Leon grabbed my hips, and he started lifting and lowering me onto Tobias' cock, at a tempo he'd chosen for us. He used Tobias' expressions as a gauge for the best angles, knowing I'd feel everything he did.

Seconds before I burst, Leon set me down, then he dug his thumb into my mark, as if fully activating our bond. I sat still on Tobias, when Leon leaned in and bit down on my shoulder. A small bit of pain to distract me from the wet, cold finger he slipped into my ass.

"Don't worry, little fireball. I'll make sure it doesn't hurt." His voice directly in my ear made me blush. Knowing he could feel everything he did to me through the bond, I trusted him completely to assure my pleasure. "Now be a good girl and hold still, won't you?"

I nodded, always wanting to be his good girl.

Strong fingers started working lube into me, before he started coating his length. I was still on Tobias' dick when Leon pressed in the tip. He entered torturously slow, testing every inch to make sure it was hitting me right. My pain was his pain, and my pleasure was his pleasure, and he was perfectly meticulous about assuring we both only experienced the latter.

Sensational. The full, tight feeling of having both of them inside me at once was amplified by the shared sensation of my own tightness on them, and both sensations had me fisting the sheets on the verge of madness.

Tobias, Leon, Talos, Crowe—they all felt so good and so different, I didn't know how I'd ever been content to have anything less than this.

"Look at you so filthy, taking two cocks at once for your audience." Crowe knelt in front of me on the bed, and he grabbed my chin to force me to look at him. I needed that extra help to focus on anything other than the ecstasy of riding up and down on both Tobias and Leon's perfect dicks. "Can you take a third, I wonder."

I nodded eagerly, to his amusement, and he rose to his knees, so his tip was in line with my mouth. Hard as it was to concentrate, I wanted to please him too. I wrangled my mind as far as I could from the ripples of orgasm between my legs, and I put all of my shaking energy into sucking him off. I tapped a light kiss on his head, then I sucked him into my mouth, using a broad tongue to pull him in. I circled my tongue on the underside of his cock, and the resulting moan was empowering.

I took him in as deep as he'd let me, tracing the vein and teasing with flicks and circles in between draws of hard suction.

Leon lifted my hips to the very tip of Tobias, so I could get the very last inch of Crowe into my mouth. I sank his cock past my tonsils, surpassing the depth of any possible gag reflex, then I caught his eye deviously as I took him an inch past *that*.

His surprise was fucking satisfying. You don't get ahead in Hollywood if you can't suck a dick, and I'd perfected the art. I lightly dragged my teeth along his shaft as he withdrew, also dragging a low, guttural moan from his chest. One more time, and I watched him snap. He fisted my hair on both sides, and he tightened down as he drew closer and closer to climax.

Crowe fucked my mouth roughly. Each thrust shoved me harder onto Leon and Tobias, and their thrusts shoved me deeper on Crowe, and the combined pleasure of all of them had my eyes watering. I dug my fingers into Tobias' shoulders beneath me, when Crowe filled my mouth with a hard grunt.

Despite my best techniques, the sudden and unexpected force of it made me choke. He pulled out under the vibrations of my wind pipe coughing for air, then he crouched down, covered my mouth, and roughly dug his fingertips into my cheeks. He stared into my watering eyes, while I shook those small coughs into his hand.

Crowe's gaze narrowed. "Swallow it, Dorothy."

He seemed to savor the surprise on my face as he pressed into my cheeks more roughly. I wouldn't disappoint him. I kept his come on my tongue as I gathered myself, then I made a show of swallowing, noting the way he watched my neck bob with such intense interest. He'd filled me from both sides, and something about that made me feel both defiled and shamefully aroused at the same time.

He eased off the grip on my mouth, then he pulled my lips to his for one more kiss. "You're the best fucking girl." He whispered, and I whimpered.

With one last quick peck, Crowe made his exit. He zipped up and waved goodbye, as if this had been the most casual encounter in the world. I was barely able to watch him go through the blurred vision of my soul leaving my body under the perfect pressure on my g-spot, my clit, and in my ass.

I collapsed on Tobias' chest, and we breathed in time until our exhales were slow and calm. I was wet, ragged, used, dripping, and satisfied.

Sex was way fucking better in Oz.

Sleep came quick and it came hard, washing away the worries that had plagued me at least for the night. It wasn't until I got up for some water, late in the night, that I found myself alone with Crowe again in the Emerald Castle's oversized kitchen.

"Hey." I said. I smiled meekly when he approached me, always feeling a touch self-conscious after a session with everyone.

Crowe said nothing in response. He stepped into my personal bubble, swept me into his arms, and he kissed me as hard as his supernatural strength let him. My cup fell form my hand, shattered at my feet, and water splashed on my legs.

"You're beautiful, Dorothy." He said as he kissed me again. "So fucking beautiful, it drives me mad. And as long as you're mine, no matter how much you change, you always fucking will be. Do you understand?"

I blinked rapidly, enjoying the compliment and even his possessiveness, but knowing it wasn't true left a pang in my chest. I'd never thought myself disadvantaged for being human until I was surrounded by magic, and now I almost wished I'd spared the wicked witches so they could curse me too. "You say that now, but in fifty years, I won't look the same. I might not even live that long. I'll age, and I'll die, and I'll barely be a speck in your eternal journey." That doubt and sadness crept up in my gut again. As much as I liked him, Crowe's company had a way of reminding me of my mortality.

He laughed, unusually light and sweet, then he kissed me again, and locked me into a hug. This kind of affection was such a treat from someone ordinarily incapable of it. "That's the point you're missing, Dorothy." The tender way he stroked my hair was so uncharacteristically loving, it made me blush. "The Devil's Queen won't ever die. You may age, or you may not, but you will never, ever die."

"What do you mean?" Always so cryptic. I needed answers.

"Exactly what I said." He pulled back then he shook a hand through his thick and wild black hair. "In a thousand years, when your heart still beats and your body heals at will, you might finally understand just how very much the same we truly are now that we've been one. Maybe then you'll figure out exactly what it means to be mine."

He stepped back and turned on his heel, while I was left trying to process the bomb he'd just dropped on me. *Wait, had he…*

Had he made me immortal like him somehow? Suddenly I understood—the need to fill me, the need to make me swallow, the need to make me his.

"Why?" I asked through a shaky voice that was more out of confused yet pleasant surprise, and less out of nerves or anxiety.

He shrugged. "Because you asked me to."

"Yes, but…" I paused. I'd been wanting to ask this for a minute, but now felt like the right time. "*Why.* Why would you do that for me, when you don't love me? When you *can't* love me. Wouldn't it be advantageous for you if I died? You could have the shoes, you could be free of all curses, and you could have anything you wanted."

Crowe lifted his chin, placing him above me with the subtlest gesture. Then he grinned wide, bearing those sharp teeth with pride. "I realized this back in Sasha's castle." He began. "I was so worried, as you wore those shoes, that you would become Grunhilda. That I was simply going to trade one evil witch for another. I thought I wouldn't care if you died, so long as I got what I wanted first.

Then Sasha put a knife to your neck. I realized in that moment she was going to snuff out your existence for good…"

He stopped himself and rubbed his neck, as if preparing for what he wanted to say next. "I'd had this unexplainable draw to protect you from the moment we met, but it wasn't until that moment that I realized my curse didn't mean I was incapable of emotions. It meant I simply couldn't feel anything for anyone… *except* you. The woman who wore the blood red shoes of the east was the only one who could tap into my heart, and the thought of someone other than my sweet girl wearing those shoes gutted me."

"Crowe…"

"I love you, Dorothy. You're the only person I can love, and the more time I spend with you, you're the only person I want to love. I don't want my emotions back, because I already have all the feelings I need."

My throat constricted, and tears burned in my eyes. "I love you, too." Those words slipped out involuntarily, but they were honest and true. I did love Crowe. In all of his trauma, his brokenness and his struggles, we were still somehow kindred spirits, and I'd known it for a long time.

I didn't need Crowe to be fixed. I didn't need any of my men to be anyone but who they'd shown me: battered, broken, and morally black. And thanks to this twisted, demonic, so-called monster, I'd be able to love them for an eternity.

How… How did I get so lucky?

I laughed through happy tears, and I shared with him a silent smile. And when I jumped into his arms for a twirling kiss, I tapped my ruby red heels together in quiet celebration.

There really is no place like Oz.

THE END (FOR NOW!)

Aftertalk

Where do I even start with this one? When I first decided I was going to write Wizard of Oz into a Dark Fantasy Reverse Harem, I thought it would be a cake walk. Multiple male characters already built into the plot: check. Plucky heroine getting spirited away: check. Big quest: check.

And then I actually read the original children's book from 1900 (prior, I'd only ever seen the movie). Hard stop, that book has zero plot or conflict for the whole first half of it. Basically they camped, they heard a cute anecdote from passersby, they camped, they camped, they camped, and— needless to say there was a lot of camping. And don't get me wrong—I love camping. Fun fact: I lived out of a tent off the back of my motorcycle for years, just for fun. I met my now partner on that trip, and he moved into my little two person tent, and we rode all over the world together.

Great, cool, wonderful—but when I do a retelling, I like to dip into the original story as the author told it, rather than using the movies (which are essentially retellings themselves). I feel like that gives it the feel of a real retelling, where you can bob along with some clue as to what events to look forward to, and be surprised by how they get tweaked and twisted.

Anywho, turned out, camping was a great vehicle for character development and sexy times, and I really got into it once the plot formed in my mind. This ended up being a way more ambitious project than I thought it would be when I first imagined it. I started falling in love with just hanging out with each of the guys, while also trying to juggle the unique challenge of having five personalities together all the time (versus Alice in Wonderland, where characters came and went, all knew each other already, and had their own lives going on). Once I got a feel for who everyone was, this book went from a lost trudge in a word document, to being finished at a lightning pace, and now I'm really going to miss these guys.

The Wicked Witches in this one ended up a special challenge though, as I wanted them to be adequately irredeemable, but also, I love writing dark, but never want to dip too far into DARK dark, you know? Like, my favorite stories growing up were things like Ichi the Killer, Berserk, and MPD Psycho, so my darkness gauge broke, and this was a balancing act of deciding what was too graphic and too disturbing to show on page, versus what was important for their characters. Juggling different trauma and the way it affects us socially and personally is always something I like to explore in my stories, but in this case, the men had some extremes to deal with.

I'd love to hear where this ranked on your Darkness scales (I'm not sure if it's more or less dark than We're All Mad Here, honestly), so feel free to let me know either in reviews or in a message! The Vicious Wonders series is me just writing what I enjoy most, and my horror movie loving brain has no clue where the line is, so it's an honest struggle I stress on in editing. Huge apologies if I missed any trigger warnings. I do my best to pick out anything I think is particularly objectionable, but sometimes I miss something.

On that note, my next story in the Vicious Wonders series is going to be a bit of a surprise (I have a couple I've got mapped and started, but I'm deciding which one has me most inspired before announcing anything), but if you have any particular stories you'd love to read as a fucked up reverse harem, I'm always excited to hear from readers!

All that said, if you enjoyed this story, it helps me a TON to leave a review! I always appreciate feedback, and

I'm always looking to improve my craft. I do read every review, good or bad, so feel free to share what you think!

Also for updates and teasers for upcoming projects, you can follow me on social media! I'm most active on TikTok, but I hop in everywhere regularly!

Goodreads: https://www.goodreads.com/author/show/19238551.Leann_Belle

Instagram: https://www.instagram.com/leannbelleauthor/

TikTok: https://www.tiktok.com/@leannbelle

Facebook: https://www.facebook.com/LeannBelleAuthor

Amazon: https://www.amazon.com/Leann-Belle/e/B07SRHFP2Z

Twitter: https://twitter.com/leannbellebooks

Join my Newsletter: https://mailchi.mp/bd337b73a316/leann-belle

Thanks again for reading! Until next time, go fast and take chances!

OTHER WORKS BY LEANN BELLE:

We're All Mad Here
A Dark and Twisted and very high heat Alice in Wonderland Reverse Harem

There's No Place Like Oz
A Dark and Twisted, High Heat Wizard of Oz Reverse Harem

Stalking Cinderella
A Dark and Twisted Cinderella Reverse Harem, with a bully step brother, a stalker prince, and a manipulative, gender-swapped fairy god mother

What Happens In Vegas
A Billionaire Office Romance Comedy (Also available in audio!)

Sing With Me
A lightly dark, erotic Battle of the Bands, Reality Show Rockstar RomCom

Rise With Me
A lightly dark, erotic Music Industry Romance with Secret Relationships and Mafia

www.ingramcontent.com/pod-product-compliance
Lightning Source LLC
Chambersburg PA
CBHW070758120726
47910CB00001B/214